THE FOREVER HOUSE

THE FOREVER HOUSE

Veronica Henry

First published in Great Britain in 2017 by Orion Books,
an imprint of The Orion Publishing Group Ltd
Carmelite House, 50 Victoria Embankment
London EC4Y ODZ

An Hachette UK Company

7 9 10 8 6

A CIP catalogue record for this book is
available from the British Library.

ISBN 978 1 4091 6657 3

Typeset by Input Data Services Ltd, Somerset

Printed and bound in Great Britain
by Clays Ltd, St Ives plc

www.orionbooks.co.uk

*To my mother, Jennifer, who made our
home the ultimate Forever House*

Acknowledgements

With much love and thanks to Julia Simonds, who inspired this book. Any mistakes are entirely mine!

'Wherever you are is my home'
Jane Eyre, Charlotte Brontë

Could this be your 'forever house'?

FOR SALE

HUNTER'S MOON

Set in idyllic gardens and grounds in the Peasebrook Valley, Hunter's Moon is in need of some updating, but its perfect proportions and enchanting features will delight the potential purchaser.

It is here that the novelist Margot Willoughby penned her most famous works, no doubt inspired by the breathtaking views.

It enjoys complete privacy yet is only two miles from the Cotswold town of Peasebrook, with regular trains to London Paddington.

It is expected that interest in Hunter's Moon will be high, so an early viewing is advised.

The Forever House

*T*wo miles out of the Cotswold town of Peasebrook, you must keep your eyes peeled for a left-hand turn into a tiny narrow road: there is no signpost, so be careful or you might easily miss it. The road is no wider than a tractor, and it meanders between high hedges for half a mile before plunging into woodland. The branches of the trees meet overhead, like a guard of honour, and the grass grows down the middle of the tarmac, leaving a trail for you to follow.

You will wonder more than once if you are on the right road, for it seems endless and to lead nowhere. Your stomach will swoop as you go over a tiny humpback bridge, and eventually you will arrive at a set of square pillars, each topped by a golden ball of stone. Moss has set in, and the gates are hanging off their hinges, but you will know you have arrived at Hunter's Moon even though there is no sign.

Swish through the pillars and along the drive. You'll find the house at the end, nestled in the cleavage of two hills, overlooking a tiny tributary of the River Pease. In spring, which it is now, it is surrounded by a swathe of bluebells.

In summer, fat bees sway drunkenly about the flowerbeds.

In winter, a dredging of snow settles upon it like a white fur stole on a woman's shoulders.

In autumn, as the last of the leaves cling to the trees in a blaze of copper glory, the hunter's moon lights up the valley at night. The hunter's moon that gives the house its name.

Hunter's Moon looks perfect in whatever it wears.

And it is just the right size. Not so large as to be unmanageable, but with plenty of hiding places. And room for parties: impromptu gatherings which turn into laughter and dancing at the drop of a hat. Yet snug and cosy when all you want is to curl up by the fire.

For the very best houses can be whatever you want them to be, depending on the mood and the season and the occasion.

Hunter's Moon is the perfect forever house.

But nothing, as we know, lasts forever.

I

Belinda was able to find Hunter's Moon easily, because she'd done a dry run the day before to make sure she wouldn't be late.

She'd been caught out once too often, lost down a country lane with no landmarks, so she always did a recce before a valuation. That way she arrived for her appointment prompt and unflustered. There was nothing worse than driving around in circles, sweating and swearing at the sat nav.

After twelve years in the business she'd got serenity down to a fine art. A dry run and a fine dusting of face powder to her cheeks, which had a tendency to rosiness, and she always appeared calm, even if she didn't feel it. Often there wasn't much time between appointments, so she was perpetually running late.

Today, though, she was bang on time. This was an important viewing. She had a feeling it had the potential for a bidding war. As far as she could make out, it was perfect. Big, but not *too* big. Plenty of land, but not *too* much – no one wanted lots of land any more because it cost so much to keep, yet everyone wanted privacy. As far as she could see, nothing awful had been done to it. There were no electricity pylons, no planning permission for a nearby housing estate, no restrictive covenants. Of course, something might become apparent when she actually got there and had a chance to look around. But she felt hopeful.

And it had one unique selling point: Hunter's Moon had once been owned by the novelist Margot Willoughby. Of course that wouldn't add much to the value, but it added to the romance. Almost every house she went to view had a copy of one of Margot's books somewhere on its shelves. No one admitted to reading them but everyone did. Belinda remembered the tattered cover of her most famous bestseller as it was passed around school. She smiled. She'd learnt a lot from that book.

A high-profile house with a bit of history in the shop window would be a fantastic marketing tool. She could already imagine her sign up on the main road: FOR SALE – BELINDA BAXTER with a little white arrow pointing down the lane.

She slowed down as she rumbled along between the hedges, the road beneath riddled with bumps and potholes. She didn't want to risk damaging the underside or to scratch the bodywork on the hedges, even though her car was a four-wheel drive, specifically bought to deal with the winding narrow lanes around Peasebrook. It was over fifteen years old, but she looked after it carefully. In her business you had to look successful, and the easiest way to convince people of that was to have an immaculate car.

As she approached the entrance she felt her pulse quicken. It was almost like stage fright, this moment, because everything depended on her performance. If she said the wrong thing, delivered the wrong line, she would lose the commission. She'd rehearsed her spiel, but of course there was always an element of improvisation.

She had to take her cues from the vendor. She could usually predict what they were going to say, but sometimes she was wrong-footed – that was why she prepared so thoroughly before she went out to do valuations. People couldn't argue with facts.

She looked at the entrance. The stone posts were impressive but the iron gates had long since fallen off their hinges, resting drunkenly in the hedge. In her head, she began her snag list: all the repairs and cosmetic touches that would need doing before the property went on the market. People protested, but presentation was paramount if you wanted top dollar. Painting and oiling the gates and putting them back on their hinges would make all the difference.

She felt her tyres bounce over the potholes as she turned into the drive. It was cool and tree-lined, reassuring oaks meeting overhead and blocking out the light. She glanced down at the passenger seat to check she had everything she needed. Her iPad in a sleek cover and a notebook and pen. Laser tape measure. Sample brochures of other high-end houses she'd handled. In the boot were a wax coat and a pair of Hunters for walking the land.

The accessories were superfluous, though, because she knew it would be her charm and her expertise that would win her the job. She made people feel safe, by allaying their fears and taking all of the hassle out of the process. 'We can do that for you,' was her favourite phrase, whether it was going to the council for a completion certificate or arranging for a delivery of freshly cut logs to put by a fireplace.

She stopped the car just before turning the final corner and pulled down the mirror to check her appearance. She wasn't vain, but she didn't want mascara smudges or lipstick on her teeth. She had to look her best for her clients: perfectly turned out, yet not a threat. Though she didn't flatter herself that she would ever be that. Belinda knew she was easier to jump over than walk around, if you were being rude like her father. Curvaceous if you were being polite. She had learned to dress for it: fitted jackets and pencil skirts or tea dresses. She had dark hair, which she wore in a French pleat, sludgy green eyes and what she'd been told was a very kissable mouth. She touched up her rose pink lipstick and pushed the mirror back.

Then she had her ritual moment of contemplation, when she wished happiness for all the people who were going to be affected by the sale. It was never just about the vendor: if it was a big chain, dozens of lives could be altered.

She still didn't know why Hunter's Moon was going on the market. The three Ds – Death, Divorce and Debt – were the most common reasons for selling a house. Those clients had to be treated with particular care. There were all sorts of emotions to negotiate: grief, stress, regret, pride, fear . . . The trouble was, people liked to lie and cover things up. They insisted on pretending everything was all right, when actually they had all sorts of skeletons in the closet.

Of course this could be just a fishing expedition. She got a lot of those. Time wasters were an occupational hazard. They saw the house of their dreams in the paper or on the Internet and wanted to put their own on the market, but all too often the numbers didn't add up, especially now it was increasingly difficult to get a mortgage.

She didn't think that was the case here, though. As she

drove around the corner, the trees finished and the pale gold April sun hit her in the eyes, dazzling her. She put a hand up to shade herself from the light, and she could see immediately that Hunter's Moon wasn't the sort of house you moved from unless you had to.

She inched over the pale chippings, manoeuvring round the fountain in the middle. It was crumbling and covered in moss – a dolphin entwined around a cherub – but she smiled in approval. These were the features that made people fall head over heels in love.

She turned to look up at the house itself, and her heart skipped a beat. If she could have described the perfect house, this was it. Built of pale Cotswold limestone and softened with lichen, she guessed it was about two hundred years old. It was three storeys high and the perfect width for its height, with large latticed windows that winked in the sunshine. A steep grey roof was flanked by two sturdy chimney pots. Wide stone steps led up to a canary yellow front door, guarded by two square lead planters holding balls of box. A thick, gnarled wisteria made its way over the top of the two ground floor windows.

In front of the circular drive, another set of steps went down to a formal garden: square herbaceous beds clustered around a lily pond. It was protected by a thick beech hedge; she couldn't see immediately beyond it, but in the distance were gentle rolling hills dotted with sheep and a glittering silver thread which must be a tributary of the River Pease.

Belinda gave a sigh that was part contentment, part envy, just as the front door popped open and a cluster of golden curls hurtled towards her with a joyous bark, barrelling into her legs. She'd trained herself long ago not to be intimidated by over-exuberant dogs, so she bent down to make a fuss.

The dog was swiftly followed by a slight woman in faded skinny jeans, a billowing white linen shirt, and sneakers.

'Teddy!' The woman admonished the dog with fond resignation, bending down to grab his collar. 'Honestly, he's the dimmest dog but such a sweetheart. Sit, Teddy.'

Teddy tried to sit but couldn't quite resist continuing to nose Belinda's shins.

'He won't hurt you.'

Belinda didn't like to say that all owners said that, even when their dogs were sinking their teeth into your hand, but she could tell Teddy was harmless. She scratched his head.

'What is he?'

'The mother's a poodle but the father is anyone's guess.'

'He's gorgeous.'

'He's a liability. He's a dreadful thief and a chewer. I was hoping he might have grown out of it by now.' The woman smiled and held out her hand. 'I'm Sally. You must be Belinda?'

'I am.' Belinda took her hand, which was dry and cool. She'd thought the woman was blonde at first, but now she could see her hair was a pale shade of honeyed grey. Her eyes were a brilliant blue, kind but observant. Her skin was relatively unlined though she must be in her late sixties. Good bone structure and a pleasant life probably accounted for her youthful looks. She wore a chunky amber necklace: it was real, Belinda guessed, rather than costume jewellery, and there was a very nice emerald on her left hand that flashed in the sunlight. Jewellery was very useful for summing people up. This woman belonged in this house – and suited it.

'Welcome to Hunter's Moon,' said Sally, and Belinda saw a momentary flicker of something in her expression. Worry, anxiety, doubt?

She wanted to tell her how wonderful the house was, how perfect, but she had trained herself not to gush.

'Thank you so much for asking me to come and see you,' she said instead.

They both stood for a moment, looking out over the grounds, a few pom-pom clouds bobbing across the blue sky. The air was sharp with the scent of a bonfire – there was a white plume rising up from further down the garden. Teddy's tail thumped up and down on the gravel. It was a moment of perfect peace, just before a conversation that was about to change the future, and Belinda sensed Sally knew that.

'Would you like a coffee?'

'Good idea. We can get all the formalities out of the way.'

She was reluctant to sit this woman down and bombard her with her sales pitch. She decided she was going to take a more relaxed approach. That was the beauty of being the boss. Somehow, she didn't think Sally was going to respond to pie charts and percentages. She recognised her type: she was a doer, a decision maker, switched on and pragmatic. Not one to suffer fools. She wouldn't quibble but she would expect great service.

A woman after Belinda's own heart.

'Come on in, then.' Sally led the way across the gravel and up the steps, pushing open the door.

2

Inside the air was cool and smelled of the lingering remnants of a wood fire, furniture polish, and a faint trace of what was probably lunch: Belinda imagined a pan of home-made soup sitting on the hob, ready for when she had gone. It made a refreshing change for a house to smell of itself. So often when she went to value houses there were cheap scented candles blazing or plug-in air fresheners pumping out chemicals: synthetic scents designed to cover up any trace of real life.

The flagstone floor in the hall was pale; a staircase made of oak curved upwards, shiny with hundreds of footsteps. A round pedestal table held a jug of narcissi. There was an enormous mirror on one wall and Belinda glanced into it. It was old and foxed and made her look radiant: a magical mirror, just what you needed to look into before setting out for the day. There were several oil paintings scattered around the other walls and up the stairwell, hung casually rather than in the measured way of someone who wanted to impress their visitors. This was a house that had evolved rather than been designed.

Already she could feel herself falling under Hunter's Moon's spell. The house almost spoke to her. She felt as if it were beckoning her inside, telling her she was home.

Which was silly, of course – she could never call somewhere like this her own. It was far beyond her reach. But just as you sometimes meet people you long to be friends with, because they exude an overwhelming warmth, so this house made her feel more than just welcome.

She followed Sally down a corridor into the kitchen. The walls were painted the same colour as the narcissi in the hall, and there was the requisite Aga tucked into an inglenook fireplace. There was a row of cream cupboards, which could have been installed at any time in the past fifty years, and a huge old dresser painted pale blue that was probably original, while well-used copper pans covered one wall. It was everything anyone wanted from a kitchen. She could almost hear its heart beat. And there, as she'd guessed, was the soup, in a Le Creuset pot.

Sally went over to a very snazzy Italian coffee machine, the only modern gadget in the room.

'My son bought it for us for Christmas,' said Sally, seeing Belinda's admiring look. 'I must admit, I'd never have bought one myself, but it's such a luxury.'

'How generous.'

Sally laughed. 'Don't be impressed. It was a totally selfish gesture – Leo says he can't come and stay without decent coffee. He's a bit of a foodie.'

She threw a handful of beans into the grinder and for a moment all conversation was halted and the rich smell of dark-roasted Peruvian coffee filled the air. Belinda's mouth watered with anticipation and delight. This was unusual – it was extraordinary how even the wealthiest people could serve you up instant coffee that tasted of gravy browning.

She raked her eyes around the room to look for clues – sometimes people left brochures from another agent lying about, just to make sure she knew there were others in the running. She knew only too well who her prime competitor would be for this instruction. Giles Mortlake of Mortlake Bassett in Maybury, whose father had founded their agency fifty years ago. Giles was smooth as a bottle of vintage claret, dressed in tweed or linen jackets depending on the season and was slightly shambolic in his battered old Volvo. He wasn't such an attractive proposition now he was heading into middle age, as the waistband of his cords was straining somewhat, and his teeth were overcrowded and yellowing. Yet his mellifluous reassurance was very beguiling. He was old school, which a lot of people wanted from an estate agent even now, especially in the Cotswolds.

Belinda had her own reasons for wanting to wrestle the listing from Giles's grasp. And she knew Mortlake Bassett weren't as upstanding and reliable as their image might indicate. She never expressed her opinion on them to clients, however. Much better to win the business with a confident, well-informed and very personal service.

She sat down at the kitchen table, which was covered in a blue oilcloth decorated with birds' eggs. There was an old wooden box in the middle crammed with jam, honey, Marmite and ketchup.

'Have you got a timescale in mind?' she asked. 'Have you found somewhere you'd like to buy?'

Discussing practicalities rather than price first helped people relax. Plus it was useful to know if they needed a quick sale, or if they could hang on for the right buyer.

Sally brought over two mugs of coffee, and put a jug of

milk on the table. Belinda helped herself as Sally answered.

'The place is too big for us. It's just not practical any more. The garden's a full-time job for a start . . .' She waved a hand to indicate the grounds outside.

Belinda nodded. This was the fourth D. Downsize.

Sally sighed. 'It's difficult when you've lived somewhere as wonderful as this. But a property has come up on the Digby Hall estate. It's not big, of course, but very luxurious. And beautiful grounds, but there's a gardener.' She laughed. 'And a management fee, of course.'

'The Digby Hall estate? It's a very special development,' Belinda nodded. Special and massively over-priced. When it was converted to a high-spec retirement village, all the units had sold off-plan in a trice. There were plenty of people around Peasebrook who wanted to carry on living somewhere lovely and not have to think too much about maintenance.

Sally nodded and voiced almost exactly what she was thinking.

'Designed for old crocks like us who are used to grand living but are slowing down somewhat . . .'

'You don't look as if you're slowing down at all.'

She didn't. Sally was one of those women who still had boundless energy and a great spirit. Belinda hoped she would have an ounce of her brio at her age.

'Yes, but it's better to move while you still have a choice about where to go, don't you think?'

'Oh, definitely.' There was nothing more distressing than an elderly person having to be rushed out of their home in a hurry because they couldn't cope. She'd seen it too many times and it was horribly sad. One minute a panoramic view, next minute some ghastly warden-controlled bungalow with two square metres of block paving to look out at.

'And my husband . . . well . . .' A cloud flittered over Sally's face. 'He can't manage stairs terribly well or surfaces that aren't level, and of course this place is huge so it takes him hours just to get out to the car . . .' She grabbed a china bowl full of brown sugar lumps. 'Sugar?' It was clear she wanted to change the subject.

'Not for me, thank you.'

'It seems serendipitous, because those properties don't come up very often, but we need to get this on the market as soon as possible. I have expressed an interest, but I want to feel confident we'll sell this easily so I can make a formal offer.'

'Oh my goodness, Hunter's Moon will fly, I'm sure of it. It's just a question of getting the price right.'

Sally gave a dazzling smile. 'Yes. But I know as well as the next person it's only worth what someone will pay for it.'

'Not everyone understands that. I wish they did. But we need a guide price.'

'I haven't a clue. I'm relying on you to tell me.'

'There are no records of the house's value last time it was sold, which can often be used to estimate.'

'Yes. It would have been years and years ago. And I didn't actually buy it. It was left to me by my mother-in-law.'

Belinda raised her eyebrows, intrigued. That must have been Margot Willoughby. 'Golly.'

Sally picked up her coffee with a grin. 'Don't worry. It didn't cause a rift, though I suppose it could have.'

She didn't elucidate. Belinda wasn't going to push her. The story would come out eventually. People didn't say things like that unless they wanted you to know more.

She opened up her iPad. 'Anyway, what you paid or didn't pay doesn't make any difference. All we're worried about is what we can get for it now.'

'Quite.' There was a wheel of home-made shortbread on a plate. Sally used a sharp knife to cut it into segments and offered her one. Endless coffee and biscuits were the bane of Belinda's life and usually she said no, but home-made shortbread was impossible to resist. She bit into its buttery sugariness and started a Hunter's Moon folder.

'Let's get the boring bit over with, then you can show me around.' She went in with the killer question. She might as well know what she was up against. 'Have you had any other valuations?'

'Of course,' said Sally, tipping her head to one side in an *I'm no fool* gesture. 'You're the third. Best of three. Isn't that what they advise?'

Giles would have overvalued. He was the most bullish agent in the area, and very annoyingly his strategy often worked. He had a nose for buyers who didn't care how much they paid for the right house. Belinda would be more cautious. She had a figure in her head, but she needed to see everything before she committed.

She was excited. Having Hunter's Moon in her window would be the perfect start to spring. And her commission on it would bring her one step closer to realising her ambition. Her own house again, at long last. It had been a long haul, but it was starting to become more than just a dream.

'Well, this is certainly the perfect kitchen,' she told Sally. 'A big kitchen is what everyone wants, now dining rooms are a bit out of fashion.'

'Oh, it's seen some fun,' Sally's eyes sparkled. 'There is

a dining room too, of course, but we hardly use it. Shall we start the tour?'

Belinda finished her coffee and stood up. This was her favourite part of the job and, as she expected, Hunter's Moon was enchanting. Light and airy but cosy, its rooms were perfectly proportioned. The living and dining rooms were about twenty feet square each, one either side of the hall looking out over the gardens. To the back of the house were a study, a snug, the kitchen and various utility rooms, and on the side was a pretty glass-roofed garden room with a tiled floor, perfect for morning coffee or afternoon tea.

'I'm afraid it's all a bit old-fashioned. No private cinemas or wet rooms,' Sally apologised.

'Oh, that doesn't matter one bit. It's unspoiled – that's the important thing.'

Belinda followed her back into the hall and up the stairs. At the top on the landing was a painting of a woman. She was lying on a sofa, dressed in a dark green dress that shone like the sea, her hair piled on top of her head. She was staring out of the painting with a half-smile on her lips, teasing, provocative, her expression full of promise. And something else. Defiance?

Belinda gasped in admiration.

'That's Margot,' said Sally. 'She still likes to keep an eye on us all.'

'She was stunning.'

'She was. And quite a character.' Sally opened the door to the master bedroom and ushered her inside. Belinda could feel Margot's eyes follow her, as if she was saying *What are you doing in my house?* and she shivered slightly. It was the first time she had felt uncomfortable.

The bedroom was large, with a small bathroom adjoining it that was pretty antiquated, so whoever bought the house would doubtless rip it all out and start again – everyone wanted rainforest showers and heated towel rails nowadays – but the point of the room was the view. Belinda imagined waking up in the four-poster bed and looking out of the window to the garden and the hills beyond.

'I'd never want to get up,' she said. 'I'd just lie here all day, staring out of the window.'

Sally laughed. 'It *is* heaven,' she agreed. 'My favourite thing in the world is Sundays. I get breakfast in bed, and I lie here planning what to do with the garden. Weed it, mostly.'

There were three more bedrooms on the first floor, each a good size, then three more in the attic, the last done out like an old-fashioned nursery – Belinda could almost imagine Wendy and Peter and John beckoning Peter Pan in through the window. There was a set of bunk beds and piles of books and puzzles.

'For my grandchildren,' smiled Sally. 'Two so far, but they live in Scotland.'

'They must love coming here.'

'They do.' She touched a ship in a bottle on the shelf, wiping off some dust with the tip of a finger. 'But there'll be room for them at Digby Hall. Not as much, but . . .'

She turned away, and Belinda sensed she was finding this more difficult than she made out.

'Shall we go into the garden?' she asked rather briskly, and Belinda followed her downstairs.

3

Alexander was following his son around Borough Market.

He felt surprisingly OK. He was a little slow, because his left leg dragged. It was this that had alerted him that something was amiss, which led to the tests, and the diagnosis. He wondered, would always wonder, if it would have been better not to know just yet, to have lived longer in blissful ignorance. After all, there was nothing that could be done. That much was clear.

But now he knew he couldn't un-know it. So the important thing was to make the most of the time he had while still reasonably fit. Which meant spending time with his offspring. He loved his son's energy, and he loved getting an injection of London.

They often did this. Alexander would jump on the nine o'clock train from Peasebrook – the one after the crowded commuter train – and they'd meet up for lunch. Sometimes they'd go to a gallery first, or Leo would take him to see his latest client or discovery – Leo's company, Fork PR, was flourishing, with an office near Borough Market, a staff of six and a huge range of clients. Last time they'd spent a blissful few hours with a knifemaker in east London, riveted by the painstaking craft. Alexander had come home with a hand-forged chef's knife with a walnut handle, and hadn't told Sally how much it had cost. Not that she would have minded, but you had to be there, to watch the skill and the love that had gone into making it, in order to really appreciate its worth.

Alexander wondered bitterly how much longer he would be able to use the knife, then reminded himself he was not going to be bitter. He dragged himself back to the moment.

'It's good to be on the ground, seeing what's new.' Leo stopped at a stall and handed his dad a creamy nib of cheese to sample.

Alexander didn't want this day to end. He loved his son's company, his energy, his knowledge, but the time was getting nearer. He was charged with breaking the news to him. He and Sally had agreed to divvy up the unpleasant tasks: she was doing the estate agents; he was going to tell Leo his diagnosis and prognosis.

Then he and Sally would drive up to Scotland to break the news to Jess together. Jess was younger than her brother – she was only just thirty – but she was settled, with two little ones, running a luxury bed and breakfast in the Scottish Highlands. Above all, they wanted to make it clear that what was to happen over the next few years should have as little impact as possible on their children's lives.

Alexander wasn't so worried about Jess's reaction or the impact it would have on her. Jess was doughty. She had her mother's practicality. But Leo was . . . what? Alexander couldn't quite put his finger on it. Not hopeless or vulnerable or incapable. He'd made a huge success of his business. He had a luxurious flat with a view of Tower Bridge.

'What do you fancy for lunch, Dad? Middle Eastern? Tapas?'

'I've had so many samples, I'm not that hungry.' Alexander smiled. He looked around at the vegetables stalls, spilling over with bright produce, some of which he didn't recognise and couldn't name for the life of him. The tantalising bakeries wafted the aroma of freshly baked breads. The rich, truffly scent of cheese filled his nostrils.

'We need a glass of something, at any rate. And you need to sit down.' Leo looked anxiously at his father. 'You seem tired.'

'No, no. I'm fine. It's just this wretched knee.' Alexander blamed his lack of mobility on a touch of arthritis – a diagnosis that was suitably unalarming and only to be expected in a man of his age. 'I'm very happy to go wherever you choose.'

'Let's get a nice plate of Iberico ham and a crisp Manzanilla.' Leo slung an arm around his father's shoulder. 'Just to start with . . .'

As they wove their way through the throngs, Alexander thought he would never admit either to himself or anyone else that Leo was his favourite, but he was the most like him: passionate, maverick, sensitive. He looked like him too: dark, chocolate-drop eyes and delicate bone structure, with thick glossy hair that always seemed to need cutting. Jess was fair, like Sally, and of a more practical outdoor nature. He felt a bond with Leo that he didn't feel with Jess, though of course he adored them both. But in different ways.

With Leo, he felt as if he was passing a bit of himself on, and never had a sense of immortality felt more important.

And as Leo pushed open the door of a buzzy tapas bar to be greeted warmly by the waitress, he realised what it was as they kissed each other on both cheeks. He would feel so much happier about all of this if he knew Leo was settled with someone. He knew that was probably madly old-fashioned and traditional of him, but what he needed was the reassurance that the line was going to be carried on. Leo was never short of girlfriends – on the contrary – but they never seemed to last terribly long.

He knew who he got that from.

Alexander managed a wry smile. It was simply a question of meeting the right girl. He knew that too, better than anyone.

He switched his attention back as Leo introduced him to the waitress, the owner and the chef. There was much hand shaking and smiling and they were settled at the best table in the house and chilled glasses of sherry appeared as if by magic. Leo had a conversation in broken Spanish with the chef about the best things on the menu.

'You're OK if I order for us, Dad? I've just asked them to bring what's good.'

'Of course,' said Alexander, and went to pick up his glass.

His fingers felt useless. They wouldn't do what he was telling them. He put his hand in his lap and reached out the other one. Happily, that was more obedient. He raised the glass, hoping Leo hadn't noticed.

Leo raised his own glass to his father's with a smile. 'Cheers, Dad.' He leaned forward. 'This is great. I needed a break. Work's been crazy for the past few weeks. Which is a good thing, obviously. But every now and then it's good to press the pause button.'

Bugger it, Alexander thought. I'm not going to tell him. Not yet. Not now. I can keep up the pretence. I love my son and I love all of this. I'm not going to burst the bubble.

4

As Sally led her outside, Belinda realised the grounds at Hunter's Moon were even more perfect than the house.

The more formal gardens were on the first tier of lawn: a pretty combination of box hedging and rose beds around a pond. A small walled garden to one side held a Beatrix Potter greenhouse, soft fruit cages, cucumber frames and sheds. And behind a manicured box hedge was the nicest surprise of all – a swimming pool, with shallow steps at one end, surrounded by a stone terrace. Belinda could imagine sleepy, sunny summer afternoons, bodies draped on sunbeds, splashing and shrieking . . .

'Of course not everyone wants a pool, and it's not heated,' said Sally. 'It's ancient. I expect the next people will fill it in.'

Belinda watched the surface of the water ripple. The bright blue of the tiles made the pool seem azure and inviting. She wondered what it would be like to be brought up somewhere like this. She had been lucky if she was taken to the public swimming baths on her birthday.

'Well, it's a lovely spot. Whatever they decide to do.'

They walked back up to the top lawn and through the formal garden, past the pond. It was still and deep green;

flashes of bright orange darted amidst the lily pads as the fish chased each other.

'The lilies will be in bloom in a month or so,' said Sally. 'They're my favourite thing in the garden. As big as soup plates . . .'

She held her hands up to show how big, then trailed off, perhaps realising that next month would be the last time she would see them.

Belinda sat on the edge of the pond for a moment to take in the view. She looked at Sally, who was gazing at the horizon. What was she thinking? Or feeling? It must have taken months of discussion and soul-searching to reach the decision to sell a place like this.

'Come on,' said Sally eventually. 'There's masses more.'

They walked up past the side of the house, where a little path led to a small courtyard, on the far side of which were the garages and a tiny coachman's cottage.

'We haven't done anything with this,' said Sally, 'but obviously you could. My mother-in-law used to work in the room upstairs. It would be a perfect home office. Careful – the staircase is a bit rickety.'

Belinda followed her up the stairs. At the top was one large room with wooden floorboards, filled with old furniture and covered in posters. An old-fashioned sound system loomed in one corner with massive speakers. The window looked out over the garden and grounds. Belinda imagined Margot Willoughby sitting here at her type-writer, gazing out over the hills. There was a shelf full of her books on one wall.

'Is this where she worked?'

'Yes.' Sally ran her finger along the spines. 'I was hoping I'd find a first edition worth millions so we wouldn't have to sell, but they're of no real value. They're out of fashion nowadays.'

'It's fascinating, though. We could make a feature of this. People love a bit of history.'

'Yes, we could do that,' agreed Sally. 'My kids used it as a party room. They could get up to whatever they wanted with their friends without us knowing.'

'Lucky things,' said Belinda. She pictured the cramped RAF quarters she'd been brought up in – she rarely had anyone back for tea, let alone for a party. She'd been shy, and making friends when they moved every two years had been torture. 'Anyway, there's heaps of potential. It's rare these days, to find something like this unspoilt. It makes the whole thing very special.'

Sally nodded

'It *is* special.' She was fighting back tears. 'But nothing lasts forever. You have to learn to let go.'

She gave a tight smile and walked past Belinda, leading her way back down the stairs.

Inside, they sat back down at the kitchen table. Belinda refused more coffee – she wanted to get some momentum.

'My strategy would be to market the property with a realistic guide price then ask for Offers In Excess Of. When people fall in love with Hunter's Moon, it will give them the confidence to make the most generous offer they can to knock out the competition.'

She named a figure. Sally nodded. Belinda had no idea what she was thinking. She couldn't tell if she was wildly off the mark, or spot on, compared with the other valuations. Usually people gave the game away, with a wince or a widening of the eyes or a mutter of approval.

'Interesting,' was all Sally said.

'In what way?' Belinda countered, eager for a clue.

'What's your percentage?' Sally asked instead.

'It's negotiable. Depending on the asking price.' She paused. 'If you sign up today, we can probably come down a bit . . .'

She felt uncomfortable trying to close the deal. It seemed crass, but this trick often worked. Sally just gave a vague smile. Belinda felt as if she was losing her. Perhaps she needed to change tack?

'If you want to exchange quickly,' she went on, 'it would be good if we could get everything on to the system and I can send my photographer over. The weather forecast is good for the next couple of days, and a blue sky really is paramount for photographs—'

'There is something I need to tell you.' Sally interrupted, putting a hand up to her neck. 'My husband has just been diagnosed with motor neurone disease.'

Belinda could see the anguish in Sally's eyes. For a moment she didn't know what to say. She had been so wrapped up in the perfection of Hunter's Moon that this revelation was quite unexpected.

'I'm so sorry,' was all she could think of to say.

'You wouldn't guess if you saw him now. Only people who know him well can see he's not quite himself. We've had a very early diagnosis. I'm not sure if that's a good thing or a bad thing.' She took in a deep breath. 'Either way, it's a terminal disease. Life is going to get very difficult. So I have to do everything I can to make it easier. Which means selling this.' She smiled. 'Like many people of our age our pension pots are sadly lacking. My husband was very successful – he was in the rag trade on the business side – but we had rather a foolish habit of spending rather than saving . . . So basically, we need to free up some capital. The difference between this and the Digby Hall cottage would go a long way towards nursing costs and whatever help we need.'

Belinda nodded. She knew Sally didn't really want her to say anything, just listen. This often happened towards the end of a viewing: the real reasons came spilling out, once the client trusted you. There was a slight break in Sally's voice as she carried on talking.

'Alexander's having lunch with Leo in London today. I didn't want him here while I was talking to agents. He would find it too distressing.'

'He does know you're selling?'

'Oh yes. He knows it's an inevitability.' Sally looked down at the table for a moment. 'I don't want to make a big thing of the sale. I don't want a sign on the road, or for it to be in the paper. Or in your window.'

'Oh.' Belinda made a face. 'Obviously that makes things difficult. Getting the best price does rather rely on exposure. But we can work around it.'

'I know it's impossible for it to be completely confidential. But I don't want a fuss. I don't want gossip and speculation. And I know Alexander won't. He's devastated about selling and he feels it's his fault. Not because he's ill, but because he didn't plan well enough. I don't want him bumping into people and having to explain. You know how small Peasebrook is.'

Belinda thought carefully before replying.

'People often want a discreet sale. It's not that unusual. But it does mean a different strategy.' She cleared her throat, twirling the sugar bowl round in her fingers. 'We could have an open house. It's hard work at the time, but it saves weeks of people traipsing in and out and constant tidying.'

Sally looked interested.

'How would that work?'

'We pick a weekend to hold it and tell all interested parties. My team will help you get the house ready. Make sure it looks as good as it possibly can. We'd have plenty of staff on hand to supervise. But we only let people come who have registered an interest and given us their financial details – and proved that they are in a position to proceed. No casual passers-by or people who just want a nose.'

'That sounds like a great idea.'

'Then we ask everyone to submit their best and final offers as a sealed bid. It really is the quickest and most secure way to get the ball rolling.'

Belinda could tell Giles hadn't suggested this avenue. She felt pleased, but sensed Sally would need time to think. She stood up.

'I'll leave you to think about it. And just call me if you have any questions at all.'

'Thank you. I can't take it all in,' Sally said. 'I do need to think. And I need to talk to my husband. This is the biggest decision we've ever had to make.'

5

After lunch, Leo was anxious about his father and wanted to put him in a taxi to Paddington. Alexander refused.

'I've never taken cabs in London and I'm not about to start now. Everyone knows it's quicker by Tube.'

'I can get you an Uber. It'll be as cheap as chips.'

Alexander wasn't having it.

Only now, as he stood at the top of the escalator, he wished he'd taken his son up on his offer. He felt daunted, suddenly. What if his leg gave out on the way down? Or his stupid hand wouldn't let him grab the rail – that was happening more often, though he hid it as well as he could. People streamed passed him, and the metal stairs rolled relentlessly downwards, making him feel giddy. Perhaps he shouldn't have had wine on top of sherry?

He could feel panic welling up and he wished Sally was with him. She'd make it all right. She'd take his arm without being asked. He felt desperate. He didn't want to become over-reliant on her. They'd always been very independent. They didn't live in each other's pockets. All that was going to change. He hated the thought.

'Are you all right, sir?' A girl in a black padded jacket

and leather leggings touched his arm, her face full of concern.

He wanted to say he was fine, but he wasn't. He wanted someone to hold his arm while he went down the escalator. He was afraid. He didn't think he'd ever felt such fear before in his life, except perhaps when Jess was born and had been a little bit blue and he'd felt so terribly powerless despite all the nurses reassuring him.

'Would you mind?' He held out his elbow for her to take.

'Take care stepping on,' she said, and guided him until his feet were firmly on a step. They glided down together. He worried they were blocking the escalator – there was always someone in a tearing hurry – but she sensed his anxiety.

'Don't worry. They can wait,' she told him.

Peasebrook seemed unreachable at the moment. He had to get to Paddington yet.

Once again he longed for Sally. He remembered when they were young, the two of them racing for the Tube hand in hand, leaping down the escalators and along the platform and then on to the train just as the door was closing, falling into their seats laughing.

They reached the bottom and he managed to step on to the ground without stumbling.

'Thank you so much. I'll be fine now,' he told the girl, and she patted him on the shoulder before racing off to her own destination.

Break the journey down in pieces, Alexander told himself. He needed to get to King's Cross, then change for Paddington, then get on the train. And Sally would be waiting for him at Peasebrook.

*

Leo hated leaving his father, but Alexander was stubborn. He would have needed a gun at his head to get him into a taxi. But there was definitely something wrong. He'd been quiet and withdrawn and . . . slow. His father was never slow. What Leo couldn't fathom was whether his father knew he was different. Was he hiding something or was he simply unaware? He'd said something about his knee – his arthritis playing up – but Leo hadn't been convinced it was just that. Maybe he should have gone back home with him? But that wasn't an option – he had a five o'clock meeting before everyone went home, then a soft launch of a new bar in Soho. Never mind – he would call home at about six and make sure Alexander had got back all right.

He felt a nagging guilt as he pushed through the crowds – the area was always buzzing with food tourists nowadays. Of course the world wouldn't end if he didn't go to the meeting or the launch. What was more important – the social media campaign of a new brand of 'artisanal' pork scratchings or his parents? His parents, obviously. The deep-fried skin of a British saddleback didn't get a look in.

His phone rang and it was the office, checking on his whereabouts. His next client had arrived.

'I'm three minutes away. Make them coffee.'

He broke into a light jog, arriving slightly breathless and charmingly apologetic. And of course, in between the meeting, and the launch, and bumping into a couple of people he'd been hoping to do business with, it was half eleven before he thought about ringing home and by then it was far too late. Anyway, his mother would have rung him if there'd been a problem. Of course his dad was all right. He knee had been giving him gyp, that was all.

6

Belinda drove back into Peasebrook after her visit to Hunter's Moon feeling unsettled.

She knew if she left a valuation without tying the deal down she probably wouldn't get it. But she could see how upset Sally was, and she hadn't wanted to manipulate her emotions. If she was meant to get the job, she would, but she knew when to back off. Sally's revelation about her husband had upset her too. So often there was sadness and grief lying underneath perfection.

She drove up the high street, and just as she did every time she felt a burst of fondness for the town that had become her home. She smiled in approval to see that it was buzzing. It had the proud boast of having the highest ratio of independent shops in the region. Of course there were a couple of chain stores, because its rising population meant a pressing need for a supermarket and a chemist, and there were the usual banks. But the other shops were a combination of long-running family businesses – the butchers, the saddlers, the greengrocer – or new enterprises set up by people passionate about what they were selling. She could see the zinc buckets of flowers spilling blooms outside the florist, and the window of a boutique filled with pastel dresses ready for spring. And her own favourite, Nightingale Books, just before the little bridge that led out of town. She promised herself a browse in there on Sunday, her only day off.

She drove over the bridge and forked right as the road split into two, then drove up a hill and pulled up outside her office. It wasn't on the high street, but that meant her rent was a quarter of what it would be if it was, and it really didn't seem to matter, and best of all there was a tiny flat over the shop, which she lived in. The basement she let to her photographer, Bruce. All in all she had made the building work well for her.

She felt a burst of pride that she had come so far. A long, long way from the shy school-leaver who had typed up property details at a faceless high street agency in Oxford, being shouted at because she had spelled 'storey' 'story'.

'A three *story* house?' her boss had shouted. 'What bloody story? The Three Little Pigs?'

She had felt tears stinging her eyes and for a moment had been tempted to walk out, but she had stuck at it, because there was something even then that intrigued her. Selling houses was like selling dreams. She loved everything about it: the personalities, the drama, the challenge.

You didn't have to be a psychiatrist to work out that moving every two years into yet another anonymous RAF quarter, where she hadn't even been allowed to paint her bedroom walls a different colour or knock a nail in to hang up a picture, had given her a fascination with the notion of owning your own house. Your own *home*. She had never really known what home meant as a child. Wiltshire, Germany, Holland, Yorkshire, then finally back to Oxfordshire – the houses had always been the same, cramped and soulless with metal windows and walls the colour of skimmed milk. Unwelcoming. Sterile. She had never walked over the threshold and felt a sense of belonging.

So once she'd been taken out to viewings, that was it: she knew what she wanted to do. She spent three years learning the ropes in Oxford, putting hundreds of houses on the market, before moving to Mortlake Bassett in Maybury, which specialised in country homes. Beautiful houses that embraced you. Even if she didn't own one, she loved living in them vicariously, mentally redecorating each one to her own taste. It almost didn't feel like work.

Thus she flourished, becoming Mortlake Bassett's best negotiator. She shook the agency out of its complacency and implemented new strategies while holding on to their *Country Life* image. She doubled, then tripled, their sales figures and set a record for the biggest bonus. Other agents in town tried to poach her, and when they couldn't entice her they copied her ideas instead, but no one had her insight or flair. Or her personality and charm: she had a way with clients that couldn't be imitated.

That was more than ten years ago. And then, they had betrayed her. Estate agency could be a dirty business. She had always known that, and worked hard to dispel the clichéd wide-boy image. Not realising that she would become a victim of it.

She didn't dwell on it now, though. Instead, she paused for a moment to look at the window where she displayed the details of the houses she had for sale in individual frames. She only listed houses she liked. That was her niche. The houses didn't have to be grand, but they had to be somewhere she'd want to live herself, from a tiny one-bedroomed weavers' cottage to a grand manor house. And, somehow, it worked: most people in the area knew if their house went on with Belinda Baxter, it was something special.

She had a brimming hot box of people looking for houses around Peasebrook. She often brokered deals without even having to put a house on the open market. She never took on houses that needed too much cosmetic surgery, but she could wave a wand and transform a house almost overnight into something really special. She'd been known to put as much as fifty thousand pounds on a house just by decluttering and revamping. She arrived with dustbin bags, empty boxes, and a man with a flatbed truck who ran back and forth to the dump. She had a contact with a warehouse full of furniture and ornaments she could hire. She could transform a nondescript garden terrace into an 'outside room' with a jet wash, a table and chairs, and two outsize pots filled with greenery. On a couple of occasions, much to Belinda's chagrin, the clients had loved their makeover so much they had taken their houses off the market.

The other agents in town couldn't offer this level of service. It was one of the things that set her apart. She could also organise a packing service, a storage service for surplus clutter, even arrange for dogs to be looked after during viewings.

In other words, if you sold your house through Belinda Baxter, you didn't have to think about *anything*. And if you bought from her, she could advise you on everything, from the best school for your children to where to put your horse in livery and how to find a reliable cleaner.

The welcome pack she put in her 'sold' houses on the

day of completion summed up her brand: a handmade wicker basket would be waiting in the kitchen, with pale blue Cotswold Legbar eggs, local sparkling wine, home-made sourdough and an apple cake from the bakery in Peasebrook.

The keys, of course, were presented to the client on a leather fob with her logo embossed in gold: two Bs back to back.

It was all about the detail.

She worked ten times harder than any other estate agent she knew. And if anyone ever accused her of being a workaholic – well, when you loved your job, that wasn't such a bad thing, and if someone broke your heart and kicked a boot through your soul, being a workaholic was better than having a nervous breakdown, surely?

She pushed open the door of her office. She was always eager to get back. She made a point of not answering her phone when she was out on an appointment, because it was too rude for words to take a call when you were with a client and there was never anything that couldn't wait.

As she walked inside, she felt the usual rush of pleasure and pride. It was her little kingdom. The reception area was warm and welcoming and relaxed: seagrass flooring, sage green walls and a highly polished oak table that served as a desk. Clients sat in plump armchairs covered in a tweedy check, the lighting was soft and there was the merest whisper of baroque music in the background. The back room was where all the phone calls were taken and the paperwork dealt with. There was no sign of actual work front of house – nothing so pedestrian.

Sitting behind the desk was Cathy, her right-hand

woman. She was an empty nester who had begged Belinda to let her help with viewings.

'I'm so bored,' she'd said. 'I've been a stay-at-home mum for twenty years and I've got no skills except for sewing in name tapes and making toad-in-the-hole. But I can't stay at home in an empty house another day or I'll go mad. You won't even have to pay me.'

Belinda had been charmed by her warmth and her enthusiasm and had taken her on. Cathy had been so enthusiastic she had taken herself to night classes and got herself computer savvy. More than savvy. She knew more than Belinda about social media and databases. Now she was her right-hand woman. She was motherly, eagle-eyed and ferociously competitive. She had a matronly bosom, stick thin legs and wore short skirts and capacious jumpers that she knitted herself. Today's featured a rearing stallion.

'Well? Did you get Hunter's Moon?' she demanded.

'She's going to let us know.'

'Who else has been out?'

'She didn't say. The usual suspects, I imagine.'

'Ugh.' Cathy regularly stuck pins in a little crocheted figure of Giles Mortlake whenever he won a house over them. And that was without her knowing the real reason for Belinda's misgivings about Giles.

'It's very sad. The husband has just been diagnosed with motor neurone disease.'

'Oh, how awful.'

'Yes. You can see it's going to be a real wrench. And they don't want too much publicity. Very under the radar.'

'Damn. I was going to do the window with a load of Margot Willoughby books. And an old typewriter.'

Belinda had to smile. 'Save your creative energy. If we

do get it, I think we're going to go with an open house.'

Cathy looked excited. They loved an open house. It was an event; a spectacle. Belinda felt a rush of affection for her, and hoped they would get Hunter's Moon. It would be something they could throw themselves into together.

'So what's been going on?'

Cathy leafed through a pile of messages.

'The Parkers have lost their buyer so they won't get Elmfield.'

'Damn. We'll have to go back to the other people.'

'Sorted. They're going to confirm their offer tomorrow. Then that peculiar man's put in a higher bid on The White House. Two thousand more. I'm sure he's buying it for his mistress.'

'OK. They'll have to accept it. They can't realistically expect more. Not on that side of town. That's a good price.'

'And Mrs Rowe's got her mortgage offer through for Lower Pitt.' Cathy did a little fistpump. 'So that's all systems go.'

'Perfect. All good then.'

'Oh – and there's another valuation request come in. Not quite Hunter's Moon, but I think it will fly. They want you to go out as soon as possible. They need a quick sale.' She ferreted on her desk for the details. 'It's called The High House? One of those lovely Georgian jobs at the other end of town? Do you know it?' She handed Belinda a piece of paper.

For a moment, Belinda didn't reply. She took the paper and turned away so Cathy couldn't see her face. Did she know The High House? She knew it like the back of her hand, every nook and cranny.

41

She walked through into the back office, sat down and started to read through all her messages. She was deliberately avoiding looking at the piece of paper Cathy had given her. Instead she tried to distract herself with emails: vendors chasing completion dates, solicitors chasing conveyancing details, buyers chasing their offers . . . Everyone was always in a mild state of panic and hysteria. She was the middleman, the mediator, the one who was supposed to take the stress out of the situation. It wasn't always possible. She'd seen it all. Gazumping, gazundering, people pulling out on the day of exchange for no apparent reason, dodgy surveys, inefficient solicitors, peculiar covenants: there were myriad reasons for a sale to fall through and Belinda had seen most of them. And so often it was just one tiny piece of paper – an indemnity or a mortgage offer or a survey – holding things up.

Yet still she loved it, because when it went right, when that call came through to say contracts had been exchanged, there was no better feeling in the world. She loved handing over a set of keys to a new owner and sending them off on their new adventure.

Eventually, she came to the end of her inbox. She had to grasp the nettle. She picked up the message and looked at the number.

The High House. She had sworn the day she'd left that she would never cross the threshold again. She had almost been tempted to leave Peasebrook altogether, but in the end she didn't have to. It was ten years ago, but she could still remember the desolation.

If she didn't take it on, The High House would go to Giles. She would be cutting off her nose to spite her face by losing the commission. She couldn't afford to turn her back on that kind of money. She had to try, at least.

For a moment, she was tempted to ask Cathy to go and value it. She could give her a guide price. She knew exactly what it was worth. But Cathy would ask too many questions. It had all happened long ago, and she didn't want anyone's sympathy.

Could she face going back there? It was only a house. Four walls. It couldn't hurt her. Although the memories might. She had worked so hard not to let what had happened break her, but instead to rebuild and prove her worth, to herself and everyone else.

She turned the paper over in her hand. She realised her fingers were trembling. Maybe she needed to go back and confront her past, to stop it haunting her. She had always known The High House would come on to the market one day; that she would probably have to face this dilemma.

She put her head in her hands. Come on, girl, she told herself. Where's your fighting spirit? You can't let Giles walk away with this one just because you feel a bit emotional about it. It's a house, not a person. It can do you no harm.

In fact, maybe it would help her to go back in there and confront her demons.

She picked up her phone and dialled the number. 'Mrs Blenheim? It's Belinda Baxter speaking. You wanted to make an appointment for me to value The High House?'

7

At Peasebrook station, Sally searched anxiously amongst the London commuters streaming off the train for Alexander. Finally, she saw him, with his distinguished sweep of grey hair and his long stone-coloured mac in case of spring showers. He looked like *someone*, she thought. He still carried himself with a certain grace. It hadn't taken his presence away from him yet.

Her heart squeezed with love and concern. She worried about him when he was out of her orbit, yet she didn't want to smother him. The urge to protect him was monumental. He'd always been agile rather than overtly strong – quick-thinking and quick on his feet, able to avoid danger. The diagnosis weighed heavy on him. His reaction times, his thought processes – they were all slower. Sally thought it was the shock rather than the disease itself.

He saw her and his face brightened and they embraced on the platform amidst the crowds. She took his arm without asking.

'I got a good parking space,' she told him. She wasn't going to ask questions yet.

'I had to stand half the way.'

'Didn't anyone give you their seat?'

Alexander grinned. 'I'd have been insulted if they had. I've still got it, you know.'

She laughed, pleased he was showing some of his old spirit.

They got to the car. Sally put on her seatbelt and her glasses and waited for Alexander to buckle up. She had to ask. She cleared her throat.

'So . . . how was Leo?'

'On good form. We had lunch at Borough Market.' Alexander paused. 'I couldn't tell him.'

She sighed. 'No . . .' She'd been afraid this might happen. But she understood.

'I don't see the point. Not at this stage. I mean, why worry him? He's just picked up a new client – a small chain of gluten-free bakeries. He's really found his feet. He's doing so well. I don't want to spoil it for him.' There was a crack in Alexander's voice.

'But he'll be angry with us if we don't tell him. And it means we can't tell Jess either.'

'Then so be it,' said Alexander. 'It's *my* disease. I'll decide what I want to do with the bloody thing.'

'But it's not yours,' said Sally sadly. 'It's all of ours.'

He gave a grunt of exasperation. She knew how frustrating Alexander found it all. 'I know. Of course I know. But . . . can we talk about it when we get back? I'm tired.'

'Of course.'

He leant his head back in the car seat and shut his eyes. 'Now isn't the right time. Not yet. The bloody awful bad news can wait. I just wanted to spend some time with my son.'

'Darling, I know.' Sally started the engine. The thing about catastrophe was you changed your mind about the

45

best thing to do on a daily basis. Hourly, even. Because there was no best way.

'Did you find an agent?'

'Yes. I think I'm going to go with Belinda Baxter.'

'Mortlake Bassett no good?'

'I didn't trust him. His eyes were everywhere. And – seriously bad breath.' Sally wrinkled her nose. 'I think Belinda will do a good job. She'll be very discreet.'

'Great.'

'Maybe when we've got a buyer, and a moving date, we can get all the bad news over at once?'

'That'll be something to look forward to.'

It wasn't like Alexander to be so defeatist. But Sally supposed he'd had a long day, and seeing Leo must have brought it home to him. She tightened her grip on the steering wheel in frustration. She kept veering from anger to sadness to helplessness, and she couldn't afford to. She had to keep it together for everyone.

Back at Hunter's Moon, Sally sat at the kitchen table while Alexander went to get changed.

Her head felt fuzzy. She'd hardly slept since the diagnosis, anxiety squeezing her chest, but she didn't want to toss and turn in case she woke Alexander, so she lay still, her mind racing during that horrible predawn time when even small problems seemed momentous. And momentous problems took your breath away. She felt as if she was lying under a mound of rocks. So by late afternoon she was nearly on her knees with tiredness, but she thought if she could keep going until bedtime she might sleep through.

She looked around the kitchen where she had held court

for so long, the scene of so many hangovers, arguments, councils of war . . . homework sessions and cakes ablaze with candles . . . hastily written letters and carefully read ones . . . champagne, cocoa, shepherd's pie, boiled eggs, asparagus dipped in butter, toast and jam . . . comfort food and midnight snacks and celebratory dinners . . .

And now, here she was alone at the table with her whole world crumbling around her. Her darling Alexander. Of course, in a marriage one always lived in the knowledge that one of you had to go first, and he was a man, and he was older, so . . . But why so soon? And why this?

She didn't want to put the house through what they were about to go through. This was a house of laughter, not tears. She had spent long enough making sure of that. It had been a Herculean task, and never dull, but it had taken a lot of time and a lot of cunning to turn things around. If she'd had one purpose in life, it was to make Hunter's Moon a happy place.

There was no choice. She picked up her phone and dialled the number Belinda had given her.

'I'd like you to sell Hunter's Moon for us,' Sally told her. 'I want to put it on the market straight away.'

She spoke quickly, as if she might change her mind if she didn't get the words out.

'Thank you,' said Belinda. 'I will personally make sure everything goes as smoothly as possible for you. It will be an honour to sell Hunter's Moon.'

As Sally put down her phone, she looked down at the sample brochures Belinda Baxter had left and hoped she had made the right decision by going with her. It probably didn't matter which agent she chose. Hunter's Moon would be snapped up regardless. It was the house of everyone's dreams. Belinda had been slick and professional, but there was also a warmth and gentleness to her the others had lacked. A genuine concern and empathy that Sally would definitely need over the next few months.

She thought about the first time she'd seen Hunter's Moon. Fifty years ago. As beautiful then as it was now, albeit . . . chaotic. That was really the only word to describe it. She had walked not into a house, but into chaos.

8

1967

There was nothing as cold or hard as a London pavement at night. Sally walked as quickly as she could in her stockinged feet, her shoes in her right hand: with their silly high heels, they weren't designed for walking on anything but plush carpet. She could feel the March iciness pass through her soles and seep upwards into her bones. Her shins ached with it.

She hadn't yet absorbed the ramifications of what she had done. It was a lot of money to give up: thirty-five pounds a week. She had thought it was too good to be true, when she'd answered the advert and they'd been all over her, taking her on on the spot. Money wasn't everything, though, and there was definitely a limit to what she would do for it. She had been naïve. She knew that now. Her brothers had warned her, but she'd been in such a hurry to set out on her new life, she'd ignored their advice.

She'd loved the Kitten Club when she started working there. It was impossibly sophisticated, with thick white carpet, curved white leather banquettes and smoked glass tables. Chunky chandeliers hung overhead, casting a low light around the silver walls. The uniform she and the other cocktail waitresses wore was a little on the revealing side – black velvet corsets over fishnet tights, very high heels and of course a pair of kitten ears on a headband. But the outfits looked fun and glamorous and Sally knew she looked good in hers: she had a tiny waist and long legs, which was the perfect combination. And Morag, the hatchet-faced Scottish woman who had hired her, and who was in charge of making sure all the girls looked their best and had eaten properly, liked her because she was a natural blonde.

'They like a fresh-faced beauty, some of them.'

Sally wasn't sure that the spiky false eyelashes and frosted pink lipstick she was made to wear were terribly fresh-faced, but it was the look. And the customers did seem to like her. They were very friendly and welcoming, as were the other girls. She felt as if she had fallen on her feet straight away. She'd sent a postcard to the boys, of a soldier outside Buckingham Palace: *Feel like a proper Londoner. Flat in Kensington and a glitzy job at the famous Kitten Club – you won't recognise me! Love to all – send sausages!! Sal xx*

She put it in an envelope so her mum couldn't see it, and sent her one of the Palace itself. *Hope you are well, Mum. I'm managing OK. Working hard. See you soon, I hope. Love Sally x*

The club *was* hard work because it was always busy, and being a good cocktail waitress meant making sure no one's glass was ever empty, so Sally spent each night on her feet running between the customers and the bar as they all drank like fish. The waitresses had to do a little curtsey with a purr when they served a drink. It was the club's signature move, and the men seemed to lap it up. Still, Sally had thought it was harmless enough.

How wrong she was.

What she hadn't realised was the purr indicated a certain willingness. Looking back now it had been obvious, but she had been too green to pick up on it. Of course, no one had spelled it out, because the Kitten Club had a veneer of class and wouldn't want to openly advertise. The transactions were discreet. They had to be or they would be shut down.

She shuddered now at the memory of the moment the penny had dropped. The man had been charm itself the first few times she had served him, but tonight something had changed. She sensed it after she brought over his second Rémy Martin, and his fingers had brushed hers as he took the heavy crystal tumbler from her. He had taken her hand and pulled her down on to the banquette next to him.

'It takes me a while to decide if I like a girl or not,' he said. 'But I knew as soon as I saw you that you were a contender.'

She crossed her legs and smiled. 'Contender?'

He held her gaze, then laughed. 'Is playing hard to get part of the game?'

He was an unattractive man, with a head of sheep-like curls, flared nostrils and a florid complexion, and his chin disappeared into his shirt collar as if he had no neck. On one little finger was a huge gold ring with three fat diamonds stuck into it. She knew he'd made a fortune after the war selling packing crates, though she couldn't really imagine what anyone would want them for.

'There's no game,' she said to him, eyes wide, then recoiled when his hand gripped her knee. She put her hand down to prise off his fingers, but he squeezed even tighter.

'I've got a room at the Dorchester,' he told her. 'You'll like it there.'

'I don't think you understand.'

His gaze was flat and hard. 'I don't think *you* understand. Come on, sweetheart. I'll get them to call us a cab.'

She stood up. 'I don't think so.' She knew she sounded prim. She was just doing the most dignified turn on her heel when the man stood up and grabbed her arm. His face was red with fury. He started pulling her across the room.

'You're coming with me. You don't get to choose. That's *my* prerogative.'

She kicked him, hard. Right in the shin with the toe of her shoe. Immediately she found herself surrounded by the two men who were employed to deal with difficult and drunk customers. They took her by the elbows and escorted her out of the club. Then bundled her down to the back door where Morag was waiting with a face like thunder.

'What were you thinking?' she hissed. 'The customer is always right at the Kitten Club. Always.'

Sally suddenly understood.

And in that moment, she remembered her eldest brother's words. 'London's a dirty place, Sal. A dark place. I'm not sure it's for you.'

They threw her out on to the street. There was no question of her being given the money she was owed: nearly a month's wages. She knew better than to bang on the door and ask for it.

She walked the several miles from Mayfair to Kensington, for she had no money for a cab and she wasn't going to flag down a car. She was exhausted, and all she wanted to do was make a cup of cocoa, fill a hot water bottle, and crawl into bed. She didn't have to get up the next day now, she realised wryly. She thought she might sleep around the clock; for the past month, her days had become nights. She wished she'd found a flat nearer to the centre of London, but she'd needed to find somewhere in a hurry and Barbara, her flatmate, had seemed, if not a kindred spirit, then at least her own age. The two girls had to share a room, but the rent was affordable and, though the flat was gloomy, the area was lovely. And gloomy could be dealt with.

Her heart lifted a little as she finally saw the black-and-white sign for Russell Gardens. She'd loved the road as soon as she saw it, with its white wedding cake houses and the communal gardens surrounded by black railings and plenty of trees. She turned the corner then jumped as she saw a figure in the gutter. A dark pile of clothes topped by a mop of hair. She still felt a little shaken by earlier events. Whereas once she would have rushed to help, she paused to assess the situation. She was, it seemed, learning fast to be wary.

She hid behind the hedge of the nearest front garden and peered through the late night gloom. The figure stirred and groaned. It was definitely a man, but she couldn't work out his age. Was he injured? Had he been attacked? Had he come out of his house and fallen?

Eventually, she decided the man was no danger, as he could barely move, and it was her duty to help. She didn't have it in her to walk on by. Her basement flat was only two doors down. She couldn't possibly walk past and leave him in the gutter.

She emerged from the shadows and went and stood over him.

'Are you all right? Can I help?'

As she spoke, she thought perhaps she should have knocked on a neighbour's door to ask for assistance. But before she could do anything about it, the figure groaned and tried to sit up, levering himself until he was perched on the kerb with his feet in the gutter.

'Shit . . . sorry . . . I don't know . . . Where am I?'

'Kensington. Russell Gardens.'

'Oh. Well, that's something, I suppose. Not too far from Paddington.'

'There's no trains now. Not till morning.'

He put his hand up to his head. There was a nasty gash on his forehead. As he lifted his face, she could see that he was about her age, maybe a bit older. Pale skin, dark hair, and a lot of blood trickling on to his white shirt.

The blood looked black in the lamplight.

He looked at the blood on his fingers and swayed, whether from the realisation he was bleeding or the fact he was hopelessly drunk, she couldn't be sure. He was only slight. Not like the hideous brute she'd fought off earlier. Instinct made her brave, so she knelt down next to him.

'Are you badly hurt? What happened?'

He looked at her, barely able to focus, his eyes rolling like marbles in their sockets, but he managed a slow and angelic smile. He gave a bewildered shrug.

She recognised the smell of brandy on him, and no doubt there had been other things before that.

'Come on,' she said. 'You need to get your head looked at. You better come in. I live just here.'

She took him by the elbow and heaved him to his feet. She looked up and down the road to see if anyone was about. The row of white houses stood silent and stiff, as if watching in disapproval. She got him to hook his arm around her neck, and walked him carefully along the pavement until they reached the railings that fronted the steps leading down to her flat. He leant against her for support as they descended, and his knees nearly buckled once or twice. As they reached the well at the bottom he lurched into the dustbin.

'Bit . . . tiddly,' he slurred.

'Just a bit,' said Sally, straightening him up. 'Where have you been?'

He gave it rather a lot of thought, digging the answer out of the depths of his fuddled brain.

'Bloody friend's bloody birthday thing. Some Italian on the King's Road for dinner. Then . . . I dunno. It all got a bit . . .'

He stood at the bottom of the steps in the well outside her door, his eyes goggling at the memory.

'Out of hand . . .' he added solemnly, nodding at the recollection. Then stared at her. 'I think I might be sick.' He was deathly pale.

'I'm not surprised,' said Sally, unlocking the door. 'I'll get you a bucket. Wait there.'

With two older brothers, neither his state nor his behaviour were shocking to her. Bucket and bed, that was the drill. She ran and grabbed the bucket from under the sink in the tiny kitchen, then took it outside.

He vomited into the bucket as she held it out, then looked up at her.

'You're a cat.' His face was puzzled.

She put a hand to her head with a laugh. She was still wearing the black velvet cat's ears from the club. She pulled off the headband that held them on and threw them into the dustbin, slamming the lid down. She didn't ever have to wear those again.

He was bending over with his hands on his thighs. He gave one more dry heave, then stood up. 'That's better. Oh God, I'm sorry. You're so sweet. Most people would have given me a good kick back into the gutter . . .'

He spoke as if that was what usually happened. He certainly had lovely manners, thought Sally, now he was able to string a few words together. He was wearing a black coat with a velvet collar, a white shirt and skintight black trousers. His hair was matted with blood, but she could see it was fashionably long. He looked as if he *was* somebody, thought Sally.

'Come on in. I'll clean up your head. Or do you think you should go to hospital?'

'I think I just hit it when I fell. It'll be fine. It doesn't hurt. Where there's no sense, there's no feeling.'

But he followed her in obediently, rather like a small child.

There was no point in apologising for the state of the flat, thought Sally. Her charge was unlikely to notice his less than salubrious surroundings. It consisted of a small living room with a tiny kitchen off it, and off that was a miniscule bathroom. To the left was the bedroom she and Barbara shared, with twin beds, a dressing table and a wardrobe. It was a bit dreary and dark, and smelled of damp, being a basement, but Sally had thought once she got some money together she would buy some things to cheer it up and make it more homely: a heater, some cushions, a rug . . .

As Barbara worked in the day and Sally at night, they barely saw each other, so Sally wasn't sure how Barbara would feel about a stranger in the flat, but at the moment she didn't care. She felt drawn to her gutter find. She didn't want him to disappear off into the night, never to be seen again. She didn't for a moment think he might be dangerous.

He walked across the room with the deliberate care of a drunk and sank into the sofa. It was sagging and ancient, in faded red brocade, but he sighed with contentment as if he was falling on to a feather bed.

'What's your name?'

'Beetle.'

'Beatle? Like The Beatles?'

'No. Beetle. Alexander Beetle. After the A A Milne poem? *I found a little beetle . . .*'

Sally stared at him. She'd never met anyone like him. He was delicate and fragile, yet confident and blasé and for some reason she couldn't take her eyes off him. Half of her wanted to look after him and half of her . . . well, wanted to do something else entirely. Was it his dark, all-seeing eyes, or his mouth, which was in a permanent half-smile, a star of a dimple to one side?

'Wait there,' she told him.

He spoke well, so she was confident he wasn't going to ransack the place while her back was turned. Not that there was anything worth stealing. She went into the kitchenette and boiled a saucepan of water, then cleaned the blood off his face with the edge of a tea towel. He sat as still as he could, only protesting when she rubbed too hard on the wound.

'There,' she said. 'At least it's clean and you're not covered in blood. You'll need some antiseptic.'

'Thank you, nurse.'

She patted the arm of the sofa.

'Put your head on here and I'll get you a blanket.'

He lay down, then reached out a hand to her before she could move away. He stroked the inside of her arm, his long, slender fingers on her pale skin, then linked those fingers in hers, holding on tightly as if he needed her. She shivered. How strange it was, she thought, that she didn't want him to let go, whereas the man at the Kitten Club had made her skin crawl. What made one person's touch irresistible, yet someone else's repellent?

His eyes were closing. She couldn't stand here all night holding his hand, so she extricated herself from his grip as gently as she could and went to fetch a spare eiderdown. She covered him up, then stood and looked at him for a moment, stretched out on the sofa, wondering who and what he was. Alexander Beetle. She smiled. He seemed to be a mass of contradictions. Man but boy. Glamorous but innocent. She wasn't sure how he made her feel, but at least she had forgotten the horrible man from earlier.

She wondered what Barbara would think if she found him in the morning. She might think an angel had been dropped from heaven. His dark lashes stood out against the paleness of his skin; a black wing of hair fell across his forehead. He didn't look very old – a little older than she was, definitely, but not much. As well as the gash on his head, she now saw his lip was swollen and bruised, which was why it looked so inviting. He was lucky not to have lost any teeth.

Sally felt a sudden urge to bend down and kiss him. She shook her head in bewilderment. Was it a sense of protectiveness that made her want to do that? She thought very probably not.

*

It was nearly four o'clock when she got into bed. Barbara was in the other, rasping away. She was a biggish girl and when she lay on her back she snored all night long, oblivious.

Sally put on two pairs of socks, pulled on a vest under her nightgown, and huddled under the covers. It had been quite a night. Her life couldn't really be further from what it had been just over a month ago, and although she wasn't sure if she liked it yet, it certainly wasn't dull. None of tonight's events would have happened in Knapford, of that she was certain.

9

1967

At ten o'clock the next morning, Sally woke with a start. It took her a few moments to work out why she felt unsettled and then she remembered. Alexander. Alexander Beetle. She'd meant to get up early to go and check on her patient before Barbara woke. But Barbara's bedclothes were thrown back and she had already got up. Sally hurried out to find her flatmate sitting on the sofa in her dressing gown, eating cornflakes with the top of the milk and two spoons of sugar, her large feet splayed into a pair of red nylon slippers. And no sign of last night's apparition. Just the eiderdown neatly folded on to one arm of the sofa.

Sally wasn't sure what to say. She didn't want to admit to letting a total stranger into the flat, now it was the cold light of day. It seemed a rash thing to have done. Last night it had seemed like the action of any good Samaritan.

Barbara waved her spoon. 'Morning!' she said through a mouthful. Then seeing Sally look perturbed: 'Are you all right?'

'I don't know,' said Sally. 'I lost my job last night.' She cast around for any evidence of Alexander, but he'd vanished without a trace. She was a tiny bit relieved, standing there with her hair all over the place in her nightdress and bedsocks.

'Oh,' said Barbara, reaching out for the cornflakes and pouring herself another bowl. 'They're looking for someone at the chemist.'

Sally made a face. Counting out pills and selling Durex to awkward men wasn't really her idea of a career path.

'Slight problem,' she said, sitting down next to Barbara. 'They wouldn't give me my wages. So I'm a bit stuck for this month's rent.'

Barbara stopped eating and stared at her through thick-lensed glasses. 'Well, I can't afford to pay for you,' she said.

Sally bit her lip. 'If you lend me the train fare, I'll go and get some money off my brothers.' They'd spot her some cash between them, even though it would be a bit humiliating.

'I'm not a ruddy bank.'

'I know. But it's either that or I move out.'

Barbara heaved a sigh and dug her spoon back into her cereal. Sally's stomach rumbled. She hadn't eaten since six the night before.

'Could I pinch a few cornflakes? I'll bring back a load of stuff from the butcher's shop. Whatever you fancy.'

Barbara looked at her, weighing up the situation. Decisions were obviously laborious for her. 'Lamb chops,' she said finally. 'And a bit of gammon. I like a bit of gammon.'

'It's a deal,' said Sally. She'd head up on the train tomorrow. She was too tired today. She thought she'd probably go back to bed for a few hours, then go to the shop and find a paper, see what jobs were going.

She found a bowl and tipped up the cereal packet. Three solitary cornflakes and a cloud of orange dust fell out.

On Sunday morning, she got up and had a tepid bath – Barbara had used most of the hot water – and put on her favourite dress: a swingy shift dress in green and yellow, with a white polo-neck jumper underneath and her white knee-length boots. The outfit would give her a lift so she would feel positive when she saw the boys. She would look the part, even though they probably wouldn't be fooled. Not when she asked them for cash.

She wouldn't say anything to her mum. Her mum would just worry. Or tell her to come home.

She was sweeping black mascara on to her lashes when she heard the sound of a car horn tooting madly outside. It was persistent – beep beep beeeeep – so eventually she went outside and up the steps to see what was happening. Russell Gardens wasn't used to disruption. Its quiet leafiness seemed affronted by the clamour, the houses looking askance at the interloper. For on the road outside was a gleaming bright red sports car, low-slung with a long bonnet. And behind the wheel, looking decidedly more human than he had the last time she saw him, was Alexander. He spotted her and waved.

'Come on,' he shouted over the throaty rumble of the engine. 'I'm taking you for lunch.'

She laughed. Already she realised it was typical of him to assume she had nothing better to do. She supposed people like Alexander knew they were always going to be the best offer anyone had. She stood for a moment on the pavement, the breeze ruffling her hair and her dress, thankful she was washed and dressed and made-up.

Of course she was going to say yes. Of course she was.

She was terrified by the speed at which he drove. London was still waking up – it was Sunday morning after all – but he seemed to have no regard for possible pedestrians as they roared down Kensington High Street. The shops were all shut and there was little traffic, but everyone who was out and about stopped and stared at them as they whizzed past.

'Where are we going?' shouted Sally over the deafening noise of the engine and the wind.

'Home!' replied Alexander. He looked sideways at her and smiled. She nudged his arm to indicate he should concentrate on the road.

'Where's home?' She'd assumed he lived in London, but they were heading out of the city, the grandeur of Kensington left behind. Here the houses were nondescript and characterless: rows and rows of red or grey brick lining the road, interspersed with the odd row of shops.

'Wait and see. It's a bit of a journey. Are you warm enough?' He slowed down and reached behind the seat, grabbing a red tartan rug.

Sally wrapped it around her and clung on to the edge of the seat, bracing herself every time they went round a corner. She had only ever been in the delivery van they used at the butcher's, or her father's Armstrong-Siddeley, which was cumbersome and slow. This car was like a jet-propelled bullet. There was no time to think about being sick, although she felt as if her stomach had been left behind miles ago.

Was she mad, driving off into the wilds with someone

she barely knew? It had seemed a better option than going home to face the questions she didn't want to answer, and the memories. They had begun to fade. Not that she wanted to forget altogether, but it was hard, trying to keep your chin up. London had helped her do that.

Eventually she relaxed, realising that Alexander knew what he was doing and where he was going. They left the outskirts of London and emerged into the countryside, whizzing through the occasional village. Sally caught a sign and realised they were heading towards Oxford, much further south than she was used to going.

After a while he pulled over in a lay-by. He dug around behind him and pulled out a thermos flask.

'Cocoa,' he grinned, spinning off the lid and filling the two cups with deliciously steaming chocolatey milk.

'You don't seem to me like a thermos flask sort of person.'

'Oh, trust me – I'm not. The person I was staying with forced me to take it.' He put the cup to his lips with a grin. 'Women do seem to love mothering me. Apart from my own, strangely.'

He laughed, so Sally didn't comment. The two of them sipped at their cocoa.

'Look at us,' said Alexander. 'Like an old married couple on a Sunday jaunt.'

'It's delicious.'

'So where are you from, then? Are you a London girl?'

'No. No, I'm from Knapford.'

'Where's that?'

'Bedfordshire.'

'Is that real? I thought it was made up. *Up the wooden stairs to Bedfordshire.*'

'It's real all right. And it's very boring.'

'What did you do there?'

Sally paused for a moment. 'We've got a butcher's shop. But I didn't want to spend my whole life cutting up slices of bacon.'

'So you ran away to London?'

'Yeah. Because the streets are paved with gold, aren't they?'

'They are. If you know where to look.'

'Really?'

'I hope so.'

'So what do you do?

'A bit of this and a bit of that. I'm chancing my arm at the moment. I suppose I should get a proper job, really.'

He took her empty cup off her and she jumped at his touch.

'Let's go. It's not all that much further.'

He screwed the lids back on, put the thermos back and started up the engine.

Eventually they turned off and the road led them through a tiny town with a wide street and high pavements. Sally gasped at the prettiness: it was like something out of a fairy tale, with its gingerbread buildings, mossy roofs and a brook running through it.

'This is Peasebrook,' Alexander told her as they flew over the humpbacked stone bridge. He slowed the car down, and now she could hear him. 'This is my home town.'

Sally gazed at the pointy windows and the wonky chimney pots; the mellow golden stone. It couldn't have been more different from sensible, upright, red-brick Knapford, which held no delights or surprises.

'It's wonderful!'

'Nothing much happens here either.' He gave a wicked laugh. 'Well, unless *we're* all home, of course. You've got to make things happen, haven't you?'

He dropped down a gear and accelerated out of the town, then a mile or so outside Peasebrook turned left into a lane that Sally would never have noticed was there. He went faster and faster between the hedges, which rushed past in a blur of bright green. She held her breath. If anyone was coming the other way, there was no room to pass.

'Don't worry – no one comes down here but us!' whooped Alexander as the car bounced along. Sally didn't feel remotely reassured.

Then suddenly they were at a set of stone gates. Alexander turned sharply and the car flew along a track lined with winter-bare trees. They turned a corner and the track broadened out, and there in front of them was a swathe of grass peppered with crocuses in front of a house that glowed gold in the weak winter sun.

'Welcome to Hunter's Moon.' He stared with pride, his hands still on the steering wheel.

'Hunter's Moon,' echoed Sally, staring in amazement. 'What a wonderful name.'

'Years ago they used to hold a huge party here during the hunter's moon, because it was so bright everyone could see to get home late at night. Only no one ever wanted to leave, so the party went on until morning.'

It was quite the most beautiful house Sally had ever seen: the yellow stone, the twinkling windows, the plume of smoke from the chimney; the trees, the fields, the hills around that hugged it.

'It's like something out of a book.'

'Well, funnily enough, in a way it is. My mother bought it with her royalties.'

Sally looked at him. 'Your mother? Is she a writer?'

'She prefers *authoress*. She says it sounds more glamorous.'

'Would I have heard of her?'

Alexander shrugged. 'Maybe. Probably. She's quite famous.'

He was so matter of fact about it. He got out of the car and came round to open Sally's door.

'Well, what's her name, then?'

'Margot. Margot Willoughby.'

'Your mother is Margot Willoughby?' Sally stared at him in astonishment. 'My mum *loves* her books.'

She could picture her mother reading them. The covers always had raven-haired beauties in revealing period frocks: all tumbling locks and heaving bosoms. Sally had packed them up when they moved but they'd thrown them away in the end because there was no room to keep them and no one wanted a pile of old paperbacks. A lump came into her throat, but she swallowed it down.

'Well, come on in and meet the family.'

Sally followed Alexander, whose long stride was hard to keep up with, across the crunchy gravel chippings and up the stone steps and through the half-open door of Hunter's Moon. As she stepped into the hallway she felt a sense of calm and warmth, as if she was coming home. But that was ridiculous, because she'd never been here before in her life.

There was no time to stop and take in her surroundings properly, because Alexander was bounding through the house: she glimpsed a wide hall, with flagstones and a gracious staircase, then followed him along a corridor, at the end of which he threw open a door.

It took Sally a while to discern that this was the kitchen, and that was only because she could see an Aga in the old fireplace. Other than that, it was like an antique shop mixed with a decadent jazz club. A table in the middle was covered in empty glasses still sticky with last night's cocktails, brimming ashtrays, books and magazines, half-burned candles dripping wax. There was a sink, and across the draining board was a cocked gun. Plates were piled up on the work surfaces, and on the other side there was a Dansette record player blaring out 'Let's Spend the Night Together' by the Rolling Stones. Another wall was covered in portraits, from the size of a postcard to imposingly large, some traditional, some abstract. Some had been added to: moustaches and spectacles had been scribbled on. The effect was of a motley crowd staring at the proceedings. There was a selection of threadbare armchairs, and on the back of one, looking beady, was a grey parrot.

At the table sat a young girl, singing along to the record, pointing a large black hairdryer at what looked to be a frozen chicken, waving it about.

'Beetle!' she cried out in delight, but didn't stop. 'There's nothing for bloody lunch so I'm trying to defrost this. But God knows how long it was in the freezer. Hello!' She beamed at Sally.

'This is Sally,' said Alexander. 'Sally, this is Annie. Otherwise known as The Afterthought.'

'Did you have to tell her that?' Annie looked indignant.

Sally could barely find words. The room was in a state of utter squalor, but somehow it didn't matter, because everywhere you looked there was something to capture your interest. A diving helmet, a mannequin, a bell jar with a little white stoat inside: she'd never been anywhere like this before.

'Hello,' she finally managed.

'Would you like a cup of tea?' asked Alexander. He said the words as if he knew that's what he should be asking but didn't feel quite comfortable saying it.

'Good luck,' said Annie. 'There's no milk either.'

Alexander's face clouded. 'Hasn't anyone been shopping?'

Annie shook her head. 'I didn't get back till yesterday afternoon because I had a lacrosse match. Dad's out and about. Mum's on a deadline. And you know what that means.'

The siblings exchanged glances. Then Alexander turned to Sally.

'Oh dear. I'm sorry. This wasn't what I was hoping for. You just can't ever tell. When my mother's under pressure everything falls apart.'

He gave a helpless shrug.

'Not that she's Mrs Beeton the rest of the time,' added Annie.

'True,' said Alexander.

Sally laughed. 'Never mind. I'm sure we can think of something.'

'I've brought back some rock buns I did in cookery. But there's no butter.' Annie turned off the hairdryer and produced a battered old cake tin. She offered it to Sally. 'And nobody can say they're not aptly named – they *are* like rocks.'

'Thank you.' Sally took one to be polite.

Alexander looked in the tin and shook his head. 'Where's Phoebe?'

'Still in bed.'

He sighed and looked around. 'Bugger. Has she finished those dresses yet? I was going to take them back up with me.'

'I've no idea.'

Annie turned the hairdryer back on and there was a loud bang. She shrieked and threw it on the table.

'You've fused it,' said Alexander. There was a strong smell of burning.

'What's going on?' There was a voice from the doorway. Sally turned. There was what she guessed was Alexander's mother.

Margot Willoughby.

'Mummy!' said Annie, her face lighting up.

'Hell's bells,' said the woman. 'What day is it?'

'It's Sunday, Mummy. All day.'

She was tiny, like a little ballerina, swathed in a man's silk dressing gown that came down to her ankles. Her chocolate-brown hair was piled up in a beehive, half of it falling down, as if she had put it up for a party two nights before, and the fringe was held back with a pair of tortoiseshell glasses. Her face was pale, her eyes huge and fringed with Bambi eyelashes – they had to be false, surely? There were freckles across her nose, and a gap between her front teeth.

Margot noticed Sally and blinked. 'Oh, hello,' she said, as if realising Sally wasn't one of her own children.

'Hello – Alexander brought me.'

'Did he bring food?'

'I'm afraid not. At least, I don't think so.'

Margot's face fell. 'I was supposed to go shopping.'

'Mummy, you are *useless*.'

'Well, we know that.' She looked at the clock. 'Where's your father?'

'We don't know.'

'Oh. In the pub, I suppose.'

Sally couldn't stop staring. She couldn't imagine anyone less like a mother than this creature. She was a million miles from her own, who at this time on a Sunday would be dressed in a flowered dress with a pinny strapped round her middle and sturdy shoes, pulling trays of puffy Yorkshire puddings from the oven while a hefty rib of beef rested on the side. She blocked the image out of her head.

Margot's eyes came to rest again on Sally.

'I'm so sorry – how rude of me. I'm Margot.'

'I'm Sally. It's lovely to meet you. My mother adores your books. I think she's read them all.'

Margot smiled in a way that indicated she'd been told this a million times before.

'Thank you,' she said. She gave an enormous yawn, stretching her arms high above her head, and looked at her watch. She floated past Annie and went to kiss Alexander. He took his mother in his arms and squeezed her tightly. Sally could see they adored each other. Margot stepped back and smiled up at her son.

'Mum. It's a bit of a hovel in here even by your standards. I've only been away three days and it wasn't like this when I left.'

'I'm fit for nothing. I've got a bloody deadline and I was up all night burning the midnight oil and I can barely see . . .'

'You know what it's like when mum's got A Deadline,

Beetle,' said Annie. She gave the word dramatic emphasis.

'But you've always got A Deadline.'

'Well, someone has to pay the school fees and the bills and for all the booze.' Margot ran her foot over the back of a ginger cat that was snoozing by the Aga. 'We'd all be dead of starvation if we waited for your father to put food on the table.'

Alexander rolled his eyes.

'Now, you're to say thank you to Sally. She pulled me out of the gutter on Friday night,' he told her, to change the subject. 'I was shamefully ratted.' He didn't seem to want to hide the fact he was drunk from her.

'Oh darling, you are such a little guttersnipe.' But she was laughing. She turned to Sally. 'Thank you. He is so irresponsible. Have you come to stay?'

'No . . . I don't think so . . . Just lunch, I think.'

'Fat chance,' said Annie. 'I think this chicken is putrid. It stinks.'

She pushed it away. Everyone stared at it.

'Fuck this for a game of soldiers,' said the parrot, making Sally jump out of her skin as she had thought it was stuffed. Everyone fell about laughing.

'So what do we do about lunch?' Margot looked around for answers, brightly expectant.

There was silence.

'Have you got a pub?' asked Sally eventually.

'Yes – the White Horse,' said Alexander.

'No! We're not going to the pub. That would mean getting dressed,' protested Margot. 'And putting a face on.'

'Most people do get dressed in the daytime, Mum. Most normal people.'

'Not if they've been up all night working.'

'What I meant,' said Sally, 'was maybe we could go and buy some food from the pub. And bring it back here. I can cook it.'

Everyone turned to stare at her.

'That,' said Margot, 'is ingenious. Alexander, drive Sally to the White Horse.' She put her cigarette in her mouth and rummaged about in her purse, producing two pound notes. 'There.'

She pressed the money into Sally's hand and she caught a drift of what she imagined an opium den might smell like – dark and exotic.

Before Sally knew it, they were back in the E-type, whizzing through the lanes, until they arrived at the pub. The landlord greeted them cheerily.

'I'll be right with you when I've finished serving this lot.'

'Have you seen my dad?'

'Not today.'

'Dad's one of his best customers,' Alexander told Sally. 'He spends all his time either here or shooting things, or helping rich people shoot things.'

'Doesn't your mum mind?'

'Anything that keeps him out of the house.'

'Doesn't he work?'

'He doesn't need to, with the books. Plus, he's totally unemployable.'

'Crikey.'

They explained their predicament to the landlord, who was obviously used to the Willoughby ways.

'I've got roast beef, but it's all in the oven already,' he told them. 'I could cut you off some slices, though. And you can take some spuds.'

They drove home, Sally carefully holding a foil-wrapped parcel of beef and a jug of thick brown gravy on her lap, a basket of potatoes and carrots at her feet. She'd managed to beg some milk, butter and eggs as well.

When they got back there was a large figure sitting at the table. A bear of a man, with wild dark hair and a scowl. Handsome once – and handsome now, probably, if he chose to shave and smile.

'So you're Sally,' he said in a lilting Welsh growl. 'Welcome to Hunter's Moon.' He held out a giant paw and she took it. He almost managed a smile. 'I'm Dai.'

'I've got him to take the gun out of the sink,' said Margot. 'I imagine you'll need it for peeling the potatoes.'

She clearly had no intention of peeling any herself.

Dai cocked the rifle and looked down it, aiming it at one of the portraits on the wall.

'Not in the house!' said Margot.

The door flew open and a girl with the longest legs and the shortest dress Sally had ever seen glided into the room.

'Phoebe,' said Alexander. 'This is Sally and she's making us lunch.'

Phoebe stared at Sally from underneath an inky black fringe, her eyes smothered in kohl. She smiled and Sally could see she'd inherited the gap in her mother's teeth. It gave her a slight lisp that made her sound like a little girl.

'Are you the new housekeeper?'

'No, she isn't,' said Alexander. 'She's an angel and you're to be nice to her.'

'Of course I'll be nice. Are you a model?'

Sally laughed. 'No!'

'You should be. You could be.' Phoebe scrutinised her. 'Don't you all think?'

74

The Willoughbys all stared at her. Sally felt awkward and picked up the potatoes.

'I'd better start these. Or we'll never eat.'

Sally was surprised by the whole family's appreciation when, within an hour, she had prepared roast potatoes, Yorkshire puddings and carrots. They sat around the kitchen table as reverentially as if she had prepared a medieval banquet complete with roast swan and suckling pigs.

'None of us can cook,' Annie told her.

'It's about the only thing I can do,' said Sally.

'That can't be true,' said Alexander.

'You look like a very capable girl,' said Margot.

Sally basked in their attention. Dai had opened a bottle of inky-purple wine, and just one glass of it made her feel woozy in the most delicious way. She felt cloaked in warmth and happiness. The Willoughbys were barking mad, all of them, but she loved being in their midst. It was like being at the theatre. Or the circus. You didn't know what was going to happen next.

'Beetle – we should take some photos of Sally in my new collection. Don't you think? It would save carting all the dresses round with you.'

Alexander looked at her. 'It's a good idea. But buyers like to feel the fabric.'

'Phoebe's a dressmaker,' Margot explained to Sally. 'And Beetle's trying to get her into all the shops.'

'Designer,' said Phoebe. 'Well, designer and dressmaker and sweeper-upper. At the moment. Until we get a firm order from someone big.'

'Wow,' said Sally. 'That must be very exciting.'

'It'll happen. Don't you worry.' Alexander speared another potato with his fork.

'So Sally – do you work?'

Margot said it in a way that made Sally realise in her world, work could be optional. A world of wealthy fathers and wealthy husbands.

'Well, I did. Until Friday. But I got the sack.'

'I can't imagine you being sacked. Where did you work? What did you do?'

'I was a cocktail waitress. At the Kitten Club? I'm afraid one of the customers was expecting more than his drink served.'

Margot burst out laughing. 'Well, of course he was.'

Sally looked puzzled. Margot stroked her arm.

'Darling, the Kitten Club is no more than an upmarket knocking shop. Didn't anyone explain what was expected?'

Sally shook her head. 'No. They trained me to pour drinks and chat and . . . look nice . . .'

'How much were you being paid?'

'£35 a week . . .' Sally said gloomily, wondering how on earth she was going to manage now.

Margot shook her head. 'You don't get paid that kind of money for making cocktails.'

'But they were all so nice. Just . . . normal.' Sally thought of the customers she had chatted to. They'd been quite interesting and perfectly civilised.

'You've had a lucky escape.'

Sally felt a bit sick. She didn't feel like going back to London. She felt foolish. Her brothers had warned her, told her she was green and to watch out, and she'd ignored them. She'd thought she was so grown up, able to stand on her own two feet.

'What are you going to do now?' asked Alexander.

'Well . . . my flatmate says there's a job going at the chemist she works in.'

She supposed that would do for the time being, until she got back on her feet. She would be safe in a chemist.

'I tell you what.' Margot leaned forward. Her eyes were glittering, as they always did when she had an idea. 'I'm looking for someone here. To sort this "bloody hovel" out and to answer my letters. I keep being told off by my publishers for not answering, but I say to them that if I'm tied up answering fan mail, how can I write books? Why don't you come and work here for a few weeks? You can have one of the bedrooms and you won't have to pay rent.'

'We promise to behave,' said Annie. 'We did have a housekeeper, but when she found two guests copulating in the drawing room she left on the spot.'

Everyone seemed to find this anecdote hilarious.

Sally looked round at them all, not sure if they were teasing her, or if it was the wine talking. Her stomach fizzed with excitement at the thought of staying here, with these gloriously alive and madcap people.

'Do you mean it?' she asked. 'Really?'

'Absolutely,' said Margot. 'I'll pay you what the wretched Kitten Club were paying and you don't have to sleep with anyone, I promise you.'

'Unless you want to,' said Alexander.

Sally tried to hide her excitement. They weren't to know how much she was already itching to restore order. She loved the kitchen, but it was completely filthy and chaotic and it could be lovely, really wonderful, with just a bit of organisation.

'So – you want me to run the house and be a sort of secretary?'

'Oh, and can you drive? Only it would be jolly useful to have someone who can pick up Annie from school at weekends.'

'Yes.' Sally had learnt to drive the butcher's van – her brothers had taken it in turn to teach her.

'Hang on, Mum – you can't exploit her mercilessly,' said Alexander. 'When's she going to sleep, in between all these duties?'

'Oh, she'll have plenty of time off, don't you worry.' Margot waved her cigarette around. 'You can come up to town with me. We'll go shopping. It won't all be pushing sheets through the mangle.'

Alexander looked at Sally. 'Don't let her take advantage. Give her an inch and she takes a yard.'

Sally laughed. 'I haven't said yes yet. What about all my things? And I owe poor Barbara a month's rent.'

'I'll pay that. You can owe me.'

Sally felt a thrill. It was wonderful to feel so wanted after the shock of Friday night. She'd thought she was on the scrap heap.

'Tell you what,' said Margot. 'Give it a month's trial. If you don't like us, then you can go.'

'But what if you don't like me?'

The whole family stared at her.

'We adore you. Already,' said Annie.

'You're like Mary Poppins,' said Phoebe.

'Only sexier,' said Alexander, and Sally's cheeks burned bright with the thought of Alexander having that thought.

'Then yes,' she said, because not in a million years could she now go back to that gloomy flat and Barbara's snoring and the thought of having to trawl through the papers for another job and risk getting herself into some other scrape.

Later that afternoon, Sally was waiting by the front door for Alexander. He was dropping her back to Russell Gardens to pack up all her things, then he was going to fetch her in the morning and drive her back down. They were dropping Annie back at school on the way.

Margot came to see them off.

'Promise me one thing,' said Margot. 'Promise me you won't fall in love with Beetle.'

'Of course not,' said Sally.

'You say that, but people do. And then he breaks their hearts. He's an expert at it. He doesn't mean to, but he does it all the time. Annie says sometimes he breaks three people's hearts before breakfast.'

Sally laughed. 'My heart is safe, I promise.'

Never mind falling in love with Alexander, she thought, as she heard him thundering down the stairs. She was in love with all of them: capricious Margot and brooding Dai and exotic Phoebe and intense little Annie.

But most of all, she was in love with Hunter's Moon.

10

1967

It was early evening by the time they set off back for London. As they left Hunter's Moon, Sally turned and looked back. Dusk was swooping in, wrapping the house in a pale grey mist, but inside the lights glowed brightly and she didn't want to leave. She felt a little giddy, from the unaccustomed wine and the sudden turn of events, and the prospect of returning to London felt cold and sobering. But she told herself she would be back the next day.

It was a bit of a squash as the three of them piled into the E-Type. Annie had to sit on Sally's knee in the passenger seat. She apologised like mad.

'I know I look like a lump but I'm only seven stone and I've got fine bones like Mummy.'

'Don't worry. I can't feel you at all,' said Sally, not wanting the poor girl to feel self-conscious. It was awful sitting on people's knees trying to be light.

Alexander started the engine and Sally felt rather than heard the roar.

'It's only a half hour drive to Larkford,' shouted Annie over the noise. 'You shouldn't lose all feeling in your legs by then.'

'Larkford. That sounds nice.'

'It's not. It's awful. It's *progressive*.' She made the word sound faintly obscene.

'What does that mean?' Sally was pretty sure Knapford Grammar hadn't been 'progressive'.

'It means we can wear our own clothes and there aren't really any rules. It's *dread*ful. Nothing ever happens. Everyone just sits around all day listening to Jimi Hendrix. And some of them smoke pot. *That's* not allowed, obviously, but no one cares.'

Sally looked shocked. 'That doesn't sound like school at all.'

'I know. But Mummy thinks it's the best place for me. She says she can't look after me properly at home and nor can Daddy so it's the perfect compromise as I can weekly board.'

'It's not that bad,' said Alexander. 'We were all sent to Larkford when Mum hit the big time,' he explained to Sally. 'She said it was the one important thing she could invest in, our education.'

'But that's the whole point. The education is terrible. No one cares if you don't do your homework. I hate it. And it didn't do you two any good. You haven't got proper jobs.'

Alexander rolled his eyes. 'Phoebe and I are doing what we *want* to do. Larkford gives you confidence. And contacts.'

Annie snorted. 'Do you know, if you haven't lost The Big V by the time you get to the sixth form, they won't let you in the common room?'

'The Big V?'

'Your virginity.' This was delivered in a stage whisper.

For a moment, Sally thought about her own. There

hadn't been time to do anything about it in the past couple of years. She'd had a few incidents at the tennis club, but nothing that inspired her to go all the way. She was horrified by the thought of Annie being under this pressure.

'How do they know?' she asked.

'They just do,' said Annie darkly.

'Annie, shut up. No one wants to listen to your drivel.'

Annie twisted her head around like an owl so she was face to face with Sally. 'Do you think if you're going to be at home I might be a day girl somewhere?'

'Don't put Sally under pressure,' Alexander chided.

'But it's ridiculous. It costs a fortune and I'm not really any bother. I would *love* to come home for tea every day.'

Sally remembered doing exactly that. Bouncing back into the kitchen with her satchel; doing her homework at the kitchen table while her mother made tea: big fat sausages that burst at the seams. Or liver and onions.

'Well, I wouldn't mind. But I don't suppose it's up to me.'

Annie sighed. 'It's all Daddy's fault that our family isn't normal.'

Alexander decided it was time to rein Annie in.

'No, it's not. And we *are* normal.'

'No, we're not. No one I know has a mother who makes things up for a living and a father who does nothing.'

'There must be loads of funny family set-ups at Larkford.'

Annie frowned. 'Loads of divorces, mostly. But definitely no other conchies. No one would admit to that.'

Sally saw a flicker of annoyance on Alexander's face. 'Shut up.'

'No. She needs to know, if she's going to work for us.' She twisted her head round again to face Sally. 'Daddy was a conchie during the war.'

Sally frowned. 'A conscientious objector?'

'Yes. Though he says he was as brave as anyone, because he was on fire watch, going in and out of bombed buildings during the Blitz.'

'Well, yes, that must have been dangerous.'

'But people think he's a coward. And it makes him angry, because he doesn't understand why not wanting to kill people makes him a coward.'

'But if everyone thought like Dad, then where would we be?' Alexander asked. 'Under German rule, that's where.'

'He's never said that *everyone* has to think that. But people should respect his right not to want to fight.'

'Oh dear,' said Sally, sensing this was an argument that the siblings had been embroiled in before, and not wanting to take sides. She wasn't sure what she thought, though she did know most people frowned on conscientious objectors. As a butcher, her own father had been in a reserved occupation, forbidden to enlist, and she knew how angry that had made him, how much he had wanted to serve his country, instead of serving out the measly meat rations week by week. He'd tried to do his bit by being an air raid warden, but it hadn't really appeased his patriotism. And then after the war rationing had hit the business hard—

She didn't want to think about her father. She thought about Dai instead. From what little she'd seen of him, she could imagine him standing his ground and sticking to his principles no matter what anyone thought. He didn't seem like a man of compromise.

'Anyway, it meant he couldn't get any work after the war. No one wanted to have anything to do with him. He was a Social Outcast.' Annie looked very serious about this diagnosis. 'Mummy already had Beetle and she was preggers with Phoebe and they were practically starving. Our grandparents would have nothing to do with them: Daddy's parents thought he'd let the family down, and Mummy's parents thought she should have nothing to do with him. They *still* won't have anything to do with us, any of them.'

'Oh dear,' said Sally.

'So that's why Mummy starting writing. And she turned out to be jolly good at it.'

'So there's a happy ending after all.'

Annie sighed. 'Well, I don't know. No one seems all that happy.'

'You're exaggerating,' said Alexander. 'Everything's fine. And you don't want to put Sally off, remember.'

Sally laughed. 'It takes a lot to put me off. Don't worry.'

Nevertheless, she was fascinated by the dynamics of the Willoughby family. Her own family seemed very uncomplicated by comparison, even after everything they had been through. Mostly they got up, went to work and came home. She supposed that having money gave you choice. Maybe that was where the problems started.

The Jag ate up the miles and Annie stopped rattling on and fiddled with the car radio until she found Radio London. Sally had never been in a car with a radio before, and she loved driving along, the three of them singing.

'You'll have to come and see the band I'm managing,' said Alexander. 'The Lucky Charms. They're going to be the next Kinks.'

'I thought you were Phoebe's manager?'

'Never keep all your eggs in one basket. Anyway, it's all linked. Music, fashion. Phoebe makes their clothes. They'll probably play in the shop when we find one.' He made it all sound so easy. They made things happen, the Willoughbys. 'I've got them a residency at a club in Soho. Come along one night.'

'I'd love to.'

She didn't tell him that, apart from her disastrous brush with the Kitten Club, she'd never been in a nightclub in her life.

'Can I come?' asked Annie.

'Sure,' said Alexander. 'We'll have a family outing.'

Annie clapped and Alexander smiled and Sally sat back in her seat, marvelling at how her life had changed in just one night. Thank goodness she had stopped to help Alexander and not just walked on by.

The driveway up to Larkford was gloomy, flanked with rhododendrons, and the school itself was a towering Gothic building that didn't look very welcoming. Sally could see why Annie wasn't keen to go back. But there were lots of youngsters milling around, and they all looked very gregarious and lively, arms around each other. Annie jumped out of the car, kissed Sally and Alexander and ran off into the crowds.

'Don't listen to her too much,' said Alexander. 'I think she's inherited Mum's storytelling capabilities.'

'Isn't it true, then?'

'Yes, but she's making it all sound much worse than it is. The Afterthought likes attention.'

'Why do you call her that?'

'She was their last resort. Mum and Dad's. She was a marriage saver.'

Sally thought perhaps Annie had been a thought of quite a different kind, given her lack of similarity to either of her parents or her siblings. She had a round, doughy pudding of a face with deep-set eyes, and mousy colouring. Sally would have felt sorry for her, but she was so cheerful and jolly you overlooked her plainness. And she was funny. Funniness went a long way to offsetting a lack of beauty. She was the dearest little thing.

'It's such a shame for her to be stuck here if she doesn't want to be. It sounds awful.'

'It really isn't that bad. Me and Phoebe survived and we're all right. And she drives Mum mad when she's at home. She's very demanding.'

'She seems sweet to me.'

'She's not as hard done by as she makes out. And she's older than she looks.'

'How old is she?'

'Sixteen next month.' He gave a wry smile as Sally looked surprised. 'I know. It suits her to put on the little girl act because that way she gets what she wants. She's quite calculating.'

'What a complicated lot you are,' said Sally. 'I've got two brothers but I always know where I am with them. They are what they are.'

'That must make life very easy.'

For a moment Sally fell silent.

'I suppose so,' she said, because saying anything else would mean telling him everything, and she wasn't ready for that yet.

She wondered what her brothers would think when she

told them her new life. Housekeeper. In what they would consider a mansion. In the middle of nowhere. She could imagine their comments:

'You'll be at the beck and call of a load of snobs with nowhere to escape to, Sal. They'll use you.'

She knew if she started to describe the Willoughbys it would do nothing to allay their fears. Even she herself thought she was being rash. Yet something was drawing her in.

'Do you want to stop off for a drink on the way back?' asked Alexander.

Sally suddenly felt awkward. Everything had happened rather fast, and now she wasn't sure where she stood with him. She'd gone from being his guardian angel and now she was . . . staff. Even though he'd asked her to go and see his band, he hadn't been asking her out as such. She looked at him as he stared at the road ahead, one arm casually slung over the steering wheel.

Was he the reason she'd said yes?

'I think I'd better get back and sort things out,' she said. 'I've got washing to do, and packing, and Barbara to placate.'

He didn't press her, which made her feel a bit deflated. He seemed quiet as they came into London, his ebullience dimming.

He dropped her off outside the flat at Russell Gardens. She didn't want to ask him in because she knew Barbara would be there and she didn't want him to see her dismal quarters sober. Nightfall had brought an icy wind and she shivered as she leant in through the window to say goodbye. Their cheeks glanced off each other. He seemed in a hurry to get somewhere.

'I'll fetch you tomorrow,' he said. 'About ten o'clock?'

She nodded, and he revved up the engine and sped off. She watched his tail lights disappear around the corner and wondered where he was going.

Barbara was very disgruntled when she told her what was happening, even when she gave her the crisp cash Margot had given her for the rent she owed and the two weeks' notice. 'Call it an advance, darling,' she'd said.

'I'm going to have to find someone else now,' Barbara complained, pocketing the money. 'I don't like change.'

'I'm sorry,' said Sally, though she wasn't particularly. Barbara had only wanted her for the rent, not the companionship. She'd even been stingy with her cornflakes.

II

It was very peculiar, standing on the steps of a house that had once been yours, staring at the paint you had chosen for the front door – Railings, by Farrow and Ball. She was surprised it hadn't been changed, but she'd left the tin behind in the shed, and she supposed the subsequent owners had liked her choice. It did indeed look very smart.

Outwardly she was her calm professional self. Inside, her stomach was roiling, her breathing was shallow and her palms felt clammy.

The High House. Her forever house. *Their* forever house. The house where they had been going to start their family, and then live with them right up until they became doting grandparents to their children's children. And maybe even great-grandparents. How long was forever, after all?

The High House was in a row of old wool-merchants' dwellings off the bottom of Peasebrook high street. It was square, double-fronted, with five steps up to the porticoed entrance, a set of black railings, sash windows, and two little dormer windows in the roof.

Belinda could remember drawing a house like this when she was small, over and over again on the big pad of sugar paper she'd had for her birthday. The sort of house she would like to have lived in if they'd had a normal life, instead of being nomads. She couldn't really draw very well, but houses were easy. Lots and lots of squares. So when she had first seen The High House it was as if she already knew it.

And as soon as she saw it, a roll of film had flashed through her head. A small girl on a rocking horse, a boy in the midst of a Hornby train-set, a towering Christmas tree in the hall, a table set for eight gleaming in the candlelight. A Hansel-and-Gretel playhouse at the bottom of the walled garden. Cast-iron bedsteads in the attic rooms, made up with soft bedding and fleecy blankets with stars on, well-worn teddy bears sitting on the pillows.

Nowadays she took the earlier turn off the roundabout to avoid going past the house, cutting into the high street higher up. She didn't want to be reminded of her shattered dreams on a daily basis.

Today, however, she was finally facing her fears. Or, to be hard-headed and rational about it, hopefully picking up another few thousand quid. She couldn't afford to be neurotic.

She picked up the door knocker and rapped it firmly, then waited until she heard footsteps on the other side of the door, trip-trapping over the tiles.

The woman on the other side of the door was petite, with pale blonde hair and a pretty face, clad in jeans and a voluminous cream jumper.

'Mrs Blenheim?' Belinda held out her hand.

'Fantastic! You must be Belinda. Come in! The house is in a state of perfect tidiness but I can't guarantee it will last so you must be quick before it descends into the usual chaos. I'm Suzi, by the way.'

'Please – don't worry about tidiness. I can see past all of that.'

'You mean I could have just left the washing-up in the sink?' Suzi feigned looking affronted.

'For me, yes. But maybe not when you have actual viewings.'

'Oh. I was going to go for the lived-in look.'

Belinda followed Suzi into the hall. It looked exactly the same, but with different photographs on the wall: Suzi and a handsome husband and two small children. But Suzi had made her laugh so much, it was not as excruciating as she'd thought it would be.

'I left you until last because secretly I want to go on with you,' Suzi told her. 'But my husband will kill me if I don't get other valuations.'

'You shouldn't be telling me.'

'I know! But I always love the houses you put on and I love your sign. I think that dark red will look really good on the wall outside.' Her eyes sparkled with mischief. 'I mean, that might as well be the reason. Aren't all estate agents the same really?'

'Well, there are other advantages to going on with me—'

'Yes, you're not a lairy pervert like Giles Mortlake.' Suzi looked disgusted. 'I swear he was looking down my top all the time I was showing him round.'

Belinda tried not to laugh, and didn't comment, tempting though it was. She warmed to Suzi immediately. She zipped around the house like Tinkerbell, chattering away and giving Belinda far more information than she needed, not least because she knew the house inside out already.

She remembered going to view The High House for the first time. This had been a rundown part of town then, a bit shabby. The house had looked uncared for, owned by an elderly woman who was going into sheltered accommodation. She clearly hadn't done a thing to it for years. The front door had been painted a dreary beige, but as soon as she walked over the threshold of The High House, Belinda knew it was The One.

Clients and customers often talked about 'the feeling': a sense of certainty that a house was right. A house could be perfect on paper, but if it didn't feel right, there was no point in trying to make it so. It was funny, she thought, that people were often more tuned in to what house was right for them than what person.

Inside, the floor of the hallway had been covered in pink carpet that was grey with dust. The windows were filthy, the doors bulged with damp. The kitchen had shiny dark brown units and a peeling lino floor. There were old milk bottles on the side, and a rust stain in the sink. It had needed totally gutting. Rewiring. Damp proofing. A new roof, probably. It was going to eat money. But she'd loved it.

It said: 'I can be whatever you want me to be'.

And it was still perfect. All the things she had loved about it were still here. The beautiful stone staircase. The light-filled kitchen. The larder with its slate shelf. The old-fashioned bell system for calling the servants still high up on the wall in the hall. She could imagine it at Christmas, the house smelling of cloves and cinnamon.

And now, in spring, the cherry tree in the back garden

was white with blossom and light flooded in through the windows.

The Blenheims had put their mark on it, but the bare bones were still the same. She barely breathed as she walked through all the rooms. She could still feel herself in here, like a ghost. So many of the things she had put in were still here: the glass pendant light in the hall, the silver mosaic tiles in the bathroom, the striped runner on the stairs. It was like rewinding through her life but without her in it.

She hesitated behind Suzi, stopping at the foot of the staircase to the third floor. This was going to be the hardest.

'The kids are up here,' said Suzi. 'I spend all my time running up and down the stairs, so it keeps me fit. But it will come into its own when they are bigger and don't need me so much.'

Belinda didn't reply. She just nodded, and followed Suzi up. She had never quite finished the top floor. She blocked out the memory, trying to maintain a professional façade, but as she saw the children's bedrooms, she felt her throat tighten with unshed tears. Suzi had done them out just as she would have liked, in soft colours, with thick curtains to keep out the darkness and keep in the warm, and carpets like clouds underfoot. Two bedrooms, for a boy and a girl, a pigeon pair.

She would never know now.

She stood in the door of the boy's room, with its Harry Potters lined up and the Lego in boxes. She could feel the pain, even now. Do not cry, she told herself. It would be so easy to break down.

She held on to the door jamb and breathed away the urge to collapse into a puddle of tears.

'Lovely,' she managed to say to Suzi. 'Two good sized rooms and a bathroom. Just what everyone wants.'

Full marks for an Oscar-winning performance, she thought, as they went back down the stairs.

'So what do you think?' asked Suzi. 'Giles Mortlake said it was "*a classic townhouse that has been lovingly restored with particular attention to period detail*". Though that's not down to me. Doing a house up is my idea of hell.'

'Actually,' said Belinda. 'It was me. I used to live here. Quite a while ago.'

'Seriously? Oh my God, that's amazing.' Suzi frowned. 'We didn't buy it from you, did we?'

'No – there have been a couple of owners in between. It was more than ten years ago.'

'You don't look old enough!'

'I was quite young, to be fair.'

Now she had confessed, she felt an overwhelming need to share the details with Suzi. She wanted to talk about the house; to exorcise it. Normalise it.

'You should have seen it. It was a complete wreck, full of awful wallpaper and terrible carpets. It was definitely a project.'

'How long did it take you?'

'About two years. I was as high as a kite on paint remover for ages.'

'Was it you who took those before and after photos?'

She'd been painstaking about recording her renovation and photographed each stage. She'd framed some of the most contrasting features and had left them hanging in the scullery when she left. They were still there, she'd noticed.

'Yes.'

'My goodness – it must have been incredibly hard work.'

'I don't think my nails have ever recovered.'

She looked down at her nails because she was finding the memories difficult. The excitement when she had lifted the hall carpet to find pristine tiles underneath. The satisfaction of stripping all the paint off the bannisters. The pleasure of choosing just the right wallpaper, the right lighting, the little touches that raised it from pleasing to perfect. And all the while she had been a little in awe of the house and its previous inhabitants and had wanted to respect its heritage.

'Well, you made it a very beautiful home,' Suzi told her.

'Thank you.'

'Why did you sell? After all that hard work?'

'Oh, lots of reasons. Property crash, a bad relationship, I wasn't very well . . .'

That was one way of putting it.

'I'm so sorry,' said Suzi.

Belinda looked out of the window. Don't cry, she told herself. It was so tempting, to tell Suzi everything. She would hug her, wipe away her tears, take a bottle of wine out of the fridge. She sensed Suzi was the sort of woman who would understand.

'Well, let's make sure we get you a good price and a quick sale,' she managed to say instead.

Suzi signed the paperwork on the spot, and Belinda promised to come round with Bruce to take the photographs as soon as she could pin him down.

As she left The High House she thought *I bloody did*

it! She'd confronted her demon and nothing terrible had happened. She felt elated, as if the dead weight that was holding her down had been lifted. Her past was no longer haunting her. She really was ready to move on.

12

1967

On Monday, Alexander fetched Sally promptly at ten. He looked tired, with black rings under his eyes, and she wondered what he had been up to, but he didn't give anything away. He was wearing the same clothes he'd been in the day before, and she thought he might have slept in them.

Her suitcase only just fitted into the boot, even though she didn't have many clothes.

'Sorry,' said Alexander. 'I don't know why Mum and Dad bought this car. It's pretty useless for anything except going fast.'

'It's beautiful,' said Sally. 'Isn't that why people buy things sometimes? Just because they're beautiful?'

She pushed her key back through the letterbox and heard it thud on to the doormat inside. She liked Kensington, but she hadn't felt at home with Barbara and wasn't sorry to leave.

Alexander wasn't very talkative on the journey. He turned up the radio so conversation wasn't really possible. Sally wondered if he was unhappy about her coming to Hunter's Moon. Eventually she plucked up the courage to lean forwards and turn the radio down.

'If you think this is a bad idea, just say,' she told him.

'I know it was all a bit sudden. And I know people some-times make offers they later regret.'

'No!' he said. 'It's the best idea any of us have had for ages. Things can't go on as they are. You are exactly what we need. I'm sorry – I'm being very rude. I had a bit of a night of it.'

'Oh.'

'It's very difficult, trying to break things off with some-one, especially when they won't take no for an answer.'

His dark brows were knitted together.

'I suppose it must be.' Sally hadn't ever been in that situation, but she'd seen her brothers negotiate several minefields. 'Nobody likes being dumped.'

He didn't elucidate and she didn't press him. She tried to imagine the girl Alexander was breaking it off with. She pictured someone with white-blonde hair and panda eyes and kinky boots, and it gave her a funny feeling inside; as she examined the feeling she realised it was jealousy. She batted it away. Alexander was never going to be inter-ested in someone like her. She was the housekeeper, she reminded herself. She mustn't forget that.

Margot came rushing out of the house when they arrived, wreathed in smiles. She had managed to get dressed today, in capri pants and a sleeveless blouse, her hair tied up in a ponytail. She hugged Sally.

'I'm so glad you're here,' she said. 'I hardly slept a wink, thinking you might have had second thoughts when you woke up this morning.'

'I thought the same!' laughed Sally. 'I was terrified you would send word to say don't come.'

Margot was holding both of her hands and looking

at her. 'I think you are meant to be here,' she said. 'The house has cheered up already. I can feel it. We haven't been treating it very well, I'm afraid.'

She spoke about the house as if it was a person as she led Sally inside. 'And now you will have to see the horrible truth. We've been living in absolute squalor. None of us is very house-trained. But the thing is, Dai and I went from living in a ghastly two-roomed flat in the arse end of Chelsea to living here. And I've never really worked out how to run a big house. I sort of get the hang of it every now and then and then it all falls apart.' Margot looked anguished, as if it was a very real failure on her part. 'And we do get people in to help but we can't keep them.' She looked pleadingly at Sally. 'If it gets too much just say.'

Sally smiled brightly.

'I'm sure I'll be fine. I'm used to looking after my brothers. Neither of them know how to wash up a cup or pick up a dirty towel.'

'Well, you're to have free rein and to run the house exactly as you want. The main aim is to keep everyone happy and fed. So I can work.' Margot began to chew on her thumbnail. 'I've got a deadline and I need to be able to concentrate. I can't worry about anyone or anything else. I know that sounds ridiculous . . .' She laughed, then looked serious.

'It's fine, I understand,' said Sally.

'Just tell me if you need money for anything. You know, if you want to buy a . . .' Margot cast around in her mind for something Sally might want. 'A vacuum cleaner or something.'

'Isn't there one?'

'Yes. Yes! There's one in the scullery. But you know, you might have a particular kind you like.'

'I'm not particular about vacuum cleaners,' Sally smiled.

'There's a chequebook in the kitchen drawer. Draw out whatever money you need from the bank in Peasebrook. And you can use the Mini whenever you like. It's in the garage. Alexander seems to have bagged the Jag. I'm not leaving the house for the foreseeable future.'

'Do you want me to bring you anything during the day? Tea or coffee or lunch?'

Margot looked appalled. 'God, no. Please don't interrupt me. I'll only want to talk.'

'Well, what time would you like the evening meal?' Sally wasn't sure what they'd want to call it. Dinner? Supper? 'And what would you like?'

Margot shrugged her shoulders. 'Ham. Lamb. Spam. Anything. Honestly, anything that somebody else has cooked would be lovely. I must go and do some work.'

Alexander came in with her bag. 'I'll show you up to your room, shall I?'

Sally followed him upstairs. On the landing was a huge portrait of Margot in a shimmering emerald green dress. There was a look in her eye that made Sally feel a bit uncomfortable, as if Margot was challenging her.

'Mum's publishers had that painted for her when she published her fiftieth book.'

'Fiftieth? Doesn't she ever run out of ideas?'

'She hasn't so far. But she does work hard, Mum. I don't think any of us really appreciate it.'

She followed him round to the next staircase.

'I know it seems as if I'm taking you up to the servant's

quarters, but these rooms are very nice. They've been done out for guests. So you should be comfy.'

The room was wonderful, in the eaves of the house, with a dormer window, and floor-length flowery curtains and a huge bed with a pink satin eiderdown.

Alexander put her case on the floor. The room felt very small suddenly, and the bed loomed very large.

'I'll leave you to unpack,' he said, very formal all of a sudden. When he had gone, Sally shivered slightly. She'd got too cold in that open-top car, she decided, and opened her case to find a cardigan.

Margot walked in the spring air to the coachman's cottage that was in the courtyard at the side of the house.

She felt filled with hope. Spring did that, for a start: it smelled sweet and fresh. The drifts of purple and white crocuses with their egg-yolk middles always lifted her heart: they were such brave and cheery little things, pushing through before everything else as if to tell them it was all right.

And then there was Sally. She felt good about Sally. Sally had been sent to her, she was sure of it. Sally was going to restore order and look after them all. The house would be calm and organised and happy. And Margot wouldn't have to worry. Sometimes she thought she was going mad because she just couldn't manage it all. Sometimes she thought that she worked her fingers to the bone so that none of the rest of them need worry and she wasn't sure that was fair.

She headed purposefully for the little coachman's cottage adjacent to the garages. On top of it was a tiny clock tower – although the clock had long been broken and stood at twenty past two – and a weathervane in the shape of a fleeing fox. Inside, the ground floor consisted of two rooms crammed with bits of old furniture left by the previous owners that after ten years they still weren't sure what to do with – a piano, several old chests, a mangle. To the right, a rickety staircase led up from the ground floor, and opened up into one big attic room with wooden floorboards.

Margot had chosen this for her study over the larger downstairs because of the view: out of the low dormer window she could see across the lawns and the gardens and the fields beyond. The view never failed to please her, as she could watch it change with the seasons, and it was the only distraction she allowed herself while writing. There was no telephone, no wireless. No communication with the outside world – just Margot and her imagination.

She thought she had finally got her study just as it should be. It was hard to strike the right balance. It needed to be comfortable, with everything she might need to hand, but not so comfortable as to be distracting. She'd had the floorboards sanded down, and the walls plastered and painted a deep dusky pink that was warm in winter and fresh in the summer. Under the window she'd had a broad desk built in, with room for her typewriter and plenty of space for her notebooks – sometimes she didn't want to type, she just wanted to scribble. There was a shelf with an Oxford English Dictionary, Roget's Thesaurus, and Brewer's Dictionary of Phrase and Fable. The wall to her left had a large bookcase crammed with copies of all the books she'd published. It was hard to believe when she looked at them – all those spines with her name up the side in curling script, translated into dozens of languages.

There were no other books, because she didn't want to be tempted to curl up and read. All the books she might read for pleasure were in the house. If she needed to do historical research she went into Oxford and spent a few days in the Bodleian, savouring its hallowed atmosphere and wishing she had been given the chance to study when she was younger. Not that she would have taken the chance if it had been offered. She couldn't wait to get away from home and go to London. That was where she had met Dai, the handsome, angry Welsh poet, reading his somewhat experimental poems in a pub in Chelsea.

He never wrote poetry now. No one wanted to listen to the musings of a man who wouldn't fight for his country. He was still angry, though. Even more angry. And somehow his anger seemed to exempt him from doing anything useful whatsoever.

It was ironic, because Dai had been the wordsmith when they met, and it had been his poetry that made her fall in love with him, and she'd never thought about writing and the power of words until they were starving – quite literally starving. And she had sat down one day and it all came trickling out. And bam! She got a book deal. It made Margot feel guilty that her own trite and meaningless words were gobbled up so voraciously by her loyal readers, but it did mean her family could live in relative luxury.

When people asked her what she wrote she gave them a typical Margot look – a flash of mischief with her Elizabeth Taylor eyebrows – and said 'Jean Plaidy with her knickers down'. Low on historical accuracy and high on drama, no bodice in Margot's books went unripped and her followers lapped them up.

And Margot didn't mind writing. There were far worse things to be sentenced to. She didn't really consider it work.

Until now, that is.

Something was wrong. She felt as if she had used every word in the dictionary, every plot, every character trait. She had used every hair colour possible – raven, flame, flaxen, russet, chestnut – and every eye colour from coal-black to ice blue.

And she sensed a sea change, a certain lukewarmness from her publishers and even her readers. And she had a sense that her agent was holding something back from her. Niggle refused to be drawn. He just told her to get on with the next book. She was supposed to write two a year; this next one was due in four weeks' time, for publication just before Christmas. A Margot Willoughby was a popular present. Thousands of copies would be carefully wrapped in jolly paper and tucked under a tree for a beloved wife or mother.

Once, the words would have flown freely from her fingertips. She was never short of ideas. As soon as she finished one book she would be on to the next. She had her magic formula, though she worked very hard to keep each book fresh and different, because she didn't want her readers to get bored or think she was just churning them out.

Today, however, she sat in front of the typewriter and stared at it. She had fed in a fresh sheet of paper with its carbon copy underneath the afternoon before. On it was typed 'Chapter One'. She had backspaced and underlined it, pecking at the underscore key eleven times, which somehow made it a bolder declaration of intent. But the rest of the page was blank.

She hadn't written a word yet. Not a single word.

There was a bitter, slightly metallic taste in her mouth. It was panic. It came up from her stomach and into her mouth. She tried to swallow it down.

Just start, she told herself. Every story starts with the first word. She cast about in her head for a sentence to begin with. But there was nothing there.

Nothing.

Sally decided she would give herself a tour of the house, to see what she had let herself in for. There didn't seem to be anyone at home. Alexander had gone off again in the Jag and the house was very quiet. She hoped no one would think she was snooping if they came across her, but she felt she needed to take stock and make a plan.

She left the kitchen behind, thinking that the detritus had been there for so long that another half an hour wouldn't make any difference, though before she left she filled the sink with hot water and put the plates in to soak. Then she ventured along the corridor and back out into the hallway.

There was a circular table in the middle covered in magazines, newspapers and letters, some of them ripped open, the envelopes crumpled, and others unopened – most of them looked as if they might be bills. There were boots and shoes and slippers kicked off by the front door and at the bottom of the wide sweeping stairs. There was a bicycle propped against a wall, a pair of roller skates and several tennis rackets. Coats and hats were strewn everywhere or hung on the newel post at the bottom of the staircase. Piles of things were perched on every stair – books, mostly, but also plates and glasses and empty bottles, a stuffed Pink Panther, hairbrushes, a hammer, several lipsticks and powder compacts.

The flagstones were covered in dirt, the pictures covered in dust, and there were cobwebs everywhere. It could be magnificent and welcoming, with just a little effort, Sally thought, and decided this would be her first project after the bombsite that was the kitchen. It was important to feel uplifted when you walked into a house.

She opened the door to the drawing room, expecting more chaos, and stopped short. It was exquisite – dainty and delicate, decorated in pale green and pink, with an elegant fireplace and soft carpet and satin curtains. But it didn't look as if anyone had been in here for months. It felt frozen in time, as if it was waiting to be discovered. Puzzled, she stepped back and shut the door, then headed for what logically must be the dining room. Would this be a stage set too?

It was quite the reverse. Except for a long table, there was nothing inside to indicate that it was a dining room. Instead, it resembled a combination of a factory and Ali Baba's cave.

There were bolts of fabric propped up against the wall: paisley, floral, houndstooth, stripes and zigzags in chiffon and velvet and silk. Some were in sludgy damsons and burgundies, others in monochrome, and there were bright pops of colour too. There were boxes full of buttons, sequins and feathers.

There was a sewing machine at the end of the dining table, and in the middle a swathe of fabric with a paper pattern pinned to it, half cut out. Everywhere there were scissors and pins, empty cups and packets of biscuits. Crumbs scattered every surface.

By the window was a long clothes rail, and on it was hung a row of finished items: dresses and jackets and skirts in a rainbow of colours.

And at the far end of the room, Phoebe was making alterations to an outfit on a dressmaker's dummy, pleating the fabric beneath her fingers until it fitted just so.

She looked up when she heard Sally step into the room. Her mouth was full of pins, but she gave her a wave.

'Oh my goodness,' said Sally. She had never seen clothes like it, not in her wildest dreams. Knapford had neither required nor supplied high fashion. This was like stepping into a magazine.

Phoebe extricated the pins from her mouth and smiled. 'Welcome to the sweatshop. I don't suppose you can sew?'

Sally shook her head. 'I can mend a tear and sew on a button, but I can't use a sewing machine.'

'That's a pity. It's all hands on deck at the moment. I have to find women in the village to run things up for me.'

'Where do you sell all this?'

'Boutiques in London, mostly. But we're looking for our own shop eventually.'

'How exciting!'

'I know! It will mean loads more work but we get to keep more of the money. Though obviously there'll be overheads too. And we'll need staff.'

Sally leafed through the clothes on the rack, silent with admiration and longing.

'Just shout if you see anything you want. You can have it at cost.'

'Really?' Sally's heart leapt with excitement at the prospect, then she realised she didn't have anywhere to wear any of the outfits. They were suited to a life of glamour and sophistication that wasn't her at all.

'I didn't think you'd come back,' said Phoebe. 'I thought you'd think we were mad. But I'm glad you did.'

She smiled shyly. She was quiet and thoughtful compared to the rest of her family, which seemed at odds with her modish image.

'Have you any idea what anyone would like to eat?' Sally asked her.

'Oh God, anything. Anything. We mostly live on bread and cheese and custard creams and peanuts. We've probably all got scurvy.'

'Do you know where I'd find the car keys? Your mum said I could borrow the Mini.'

'Oh, they'll be in it, I should think. No one bothers to take them out. Oh, anything but cod in parsley sauce. That makes me retch.'

'Fish will be on a Friday.'

Phoebe looked startled. 'Oh.'

Sally laughed. 'I'm only joking. Don't worry, I'm not going to be like a proper housekeeper. But I had better do some shopping or I'll get sacked after my first day if there's nothing on the table.'

'Don't worry,' said Phoebe. 'You'll never get sacked. The danger will be you walking out on us. That's what usually happens.'

It took Sally a while to get used to driving the Mini, and get the hang of the tiny winding roads, as she'd only ever driven the butcher's van in and around Knapford, but before long she'd reached the outskirts of Peasebrook. She managed to park, and looked up and down to assess the calibre of shops available. What she saw delighted her. It was a proper old-fashioned high street. There were three butchers to choose from, two bakers, a large greengrocer and a fishmonger, a post office – everything she could possibly need. She took note of an ironmonger as well, for her next trip in. The rest of the high street was a mix of antiques shops, a hairdresser, a saddler – she got the feeling that blood sports were the main entertainment in Peasebrook – and a big old coaching inn. It felt a lot more countrified and slower than Knapford. Everyone seemed to have time to stop and chat, whereas people in Knapford always had somewhere or something to get to.

She chose the butcher with the most attractive window display with a knowing eye: she could see the meat was pink and fresh, the sausages plump, plenty of fat on the joints. Inside, she joined the queue, and breathed in the familiar scent of sawdust and blood while she decided what to cook. She thought a beef casserole. If she made one big enough she could leave it for people to help themselves. She thought Hunter's Moon was probably not used to any sort of routine and the Willoughbys were used to coming and going as they pleased. She could cook a big gammon later in the week, and perhaps a roast chicken . . .

It was her turn, and she gave her order to the butcher: two pounds of stewing steak, a dozen sausages, half a pound of bacon. It was while he was wrapping up her order that the feeling came upon her: a swell of home-sickness mixed with a sudden longing for her father. The butcher was nothing like her dad, really, but something in his manner, the deft way he rolled up the meat and wrote the prices down on a brown paper bag in pencil, brought the memories back. She fumbled for money, horrified to find her eyes filling with tears she couldn't blink back, and she could barely say thank you and goodbye.

She fled the shop and stood on the pavement in the high street, trying to gather herself together but she couldn't, and suddenly the tears were gathering pace and rolling down her cheeks and she was heaving with sobs.

What on earth was she doing here? Miles from her own home, amongst people she had barely met? How could she possibly think this was going to be a new life? There was nothing familiar to cling to. No one who knew who she was, or even cared. The Willoughbys were obviously taken with the novelty of having her in their midst, but she wasn't one of them. She was an outsider. She didn't belong in their house or to their family.

She stood clutching the handle of her shopping basket. She was mad to think this was a good idea. She should go back to Knapford. She would be able to find a job there easily enough, and maybe a flat. She had her brothers, and plenty of old friends, and she knew nearly everyone in the town. And her mum. Her poor mum. How on earth could she have left her?

She was crying too hard to find her way back to the car. She stumbled blindly up the street, thinking she still needed to get vegetables for this evening, when she found a pair of arms wrap themselves around her.

'Hey. Hey hey hey. What's up?'

It was Alexander. He looked down at her, his face full of concern.

Sally tried to pull herself together but she just couldn't. She buried her face in his chest.

'It's OK. Nothing's happened. I went to the butcher and he reminded me of my dad, that's all.'

'Poor sweetheart.' Alexander stroked her hair soothingly. 'Why don't you give him a ring tonight? You can use our phone. Mum won't mind.'

'I can't.' Sally looked up at him. She hadn't meant to tell him. But she had to explain now or Alexander would think she was unhinged. 'He's dead . . . He died. Two years ago.'

'Oh Christ.' Alexander looked shocked. 'I'm sorry. I had no idea.'

'I should have told you earlier.'

'No. Not if you didn't want to. There has to be a right time for those sorts of things.'

He was so sweet. So understanding. For a moment, Sally was tempted to tell him everything. But then she realised they were in the middle of the high street. Here was not the place for a story like that.

'It's OK. Sometimes I get used to it and then something makes me remember him.'

'Of course it does. It's OK. You're allowed to cry. Poor you.'

Alexander hugged her tighter, then looked around. 'This doesn't look good. People are giving me disapproving looks.'

Sally wiped her eyes and managed a giggle. 'Perhaps they think you've broken my heart.'

'Probably,' said Alexander. 'Come on. What you need is one of the Corn Dolly's cream teas. I've never known a girl not to be cheered up by one of them.'

He led her off down the street to a café with a bow window crammed with cakes and buns.

'I think we've brought the average age down by fifty per cent,' he remarked in a stage whisper as they took a seat by the fireplace. The rest of the customers seemed to be dressed in tweed with dogs at their feet. A waitress with a mob cap and a frilly apron arrived at the table to take their order, and Sally realised that she'd hardly eaten since lunch yesterday.

'She'll have one of those big scones with the sultanas in, with cream and jam,' said Alexander. He patted the back of Sally's hand. 'I guarantee you'll feel a hundred times better afterwards.'

Sally gazed at him in amazement. For all his good looks and his glamour and his wicked ways, Alexander was surprisingly kind.

And he was right. The hot tea, and the scone the size of her fist, and the thick golden cream spread on top followed by strawberry jam lifted her spirits no end, and she soon found herself laughing as Alexander gave her a potted background on the other customers and their peccadilloes.

'Most of the old bags in Peasebrook disapprove of Mum because she doesn't go to church or belong to the WI and she works. But they suck up to her like mad because she's famous, and they're always trying to get her to open the fete or do a reading at the carol service.'

He reached out and brushed a dollop of cream from Sally's lip. She blushed and moved away, wiping her mouth herself just to make sure it was all gone.

'Alexander Willoughby.'

The pair of them looked up to see a woman with short dark curly hair standing by their table. She was in a fitted hacking jacket and tight jodhpurs.

'Long time no see, you naughty boy.' Her brown eyes were laughing and a smile played around the corners of her mouth.

'Hilly.' Alexander stood up, and indicated Sally. 'This is Sally. Sally, this is Hilly, a friend of the family.'

'What a very dull description.' Hilly swept Sally up and down with an appraising glance. Then she turned back to Alexander. 'What have you been up to? I haven't seen you for months. I've missed you.'

There was definitely a tone of reprimand in her voice. Was it wistful? Sally couldn't be sure.

'It's been hectic. I've been trying to sell Phoebe's clothes. And the band take up quite a bit of time. I'm in London a lot.'

Sally could sense he was making excuses.

'Well, lucky you. Think of us poor country mice with no excitement in our lives.' She turned to Sally. 'Look after him. I hope you know how very lucky you are.'

Her voice dripped innuendo, and she gave a wink before turning and leaving the café.

Sally looked at Alexander, who couldn't meet her eye.

'Did you want her to think I was your girlfriend?' she demanded.

'Honestly, I was only trying to protect myself. You don't know what she's like.'

'Is she an old flame?'

'Well. Sort of.'

Sally's eyes widened. 'She must be much older than you.'

'Hilly doesn't take no for an answer.'

'And isn't she married? She was wearing a wedding ring.'

'She's very predatory. She's like a sparrowhawk.'

'And you're the poor little defenceless mouse?' Sally raised an eyebrow.

Alexander fiddled with his teaspoon. He seemed a bit abashed.

'I know. I know. To be fair to me I had no idea at first. She chatted me up at some drinks thing Mum made me go to, and then it all got a bit . . . well . . . By the time I clocked she was married she'd got rather attached.' Alexander pulled some money out of his pocket to pay for the tea. 'I haven't seen her for a while. I've been trying to avoid her. I don't want to hurt her but I couldn't carry on.'

'Gosh.' Sally sat back. 'I didn't think things like that went on in the countryside.'

'I'm sorry if you felt I was using you.'

'It's fine.' Sally grinned. 'At least I've saved you from her clutches.'

Alexander pretended to shudder. 'Or her gun-wielding husband. Anyway, at least you look happier now. I've given you something else to think about.'

This was true. She felt much more robust, reinforced by the tea and distracted by the exchange. She picked up her basket, where she'd left it by the café door.

Alexander took her by the arm and led her outside. 'Now,' he said. 'Are you going to be all right?'

He looked down at her, genuinely concerned, his dark brows knitted in consternation. Sally could see why someone like Hilly would crave his attention. He made you feel like the only person on the planet who mattered.

'I'm fine. I'll see you later,' she said. 'Supper's at seven thirty.'

Or it would be, if she went and got the vegetables she needed. She'd better get her skates on or it would be custard creams all round again.

*

It took Sally more than an hour to restore order to the kitchen when she got back to Hunter's Moon.

It was a curious mixture of brilliantly well equipped and totally antiquated. In the cellar there was a twin tub and a washing line strung up, but it was far too damp and cold down there for anything to dry. She went outside to see if there was anywhere she could hang a washing line. How could anyone not have a proper washing line? She had found a pile of bills in the kitchen for laundry – washing and ironing and dry cleaning. The amount per week was astronomical – almost as much as Margot was paying her.

There was a brand new refrigerator and a large chest freezer, but they were both almost empty – the chicken Annie had been trying to defrost must have been one of the last things in the freezer's cavernous depths. Sally made a mental note to gradually fill it up with soups and stews. There were mouse droppings in the pantry, and about twenty pots of raspberry jam lined up on a shelf with handwritten labels, but nothing else. The Aga would need servicing and the chimney sweeping.

It was all going to need a proper spring clean, but she cleared up enough to get the casserole on. She'd already told Alexander it would be ready for half past seven, so she went and told Phoebe in the dining room.

'I'll tell Mum,' said Phoebe. 'She's savage if she gets interrupted. I'll tell Dad as well.'

Sally went back to the kitchen, then dug about in the drawers for a pen.

'I thought I told you not to do that,' said a voice, and she jumped out of her skin before remembering the parrot was surveying her from his cage. That definitely needed cleaning out, but she was a little nervous of him so she decided that could wait.

She sat down at the table with an old envelope. What she needed was a list.

FOOD	ESSENTIALS
Cereal	Dusters
Butter	Fairy Liquid
Sugar	Vim
Eggs	Mousetraps
Bisto	Lux
Cornflakes	Pegs
Marmalade	Iron and ironing board

Once she'd started, she couldn't stop. Brillo pads. Cocoa. Bovril. Mop and bucket. She thought of the kitchen at home, and how ordered it had been. How comforting. Whatever you wanted, you could find. She thought of the piles of ironed clothes her mum would leave for them. Cups of Horlicks on a cold winter's night; jugs of squash in the summer. Plates of sandwiches. Home-made flapjacks. She thought how safe it had made her feel. She wanted, desperately, to recreate that feeling here, for the house was crying out for it. Never mind the Willoughbys, Hunter's Moon needed looking after.

Dai was the first one into the kitchen, just after seven o'clock. He poured himself a glass of beer and offered Sally a cocktail, but she refused. It was Monday. She never drank on a Monday: in fact, she rarely drank at all. She thought the Willoughbys probably had no notion of what day of the week it was between them, nor cared.

Dai sat at the table while she put the finishing touches to the meal and set a proper place for everyone. With his broad shoulders and his head of wild shaggy black hair, he was like a gentle giant, and she found his rumbling voice tinged with the traces of singsong Welsh rather soothing.

'How are you settling in?' he asked, watching her with fascination, as if she were an illusionist, rather than simply putting a pan of water on to boil for the peas.

'There's a couple of things I'm confused about,' she said to him. 'Why does the drawing room look as if no one ever goes in there?'

'Because no one does. Margot had it done by some mad posh woman who does up houses, and we're all too scared to go in there. She uses it for photo shoots. And that's about it. We don't even go in there on Christmas Day. We hate it.'

'But that's such a waste.'

Dai nodded in agreement. 'Yeah, well, it's OK, because we told her to sling her hook after she'd done the drawing room. This is supposed to be a house, not a museum.'

Sally thought there was probably a compromise between a house feeling like a museum and looking like a bomb had hit it, but she didn't comment.

'What's the other thing, then?' Dai tipped the rest of the bottle of beer into his glass.

'The raspberry jam. There's twenty jars of raspberry jam in the pantry and nothing else.'

'Ah. That was Margot's attempt at being domesticated. We had a glut of raspberries so she decided to make jam.'

'She made all of that?'

'Yes. But none of us wants to see another spoonful as long as we live.'

Sally lifted the lid on the casserole and the rich scent of stewing beef curled around the kitchen. Dai groaned in appreciation.

'Proper food. I can't remember the last time we had a decent meal.'

'Can't you cook, then? Isn't it all about equality these days?'

Dai looked at her as if she'd asked if he could fly. 'No.'

'I could teach you.'

He frowned. 'What would be the point of that? You don't keep a dog and bark yourself.'

Sally raised her eyebrows. 'It might come in useful if I ever decide to leave.'

Dai chuckled. 'You're not leaving, cariad. Not now we've got you. Not a chance.'

Sally was surprised when all of the others arrived in the kitchen by twenty past seven. Even Margot, who was astonished to see knives and forks set out and a glass at everyone's place.

'You've laid the table properly. Napkins and everything!'

'Actually,' said Dai, 'she made me do it.'

Everyone stared at Sally in amazement. She laughed.

'Everyone's got to pull their weight, I'm afraid.'

Margot sat down. 'Everyone who's not in paid employment, you mean.'

'Listen to Lady Muck.' Dai threw his napkin at her, and she threw it back with a smile.

'Darling, don't forget it's the agency party tomorrow night. Shall we stay in town?'

Dai frowned. 'Do I have to come?'

'Please. It'll be no fun on my own. I hate talking shop.'

'I don't fancy it.'

'You had a fantastic time last time.'

'I did not. That awful woman with the glass eye would not leave me alone.'

'Edith? You were flirting with her.'

'I felt sorry for her. You'd think with all her money she'd get an eye that swivelled.'

'She's eccentric and lonely.'

'Will she be there?'

'Of course. All Niggle's clients will be.'

Dai shook his head.

'I'm not in a London mood.'

'You are so boring these days. What's the matter with you?'

'I'm boring because I don't want to be mauled by a woman with one eye?'

'There'll be stacks of other people there. She won't notice you.'

'She damn well will. Her other eye doesn't miss a thing.'

'Well, you shouldn't be so irresistible.'

'Go on your own, Mum,' said Phoebe. 'You know what Dad's like when he's in one of his antisocial phases. He'll only be a ball and chain.'

Dai raised an eyebrow. 'I am here, you know.'

'I'll come with you,' said Alexander. 'Liven things up a bit.'

'It's OK,' sighed Margot. 'I'll go on my own.'

Sally was looking round at them all in amazement. She was used to her brother's banter at the table, but this was something else.

Phoebe caught her eye. 'It's always like this,' she said. 'I wouldn't be surprised if you've gone in the morning.'

Sally put a large cast-iron casserole in the middle of the table and lifted the lid.

'I hope you like this. It's my mum's recipe. Hopefully there'll be enough for lunch tomorrow.'

There wasn't a single spoonful left over.

13

'Ooh. What about him? He looks nice. Very handsome and he's got a nice shirt on. Oh, he's a widower, poor thing. *Lost my wife five years ago but finally feel ready to go out into the big wide world . . .* Aaaah.'

'Cathy – please stop. Nothing would induce me to hook up with someone when I have no idea who they are.'

'But he's got kind eyes. And a Labrador. So he must be all right.'

Belinda sighed. Every morning Cathy trawled through various Internet dating websites for the latest additions on her behalf.

'Just send him a message. It can't hurt,' Cathy pleaded. 'He's thirty-nine. That's the perfect age for you.'

'Where the bloody hell *is* Bruce?' Belinda frowned at her watch.

Cathy clicked off the site. She could see there was no cajoling Belinda.

'He knows your appointment's at ten. I reminded him last night before I left the office.'

'If he's got a hangover . . .'

'He promised he'd be on time. It's only just gone half nine and it won't take you long to get to The High House.'

Belinda loved Cathy for her calm reassurance. She

knew not everyone worked at her pace, Bruce in particular. He was cutting it fine, though. The sun was out but there was no guarantee it would stay out, so they needed to get going.

Photography days were her favourite days. Most agents didn't bother going out with their photographers, but Belinda loved being part of the process. She didn't interfere with Bruce – she respected his talent far too much to micromanage him – but she used the opportunity to get to know the house she was selling a little better.

The only thing that enraged her about Bruce was his timekeeping. Or lack of.

'I'm going to kill him,' she said, looking at her watch again, just as Bruce loped into the office, his long legs in faded skinny jeans, shrugging off his black leather jacket, his hair windswept from roaring around in his battered vintage Porsche.

He was fifty if he was a day but he still looked as if he'd just walked offstage after kicking over a drum kit. He was an anomaly in genteel, countrified Peasebrook. He'd taken refuge back at his father's house three years ago when he was careering off the rails – 'It was Peasebrook or the Priory,' he was fond of saying – but he still dressed like an off-duty rock star. He was constantly being pursued by middle-aged faded blondes, who sported a tad too much leather and leopard skin, and Belinda was always getting him out of scrapes.

Bruce usually did weddings: glorious tableaux that looked like something out of a fairy tale. Belinda had seen some of his wedding photos, hunted him down and begged him to come and work for her. She was surprised when he said yes, because she couldn't afford to pay him anything like what he got for a wedding, but she threw in her cellar as a studio and that tipped the balance.

'It'll get me out of the house,' Bruce told her when he agreed. 'I work most Saturdays, but the rest of the time I'm stuck inside editing and touching up. This will suit me down to the ground. And it stops me ending up in the pub.'

Belinda could see from day one that Bruce might be trouble, but working for Belinda gave him more structure to his week. And he couldn't pour himself a stiff Jack Daniels in the morning in case she called him out – he had a habit of turning to the bottle when self-doubt set in, because, like her, he was an obsessive and a perfectionist.

'I don't drink at weddings, though, ' he told her. 'Not any more.'

There had been an incident with a bridesmaid, apparently. For all his observance, Bruce had failed to notice one of the ushers was her husband.

'I thought bridesmaids were unmarried,' he had protested. 'Isn't it matrons of honour you're not supposed to bang?'

Potential troublemaking aside, Bruce made her brochures look like a magazine spread. Other agents tried to copy their style, but without Bruce's eye, they couldn't pull it off. He was the David Bailey of house photographers, and her clients loved him. All of a sudden they saw where they lived through fresh eyes.

Belinda went to hug him. His cheeks were cold: the spring air still had quite a bite to it.

'Come on. We've got two to do this morning. One in town, then we're going to the most beautiful house, Hunter's Moon. Out on the Maybury road?'

Bruce's eyes gleamed. 'You know who that used to belong to?'

Belinda nodded.

'Yes. Margot Willoughby.'

'She was an absolute stunner. My father knew her. He was utterly besotted.' Bruce gave a wicked grin.

'But he must have been way younger than she was. She's long dead, isn't she?'

Bruce just laughed. 'You know my dad. He's still got an eye for the ladies, even now.'

'Your father's a poppet.' Belinda adored Bruce's father, a sprightly octogenarian with twinkling eyes and a story to tell. He was always in Peasebrook high street, in his tweed cap with a walking stick – he'd broken his hip out hunting at the age of seventy-four.

'Get him to tell you about the parties. They were quite wild. Lots of fancy dress and bad behaviour.'

'I will!' Belinda was fascinated, and now Bruce had begun to paint a picture of life at Hunter's Moon, she wanted to know more of its history. 'Come on. Chop-chop.'

Bruce grabbed his camera bag. 'Am I driving or are you?'

'Me,' said Belinda, who knew only too well Bruce's disregard for the speed limit. 'I'd like to get there in one piece.'

They did The High House first.

Despite Suzi's protests that she was some sort of domestic slut, it was immaculate. She welcomed them in.

'I'll leave you to it,' Suzi said. 'There's probably nothing more annoying than a vendor trotting round after you making helpful suggestions.'

Bruce eyed her approvingly. 'You can trot round after me if you like, darling.'

Belinda nudged him with her elbow to shut him up. Not everyone appreciated Bruce's innuendo. 'You're right. It's best if you leave us to get on with it. We won't be more than an hour.'

Somehow, going back into The High House for the second time felt less traumatic. And having Bruce there, with his constant banter and his enthusiasm, chased away any ghosts. He bossed her around, getting her to move furniture and put vases of flowers in strategic positions.

'This will fly,' he said. 'Nice gaff. They must have put a lot of hard work into this.'

Belinda found it tempting, for a moment, to drop it casually into the conversation. That the staircase had been stripped by her own fair hands. And the tiles in the hall. That she had painstakingly designed the sleek cream kitchen with the wooden worktops. But if she told Bruce The High House had been hers, she'd have to tell him more.

'It's gorgeous,' she agreed. 'Someone's dream home. It'll be snapped up.'

'Why don't you buy it? I can totally see you here.'

'Ha ha.'

'You're looking for somewhere though, right? You've been saving like mad.'

Everyone at the office knew about her Forever House fund.

'This is way beyond my budget.'

She was just a few thousand pounds shy of her target deposit. That, combined with her income, wasn't nearly enough for a house like this. She would only be able to afford a small cottage. Although that would do for her. As long as it was hers, a house she could call her own, and put her own stamp on.

'You've got to think big, babe. You could get a lodger.'

'I do *not* want a lodger. I've got enough to worry about.'

'You never know, you might get some hot young guy.'

'I don't have time for a guy, hot or otherwise.'

Bruce looked at her thoughtfully.

'You need to get back on the horse before it's too late. You know that, don't you?'

'Bruce – I've had enough of Cathy trying to match me up every morning. Why can't you both accept I'm quite happy as I am?'

'How long's it been?'

She looked at him. 'How long's what been?'

'You know.'

Belinda rolled her eyes and refused to answer his question.

'You're obsessed.'

Bruce sighed. 'I'm not talking about sex.' He lifted a strand of her hair. 'I'm talking about you having someone who cares about you. You're a gorgeous, amazing girl, Belinda.'

'Not really.'

'You're hot, babe.' Bruce could never understand why she was single. 'You've got that sort of naughty netball captain thing going on.'

Belinda rolled her eyes. 'I've never played netball in my life.' Bruce was so un-PC. And he called her babe without a trace of irony. But somehow he got away with it, and secretly she was flattered, because Bruce didn't dish out compliments unless he meant it. 'If I wanted a boyfriend, I'd go and find one.'

'I think you're scared. I think you're scared of being hurt again.'

'Who says I've been hurt? You're just making assumptions.'

'You have. I can tell. Why else would you lead the life of a nun? But you know, not all men are bastards . . .'

'I know. But I haven't got time.'

'You have to make time!' His voice was low, caring. 'I think it's a waste, that's all. You deserve to have someone to look after you and worship you. And just because somebody hurt you once—'

'Please, Bruce. Pack it in.' Belinda was starting to get agitated and she knew why – because Bruce was right. 'I don't go banging on about you being unattached.'

Bruce chuckled. 'No one would have *me*, darling. I'm bloody impossible. We know this.'

'You could choose not to be. You could make a lovely husband. You're kind, funny, fun. Quite nice-looking.'

'Quite?' Bruce feigned hurt.

'OK – very. There's loads of fifty-something divorcees and widows out there who would leap at the chance.'

Belinda couldn't help laughing at Bruce's expression. He was looking very disgruntled. He could dish it out but he couldn't take it.

'It's way too late for me. I'm set in my terrible ways.'

'Well, there you go. You and me both. Let's agree to differ.'

Even when he was scowling, he was handsome, she thought. If he wasn't such a reprobate, if he wasn't so much older than her, if they didn't work together, she might be tempted.

She was glad she'd dodged the bullet, though. If she

told him the truth, Bruce wouldn't let it drop, and she didn't have the strength or the heart to revisit what had happened. Some things were best left in the past.

'Are we finished here?' she asked. 'Because we need to crack on.'

Twenty minutes later, as they turned off the main road and into the lane that led to Hunter's Moon, she grinned at Bruce. She felt excited by the thought of his reaction.

'Prepare to be dazzled.'

Bruce gave a low whistle as they turned the corner and he saw the house for the first time. 'Wow. My father always said it was the most beautiful house he'd ever been in, but this is something else.'

'I know. Isn't it gorgeous?'

'Oh, man – they'll be falling over themselves.' He scrambled out of the car and grabbed his camera bag. 'Look at it! Look at the fountain! Can you imagine what fun you could have in that?'

Belinda could only imagine what he was imagining: six supermodels and a bottle of Fairy Liquid, probably.

'Calm down, Bruce. We're keeping it classy, OK?'

Bruce nodded, slightly in awe of the view in front of him. 'I'll have no problem. This is perfect. Oh God, I hope you find someone nice to buy it. I mean, what would you change? Nothing.'

'I know, right?'

'It would break your heart, moving from here.'

'Yes,' said Belinda softly. 'I think that's exactly what's happened. So I want to make the whole thing as painless as possible.'

Bruce looked at her, a quizzical expression on his face.

'Why are you looking at me like that?'

'Most people would be rubbing their hands together with glee thinking about the commission.'

'Don't worry; I'll get my commission. It doesn't mean I can't look after my clients. Their peace of mind is more important to me than my percentage.'

'You're a softie really, aren't you?'

'Maybe.' She crunched across the gravel towards the front door, just as a tall, slender man emerged.

'You must be Belinda.' He smiled, and she was struck by how attractive he was, although he must be in his seventies. Dark, arresting eyes and swept-back grey hair. 'I'm Alexander Willoughby. My wife tells me we are in very safe hands.'

'I hope so. This is my photographer, Bruce. We'll try not to intrude.'

Bruce held out his hand. 'Pleased to meet you. My old dad used to come to parties here when he was a youngster.'

'Oh God.' Alexander gave an impish grin. 'Did he survive to tell the tale?'

'He was head over heels in love with your mum.'

Belinda cringed. Bruce was being his usual indiscreet self. Alexander didn't seem to mind, though.

'Who wasn't?' He indicated the house and grounds with a sweep of his hand. 'Anyway, help yourselves. Sally's out, but she'll be back soon so don't go without saying goodbye. Come and have a coffee in the kitchen.'

He walked back inside.

'What a legend,' said Bruce admiringly. 'I hope I wear as well as him.'

All Belinda could think was: what a wonderful man and how terribly sad.

Usually Bruce's time was spent trying to make houses look more enticing than they really were, with filters and wide angles. He needed no such trickery for Hunter's Moon. The difficulty was narrowing the pictures down: they were spoilt for choice, between the fountain and the lily ponds and the swimming pool; the clock tower, the walled garden – and that was before they even went inside.

When Sally saw the pictures, they made her cry. Bruce loaded the best shots on to her iPad and she and Alexander scrolled through them in the kitchen.

'They're like something out of a magazine,' she said.

'I've contacted everyone on my books who's after a property like this,' said Belinda. 'There's been a lot of interest. We've got several bookings for the open house already.'

They had agreed a Saturday in a fortnight's time. Belinda felt it was important to create a sense of urgency, to instil in potential buyers a fear of missing out.

'I think it's probably best if Alexander and I aren't here,' said Sally.

'Definitely,' said Alexander. 'We'll go away for the day.'

Belinda felt relieved. It would be awkward for the Willoughbys, watching prospective purchasers crawl over their beloved home. She had done her best to make sure there weren't any property tourists – it was surprising how many people spent the weekends viewing houses they could never afford to buy – but people were naturally curious.

'I agree,' she said. 'I'll look after your house, don't worry. I can report back the next day. We should have got a fairly good idea of interest levels.'

'Perfect.'

'Oh, and it might be best if you took Teddy with you too. I'm sure whoever buys Hunter's Moon will be a dog lover, but it might be less disruptive on the day.'

Sally bent down and ruffled the dog's head. 'There's no way I'd leave Teddy here – he'd take great delight in causing as much chaos as he possibly could.'

Later that evening Alexander scrolled through the photos again. It was strange, seeing all the settings without any people in them. The pool, so still and silent: he could imagine the heat of summer and all of them lounging around, himself and Phoebe and Annie and their friends, revelling in the luxurious torpor of nothing to do. The drawing room, crowded with people at Christmas, logs snapping in the grate. And he didn't think he had ever seen the kitchen as empty as it was in the photo Bruce had taken – though he had artfully positioned Teddy in front of the Aga. The photos were stunning but somehow lifeless.

He tried to imagine who might be buying the house, but stopped. It was too painful.

'Are you all right, darling?' Sally came up behind him and ran a caring hand over his shoulder. 'They're wonderful, aren't they?'

He took in a deep breath. He wasn't going to drag Sally down with him. He knew she found it as hard as he did. That she was fighting to make this part of their journey together as painless as possible. She was smiling down at him and he thought: she looks just like she did the first night I met her. He might have been drunk, but he could remember the care and concern in her eyes as she looked down at him. And how utterly adorable she'd been, with those kitten ears, her mascara smudged, her lips still sugary pink.

He could remember it as if it was yesterday, the night he'd fallen in love with Sally. It had frightened him. He'd never been frightened by a girl before. Frightened of the feelings she unleashed in him that he didn't know quite what to do with.

He'd fallen in love that night, but it had taken him a long time to admit it to himself, over that summer. It had taken him even longer to admit it to her.

14

1967

'You don't think it's too much?' asked Margot. 'I mean, it's quite a tricky colour.'

She was standing still, with her arms out, while Phoebe adjusted the hem of the dress she had made for her. It was in burnt-orange chiffon with bell sleeves, and was dangerously short, finishing halfway up her thighs. Luckily Margot had good legs, and she had teamed it with her patent Roger Vivier shoes with the silver buckles.

'Well, nobody else will be wearing it.' Dai was surveying his wife with the look of a man who didn't understand fashion and never would.

'You look wonderful,' said Sally. 'You'll be the belle of the ball.'

'Is my hair OK? That hairdresser in Peasebrook is out of the ark. I gave her a picture but I don't think she even looked at it.'

Her hair was piled up in an elaborate bouffant of curls.

'Hang on,' said Phoebe. She grabbed a comb and gently teased out some strands of hair with the tail. 'That's better. It's a bit less of a helmet.'

Margot went to stand in front of the mirror Phoebe had propped up. She looked happy with the result.

'Darling, you are a genius. Every woman should have a Phoebe.'

'Every woman will have soon – if I play our cards right,' said Alexander. 'I'm showing her winter collection next week.'

'Winter?' said Dai. 'But it's only March.'

'We work two seasons ahead in fashion, Dad.' Phoebe ruffled her father's hair. 'And I know you know. Why do you pretend you don't?'

'I don't know,' said Dai. 'I'm bored, I suppose.'

'Only boring people get bored,' said Margot crisply. 'And I *have* offered. It's not too late for you to go and have a bath and come with me.'

'Yes, it is. It would take me too long.'

Margot sighed and rolled her eyes. 'Girls, never marry a man who won't take you to a party. It's too tedious for words.'

Sally winced. She had noticed that Margot could be cruel. She didn't think she meant to be – it was just her manner, to be tart. But she felt sorry for Dai. It must be difficult living in Margot's shadow. She was so glittery and certain and sure of herself.

Actually, Margot wasn't as sure of herself as everyone thought.

She might earn more money for Niggle than most of his clients, and was probably his best known, but she couldn't help feeling that a lot of them looked down on her for it. So she found his parties quite difficult. She made up for it by endeavouring to be the most glamorous person there, but perhaps that only proved what she feared people were thinking: that she was rather superficial.

She was also feeling a little unsettled by Sally. She thought her wonderful, and what she had already done, in just a few days, was marvellous, but she rather showed up how useless Margot was. She scolded herself for being insecure. She couldn't do everything. She couldn't be a doting wife and mother and run a house *and* write best-selling novels.

Only she wasn't doing any of those things at the moment . . .

She wasn't going to let her doubts spoil the evening.

If her agent did one thing well, it was give excellent parties. Nigel (or Niggle as his clients called him) Rathbone knew the job of a writer was a lonely one, and that most, if not all, writers liked a drink, so he threw open the doors of his Fitzrovia office several times a year, shipped in vats of booze, got a girl in to do cheese and pineapple on sticks and stood back. It was always a Rabelaisian affair. Over the years, the parties had ended in three marriages, two divorces, a birth and a lot of lunches – some clandestine, others lucrative, as he invited publishers and producers too. He was unusual as he represented both novelists and screenwriters, but his argument was that it was all story-telling, so what did it matter?

Margot had skittered around all the people she knew, kissed them and exchanged pleasantries. Including the hideous Edith, Dai's bête noir, who wrote abstruse feminist diatribes – which Margot couldn't get through to save her life.

'Is your charming husband not here?' Edith raked the room with her good eye.

'He's in the country,' said Margot. 'Excuse me – there's someone I must say hello to.'

She'd spotted a newcomer. Terence Miller was a recent client. He'd famously fallen out with his old agent – it had actually got to fisticuffs in the bar of a hotel late one night – and Niggle was reticent about taking him on because he was a bit of a firebrand and a hellraiser, being a champagne socialist.

'Only there's always more champagne than socialism with Terence,' Niggle confided in her. 'Except when it comes to his scripts, which are brutal. But brilliant. Which is why I'm taking the risk. I can always sack him if he gets out of control.'

Miller also had a reputation for being arrogant, and a womaniser. Margot wasn't intimidated by either trait. She was used to brooding, acerbic, principled Dai, and she radiated under the attention of men, being a natural flirt. She considered Miller fair game.

She saw him meet her gaze and he assessed and dismissed her in one second before he turned away. It was all she could do not to let her mouth fall open. No one *ever* dismissed her, especially not men. Even in middle age, she was still catnip; still irresistible. And while she never did anything about it, she revelled in the attention.

She was not going to be ignored.

She got one of the waiters to freshen up her brandy and soda and cornered Miller by the food table. He was examining a plate of prunes wrapped in bacon with a worried expression.

'Welcome to the Rathbone Agency,' she told him. 'I loved *The Runaway*. I cried from start to finish.'

He gazed at her with pale grey eyes, paler than the moon.

'What are these?' He pointed at the plate.

'Devils on horseback,' Margot told him. 'Standard party fare.'

'I don't see the point of this sort of thing,' he said. 'Waste of bloody money. But Nigel told me he would only take me on if I came.'

'Niggle likes everyone to mix and share ideas and collaborate,' said Margot.

'Collaborate?' He managed to fill the word with innuendo. He had a flat Nottinghamshire accent that came and went to suit the occasion and the company.

'Yes,' twinkled Margot. 'Lots of us have worked together on projects. Well, not me, because, well . . . no one wants to collaborate with me.'

'Oh.' He raked his eyes up and down her. 'Nice dress.'

She was slightly taken aback that he would notice. 'My daughter made it.'

He put a hand out to feel the fabric, rubbing it between his fingers. She pulled away as if she'd been burned. He put his hands up in apology.

'My mother was a lacemaker. I was brought up to appreciate beautiful fabric.'

Margot smoothed the dress down as if to wipe away his touch.

'I wouldn't have thought you'd be interested in something so superficial.'

'Why not? You can have a social conscience and still appreciate beauty or talent or quality.'

'Yes, I suppose so.'

'So who are you? You obviously know who I am.'

Margot looked at him suspiciously. Was he goading her? If he had joined Niggle's agency he would know who she was, because she was the star turn. The man on the street might not recognise her face, but they would know her name. She wasn't going to play his game.

'Oh, I'm Margot,' she said. 'I've been with Niggle yonks.'

'Margot who?'

She blinked. There was only one Margot.

'Willoughby,' she managed finally.

He turned the corners of his mouth down and shook his head. 'I haven't heard of you.'

'Well, to be fair, you wouldn't be my target reader.'

'What do you write?'

'Historical romance.'

'Ah. More cleavage than historical accuracy?'

She tried not to bristle. 'My readers enjoy them very much.'

'I'm sure.'

She swallowed, suddenly feeling the need to defend what she wrote. 'It gives them an escape.'

'Not really.' He stared, his pupils boring into her. They were very small and very black. 'It gives them the *illusion* of escape, which is a very different thing.'

'Different from what?' Margot felt her indignation rise.

'From writing something they can relate to.'

'Why would I want to do that?'

'You're an intelligent woman. Why don't you write something about how women really feel? What they are really going through?'

'Why don't you?'

She stood in front of him, hands on hips, outraged. Like one of her own heroines, she thought, and felt foolish. He made her feel foolish.

'I am,' he said. 'I'm writing a screenplay. About three women who work in a knicker factory.'

'Oh.' She was quite nonplussed.

'There's a single mother, a widow, and the boss's wife. They kidnap the boss, then give all the women better pay and working conditions and start making the kind of underwear they want to wear.'

'How very enlightened.'

'It is.' He smiled. 'I love women. I want to write things that help them make their lives better.'

He was smug. Patronising. He was goading her.

She felt flustered.

In less than two minutes he'd managed to hone in on her greatest insecurity (and she was particularly riddled with them at the moment): that what she wrote was trite and meaningless.

'Well, good for you,' she managed finally. 'But I know what I write makes women's lives better, because they write and tell me. I get sacks of fan mail. Sacks.'

She realised her voice was getting higher.

He looked at his watch and looked at the door.

'I think I've done my bit here,' he said. 'I'm off. Very nice to meet you.'

He put his hands in his pockets and loped off. Margot didn't think this had ever happened to her before. Men never voluntarily walked off and left her standing there. It was a new experience and not one she liked. Had she lost her touch? Was the orange dress too much? Or did he not like women full stop? Was he off to some nefarious Soho den to pick up young boys?

She looked around the room. She actually wished Dai was here and they could slink off to her favourite Italian for dinner. She wished she hadn't been quite so horrid to him.

She was finding him difficult these days, though, if not impossible. She never knew what mood he was going to be in. He went from introverted, almost inert, to being the life and soul of the party, with no apparent reason. Some days he wouldn't get out of bed at all. He would sleep and sleep, right around the clock, and she couldn't tell him to get up because he would only ask what was he getting up *for*? And she couldn't answer that. He kept the curtains shut all day and by the time it came for her to go to bed, the sheets were wrinkled and the room smelled airless. Those were the days when she wished she had a day bed in her study she could escape to, but she knew if she did she would be tempted to have little naps whenever she couldn't write, and that would be the beginning of the end.

He was occupied in the winter, because he was in with all the gamekeepers who went drinking at the White Horse, and he loaded guns for the local shoot, which would keep him busy from dawn until well after dusk, as they all went off and drank themselves stupid in the pub afterwards. Margot didn't think it was a very constructive way of spending his time, but she didn't say anything. He seemed to enjoy being out in the elements.

The downside of that was he knew everyone there was to know around Peasebrook and would invite them back to the house at the drop of a hat. Often Margot would come in from her study and find a curious mixture of landed gentry and local bits of rough in the kitchen, music blaring. Dai would be mixing cocktails – they might run out of food but they *never* ran out of drink – and he would end up on the kitchen table reciting Dylan Thomas. There was no fear of Dai going gently into a good night, or gently anywhere, but everyone lapped it up and there was uproarious applause and demands for more. At least, thought Margot, he wasn't reading his own poetry.

And as Dylan Thomas had said of himself, Dai had a beast, an angel, and a madman in him. Only the angel appeared less and less often these days . . . Dai needed a lot of attention, and Margot didn't have enough time to humour him *and* write enough books to keep them in the manner to which they had become accustomed.

Although maybe what they needed was a holiday. They hadn't been away together, just the two of them, for an age. Perhaps a little trip around Italy? She brightened at the idea. As soon as she'd finished this wretched book, she would organise it.

She looked around the room. She didn't think anyone would notice if she slipped away. She'd done her duty and there was no one here to amuse her, so she might as well get away and have a good night's sleep. Then she could get up in the morning and start writing. Time was, after all, marching on and the deadline was getting nearer and nearer.

'The thing is, I want my dresses to turn ordinary girls into extraordinary ones. Just for one night. I want to turn them into who they want to be.'

Alexander and Phoebe had persuaded Sally into modelling for them so they could take some pictures. She had protested, but for some reason they seemed to think she was the perfect representative of the girl on the street.

'We need a catalogue,' explained Alexander. 'I can't cart

the actual dresses around with me everywhere. If I've got pictures, with a real girl in them . . .'

'A *real* girl,' laughed Sally. 'You make me sound like Pinocchio.'

'But you *are* real,' said Phoebe. 'I don't mean you're not beautiful, because you absolutely are. But you're not a freak, like me.'

'You're not a freak.'

'I've got a gap in my teeth and my ears stick out. No one would want to look like me.'

Sally frowned. She thought Phoebe was stunning. But then, she hadn't met a girl yet who was happy with how she looked.

'You don't have to if you don't want to,' said Alexander.

But his smile was so winning that ten minutes later she was standing on the table in the dining room, which they were using as a makeshift catwalk, in a white dress with hundreds of silver discs stitched on to it. It was far shorter than Sally would ever dare to wear. It would be no good for a night out in Knapford.

'This is the perfect party dress for Christmas 1967,' Phoebe was saying as if she was commentating a fashion show. 'Silver and white – to represent snow and starlight.'

'Snow and Starlight,' said Alexander. 'That's what we'll call the collection.'

Sally struck what she thought was a model's pose. She felt self-conscious. She was no Twiggy, she knew that. But she was eager to please.

'It's just too dark in here,' complained Phoebe, fiddling with her camera.

'Just keep taking pictures. You won't know if they're any good until we get them developed.'

The door opened and Margot stood in the doorway.

'Mum! You're back early. Was the party no good?'

'It was too boring for words. What are you three up to?'

'Shooting our winter catalogue,' grinned Alexander.

'How very grand. Sally, you look out of this world.'

'I feel a bit silly.' She felt even more self-conscious now Margot was here.

'Where's Dad?'

'Gone to the White Horse.'

Margot tutted. 'Does he really find all those grubby gamekeeper types more interesting than me?'

'No, Mum. It just meant he didn't have to get changed. Or pretend to be something he wasn't.'

'Your father's got more talent than most of the people at that party. He just won't do anything about it.' Margot put down her handbag. 'You need some more light. Alexander, go and get the lamps from the drawing room. And we need cocktails. You'll never relax otherwise, Sally.'

Sally had to admit to herself she was never going to relax under Alexander's scrutiny. She felt self-conscious, because she cared terribly much what he was thinking but couldn't tell at all by looking at his expression. But by the time she'd had two of the Snowballs Margot mixed, to get them in the Christmas spirit, she found all her inhibitions falling way. The creamy, sugary, boozy mixture was too delicious.

When Margot threw herself into something, it came to life. She completely took over the shoot. She arranged the lighting, told Sally what to wear and how to stand, made Alexander go and fetch props and jewellery from her jewellery box.

Dai looked in at one point and beat a hasty retreat. He could see straight away he couldn't make a contribution.

'Have a Snowball!' Margot tried to lure him in.

'You're all right.' He slunk off to bed.

It was three o'clock in the morning before they finished taking the photos. Phoebe had used up several rolls of film.

'Bugger,' said Margot. 'I wanted an early night.'

'Thanks, Mum,' said Phoebe. 'I'd have given up hours ago if it wasn't for you.'

On the landing, before she went up the next set of stairs to her little attic room, Alexander stopped Sally.

'Thanks for being a good sport.'

'It was fun.'

'I know it wasn't part of the deal. But I think the photos will make a lot of difference. You looked really beautiful.'

Sally blushed. She wasn't at all sure if he meant it. She blushed even more when he gave her a hug. She felt an extraordinary warmth rush through her. But then he was gone, disappearing down the corridor to his own room, leaving her somewhat bedazzled.

She didn't think the hug meant anything. Alexander was just being kind, and that was one of the things she liked best about him, even though she thought he might be a bit of a monkey where girls were concerned. It was a very confusing combination.

As she climbed up the stairs to her bedroom, she realised she felt happy for the first time in a long while. Properly, deep-down happy, not just the momentary happiness that a new lipstick or a bag of chips brought you. The ball of sadness she had been carrying around with her felt less heavy. It would never go all together – how could it? – but at least she could bear it now.

For the first time since it happened, she slept a dreamless sleep. No nightmares. No waking up drenched in sweat or crying. No reminders at all of that terrible day.

15

Leo woke at exactly the same time he always did – 6.15 – even though it was Saturday and his alarm wasn't programmed to go off. He stretched for a moment and thought about what to do. It was the first time he had been able to give thought to the fact he had a free weekend. Work had been full on, which was great, except it meant he had to put all the things he wanted to do with his life on hold.

So he was going to do some of them today. He was going to go to the gym, get a proper workout followed by a swim and a sauna. Although he ran every other morning it wasn't enough. His body needed attention. Especially when so much temptation was put in his way on an hourly basis. He was far from running to fat – Leo had inherited his father's lean physique – but it could creep up on you if you didn't take care.

Then he was going to drive down to Peasebrook and see his mum and dad. He decided he would surprise them, because if he phoned to tell them his mum would go into overdrive and start cooking and he didn't want that. In fact, he was going to cook for them. He could stop in Peasebrook and do the shopping. It would be fun, sourcing everything in the high street. There was a fantastic cheese shop, for a start. And no doubt there would be new places open since he last shopped there. Peasebrook was flourishing.

Maybe he could get a few more Cotswold clients? He had Honeycote Ales already, with their gastropubs and the delicatessen and café they'd opened in the converted brewery. There was lots of other foodie businesses springing up in the area. If he got a few more contracts down there he could spend more time at home – he still considered Hunter's Moon his home even thought he'd had his flat over five years – and keep an eye on his parents. His dad had definitely been off colour the last time he had seen him, more than three weeks ago now, and although they had spoken on the phone, Leo still felt guilty. A visit was long overdue.

He jumped out of bed, galvanised by the prospect. He might as well admit it. The relentless hubbub and competitiveness of London was starting to pall. He didn't want to go out five nights a week any more and have the same old conversations over and over again. He'd much rather loll about in the countryside. Go to the pub, have a nice walk, potter about. He needn't go back to London until Monday morning if he didn't feel like it. He could have Sunday lunch and snooze it off. What absolute bloody bliss.

He laughed at himself. You're getting old, Leo, mate, he thought, as he stuffed a few things into a leather holdall and put on his gym kit. It was true. He'd even turned down a trip to Ibiza with his mates. They went every summer but he couldn't face all that eternal sunshine and clubbing and the wretched infinity pool with the girls in their impossibly small bikinis. He wanted something more . . . nourishing.

Outside, he could see it was a perfect spring day. Hunter's Moon would be looking at its best. He slung his bag over his shoulder and grabbed his car keys. He couldn't wait.

There were fourteen interested parties booked in for the open house.

That was without a single advert in the papers or any display of the particulars in the window, although Belinda and Bruce had put together a stunning brochure which they'd released discreetly to interested parties. So considering they had done no publicity, the response had been overwhelming.

In the end, the only thing Belinda hadn't had any control over was the weather, but the morning dawned pearly bright. It was the kind of day that inspired poets to pick up their pencils and artists to rush outside with their brushes. The kind of day that put a smile on the face of even the most curmudgeonly.

Belinda and Cathy arrived at seven o'clock to find Alexander and Sally, with Teddy on a lead, ready to set off for the day.

'I feel awful hounding you out of your own home,' Belinda said.

'We're looking forward to a day out,' said Sally.

'I'll come and see you in the morning,' said Belinda. 'Midday?'

'Oh gosh – that's beyond the call of duty on a Sunday.'

'It's no trouble. You'll want to know how things have gone.'

'Why don't you come for lunch?' said Sally. 'Or is that blurring the edges?'

Belinda laughed. 'I'd love that. I never have Sunday lunch. It's far too much effort for one person. Thank you.'

In the car, Sally worried she'd stepped over a line.

'Do you think I was wrong to ask her for lunch?' she asked Alexander.

'Not at all,' he said. 'If this bloody disease has taught me anything, it's to spend more time with people you like. She's definitely gone the extra mile for us.'

'It's a pity—' Sally began, then stopped. 'No, never mind.'

'I know exactly what you're thinking,' said Alexander. 'And I thought the same.'

Sally started the car. They'd booked in for lunch at a restaurant they'd heard good things about, then they were going to call in on friends later in the afternoon. She was worried that Alexander would be tired. It had been a tough couple of weeks. They had started going through the house and chucking things away. It was good to declutter for the open house, but they'd also need to get rid of a lot of stuff before they moved, so it was an opportunity to make a start.

Going through everything was exhausting, though. Not so much physically, but emotionally. So many memories. And it was hard deciding whether to throw things away or keep them. They were both attached to so many different things for so many different reasons. But there wasn't going to be room at Digby Hall for even half of their clutter.

There was decades of junk. All Alexander's records, heaps and heaps of Phoebe's clothes – ones she'd bought and ones she'd made and piles of stuff she'd collected

– scraps of fur, and old hats and scarves and buttons. And of course Margot's books. She couldn't even begin to count them. She wondered if the new owners would like them as part of the house's history. Probaby not. It wasn't as if Margot was Jane Austen or one of the Bronte sisters.

Leo and Jess might want some of the stuff, but even so they had a monumental task ahead of them. And if things went quickly, they might not have long to sort it all out. If Belinda found them a good buyer, it could take less than six weeks.

Sally gulped. She wasn't sure if she was ready.

She put the car into drive and drove off. She caught Alexander's gaze in the rear-view mirror, looking back at the house. She put her hand down to hold his, but for the first time ever his fingers didn't close around hers. How thoughtless of me, she thought. She left her hand there as long as she could, before she needed to put her hand back on the wheel, but she didn't draw attention to the incident. She wasn't going to dignify the disease with any recognition of what it had done. Not today.

16

The Willoughbys had left Hunter's Moon immaculate. They'd had help, using a cleaning service and a gardener recommended by Belinda, because Alexander certainly wasn't up to it, and Sally had found overseeing things was a job in itself, as Belinda had given her an exhaustive list of chores to be accomplished to a higher level than most people's housekeeping standards. Not least to double dose the fabric conditioner on the bed linen so everything smelled sweet.

The house was gleaming. Outside, every weed had been pulled out of the chippings. The edges of the flowerbeds were sharp. The grass was cut to velvet perfection, with immaculate stripes.

And now Belinda and Cathy had just over two hours to dress Hunter's Moon before the viewers started arriving at ten.

It was the first time Cathy had been to the house and she was blown away.

'I can't believe I can't Instagram this. It's such a waste.' At the age of fifty-three, Cathy had become a social media freak. There was nothing she didn't know about search engine optimisation and analytics. Belinda found it amusing, but also useful. She couldn't deny

Cathy had raised their profile through her prolific posting.

'I know, but you can't,' said Belinda. 'We have to respect the Willoughbys' need for confidentiality. Come on – we've got lots to do.'

'It's a bit like trying to improve on Angelina Jolie,' said Cathy.

'Everyone can benefit from a little make-up and a few well-chosen accessories.'

Belinda had come armed with several bunches of fresh flowers – brightly coloured tulips and sweet-smelling freesias and cream roses. There were stacks of vases in the scullery, so she made sure there was one in each of the main rooms and the master bedroom, and one big display of roses in the hall.

She laid the table in the dining room, and lit slow-burning candles. Today's papers and the most current magazines were laid out on the coffee table in the drawing room, together with a bottle of champagne and four glasses waiting to be filled. She deployed the oldest trick in the book in the kitchen – she'd bought a bag of frozen pains au chocolat to pop in the oven throughout the day, as the scent of them cooking was irresistible, and freshly roasted coffee beans. She put Classic FM on the radio in the kitchen, very quietly. As a finishing touch, Belinda hung a pair of caps from the local prep school and a satchel on the pegs in the cloakroom, for aspirational parents.

Cathy was trying to lay out a croquet set on the top lawn, bashing the hoops in with a rubber mallet while trying to read the instructions.

'I'm getting confused,' she wailed. 'I don't think I've got it right.'

'Don't worry if it's not exact,' laughed Belinda. 'It's only for show.'

'Are you kidding?' said Cathy. 'There'll be someone who'll pick me up on it.'

'It's not going to stop them buying the house, though, is it? Come on, let's have a quick coffee before they all get here. We won't be able to stop for lunch.'

They stood on the doorstep with their mugs. It looked perfect. There was even a flock of fluffy white sheep in the field in the distance, with a few spring lambs jumping around.

'I didn't actually organise the lambs,' admitted Belinda. 'That was just luck.'

'I feel as if we're putting on a play,' said Cathy. 'It's like something out of Agatha Christie. I feel as if some great drama is going to unfold any minute. Miss Peacock on the lawn with the croquet mallet.'

'I hope not,' said Belinda. Desirable houses did sometimes bring out the worst in people though. They would stop at nothing: bribery, corruption, subterfuge, sabotage. She'd been offered crates of champagne and envelopes of cash to sweeten a deal. She'd also been on the end of threatening phone calls. Property could be a dangerous game.

But she was ready for anything.

At nine, the half dozen teenagers she had hired arrived. They were all doing business studies at the sixth form college, so it would be useful for their CV and she was paying good money. There were two stewards for parking, two girls who were serving tea and cucumber sandwiches from an open-sided gazebo, and another two in the house on hand to hand out information and field questions.

Bruce had insisted on coming to help too, as by luck he didn't have a wedding that day.

'Don't be surprised if my dad tips up,' he warned darkly. 'He's desperate to come round for a shufty. Any errands you want running, just give me the nod.'

'We should have dressed you up as lord of the manor,' giggled Cathy.

'Oh please. I love a bit of role play,' said Bruce.

'No.' Belinda knew she had to nip the two of them in the bud, but she couldn't help smiling. 'Just keep an eye on everyone. Chat to them. See if you can get any inside info.'

The viewers were scheduled to arrive at half hour intervals, so that it never felt overcrowded. Everyone was checked as they came in. No one was allowed to view if they hadn't registered. They all had to be in a position to proceed, with either a letter from a solicitor confirming their own property was sold, or evidence of money in the bank. There had been no compromise on this; no promises that their own house was 'about to go on the market' or 'we can get a mortgage' would do. Belinda was strict on this, after years of dealing with time-wasters. It was amazing how many people pretended, even to themselves, that they could afford a house they clearly couldn't.

Then Cathy would do the guided tour, which lasted about half an hour. This ended in the drawing room, where Belinda would have a conversation with each set of viewers and answer any questions they might have, and give them the paperwork they needed to submit their sealed bid.

'I'll text you info about each client before they get to you,' said Cathy. 'I'll do a heart emoji if they're nice, and a scream one if they're awful.'

They would be on their knees by six o'clock, when the day was scheduled to finish.

From ten o'clock cars began to swish along the drive. Some viewers brought their entire family – sometimes three generations. Belinda knew from experience you could never tell how much money someone had by what car they drove – a top-of-the-range vehicle didn't always mean cash in the bank, while some of the wealthiest people she had known drove around in beaten-up old bangers. The parking area began to fill up, and the hordes began to crawl over the house and grounds.

She was grateful once again that Sally and Alexander weren't there. She thought how awful it would be for them to see their house treated like a tourist attraction, and worse, to overhear the remarks of those looking round. People could be less than sensitive.

She and Cathy always had a favourite contender. Every house had a buyer that was perfect for it, but sadly they weren't always the ones who got it in the end. They would often cheer for their preferred buyer throughout the ne-gotiation process.

It was a game, matching houses to buyers, a game of hopes and dreams, high figures and higher emotions. It was up to Belinda to steer everyone through the legal and financial knots, the dramas, the logistics. Everyone moaned about estate agents but she knew she earned her commission. People expected her to work miracles, to quite literally open doors. And Belinda always went the extra mile to make sure the right person was holding the key.

Today, she could see in the viewers' eyes the lengths

they would be prepared to go to in order to get Hunter's Moon. Everyone fell in love the moment they drove in and saw it in front of them. Sometimes on a viewing people would turn around and drive off without even getting out of the car. This was not going to happen today.

Throughout the day Cathy kept in touch with her by text, giving her the heads-up on any useful snippets of conversation. People often thought they couldn't be heard while they discussed their personal lives.

'Flashy Brummie – second-hand car dealer with more money than sense – this is a marriage saver for him. He's told his wife he doesn't want any more whining if he buys it for her.' Scream emoji.

'Horsey woman who wants to move here from London – husband not too keen but she's got something on him for sure.' Smile-through-gritted-teeth emoji.

'Really lovely family who would be breaking the bank to buy it but they love it!!!' Heart emoji.

Some people seemed to find the notion of a sealed bid difficult to grasp, no matter how carefully Belinda explained it. In particular the second-hand car dealer who had small-man syndrome and was very heavy-handed in his negotiations.

'I'll pay fifty grand more than the highest bidder,' he told Belinda.

'Um – I'm afraid that's not quite how sealed bids work.'

'You want the most money you can get, don't you?' The man puffed himself up like Toad of Toad Hall.

'Of course we want to achieve the best price we can for our vendors. But this is the fairest way with a property that is clearly going to attract a lot of interest.'

She fixed him with a stern gaze. He looked back at her thoughtfully, then smiled.

'My wife wants this house. I will get it. Because I always get what I want.'

'Then I suggest you make your best offer and back it up with a letter from your solicitor so we can be sure everything is in place.'

He went a slightly darker shade of burgundy.

'Everyone has a price. Just name yours.' He gave a smirk. 'I know how this game works. I know you can influence the outcome. I know you can pick whoever you want.'

Belinda ignored his overture.

'You have the information pack. You've registered your interest. We will be in touch with further details.'

As politely as she could, Belinda indicated the door. He started spluttering with indignation, but Belinda was having none of it. She knew his type, and he had no place at Hunter's Moon, that was certain. He was right. She could influence the outcome. He would get the key of the door over her dead body.

She had a few moments before the next viewers came in. She checked her appearance in the mirror over the fireplace, running a finger under her eyeliner, which was getting a bit smudged, and smoothing down her hair. Cathy texted her the inside info on the next lot.

'He is gorgeous. She is a yoga freak. She wants HM as a yoga retreat.' Eye-roll emoji.

Belinda smiled, then turned to greet her next viewers.

She froze as a familiar voice floated through the door.

'Let's make an offer, darling. If you think it's right.'

It couldn't be. But she knew that voice only too well,

even though she hadn't heard it for nearly ten years. And then suddenly, there he was in front of her, as bold as brass, not an iota of shame on his face, a tall, willowy girl by his side.

'Belinda.' He gave her his most charming smile, the one that had lured her in, the one that covered up his insecurities and weaknesses.

It took all of Belinda's self-control to hide her shock.

'Charlie,' she said.

'I did wonder if you would be here.'

'It can hardly be a surprise,' she said. 'Given my name is all over the details.'

'I thought you'd be far too grand to actually turn up to the open house.'

'No. No. I'm all about the personal touch.' She turned to his companion with a smile. 'Hello. I'm Belinda Baxter.'

The girl was wide-eyed and extremely pretty – but nervily thin; too thin to be healthy. She was dressed in designer hippy clothes: silk harem pants and drapey cashmere, with an armful of silver bangles and a diamond in her nose. Her skeins of caramel hair were scooped into a topknot with several fake plaits spilling out. Belinda could smell the £200 equivalent of a bottle of patchouli on her.

Vegan, teetotal, tattoo on her bottom, she guessed.

'I'm Natasha. What a beautiful house. Is it yours?'

'I wish,' said Belinda. 'I'm just the estate agent.'

'Oh.' From her reaction, Natasha had no idea who or what Belinda was or had been.

'Well,' said Belinda. 'Welcome to Hunter's Moon. Are you thinking about it for yourselves?'

'Well – not *just* us,' said Natasha. 'We're looking for somewhere we can hold yoga retreats.'

Belinda nodded. 'Yoga retreats?'

She tried not to raise her eyebrows. Charlie and yoga? He was looking at the floor.

'I've got a lot of private one-to-one yoga clients,' Natasha explained. 'But what they really want is two or three days when they can really get into it and immerse themselves. This place would be perfect.'

'It's certainly very peaceful,' agreed Belinda. 'And there's plenty of space.'

Her mind was racing. What was Charlie's game? What was this girl to him? Was this his idea of a joke? She looked at him and he had the grace to look a little shame-faced.

'Tash – why don't you go and have a quick look at the outside again? I'll chat through the boring bits with Belinda.'

Natasha looked at Belinda and back to Charlie. She seemed a little puzzled. 'I don't mind if it's boring.'

Charlie looked at her. 'We could do with some more pictures to show your father. You know what he's like.'

For a moment it looked as if Natasha was going to protest. She looked between Charlie and Belinda again.

'OK.' Her tone indicated that she wasn't happy.

Belinda raised her eyebrows as she left the room.

'So. She seems lovely. Is she your . . . girlfriend? Wife? Mistress?' She couldn't help but be scathing.

'She's my fiancée.'

'Lucky her.'

'I work for her father.'

'Wine advisor?'

'No. All that's behind me.'

'Really?'

'I'm a different person. I've been dry for five years now, Belinda.'

'Well done you.'

Charlie nodded, looking pleased. 'We met at AA. In Fulham.'

'You went to AA?'

'Go. I still go. Every week. Apparently a lot of people meet their partners there.'

'Great.' She thought about what she'd told him. 'So was Natasha a raging drunk too?'

He didn't flinch at her barb.

'She was a bit of a party animal. Her dad threatened to cut her off. He refused to pay for her to go to rehab so she sorted it out for herself. And now I look after Natasha for him.'

Belinda felt that saying nothing was best. Charlie in charge of security? She couldn't think of anyone less suited.

'A bodyguard?' She managed finally, trying not to laugh.

'Well . . . no. I'm supposed to make sure she doesn't drink. Or do anything worse.'

'That's . . . quite a career change.'

'Don't mock me. It's been a long journey.'

He looked at her and she could see he wanted her approval.

Now she looked more closely at him, she could see his eyes were brighter, his skin smoother, he looked trimmer. He had gone off the boil in the last couple of months they were together: bloated, red-eyed, double chins. He'd been a mess.

'So you fell in love? Like Whitney Houston and Kevin

Costner? Wasn't part of your job making sure she didn't fall for anyone unsuitable?'

He looked pained.

'I know I was a shit to you. And I'm sorry.'

'A shit to me? Charlie, you *crushed* me.'

'I wasn't in control of my life. I was in a bad place.'

'How did that give you the right to treat me the way you treated me?'

'Don't think I don't feel bad about what I did. Don't think I don't think about it.'

'I don't think you do. Look at you. You've reinvented yourself. Found yourself another victim.' Oh God. She sounded really bitter.

She'd never been bitter. She'd been destroyed, but not bitter.

She was aware that time was slipping by. That the next viewers would be coming in any moment.

'Anyway, I don't think now is the time for this discussion,' Belinda said.

'No.'

He seemed genuinely remorseful. He was silent for a moment, then looked up, holding the brochure.

'Anyway, here we are, two alcoholics about to open a yoga retreat. It's a chance for a new beginning for us both, and a chance to pay it back a little. Help people out.'

Belinda looked at him. She didn't suppose the yoga retreats were going to be free, so the people they'd be helping would be as privileged as they were. She could feel the rage inside her, starting as a tiny flame, and every time he said something it fed the flame. She could hardly breathe with it now. She told herself she mustn't react.

'We are really interested in Hunter's Moon,' said Charlie. 'We've been looking for months. I kept telling Tash she would get more for her money out of London. This is sensational.'

'Well, here's a form. Feel free to register your interest,' said Belinda. 'We will be doing sealed bids in a couple of weeks.'

'Couldn't you—'

Belinda looked him in the eye. 'No, Charlie. Whatever you're going to ask. I couldn't.'

'Money isn't a problem. We have a generous budget.'

'You'll have to go through the official channels.'

'I didn't have you down as someone who bore grudges.'

He was beyond the pale.

'Namaste, Charlie,' she said. 'Or as we say in the real world, fuck off.'

She pushed past him and out of the door of the drawing room, past the next couple who were milling in the hall. She walked past them and down the corridor into the kitchen. She felt safe in here.

She took in several deep breaths to calm herself. *Bloody* Charlie. How dare he? How *dare* he? He must have known she would be here. What was he thinking, rubbing her nose in it like that? Parading that poor creature in front of her? 'Generous budget'?

She tried to collect her thoughts. She tried to remind herself that she had got over Charlie long ago. That she had made a huge success of herself despite him, and that she was a better person for it. That he was never in a million years going to be as good a person as she was, and that he couldn't hurt her any longer.

Bruce came into the kitchen.

'Babe, there's about a million people looking for you. What's going on?' He stared at her. 'Are you OK?'

'Just give me a minute.'

'What's happened? You look as if you've seen a ghost.'

'I sort of have,' said Belinda. 'Well, not a ghost. More of a skeleton.'

Bruce grinned. 'Oh. So you're not whiter than white. Which one, darling? You must show me.'

Belinda shook her head. The last thing she wanted was Bruce interrogating her about her past. She had to gather herself together. With a bit of luck Charlie would have got the message, and spirited himself and Natasha out of there.

'It's fine. I'm OK. It was just a bit of a shock. I'm coming.'

She swept past him before he could ask any more then went back along the corridor to the drawing room, where the girls from the tea tent were looking for her.

'We've run out of sandwiches,' said the waitress.

'I'll nip to the Co-op for some more bread and cucumber,' said Bruce.

'Thank you,' said Belinda, thinking that, despite his nosiness, Bruce was a diamond and a trouper and she didn't know where she'd be without him.

17

Leo spent longer than he meant to at the gym, then the traffic had been bad out of London. The nearer he got to Hunter's Moon the more he knew he'd made the right decision to come away for the weekend. The air was sweet. The sky was . . . well, sky blue. The sun cast a rosier glow down here than it did in London. He'd bought a leg of lamb and vegetables and cheese for Sunday lunch. He turned up Ella Fitzgerald singing 'Feelin' Good'. He was coming home.

Leo frowned as he arrived at the entrance. The gates, which been lying in the verge for as long as he could remember, had been put back on their hinges. The Willoughbys didn't worry about appearances or security. The gates wouldn't keep anyone out anyway.

There was a freshly painted sign too. They had never needed a sign.

There was a pair of teenage boys standing there, both with sunglasses on, managing to look both awkward and self-important.

He rolled down his window.

'What are you two doing?'

'Could I see your registration documents, sir?'

'What?'

'For the open house? You can't come in if you haven't registered.'

Open house? What was this? Some sort of garden scheme his mother hadn't told him about, where the public crawled over your grounds and pinched cuttings? He wished she'd told him. He'd have come to help. Though it wasn't too late.

Through the trees he could see a gazebo on the lawn, and someone serving tea. He sighed. This was going to take the edge off his surprise. But never mind.

'Sir, I'm going to have to ask you to turn around. If you would like to register to view on another occasion, you can contact the estate agent.'

He handed Leo an envelope. Leo drew out the paper-work inside. On the top was a glossy sales brochure.

He looked up at the boy.

'You have no idea who I am, do you?'

'No, sir.'

'I'm Leo Willoughby. This is *my* house. My *home*. You'd better get out of the way.'

And before the boy could protest, he accelerated off.

Belinda was talking to an earnest young couple with a dear little boy who sat on the sofa running his toy trains along the back.

'We went through a lot to get Gideon,' the man said. 'We want to give him an idyllic childhood, so we're leaving Shepherd's Bush.'

'I want ponies and dogs and chickens.' The woman smiled. 'I spent twenty years working for London's biggest divorce solicitors. I want my life back. I want to make jam.'

'Well, there are plenty of soft fruit cages in the walled garden,' Belinda told them.

'Oh, I know. This house is perfect.'

'What's the deal?' said the man.

'We will do anything. Anything.' His wife fixed Belinda with the gimlet eyes of one who was used to ferocious court battles.

Yet again, Belinda found herself outlining the rules of a sealed bid and making sure they knew there was no way around it but to put in their best offer, then she heard the sound of a car roaring up the drive and coming to a halt outside the front door. No one was supposed to do that.

'Excuse me,' she said to the couple, and made her way out into the hall, just as a man strode in through the front door.

'What is going on?'

He was in his thirties, probably about her age, she guessed. Despite his angry scowl he was good-looking: dark, good bone structure, glossy hair cut to look tousled, jeans and navy blue suede brogues and a moleskin jacket with a flash of bright lining.

He saw the hall table with the brochures lined up neatly in front of the vase of flowers.

'Who are all these people and what are they doing in my house?' he demanded. 'Who's in charge here?'

Belinda approached the man. 'I'm Belinda Baxter. I'm the estate agent. I'm supervising the viewings. Who are you?'

The man glared at her.

'I'm Leo Willoughby,' he told her. 'Where are my parents?'

He looked around as if expecting them to be walking down the stairs. Belinda hesitated. She should ask him for identification, but she could see he was who he said he was. His resemblance to Alexander was noticeable, and Sally had spoken of her son Leo. She didn't want to antagonise him further.

'Shall we go and have a chat in the kitchen?' asked Belinda.

'Right after you get rid of all these people,' Leo bit back.

'I'm afraid we can't do that.' Belinda tried to keep her voice as soothing as possible. 'The viewings are scheduled until six. Your mum and dad should be back about seven. I've made arrangements with them to lock everything up and leave before they get back.'

He wasn't really listening.

'I've got the weekend off. I came down this afternoon to surprise them,' he told her. 'How could they do this?'

'I can't explain their decision,' said Belinda. 'I took instruction from them. They wanted it to be discreet. That's all I can tell you.'

'It's a terrible thing to do. I just don't understand.' He looked utterly bewildered.

Belinda didn't know what to say or do. It wasn't her place to tell him the truth about his father's illness. His parents had obviously decided to hide it from him, for the time being.

'Does my sister know? Does Jess know?'

'I don't know. I really am just the agent. And I'm very sorry this has caused you such distress . . .'

'Have they gone mad? Have they actually gone mad?

They *can't* sell Hunter's Moon. Has anyone made an offer yet?'

'There's been a lot of interest.'

'Of course there has.' He looked at his watch. 'Would you mind clearing everyone out as quickly as you can? I don't want anyone here when my parents get back. I need to talk to them alone.'

Belinda nodded.

'Of course.'

'Thank you.' He looked at her, his face bleak and full of fear.

Belinda felt hypnotised. She felt as though she'd seen him before.

And then she realised, of course she had. He had his father's eyes.

'Would you like a cup of tea?'

It seemed such a trite, useless, meaningless thing to say. He gave a wintry smile.

'A stiff drink more like.'

He turned and walked away, heading down the corridor towards the kitchen. Belinda wasn't quite sure what to do. The couple she had been talking to appeared in the doorway of the drawing room.

'Everything OK?' said the man.

'Fine,' said Belinda. 'I'm just coming. I'm sorry to keep you waiting.'

As dusk started to fall, Belinda dished out six cash-filled envelopes to the teenagers and sent them on their way.

Cathy and Bruce were pulling up the croquet hoops. She'd filled them in on Leo's arrival, swearing Bruce to secrecy on the background to the drama. She trusted him.

He liked idle gossip, but he knew when to keep his mouth shut.

'The poor love!' Cathy's eyes were wide with sympathy. 'Did he really have no idea?'

'None. I feel terrible. Do you think I should call his parents and give them the heads up?'

'I do,' said Bruce.

She tried to call Sally's mobile, but it went straight to voicemail.

'Mrs Willoughby, it's Belinda. Everything has gone well, but I thought you should know that Leo is here. So I won't have locked up. I hope that's OK.'

She hung up with a sigh.

'I'd better go and say goodbye to him. You two go off home.'

'There were some nice people today, though, weren't there?' Cathy sounded plaintive, as if she needed reassuring. 'This house *has* to go to someone nice.'

Belinda didn't want to think about the alternative.

'Ever Mr and Mrs Nice from Niceville wouldn't be nice enough,' she said.

There was an air of gloom. It was a shame. Usually after an open house they would have fun dissecting the day and guessing who would put in the highest bid, as well as choosing who they would like as the new owners. But now didn't seem the time for speculation.

Belinda went through all of the rooms to make sure everything was in order. She was satisfied that the house looked pristine, with no evidence that there had been people tramping through it all day. She drew the curtains in the drawing room and put another log on the fire.

She went down to the kitchen to say goodbye to Leo. He was sitting at the table, an empty glass in front of him, scrolling aimlessly through his phone.

'We're off now,' she told him.

He raised a hand in farewell but didn't look up. She wanted to reach out to him, but what could she say?

Bruce was waiting by her car. He had stayed on to make sure she was all right. He realised she'd been unsettled by the afternoon's events, and she appreciated him caring enough to hang on for her. Just as long as he didn't start an inquisition about Charlie. But somehow the drama of Leo turning up had overshadowed that event.

'I feel so terrible for him. What an awful way to find out. And his poor parents.'

'Maybe they should have told him? But it's classic isn't it? My dad was the same. Never let on he had Parkinson's for ages. *I didn't want to worry you* . . .' Bruce shook his head. 'He's still going strong though.'

'It's still very sad,' said Belinda. 'Mr Willoughby is so lovely.'

'It's life, I'm afraid, love,' said Bruce. 'We're all going to die.' He slung an arm around her shoulder and squeezed her to him. 'Which is why we've got to have as much fun as we can while we can.'

Belinda couldn't help laughing. 'Well, I know that's your motto.'

'Yes. It is. And it should be yours too. But what do you ever do but work your arse off?'

'Don't start.'

'I'm not letting you get away with it this time. You've had a long day. A difficult day. You are going to go home

170

and have a long bath and then you're coming out with me for a Chinese.'

Belinda's instinct was to protest. She wanted to go back to the office and go through all the details, making notes about everyone she had spoken to while they were still fresh in her memory.

She opened her mouth to refuse, but he put a hand up. 'I'm not taking no for an answer.'

Bruce was right. She never had any fun. She *had* had a difficult day. And he'd been a sweetheart and she didn't want to hurt his feelings by saying no.

'You win,' she laughed. 'But it's my treat. The company can pay.'

Bruce rolled his eyes.

'We can argue about that later. Now go home and get out of your Margaret Thatcher uniform and I'll meet you at the Hong Kong Garden at eight.'

18

Leo was standing on the doorstep when he saw his parent's Volvo come along the drive. A safe and sensible car on the surface, but this was one of the snazzier sporty models and had a tiger in its tank. It suited them, as it combined his mother's reliability with his dad's derring-do.

His mother saw him first. She was driving, which was unusual. Alexander loved to drive fast, which was why they had the turbo. Leo's heart was pounding. He hated confrontation, but that's what this was going to be. He was afraid, too, because he knew that selling Hunter's Moon – or at least putting it on the market; the show wasn't over yet – wasn't just a whim. There would be a reason, and he was pretty sure he wasn't going to like it.

Sally pulled the car up right in front of the house and he heard her pull on the handbrake. His father rolled down the window before she switched off the engine.

'Hey,' he said softly. He looked tired, thought Leo, and remembered thinking he looked tired at Borough Market. He looked sad too, his dark eyes lugubrious where usually they snapped and crackled.

He stepped forward to open the car door for his father as Sally got out the other side.

'Leo,' she said, and came around to hug him. He breathed in Calèche. She was still as slender as she had been when she arrived here – he'd seen the photographs of her from Phoebe's first collection. Alexander had framed them for Sally one Christmas. But suddenly now he held her she felt frail rather than slim. He supposed that was just his protective instinct. His heart stalled for a moment. Was it his mum? What would he do without his mum? Jesus, what would he do without his dad? Either of them.

He was terrified.

The three of them stood on the gravel. It was starting to get dark, and a malicious April breeze made them shiver.

'I came down to surprise you.'

'Oh, darling . . .' Sally looked tearful.

'You better tell me what's going on.'

'Of course,' said Leo. There was silence for a moment, but there was no sense of accusation or recrimination or defensiveness. Just a heavy sense of foreboding.

'Go and sit in the drawing room, you two,' said Sally. 'Light the fire. I'll bring in tea.'

What unnerved Leo was the lack of platitude. He realised he had been hoping for his mum to say 'Oh, we were just having a silly moment – thinking we would sell up and go around the world'. He could tell by their demeanour this was not the case.

There was a hard lump of dread between his heart and his stomach. He followed his father into the drawing room. There he saw that the curtains had been drawn and the fire lit and the guard put in front of it. Belinda must have done that, which was thoughtful. He felt a twinge of guilt that he had been so curt with her.

'Sit down, Dad.' He patted the back of the leather club

chair that his father usually sat in and went to put another log on. It might be late spring, but there was still a chill that needed keeping at bay.

Leo looked around the room and thought of all the Willoughby rituals that took place in this room. They always opened their stockings in here, even now. They always had champagne in here at six o'clock when it was a birthday; all the cards would be lined up on the mantelpiece. Sally would bring in a cake – always chocolate with shiny icing and the name piped in white on the top. Engagements – not his, not yet, heaven forbid – and imminent babies had been announced. Toasts had been made to the newly departed. The formal events had been confined to the drawing room, but it was the kitchen where the real dramas had taken place: the drunken arguments, the midnight feasts, the illicit kissing. The kitchen . . . the beating heart of Hunter's Moon.

'So what is it, Dad? You better tell me before Mum gets back. I need to know.'

If he was going to cry, he didn't want to do it in front of Sally.

Alexander sat down on the sofa facing the window. Leo sat opposite him, leaning forward, his elbows on his thighs, his fingertips touching.

Alexander tipped his head back and shut his eyes. 'I've been diagnosed with motor neurone disease.' He waited a moment, then opened his eyes and looked at Leo. 'I know you'll be cross with me for not telling you as soon as I found out. But . . . I just wanted more time with you without you knowing. I was going to tell you the other day but I didn't want to spoil things. I wanted . . . *needed* . . . longer. I'm sorry if that was wrong.'

He shrugged his shoulders. He looked utterly defeated.

'Motor neurone disease. That's the Stephen Hawking thing, right?'

'Yeah. But he's an outlier. Most people don't last nearly as long as him.' Alexander pressed his lips together. 'By a long chalk.'

'Oh God.'

'I can give you leaflets. Or a website. Or you can talk to my neurologist if you like. But the only things you really need to know are it's going to be tougher on everyone else than me, and I've probably got three years max.'

Leo flinched.

'It's OK. You don't have to say anything. It's a shock. And it's awful. But we have to find a way to get through it. For your mum.'

Leo nodded, not trusting his voice. 'Of course,' he managed. 'Dad. I'm so sorry.'

'I know.' Alexander's smile was wintry. 'Shh – your mum's coming. So . . . brave face. OK?'

As Sally came in through the door with a tray Leo jumped up to help her.

'I thought tea was a waste of time. I've done gin and tonics . . .'

She took one off the tray and took it over to Alexander, who looked up at her.

'I told him.'

Leo put the tray on the coffee table and took his mum in his arms.

'I'm so sorry, Mum.'

'I know. I know.' Sally held her son as tightly as she could.

'But I don't understand why you didn't tell me. Why

you tried to sell the house behind my back?'

'Not behind your back,' Sally looked pained. 'It's been very difficult for us. You must understand that, Leo. We wanted everything sorted and organised before we told you and Jess.'

'OK,' said Leo. 'But I wish you'd trusted me. I want to help.'

Sally sighed. 'Of course. But the point is we don't want this to affect your life.'

'How can it not?'

'I mean we want to be as independent as possible. We've taken as much advice as we can about the future. Life will get very difficult as the disease progresses.'

'The bottom line is we're strapped for money. There's a reason I keep nagging you about your pension plan,' said Alexander. 'It never occurred to me to do a proper pension plan when I was younger. I thought money just reproduced itself somehow. I did very well for myself, for all of us, but I did nothing about the future. And now it's come to bite me on the arse.'

'We're not stony broke,' said Sally. 'But we do need to release some capital. We will need help eventually.'

'So that's why we want to sell the house. We've seen somewhere we want to buy. Well, a bungalow—'

'A bungalow?' Leo looked horrified.

'That makes it sound awful. It's not a bungalow in the conventional sense, though it is all one level – very open plan – but it's very nice. They call it ranch-style, I think.'

'Ranch-style? In the Cotswolds?' Leo frowned. 'It is around here, right? You're not moving somewhere else?'

'It's on the Digby Hall estate – just the other side of Peasebrook. I can show you the brochure . . .' Sally jumped up. Leo could see how hard his mum was trying to make everything sound OK. That was so very much his mum. Alexander was being matter of fact and trying not to show how scared he was.

Leo didn't know how to react. He was devastated. Of course he was. Who wouldn't be? His smart, funny, clever, kind father. And his sunny, caring, beautiful mum. He had to find a way through this. To be as supportive as he could. To enjoy them as long as he could. To make their lives less terrifying and difficult and miserable. He couldn't even think about what this disease meant to them all.

'Have you told anyone else? Annie? Or Phoebe?'

'No. No . . . We wanted to sort things out before we told anyone else.'

'But they're family, Dad. They'll all want to help. That's what families are for. They *must* know.'

Alexander looked distraught. 'But as soon as everyone knows . . . That's when everything changes. Nothing will ever be the same.'

'Oh, Dad.'

Leo jumped up and went to hug his father. He couldn't remember the last time he'd hugged him like that. They were a perfectly affectionate family – but this embrace was different. This embrace said everything. How much he loved his father. How he was going to do everything in his power to help him. And how he never wanted to let him go.

Or Hunter's Moon. The Willoughbys were Hunter's Moon. Hunter's Moon was the Willoughbys. It was a member of the family, as much as Alexander and Sally and Leo and Jess. And Annie and Phoebe.

Hunter's Moon belonged to them and no one else.

19

As Bruce had instructed, Belinda ran herself a deep bath after the open house and lay wallowing up to her neck in Badedas. She was exhausted. It was tiring enough talking to prospective buyers, let alone the horror of Charlie turning up.

Although somehow that horror had been overshadowed by Leo's arrival. Belinda had been so anguished by his predicament. And frustrated by the fact she could do nothing to help him, for he was going to find out the truth about Alexander. She imagined them all together, curled up in the living room by the fire.

The Willoughbys were good people. They would be kind to their son, and he to them. The house would hold them tight, she thought. Hunter's Moon was a safe place.

Oh God. But not for much longer. And over her dead body would Charlie get it. How did he manage it, she thought? How did he worm his way into the hearts of girls who could get him what he wanted?

She'd fallen for it, she reminded herself. To be fair, she didn't suppose it was premeditated. Charlie wasn't together enough to have an actual plan. But when an opportunity presented itself, he clung on with both mitts, squeezing as much out of the situation for himself as he could, and leaving nothing for anyone else.

She had been that girl. She had been where Natasha was now. Charmed, enchanted, beguiled – and totally taken in. She sank a little deeper into the water as she remembered.

Their eyes had met not across a crowded room but a crowded marquee.

One of the things Belinda had introduced when she'd worked for Mortlake Bassett in Maybury was arranging promotional events. She'd organised for them to have a hospitality tent at the Peasebrook May Day Hill Climb.

The event attracted thousands of spectators happy to spend their bank holiday watching vintage cars whizz up Peasebrook Hill in the shortest possible time. Some of the cars were glorified bathtubs, battered and worn, others were gleaming and in concourse condition, but they were all beloved of their proud owners. The racetrack ran up the steep winding hill, and beside that was a path behind a safety fence so spectators could choose their position: some liked to watch the start, some gravitated towards the finish line, others hovered in between. It was a typically English, slightly eccentric pastime.

The Mortlake Bassett marquee was positioned halfway up the hill. They had a champagne bar and served deliciously sticky sausages in floury rolls to their clients, old, new and potential. Belinda was in charge of the invitation list, advised by the boss Richard Mortlake, Giles's father, who had a vast network of influential friends and acquaintances around Maybury. Most guests were either people who had bought or sold their houses through them, or people they had done business with, or local faces. Belinda had notified the local press and made sure there would be pictures in the weekly paper and the county magazine. People loved to be seen at this sort of thing.

Her role on the day was hostess, discreetly checking everyone had an invitation and making sure everyone mingled and took home a goodie bag with a chocolate racing car, a Mortlake Bassett key ring and the all-important brochure outlining their services. Although she and Giles had technically the same job description, and even though the event had been her brainwave, it seemed that because he was a man (and presumably because he was Richard's son) he didn't have any duties on the day other than to schmooze. Belinda was becoming used to these discrepancies, and recognised she had to grin and bear it.

There were two couples coming in through the marquee entrance, looking a bit sheepish. Belinda recognised the look – it was the classic gatecrasher expression. They looked nice enough, and the right kind of client – well dressed in city-does-country clothing: smart jeans and tweedy jackets and un-muddy boots – so she probably wouldn't quibble. She went over to greet them.

'Hello,' said one of the blokes. 'Charlie said to drop in for a glass of fizz.'

'Charlie Fox?' said his girlfriend. 'Or as we like to call him, Charlie Bar.'

Charlie Fox was indeed running the bar. He had recently opened the Peasebrook Wine Company, but it was as if he had been in the little town for generations, as he integrated himself so well. He had a mop of blonde hair, twinkling eyes and a winning way with customers. With his pale cords, brogues and checked shirt, his clothes sat well on him and he had a raffish air that set him apart from the usual hunting/shooting/fishing brigade. There was a rumour of some sort of wrongdoing in the City – insider dealing? – but nobody much cared. Charlie Fox fitted into Peasebrook very nicely, and Belinda had thought him the ideal choice to supply the wine.

'No problem,' she told them. 'There's champagne and hot dogs and—' she lowered her voice '—we've got a very posh Portaloo round the back.'

She grinned at the girls. Decent loos were gold dust at events like this.

Charlie came over with a bottle of champagne to greet his friends.

'Guys! Hi. You made it.' He turned to Belinda. 'Don't worry, I won't be charging this one out. But be nice – these chaps are looking to move out of the big smoke.'

'It's fine. Honestly. Have the champagne on us.'

'You'll have a glass, yeah?'

Charlie brandished the bottle at her.

Belinda never drank while she was on duty, though everyone else was necking as much free booze as they could. She liked a clear head and to keep her tongue firmly tied. She knew only too well that gossip and speculation were rife once a few glasses had been down, and idle chatter could be fatal to her business. Discretion was her watchword.

It mystified Charlie, though, that he couldn't persuade her to have a glass of the champagne he had sourced himself on his last buying trip to France.

'Come on. Just the one! It's glorious – as good as Dom Perignon and a fraction of the price. Heaven in a glass.'

'Elderflower cordial for me,' she insisted, knowing she sounded prim. 'I have to keep a clear head. And I don't want my tongue loosened. You know what they say, careless talk costs lives. Or in this case, house sales.'

He looked at her, bemused, and gave a little sigh. 'OK,' he said. 'But promise me you'll have a glass with me when this is over.'

He looked at her so winningly she couldn't refuse. His charm was infectious and under his gaze she felt like a more interesting person. For some reason he seemed drawn to her, though she would have had him down as fancying the leggy young girls he employed as waitresses. She wasn't used to the attention. She rather liked it.

Since leaving her parents' house on the RAF base the minute she left school, Belinda had found being single by far the easiest route to survival. She took her career very seriously. She wanted to be independent and autonomous: it was the first time she'd had control over her own life. She had a ten-year plan: five years to get herself on to the property ladder and ten to open her own agency. Once she had her own house and was her own boss, then she could think about her love life.

She had started making proper friends, though, for the first time, because she was growing in confidence.

'You're so *driven*,' they would complain. 'You do nothing but work.'

She just laughed. 'I love my job,' she explained. 'So it makes perfect sense. Once I'm established I can drop down a gear if I want to.'

They rolled their eyes but they still asked her out when they went to the movies in Oxford or had Sunday lunch at the pub or organised weekends away, and if she could make it she did. They were different, though – they lived for the weekends and their holidays and were obsessed with finding The One. Belinda went on the occasional date, but no one really lit her up from the inside. She was too exhausted to be much fun in the evenings, and she worked most weekends, so she didn't consider herself to be a particularly enticing option.

So it was unlike her to feel drawn to someone. There was a sparkle and levity to Charlie that she liked. Something about him that felt easy and relaxed. She didn't feel hunted, like she did with some men.

She was conscious of his gaze on her all afternoon in the marquee. She was wearing a pink Harris tweed jacket with a velvet collar, nipped in at the waist and tightly buttoned, over a black pencil skirt and suede ankle boots. She knew she looked good. She blushed when she caught Charlie's eye more than once – she never blushed! – and when the last of the guests had gone, and he was supervising the waitresses putting the glasses back into boxes for him to take back to the shop, she wasn't sure what to do; how to keep herself casually busy until there were so few people left they could no longer ignore each other and she could go and say thank you.

She was just rehearsing what to say to him when he came over.

'Would you do me the most enormous favour? Have you got a car with you?'

'Yes.' She looked wary.

'I haven't got enough room in mine for all the boxes. A friend dropped them off for me this morning but he's buggered off for the weekend. Would you take a few boxes back to the shop? I would be eternally grateful.'

She could hardly refuse. She would have to drive through Peasebrook on the way back home. Besides, she didn't want to refuse. She knew perfectly well it was a trap.

She drove into Peasebrook and pulled up on the pavement outside the shop. Until recently it had sold knitting wool, but Charlie had transformed it with burgundy paintwork and two giant urns with box spirals outside the door, and where once there had been balls of gaudy wool and patterns for Fair Isle jumpers in the window, now there were tempting bottles of Chablis and Sancerre and Meursault. She carried the boxes inside: the interior was warm and rustic, all wooden floors, copper lights hanging from the ceiling, and chunky oak poseur tables to sit at while you tried your wine.

'You have to have a drink now, so I can thank you.' He took the boxes from her with a smile.

She didn't even pretend to protest. She knew she would have to drive home, so she would drink just enough to take away her nerves and give her the courage to flirt with him.

He produced a long slender bottle. 'This is a really gorgeous light Australian Riesling. It won't make you do anything you don't want to do.'

He poured the merest inch into a pristine, long-stemmed glass and handed it to her.

'Taste this. I love it. You'll get grapefruit and lime-blossom.'

It was crisp and cold and delicious. As Belinda rolled it round her tongue, she realised there was a whole world she didn't know about. She was used to flaccid, acidic pub wine at best.

'Please, stop me if I ever start boring you,' said Charlie.

'But I'm passionate about wine. I couldn't live without it.'

'I don't know that I've got a passion,' said Belinda, suddenly realising that apart from work, she had no interests.

'That,' said Charlie, 'is the saddest thing I've ever heard. Surely you have? All girls have. Shoes? Books? Frank Sinatra? Vintage teapots?'

Belinda thought about it. 'I quite *like* a lot of things, but there's nothing I couldn't live without.'

'We need to find you one, immediately. I shall make it my mission.'

'Houses,' said Belinda. 'I love houses. I could spend all day looking at them. Dreaming about them. Imagining they are mine. Fantasising about how I would decorate them.'

'Well, there you go, you see.' Charlie clinked his glass against hers. 'Everyone has a passion. You just have to dig deep to find it sometimes.'

It felt so right, the two of them sitting in the middle of the shop on high stools. Charlie brought out a slab of Taleggio cheese he'd bought at the cheesemonger, and they ate it with a couple of ripe pears. And before she knew it, they had finished the wine.

'Oh no,' she said. 'I can't drive home yet. I've probably only had two glasses but it's not worth the risk.'

'Oh dear,' said Charlie. 'Well, you'd better come up to my flat and watch telly while it wears off. You can't afford to lose your license.'

'No, I can't,' she said, following him up the steep winding staircase.

They didn't even get as far as putting the television on.

She found herself letting him unbutton the bone buttons on her jacket. He drew in a long breath when he saw that all she had on underneath was a pink silk push-up bra. Like houses, Belinda knew how important foundations were. She didn't expect anyone to see, necessarily, but she always wore perfectly fitting matching underwear.

And she liked his appreciation, as he ran his fingers over the silk, gently brushing against the skin underneath. She shut her eyes and let him put his lips to her breasts, relishing their warmth, the butterfly gentleness of his kisses.

And before she knew it he had peeled away the rest of her clothes, and pulled her hair out of the velvet ribbon that held it back, and she was lying on the floor of his flat, on a rug, her limbs entwined with his, and it felt perfect.

Afterwards they lay tangled up in each other. She could hear music playing in the background, and she felt as if she was in a film. He was looking at her, a mischievous grin on his face.

'That was a bit wow,' he said.

She wasn't sure what to say. Agreeing felt contractual, as if they were going to be bonded in something. But she could hardly say it hadn't been.

'Yeah – it was pretty good,' she said, gathering up her clothes.

'Pretty good?' he looked affronted. 'That was more than pretty good. That was . . . special.'

She smiled as she did up her bra, then slid on her jacket and started to do up the buttons.

'I bet you say that to all the girls.'

'I don't,' he said. 'I really don't. Where are you going?'

'Home. I think I've sobered up now. All that exertion.'

He grabbed her by the arms. 'Stay with me. Stay the night. I want to hold you in bed. I want to wake up next to you.'

She shook her head. He looked really upset.

'That's never happened to me before.'

'What?'

'I don't know. It felt . . . different.'

Belinda laughed. 'Maybe you've just never had great sex before.' She reached out and tousled his already messed up hair. She'd gone further than she meant to. She never slept with people she hardly knew, but there was a spark between them that had made her behave out of character. Now she was having to backtrack. She didn't like giving too much of herself away.

She zipped up her skirt and slid her feet into her boots. In some ways it would have been nice to tumble into his bed, but it indicated a level of commitment she wasn't prepared to give.

She picked up her bag and moved towards the door. He stood behind her, then hooked his arms around her waist and kissed the back of her neck. She felt all the little hairs ripple, but she put her hand on the latch.

'When can I see you?'

'I've got a very busy diary.' She was going to play hard to get if it killed her.

'Surely you have to eat?'

'Occasionally.'

'Can I call you? I've got your mobile number because it was on the information sheet for the Hill Climb.'

'Stalker.'

'Yes. Probably.'

She laughed and shut the door behind her. Then shut her eyes and did a silent scream. She couldn't even blame the wine. He'd drunk most of it.

*

She was distracted at work all the next day. Images of Charlie's smiling face flashed up in her mind. She could feel his hands on her. She drifted off at the memory in the middle of conversations.

'Belinda?' Richard Mortlake looked at her in consternation in the middle of their weekly target meeting.

'Sorry.' She snapped out of her reverie and shuffled through her paperwork. 'We've put on seven houses this week – we've definitely got the market share . . .'

He called her that evening. They went out for dinner, even though it was only a Tuesday. They went back to his flat.

And this time she stayed over.

Her friends crowed with delight when she admitted she was head over heels and she and Charlie were a proper item.

She supposed it had just been a question of finding the right person. The one who allowed her to be her, and didn't push for attention, but was interested. Charlie loved talking houses with her. He loved all the gossip about the owners, and the wrangling that went on. He introduced her to lots of people – having a wine shop made you very popular, it turned out, and even though he'd only been in Peasebrook just over a year, he seemed to know everyone that was everyone.

Suddenly life had a different dimension. It felt fuller and richer and more fun to be sharing it with someone. Her social life went up a gear, and her sex life went into overdrive. Luckily it didn't affect Belinda's work. On the contrary, it made her even more determined to succeed and do well. She and the boss's son, Giles, were constantly pitted against each other, and she was determined to outdo him.

The only thing she found disconcerting was Charlie's spending.

'There's no pockets in shrouds,' he would say in a cod Yorkshire accent, egging her out for yet another evening where he would think nothing of spending over a hundred quid on cocktails, dinner and wine. She tried to rein him in but he wouldn't have it. He was generous to a fault, and always picked up the bill.

Maybe that's what normal people did? Maybe she was the weird one? It wasn't that she was stingy. She was just tactical about what she did with her money. How else were you supposed to get on?

'I don't know – everything just seems to fall into place,' Charlie said when she asked him how he managed financially. 'I've never made a plan in my life and I've done all right.'

He did seem to be doing all right. The wine shop was always busy and he was working hard picking up contracts with restaurants and hotels. She tried not to worry and told herself it was good to have opposites in a relationship. It would be awful if they were both spendthrifts. And she supposed it would be boring if they were both like her.

Besides, she was happy. *They* were happy. They were a good match, she thought.

Charlie had been worth the wait.

One day, he told her he had a surprise.

'I've got something to show you.' He held up a key.

She went to grab it. 'What? What's that for?'

He pulled it away, laughing. 'You have to follow me.'

He led her out of the wine shop and down the high street to the far end of Peasebrook. Belinda frowned when he stopped outside one of the old wool-merchants' houses.

'This belongs to one of my clients,' he told her. 'She's had to go into sheltered accommodation and they're putting it on the market. We've got a sneak preview. If we want it, it's ours.'

She fell in love at first sight.

The High House was what she would euphemistically call 'a project' if she was listing it. She didn't feel daunted, though. She would far rather have a wreck that needed to be done up from scratch than have to undo someone else's hard work that wasn't to her taste. Some of the eye-wateringly expensive kitchens she saw on her viewings would be impossible for her to live with, but to rip them out would be a waste. The High House was a blank canvas. It was structurally perfect – well, obviously it would need a thorough survey, but Belinda couldn't see any obvious horrors like subsidence – and therefore just waiting for her to put her stamp on it.

Well, *their* stamp.

'What do you think?' asked Charlie. 'Can you see us here? Because I can.'

She swallowed. This was a turning point. Buying The High House together would be a huge step. It was begging to be filled with footsteps and laughter. Already she could imagine it. When she looked in the bedroom, she imagined a giant sleigh bed and her and Charlie gently sleeping. When she looked in the kitchen, she saw them sharing tea and toast with the radio on in the background. She could picture them in the garden, Charlie bringing out a bottle of something new he'd discovered, sitting and sipping it in the early evening sun.

She looked over at Charlie, his arm resting on the mantelpiece. The fireplace below had been bricked up and an ugly gas fire put in, surrounded by shiny beige tiles. She fast-tracked to a year or more later, the Artex paper on the walls stripped off, the floorboards exposed and sanded and polished, the woodwork, currently sticky with a brown gloss, picked out in a subtle, dead flat oil. Apple logs burning in the grate and the mantelpiece groaning with photographs and invitations.

She could picture it so clearly. It felt so right.

'Yes.'

'So how do we do this?'

Looking back, this was the moment she should have heard alarm bells. But her brain was fuzzy with the thrill of being in love for the first time, the prospect of a house to call her own, the thought of a bright future.

And even perhaps a family. That was her ultimate dream. She could already picture her slightly unruly but enchanting offspring sliding down the bannisters. And she was so sidetracked by the second half of what Charlie said next that she ignored the warning signs.

'There is only one snag. All my money is tied up in the wine business at the moment,' he told her. 'I can't take any of it out. Of course I can contribute to the mortgage payments, but I can't put anything down as a deposit.' He put his arms around her neck. 'But nothing would make me happier than being Mr and Mrs Fox of High House, Peasebrook.'

A thrill ran through her. At the same time, she was doing the maths. This was why she had been saving all these years. This was her game plan, and it was time for the pay-off.

All she wanted was her own four walls around her. A house she could call her own. Only then would she feel happy and settled and secure. Where she could drive a nail into her own freshly painted plaster and hang up a picture. A house that was hers, forever. A house that was an extension of her personality and reflected who she was. A house that looked after her. A cocoon. A haven.

It took six weeks of wrangling with solicitors, banks, building societies and surveyors. More than once Belinda sank into despair, convinced the figures didn't stack up. The mortgage would have to be in her name only, as it turned out Charlie had a raft of County Court Judgements thanks to the myriad parking tickets he had racked up while living in London.

'I know I'm an idiot,' he told her. 'But I'll be able to help *pay* the mortgage. I just can't have my name on one. But because you're sensible and a genius, it will be all right. And I can pay for the building work. Don't forget this place is going to be worth a mint when it's done up. Peasebrook is on the up.' He grinned. 'You always know when a decent wine merchant moves into town that the property prices are going to soar.'

She juggled figures and had endless meetings and photocopied a million pieces of paper – payslips and bank statements – but eventually she got the mortgage offer and took out some money on her credit card to pay the stamp duty.

And then suddenly, one Friday afternoon, the solicitor rang to say they had exchanged contracts and she and

Charlie stood on the pavement outside The High House with the key in their hand, just as they had done the first time they had come to see it, only this time it was theirs.

Every day, Belinda seemed to get further away from who she had been and turned into someone new. By the end of the year, they got married. They barely spent any money on the wedding, because it was all going to go towards the house, but they did a very relaxed and casual wine and cheese evening for all their friends in the shop, and Charlie promised her a proper reception when the house was done up.

'I don't care about that sort of thing. You know I don't,' said Belinda, surrounded by paint charts. 'I am as happy as a pig in the proverbial.'

'That's why I love you. Because you are so undemanding.'

'Just you wait,' said Belinda. 'I can do demanding, when there's DIY to be done.'

She couldn't pretend that the first year of marriage wasn't hard. The house was cold and dusty and noisy to live in. Somehow she managed to commute to Maybury, hold down her job, and supervise the renovation. Charlie was very tied up with the shop and was reluctant to take on more staff, and so much of his business was done at weekends that it was left to Belinda to manage.

'I know I'm not much use, but hopefully it will pay off,' he told her, when he'd come back from yet another delivery, yet another wedding, yet another tasting to find her up a ladder. Sometimes she wondered if perhaps he drank a little too much, but it was part of his job.

'It actually *is* my job,' he said, when she questioned it once. 'I can't be a teetotal wine merchant.'

Of course he couldn't, and actually it made the

renovation easier, for she was able to get on and do it her way without asking for a second opinion.

'I totally trust your taste,' said Charlie. 'It's impeccable.'

She was flattered, and it didn't occur to her that he just wasn't all that interested.

She spent Saturday nights with a paintbrush in her hand, or pushing a sander over the wooden floorboards, while he was out at events. She would fall into bed at midnight; he would come in at two.

'You reek of booze,' she said, pushing at him, but in a fond way.

'You stink of paint,' would be his riposte, but they would curl up with each other, because they were still slightly in awe of how they could make each other feel between the sheets.

Belinda started awake. She had fallen asleep and her bath had gone cold. She shook away the unwanted remnants of her reverie. Reliving those days always made her feel unsettled. She had worked so hard to put them behind her.

She never thought about what had happened next if she could help it. Perhaps it was unhealthy to block it all out, but that was the only way she could manage.

And she was doing fine, she told herself as she jumped out of the bath and wrapped herself in a towel. She was a success, against the odds.

And now she only had fifteen minutes to get ready and get to the Hong Kong Garden. She grabbed a pair of jeans and a cardigan and rough-dried her hair. It was only Bruce. He wouldn't mind if she didn't look top dollar.

20

Peasebrook had a great selection of restaurants for a small town. Its jewels in the crown were A Deux, a tiny little pop-up restaurant for two, and the Cardamom Pod, a funky, upscale Indian. And then the Hong Kong Garden, a traditional Chinese that was always packed because the food was as fantastic as the décor was excruciating: shiny red and black plastic with lots of backlit photographs of the food they served.

Bruce was waiting outside when she arrived. He gave her a hug, then looked at her appreciatively.

'You look stunning, darling. You've increased your chances of getting laid a hundredfold. All those stiff jackets – they're not doing you any good. Come here. You've done your cardi up wrong.'

He buttoned it up properly for her. Belinda grinned, because she was used to Bruce and his un-PC banter, but she had to admit it was nice to be appreciated, even when you hadn't done your hair properly.

As they made their way to their table inside, she spotted someone she wanted to avoid. Giles Mortlake, sitting in front of a mound of egg fried rice and chicken in black bean sauce, his rabbity wife opposite him. Could she sneak past without him noticing?

Not a chance.

'Belinda!' Giles heaved himself to his feet and stretched out a meaty paw. He must have put on three stone since she'd last crossed paths with him.

'Giles. How lovely. We're just about to sit down . . .' She indicated her table where the waiter was hovering.

Giles pointed at Bruce. 'You're the chappie who does the pictures. You did a nice job on Hunter's Moon, I must say. Very *House and Garden*.'

'How did you get a brochure?' Belinda felt indignant.

'Oh, Belinda, come on. Industrial espionage. You know you're guilty of it too.' Giles smirked. 'Congratulations on getting it.' He winked at Bruce. 'I taught her everything she knows.'

Belinda wasn't going to dignify this claim with a protest. 'Enjoy your meal,' she said, and went to move on.

'I see you got your old place as well. The High House.' Would this blithering idiot not shut up?

'Yes.'

'Must have been a trip down Memory Lane. But good to make some money out of it after everything you lost.'

'That wasn't really my motive.'

'Come, come – revenge is a dish best eaten cold, no?'

'It wasn't revenge, Giles. It's just business.'

'Well, good to see you doing so well.' Giles sat back down in his seat and picked up his chopsticks. 'Enjoy!'

Belinda was seething as they made their way to their table.

'How did you not punch him?' asked Bruce.

'I've no idea,' she said tightly as they sat down.

'There's no love lost between you and Giles, is there?'

'No, there bloody isn't.' Belinda picked up the menu.

There was silence for a moment, then Bruce couldn't bear it.

'So The High House was yours?'

'A long time ago. For a very short time.'

'You didn't tell me.' Bruce looked hurt.

'It's not relevant.'

'No, but it's interesting.' He leaned forward, eager for more information.

She sighed. She knew Bruce. He would winkle it out of her eventually.

'OK. The guy at Hunter's Moon this afternoon? That's Charlie Fox. My ex-husband. We were married for about five minutes. We had The High House for about five minutes. We got married far too quickly and we had nothing in common. That's all there is to it and I don't want to talk about it.' She stared at Bruce, defying him to pry any further.

'You were married?'

'End of conversation.'

'Right.' He picked up the menu and looked down it. 'I reckon we should go Set Dinner for Two, because it's fricking awesome and if there's anything left you can take it back home.'

'Lovely,' said Belinda, thanking God he'd got the message.

'The duck in black bean sauce is amazing; the salt and pepper squid is amazing. It's *all* amazing.'

'Then bring it on. And could I please have a very large glass of white wine? In fact, make it a bottle.'

The service at the Hong Kong Garden was unfailingly cheery, and with a towering bowl of warm prawn crackers and a goldfish bowl full of Pinot Grigio in front of her, Belinda started to feel as if the day had barely happened.

By the time they had chomped their way through their banquet, Belinda realised she had polished off a whole bottle of white wine to herself as Bruce was drinking Chinese beer. Luckily she'd had plenty of food, so she didn't feel as out of control as she might, given she rarely drank more than a glass these days, though once upon a time a bottle a night had been the norm.

She wasn't thinking about that, she reminded herself. She'd managed to dodge the bullet. As Memory Lanes went, that wasn't one she wanted to go down.

After pineapple fritters, the bill arrived with two fortune cookies. She crushed hers open and unravelled the tiny strip of paper.

'What does it say?' said Bruce.

'A dark stranger is going to enter your life and bring you untold happiness,' she read.

'Why are they always dark strangers? Why are they never ginger?'

'What about yours?'

Bruce unravelled his. 'A beautiful brunette will end up in your bed tonight.'

Belinda laughed. He was incorrigible.

'You better get out there and start looking for one then.'

She held on to Bruce's arm as they came out into the high street. She was a tiny bit unsteady on her feet, and he laughed at her.

'Darling, you need a coffee. Come back to mine. And don't worry, I'm not going to pounce. That would be very bad form,' he chuckled.

'You *are* Peter Pan,' murmured Belinda. 'That's who you remind me of.'

'Oh gawd, don't. You make me sound like Cliff Richard.'

Bruce had an apartment in the converted glove factory just off Peasebrook high street. Belinda had been the agent when they went on the market and had talked him into buying one of the first releases, but she hadn't been to see it since he'd moved in.

There was an open-plan main room with rough bare brick walls and large arched metal windows. A U-shaped white linen sofa sat in front of a wide screen TV, hundreds of vinyl LPs lined up against the back wall, and there were black-and-white photographs everywhere.

'This is my diary,' Bruce told her proudly. 'The gallery of me and my life.'

He went over to an art deco cocktail cabinet while Belinda scrutinised the photos. It was like looking at a gossip column mixed with a travel magazine. Bruce's life had certainly never been dull: beautiful people in beautiful places, having the time of their lives; cowboys and flamenco dancers and graffiti artists.

He came and stood by her, handing her a Cointreau on ice cloudy with promise.

'That's not coffee,' she said.

'No,' he said. She took it and sipped, enjoying the fiery orange sweetness slipping down her throat and the glow it gave her. It was great, being out, letting her hair down. She couldn't remember the last time she'd done it. She'd drunk more this evening than she'd drunk this year.

She waved her glass at all the photographs.

'This makes me realise I've never done anything or been anywhere.'

'Well, do something about it. Go travelling.'

'I'm not like you. I can't give up everything and take a camera and make money.'

'No, but you can go on holiday. When did you last go on holiday?'

'I don't know.' She felt the need to defend herself. 'I'm saving for a house, remember?'

'Don't you ever give yourself a break? You're not indispensable. No one is. You've got a great team. Today proved that.'

She didn't want to answer. She carried on looking at the photographs. There was a girl who appeared repeatedly; a girl with messy blonde hair and shining eyes who was always laughing and flirting with the camera.

'Who's this?' she pointed to a picture of the girl in a bikini, wearing a false moustache and a sombrero.

Bruce stood for a moment looking. 'That's Caroline,' he said. 'My girlfriend.'

'Oh.'

'She drowned. In Mexico.'

'Oh Bruce. I'm so sorry. I had no idea.'

This really was an evening of secrets for them both.

Bruce came and stood next to her.

'She was wonderful. I adored her. She was the funniest, kindest, most alive person in the world. She was twenty-four when she died. I was twenty-six.'

Belinda put a hand on his shoulder, not knowing what to say. She'd had so much to drink she was terrified of what might come out. She hadn't had enough not to think it didn't matter.

'She's the reason I've never settled down with anyone. I can't face losing someone I love ever again.'

'Oh, Bruce . . .' His revelation explained so much. He wasn't just a jack-the-lad, a player. He was masking a broken heart. 'You can't live the rest of your life not falling in love just because you might lose someone.'

He shrugged.

'I guess I'm just risk averse.'

'I suppose so. But it just seems very sad. You deserve someone special . . .'

She stopped, because her words sounded sugary and sickly. And because the expression on his face told her to stop. She wanted to hug him, dear funny crazy Bruce.

'I could say the same to you,' said Bruce eventually. 'You can't live the rest of your life not falling in love just because someone hurt you.'

He was standing very close to her, looking down. He was in his jeans, and she could see how toned his arms were in his old Clash T-shirt, and how flat his tummy was, and she thought if Bruce knew about anything – well, apart from photography – he probably knew how to make a woman happy in bed.

She felt a sudden rush of longing to be held, to feel warm, and to connect with someone, to get rid of the memories . . .

21

Belinda was woken by the smell of coffee and the sound of Bon Jovi pounding through her. To say she was living on a prayer was an understatement. She couldn't work out where she was at first: she could see the familiar golden stone of Peasebrook through an arched window. The bed she was in was low with a distressed headboard, and there was a leather punch bag in the corner of the room next to a large framed poster of Marlon Brando in *On the Waterfront*. The room was minimalist and decidedly masculine. She breathed in the pillow next to her and her stomach flipped. Aramis. There was only one person she knew who wore that.

'Hey.'

She looked over at the doorway. Bruce was standing there with two mugs. He was wearing a tight white T-shirt and a pair of grey sweat shorts. He was smiling at her with his inimitable wicked grin.

'The fortune cookie was right.'

She threw the duvet over her head and hid. It was coming back to her. In fact, she could still taste the monosodium-glutamate. Chinese. Wine. Cointreau. A deadly combination.

She felt Bruce come and sit on the bed.

'Babe. There's nothing to be ashamed of.'

She peeped out. He put the coffees down on the bed-side table and stroked her hair.

'How are you feeling?'

'I don't know.'

She knew if she sat up, her hangover would kick in.

'I'm really sorry,' she managed in a strangled voice.

'What for?'

'I don't usually behave like this.'

He stared at her. 'It's OK.'

'This is so embarrassing.'

He touched her arm and she nearly jumped out of her skin.

'Why are you so jumpy?'

'Because – what are we going to do now? Can we just forget it ever happened?'

'Forget what? We had a great night.'

She put her hands over her ears. 'I don't want to hear.'

'Oh my God!' Bruce started laughing. 'You think we had sex.'

He flopped back on to the bed and started cackling.

'What's so funny?' Belinda was nettled.

He finally managed to stop.

'I am not into necrophilia,' he said solemnly. 'You passed out. I just about managed to get you in here. And don't worry. You still have your clothes on.'

She looked down at herself and realised with relief that she was fully dressed.

'I slept on the sofa. And, for the record, I would never take advantage of you. I respect you way too much. There's not many women I can say that about.'

For a split second, Belinda felt disappointed. Then she

worried that what Bruce was effectively saying was he didn't fancy her. She was puzzled. When had she become so insecure?

'Coffee,' she croaked. 'I've got to go to Hunter's Moon for lunch at midday.'

She had never turned up to an appointment with a hangover. What would the Willoughbys think of her?

Bruce handed her a cup.

'Do you mind if I do my work out?' Bruce nodded towards the punch bag. 'I have to get it out of the way first thing or I won't do it. I need to sweat out all that booze.'

'You go ahead.'

She watched in awe for the next twenty minutes as he punched and jabbed, wincing at the thwack of leather against leather. He didn't stop for a moment, dancing on his feet, the sweat gathering as the bag swung wildly from side to side. It was exhausting just watching him. No wonder he was in such good shape. He might be fifty, but his arms were toned, his abs defined, his thighs like rock.

She ventured out of bed, stepping gingerly on to the carpet. So far, so good.

He turned to her, taking off his gloves and handing them to her.

'Here,' he said. 'Best hangover cure ever.'

'I can't.'

'Sure you can. Come on. Just ten minutes. You'll feel on top of the world.'

She pulled the gloves on, and he tightened them and did up the straps.

'Right. Stand with your feet apart, one foot in front of the other, like this. Then jab – boof boof boof boof. Think of someone you want to punch.'

'That won't be hard,' said Belinda, swinging her arm through the air and imaging Charlie's face. The smack as she hit the punch bag was extraordinarily satisfying.

'Come on. Faster. Give it everything you've got. Pull your elbows right back. Bend your knees.'

Belinda tried to follow his instructions, laughing.

'Come on! You can punch harder than that. Pull your abs in. Twist at the waist.'

In the end, she kept going for about fifteen minutes. And Bruce was right. By the end of it, her heart was racing, her head felt clear and she was high on endorphins.

'OK if I use your shower?' she asked Bruce, panting and pulling off her gloves.

He stopped for a moment. 'Sure. Do you want clean underwear?'

She looked taken aback. He pointed at the chest of drawers.

'Top left-hand drawer.'

She opened it up. Inside was a pile of brand new knickers, with the tags still on.

'Please tell me they're not for your conquests.'

He grinned. 'They're for photo shoots. You would be amazed how much VPL I have to contend with. Those are seamless. Rifle through and find your size.'

He carried on punching. Belinda picked out a pair of knickers, laughing to herself. Bruce cracked her up.

In the shower, her head began to clear and she started running through what she needed to do. She might have time to go to the office and do emails to everyone who had gone to the open house. And then go for lunch at the Willoughbys. The thought gave her a heavy heart. Poor Leo. She had really felt for him yesterday. She hoped he had been able to sort things out with his parents. She felt for them all, in fact. It was a horrible situation.

If anyone knew what it felt like to lose the home you loved, it was Belinda.

22

By the time she drove up the drive to Hunter's Moon, she felt almost human.

'All hangovers have gone by midday,' Bruce had assured her. 'Except the stealth ones that hit you a few hours after you get up. Because you're still drunk from the night before.'

'Are you an expert?'

'I could write the manual.'

She'd gone back to her flat and changed into a grey sweater dress and boots. She left her hair down and put on the light-diffusing foundation she only used in emergencies. Then she went through her notes, ready for the debrief.

At Hunter's Moon, Sally and Teddy greeted her at the door. Sally was a little subdued, but exuded her usual warmth.

'I'm so sorry – I didn't pick up your message until we got home yesterday. I'm sorry you were put in such an awkward position.'

'I hope everything's OK?' It was hard to know exactly what to say in the circumstances.

'We should probably have told Leo on day one. But it's all out in the open now.'

'Just say if you would rather be alone today. I can update you tomorrow.'

'No, it will be lovely to have you. Come in.'

Inside the hall, Belinda could smell the delicious waft of Sunday lunch and her stomach rumbled. She had only managed coffee and water this morning. She needed food.

Sally pushed open the door of the drawing room. Inside, Leo was sitting on the sofa with the Sunday supplement. He stood up as soon he saw her.

'Darling, would you get Belinda a drink?' asked Sally. 'I'll go and give Dad a shout.'

And she was gone. Belinda and Leo looked at each other.

'Would you like a glass of champagne? To toast us starting over again?'

'Actually, just water for me, please. I'm driving.' Just one glass and she'd probably be back over the limit and goodness knows what might happen.

'I know. It's a bore. I'm not going to go back until tomorrow now, so I can indulge.' Leo walked over to the drinks cabinet and started finding glasses and ice. 'Anyway – I need to apologise for yesterday. I think I was probably very rude to you and made a bit of a scene.'

'Please – don't give it a second thought. It must have been horrible, seeing strangers crawling all over your home.'

Leo sighed. 'It's been the worst weekend of my life. My poor parents.'

'I am very sorry.' Belinda wasn't sure what to say other than that. She had trained herself to be neutral and keep a respectful distance, though her instinct was to engage with Leo.

He brought over a glass of sparkling water with ice and lime. Again, she was struck by how very like his father he was. The same bone structure; the same soulful eyes. As he handed it to her, she caught a trace of his cologne: something Eastern and exotic, dark with promise.

'I spent all morning on the Internet looking for miracle cures. Needless to say, there aren't any. Then I tried to work out if I could buy the house from them so they could stay here . . .' He looked rueful. 'I've done well on my flat in London but not *that* well.'

'If it's any consolation, the development they are moving to is very nice. Very well appointed and everything is high spec.' Oh God. She sounded as if she was one of their sales reps.

He made a face.

'I can't stand the thought of them living there. It looks like a bloody golf club to me. I know they've got all the facilities and it's very convenient but . . .'

'It's not Hunter's Moon?'

'No. When you've been brought up somewhere like this you just assume it will go on forever. I always imagined my kids swimming in the pool and eating their fish fingers in the kitchen . . . Not that I have kids but you know . . . one day.' He gave a half-hearted laugh. 'First world problems . . .'

Leo looked away.

'Sorry. It's just – I've had to keep a brave face since yesterday . . .'

He tried to smile.

She put down her glass and walked over to him. She put a hand on his arm.

'Hey.'

He wiped at his eye with the side of his hand, rubbing away a tear.

'Shit . . .'

She could see he was really struggling to keep his composure. Her instinct was to put her arms around him, but she couldn't possibly. It wasn't professional. Then she saw another tear escape from the corner of his eye. To hell with being professional: it was only human to give him a hug.

So she did. And for a moment he let her hold on to him. He breathed in deeply a couple of times. She didn't say anything because what could she say. Then he stepped out of her embrace. He smiled, and in that smile was his unspoken thanks.

'I feel so guilty. There was me, swanning about, and all the time they were going through this.'

'But you're here for them now,' said Belinda. 'I know you feel as if there's nothing you can do, but that's all they need.'

'I just can't bear the thought of the house being sold.'

Belinda took a sip of her water before she replied.

'Look, I know it seems like a terrible thing, to lose your family home. But I promise you, you will survive. I see it all the time. I know it's momentous, but—'

'And it should be me looking after him. Not Mum.' Leo cut her off, as if he wasn't listening. 'She's spent her whole life looking after us. She should be winding down now, just worrying about the garden and what cake she's going to make for the summer fete. Not having to watch her own husband deteriorate and be his bloody carer!'

'I understand you want to do your duty. But it's not always possible, is it? Not when we all have jobs.'

'Yes, but really – how can I give a fuck about promoting an artisanal gin bar when all this is going on?'

'Is that what you do, then?' Belinda knew perfectly well what he did because Sally had told her, with great pride.

Leo nodded. 'I've got a PR company. Anything to do with food or drink or restaurants or bars or eating. But I'm worried – I really need to be here for Mum and Dad and I'm busier than ever. I suppose you know what it's like, working for yourself. I mean, I've got a great team but . . .'

He spread his hands as if to indicate she must understand.

'I hear you. There's no such thing as time off.'

'Yes. People think because you're your own boss you can do what you like, but you can't really. I mean, yes – I'm going to take tomorrow off, but I should be back in London and my voicemail and my inbox will be full to bursting and everyone will be screaming at me to make decisions.'

'Tell me about it,' said Belinda. 'Sometimes I shut my mobile in the kitchen drawer and turn the music up. But you shouldn't beat yourself up. We can't do everything. I know you want to help your parents but you have to be realistic. You've got your own life. And they know that. Which I guess is why they said nothing.'

'Do you really think that?'

Belinda took a sip of her water. 'What I actually think is . . . it's one of those shit situations where there isn't an answer. In this case, your parents are doing the most sensible thing.'

Leo looked at her. 'Said the estate agent selling their house.'

Belinda raised her eyebrows. 'Trust me, if they told me they wanted to take Hunter's Moon off the market, I would be delighted.'

'Somehow I don't think that's going to happen. They need the money. I mean, I can help them out with the garden and practical stuff, but at the end of the day it comes down to cash.'

Leo seemed to have composed himself. He seemed altogether a much softer person than the angry man she had met yesterday. She supposed her first impressions of him had been the worst possible. It had been a stressful situation.

'Listen, I wanted to ask you to keep me in the loop.' He pulled a card out of his wallet and handed it to her. 'It's not that I don't trust Mum and Dad, but I'd really love to know what's going on, and if there's anything you think I should know about, just call me. I know they're trying to protect me. But whenever they say *we didn't want to worry you* it makes me want to tear my hair out.'

Belinda looked at his hair. It was as black and glossy as a raven's wing. She swallowed, and took his card.

She wanted to say that she thought his parents were perfectly capable and he should let them get on with it, yet she could also sympathise with his desire to be involved.

'Of course,' she said, and put the card in her pocket.

In the kitchen, Alexander was staring at the rib of roast beef resting in the tin.

The carving knife and sharpening steel were sitting on the side next to a large white meat plate.

He put out his hand to lift the knife, but he couldn't.

'You're going to have to ask Leo to carve,' he said stiffly to Sally, and walked out of the kitchen.

Sally stood with a pot of horseradish in her hand. She felt tears come to her eyes. How tactless of her. She hadn't thought. She should have steered Alexander towards Belinda then commandeered Leo discreetly. She'd forgotten, just for a moment. Not the situation, of course not, but the practical implications.

She wanted to go after Alexander and hug him. Tell him it was going to be all right. Hold him tight and make him feel safe. Just as he had made her feel, all those years ago . . .

23

1967

S ally couldn't believe it when she woke the day after the photo shoot and it was just after nine. She didn't think she'd ever woken up so late, but it had been after three before she went to sleep. And it turned out that having your photograph taken was exhausting. Plus she had never slept in a double bed before and couldn't get used to all the room. It was heaven.

She ran to the window and looked out across the garden to the fields beyond. Today was a crisp and bright spring morning, though still very cold, and everything glittered with frost. The house almost seemed to be breathing itself, in tandem with its slumbering inhabitants. Sally could sense she was the first one awake. She dressed quickly, in an old pair of slacks, a polo-neck jumper and her plimsolls, because she was going to be on her feet all day. She tied her hair back in a ponytail and slapped on some Ponds cold cream, her only nod to a beauty regime.

In the kitchen she put on the kettle to make a pot of tea, then began to cook, knowing there was nothing better than being woken by the smell of frying bacon.

By half past nine she had made another list of things she needed and no one had appeared. She put the bacon in an enamel dish in the warming oven of the Aga – it would keep there quite nicely – and she could do the eggs when someone appeared. She gathered up dusters, sponges and a mop and went to tackle the hall.

Before she started to clean, she dealt with the big pile of post on the table. It made her blood run cold to see all the unopened brown envelopes, with some of the postmarks dating back weeks. Some of them were stamped URGENT or FINAL DEMAND. She didn't open any of them, but she could tell just by feeling them that they needed attending to. She could tell Margot had an instinct for invitations and just left everything else.

She didn't suppose Dai had attended to a piece of paperwork in his life or even stopped to look at what was on the table.

She sorted the letters into piles, depending on who they had been addressed to.

She looked up and saw Margot coming down the stairs, yawning. She was wearing men's pyjamas with the sleeves and legs rolled up, her tangled hair falling down to her shoulders.

'Morning!' She beamed at Sally. 'Can I smell bacon?'

'Yes. I'll come and do you an egg too.'

'My goodness, it's like being in a lovely hotel. Yes, please.'

Sally held out Margot's pile of officialdom.

'I've sorted through all the post. You might like to have a look through these while you're having breakfast.'

Margot looked slightly puzzled. 'Oh, I'd just throw the whole lot in the bin. If it's important, they'll write to me again.'

'Don't you think you should open them? Some of these are from the bank. And there are bills too. I think.'

Margot flipped through them, just putting aside the ones marked Personal. 'Oh dear. Yes. This is mostly my Christmas shopping. I suppose I should pay – it's been a month or so.'

'Over three months.' Sally corrected her.

Margot handed her back the pile.

'Let's just bin all of them and start again and I promise I will turn over a new leaf and open everything. I've got the fan mail. That's all I need to worry about, really.'

Sally looked at the remaining envelopes. She felt panic pool in her stomach. She knew the consequences of unpaid bills better than anyone. The fear had never left her.

'Are you sure you wouldn't like me to open them? And pay them? You said there was a chequebook in the kitchen drawer. If you sign the cheques, I can settle all these ac-counts and then you're square. Otherwise you might get into the most awful trouble . . .'

To her huge relief, Margot smiled. 'That's not a bad idea. Yes, why not?'

'I mean, you don't want them to cut off the electricity or the telephone.'

'Would they do that?'

'Of course. If you don't pay.'

'Oh yes. That would be awful. You go ahead.'

Sally took the envelopes back to the kitchen and put them on the table, then made Margot breakfast. Alexan-der and Phoebe appeared soon after, but not Dai, and they were so appreciative of her cooking it made her smile.

'Oh my goodness – a butter dish and butter knife?' said Phoebe in admiration.

'And a jam spoon. We are total savages, you know that,' said Alexander, carefully scooping out some marmalade on to his toast.

'No, darling – we're just busy,' said Margot. 'It's nothing to be ashamed of.'

Sally worried that Margot felt as if she was being got at for not being a good housewife. She had noticed moments of prickliness and reminded herself to be careful. The last thing she wanted was for Margot to feel threatened.

When they had all disappeared off – Margot to her study, Phoebe to the dining room and Alexander goodness knows where – she sat down with a pen and made a note of every bill, then took the chequebook out of the drawer and wrote out seventeen cheques for the seventeen unpaid bills.

Electricity. Telephone. The butcher in Peasebrook – not the one she had been to, she noticed. Harrods. Fortnum's. Hatchards. Margot's room service bill at Brown's. Petrol from the local garage. It went on and on. It made Sally's blood run cold, the thought that anyone could ignore the fact they owed money.

But then she supposed the Willoughbys didn't really understand the consequences of debt.

She put the lid back on the pen. She wasn't going to think about her father. This was her chance for a new adventure. She wasn't going to live in the past, or let what had happened overshadow her.

She put the cheques into a pile ready for Margot's signature. She would have to go to the post office for envelopes and stamps – there was no point in looking for any here.

She hadn't opened Margot's bank statements. That was

going too far and they were really none of her business. She would find another way of getting her to give them her attention.

Later that week, Margot reached out for her pile of post. Sally had taken to giving it to her each morning at breakfast. She tutted as she realised Sally had put two letters from the bank on the top. She was only interested in her fan mail, so she put those to one side and leafed through the rest.

Letters from readers often cheered her up and reminded her why she wrote. People mostly wrote nice things, although they did love to point out mistakes and inaccuracies. She liked it best when a reader told her one of her books had got them through a particularly hard time: a bereavement or an illness. Those letters always made her feel as if what she was doing was truly worthwhile.

Today there was one letter that particularly intrigued her, which had been sent on from Niggle. It was in a long white envelope with thick black writing: Margot Willoughby c/o The Rathbone Agency. She opened this one first, curious, because it looked interesting.

She spread the letter, neatly folded in three, open. It was brief, but emphatic.

Dear Miss Willoughby
Following on from our meeting at the party, I took the liberty of reading one of your books today. I have to admit to finding it highly entertaining. I think I owe you an apology. I was rude and dismissive of your work, and I would like to take you out for lunch to make up

for it. I don't always behave terribly well when I'm nervous. My number is at the top of this letter. Please do telephone me next time you are in town.

With my very best wishes
Terence Miller.

Margot stared at the letter in amazement. She read it over and over again, and as the words finally sank in, she found her heart was beating faster and faster, and a feeling washed through her. She finally managed to identify it. It was pleasure. Pleasure at his validation, and even greater pleasure at his invitation. Why? she wondered. He wasn't handsome or charming. He'd been vile to her. Yet something drew her to him. Was she being perverse? Was it because he seemed to be the only man on the planet who didn't find her attractive, and if Margot liked anything it was a challenge?

She felt flustered. She didn't know what to do with her feelings, or his invitation. Of course, she didn't have to answer it. He'd been so rude she was well within her rights to ignore his overture. She fished about in the drawer of her desk for her cigarettes, only to find the packet empty. She needed something to calm her nerves. Nerves? Why on earth did she feel nervous? She should chuck the letter in the bin and crack on with her book.

But his sardonic tones, those pale grey eyes behind his thick glasses, wouldn't leave her.

At three o'clock, she drew on her cardigan, went out to find the Mini, then drove to the post office in the nearby village to buy cigarettes. She came out, lit up and stared at the phone box over the road as she inhaled the smoke.

Something dark and potent pooled in her tummy. Something dangerous.

She tossed her half-finished cigarette into the rubbish bin and walked over to the phone box. She tried to look casual but she probably looked anything but. She dug in her purse for the right coins, then picked up the receiver and dialled the number, listening to the whir of the dial as it spun round like a wheel of fortune. She pushed in a coin as she heard the pips.

'Three-five-eight-eight,' growled Terence Miller. She would recognise his voice anywhere.

'Hello. Mr Miller? It's Margot Willoughby.' She sounded far more self-assured than she felt.

He didn't reply for a second, then his reply held a mixture of surprise and amusement. 'Oh.'

'I got your letter. Thank you.'

Again, he was slow to reply. She wondered if he was embarrassed. Perhaps he'd been drunk when he wrote it, and was now regretting it.

'Good,' he said.

She ploughed on.

'I've a morning meeting in London on the seventeenth,' she lied. 'I wondered if you were free for lunch afterwards?'

Again, a few seconds' silence. Did he do it to unnerve people, or was he genuinely slow to react? Margot wound the thick telephone cord around her fingers while she waited for his reply, biting her tongue despite the urge to babble, wondering why on earth she had phoned him. Was she mad?

'That's fine,' he said, sounding as if it was the most boring proposition he'd ever had. 'One o'clock at Mirabelle.'

And he rang off.

Margot put the phone down and leaned her forehead against the cool of the glass. She could see the children leaving the school playground, skipping around, laughing, pushing each other. Her heart was beating and there was blood in her veins and she felt as if she had done something for herself for the first time in a long time. She felt exhausted and frustrated and daunted, and she wanted to speak to someone who understood how it felt to stare at a blank page day after day, and she thought that Terence Miller, for all his posturing, probably did.

It took a fortnight for Sally to get the full measure of the Willoughbys.

There had been no structure, no discipline, no routine at Hunter's Moon, but what pleased her was how they responded to her attempts to organise them. They started to come down to breakfast before nine, because she had told them she wasn't going to cook after that. And she found that if she asked them to do things, they would help. Phoebe happily pegged out the first wash of the day. Alexander fed the cat and kept its bowls clean and cleaned out the parrot. Margot remembered to bring all her cups and plates over from the coach house. Dai was a shadowy figure who hadn't quite engaged with the new status quo. He stood apart from the rest of the family, awkward and possibly even a little shy. It was as if he didn't quite belong.

And when Annie came home at the weekend, she was eager to help with the cooking. Sally taught her how to make scones and Victoria sponge and pastry.

'The cookery teacher at school is rubbish. She's got awful BO,' Annie informed her, rubbing butter and lard together into a mound of flour. 'Why are you such a brilliant cook?'

'I'm not. I'm nothing like as good as my mum. I learnt everything from her, really.'

Sally had stood on the stool in the kitchen next to her mother from a very young age, watching her deft fingers knead bread or roll out biscuit dough. She felt a momentary pang of guilt. She'd been away long enough. It was time to go home soon, just to see how everyone was. She couldn't stay away forever.

Not yet, though.

One of the first things Sally wanted to do at Hunter's Moon was reinstate the drawing room. It was such a waste for it to be sitting there unused. She could understand why no one wanted to go in there, because it was so cold and unwelcoming. It might look stunning in the pages of a magazine, but it wasn't conducive to socialising or relaxation.

She started by taking off all the plastic covers on the sofas and chairs – they were still on there from when they had been delivered – then rearranged them into a less rigid setting. She decluttered the mantelpiece of all the fussy china ornaments the designer had placed there. Flowers, photographs, cushions – that was what the room needed, not awful china figurines, a sense of family rather than formality.

People, too – that was what it needed and a few scuff marks and creases. It needed to feel lived in.

A real fire. That would bring it to life.

She went to find Dai, who was sitting at the kitchen table. She wasn't sure if he was dressed or if he had slept in what he was wearing. Sally was used to boys. She had seen how her mother had handled her brothers: quietly and firmly. They needed to be told what was expected of them and to be given a time frame. There was no point in expecting them to guess. Men were not mind readers. They needed clear instructions.

'I've got a job for you,' she said brightly. 'I need some logs. I want to start using the fire in the drawing room and there are loads of fallen branches around the place. I wondered if you would collect them up for me? Maybe chop them up and put them into a nice pile somewhere dry?'

Dai stared at her. He frowned, and for a moment Sally was afraid she had gone too far too soon. Her mother never gave her brothers an opportunity to say no when she asked them to do something, so she was trying to employ the same tactic. She wasn't sure that Dai quite had the same respect for her that her brothers had for her mum.

It took him a moment to reply. He seemed to be turning her proposition round in his mind. Then he smiled. 'Good idea,' he said. 'I reckon there's an axe lying around somewhere. Nothing like a proper fire.'

'Exactly. But fires are very hungry things, so I'll need a good supply.' She felt a rush of jubilance.

He swilled the rest of his tea back, put his cup down on the table, and stood up.

He nodded at her.

'It's nice to feel wanted,' he told her.

She watched him amble out of the kitchen, scratching his head as he went, obviously slightly bemused by the exchange.

*

At supper that night, Dai was absent.

'Oh, he'll be off wrapping hedgehogs in clay with one of his shadowy friends,' said Margot. 'He's part gypsy these days.'

Sally worried that he was cross she had asked him to do the logs, and this was his way of showing his annoyance. Had she overstepped the mark? She felt sure he'd seemed quite happy to do it. He'd said it was good to feel needed! Was he being sarcastic? Some men didn't like being told what to do by a woman. Dai certainly seemed to do what he pleased with little regard for anyone else, but she didn't think he was a chauvinist. Oh dear. It was very difficult to work out the balance of power in this house.

But just as they were all finishing the queen of puddings she had made – she thought she better start using up that raspberry jam – he walked back in.

He chucked an envelope on the table. It was bulging.

'That's for you,' he said to Sally. 'With a bit extra for compensation, shall we call it?'

She opened it. There was nearly a hundred pounds in there, and a piece of headed notepaper.

'You went to the Kitten Club!'

Dai laughed, and she thought how handsome he was when he smiled. If only he would smile more often.

'Bunch of lily-livers. Didn't take much to get it out of them. They're all talk. What a horrible place.'

Sally could imagine him towering over them all. She imagined Morag, panicked and flustering. She felt a thrill run through her. Dai had been all the way up to London to get her wages for her. She turned to Margot.

'Well, I need to pay you back. For the rent you gave me to give Barbara.'

Margot waved her hand. 'Oh, don't be silly. It's very important for a girl to have a bit of a nest egg. You keep it.'

'For clothes!' said Phoebe. 'Imagine what you could get.'

'Thank you,' said Sally to Dai, who gave a shrug.

He sat down. He looked at their empty plates. 'Don't tell me there's no food left. I've been looking forward to this all day.'

'There's loads,' said Sally. 'I saved you some and I made two puddings.'

Dai looked pleased and smiled for the second time.

'Goodness me,' said Margot. 'You really are a marvel.' She looked at Sally through slightly narrowed eyes as she blew the last of the smoke out of her cigarette and stubbed it out on her pudding plate.

24

1967

M argot had never been to Mirabelle.
　　She had thought of nothing but her lunch with Terence since the day she had made the arrangement, which had done nothing for the progress of her book. She told herself that she would be able to concentrate once she'd seen him again.

She took the train up from the tiny station at Peasebrook to Paddington. She felt a little self-conscious standing on the platform as she stood out from everyone else in their drab workaday clothing. Phoebe had worked her magic again. She'd made her a little suit in pale pink with gilt buttons that was so demure it would make Jackie Kennedy look like Diana Dors. Some men found demure sexy, and Margot had a feeling that Terence Miller was one of those men. On top of it she wore her fox coat. April was a fickle madam. You never knew where you were with the weather.

The 11.18 pulled in to the station. It would get her into Paddington just in time to get a taxi to Mayfair and then she would probably get the 4.45 home again. She knew the timetable back to front: life as an author seemed to consist of an awful lot of lunches.

Niggle always took her to 'the Trat' – La Terrazza – in

Soho because he loved its casual chaos and the fact there was always someone in there he knew as well as a good arty smattering of actors or singers or photographers. Niggle was a shocking star-fucker on the quiet and loved to drop names, but he was also good at spotting talent, and had taken a punt on more than one hopeful penniless writer he had ended up getting drunk with at the Trat – they kept the prices deliberately low because they knew critical acclaim didn't always mean money.

Mirabelle was just as starry but a little quieter and pricier than the Trat, tucked away down Curzon Street in Mayfair. She gave her coat to the maître d' and checked herself in her compact, feeling nervous. She had come here for professional advice, not a liaison, she reminded herself. Yet when she saw Terence Miller already at the table she felt such a burning curiosity and fascination, she had to stop and gather her thoughts. It had seemed such a good idea when she'd been standing in the telephone box, but now it seemed like madness. What on earth was she expecting to come of it? She felt foolish and impulsive but it was too late now, because he had seen her. He didn't wave or stand up. There was just the merest flicker of recognition with no smile. His face was carved from granite.

She was going to make an idiot of herself.

Then she remembered: *he* had written to her. *He* had invited her to lunch. Which must mean he wanted to see her, surely? He had made the first move.

The maître d' escorted her over to the table and pulled out her chair. All the other customers were far too busy perusing their menus or knocking back their drinks to notice her. Terence stood up, a glass in one hand, until she had settled herself, then sat down.

'Hello. Good journey?'

'Uneventful. I didn't see any murders out of the window. No mysterious handsome strangers sat in my carriage.'

'How was your meeting?'

She remembered she'd told him she had a meeting. 'Oh,' she said. 'Fine. Just a catch up with my editor.'

She took out a cigarette, which he lit for her. She inhaled deeply. Nervous. Come on, Margot. You're not frightened of anyone.

'So. You eat your words, then?' she ventured. 'Not such a load of old rubbish after all?'

'*Enjoyable* rubbish,' he corrected her.

'Cheek!'

A black-jacketed waiter came to take her drink order. She asked for a whisky and soda. That might make her feel less . . . awestruck. She realised she was a little in awe of Terence. Not his intellect. She wasn't intimidated by his intellect. It was his assuredness. His self-control. His . . . *almost* disinterest in her. He couldn't be totally disinterested, or why write to her? Yet he seemed profoundly unmoved by her presence. Most men were transfixed. It was a new experience.

She opened the menu. The last thing she wanted was food.

'You sounded a little overwrought when you phoned.'

She looked up. Those eyes. She'd forgotten those eyes. If she was putting them in one of her books, she would call them silver. She wondered what he would do if she told him that. Laugh, probably.

She stubbed out her cigarette in the ashtray. 'I just can't write at the moment. I just can't do it. I stare at the paper in my typewriter and it's as if my mind is empty. I feel as if I've used up all the words I know.'

He seemed intrigued by her predicament. 'I don't have the luxury of writer's block. I have a huge team of people waiting for me to deliver.'

She raised her eyebrows. How arrogant he sounded.

He softened, realising his tone was inappropriate.

'I just feel the pressure, that's all. You know all those names at the end of a film? They all rely on me to turn it in before they can get paid.'

'Well, I have people waiting too. Hundreds of thousands of readers. Obviously they won't starve if I don't deliver . . .'

If she was a little spiky, it's because he deserved it. He laughed, knowing that he did.

'I've never had writer's block. My problem is knowing when to stop.'

'Maybe I could steal some words from you?'

'Help yourself. But I don't think they'd fit very well.'

'Oh, you mean they're too long?'

'Don't be so touchy. No. I mean they're not very descriptive. I really only write dialogue. It's very different from writing a book, writing a script. You have to leave as much as you can out. You have to leave room for everyone else. The actors and so on.'

'Oh.'

'Whereas you have to paint pictures with your words.'

'I suppose so, although I do like my readers to use their imagination a bit. I can't do it all for them. Have you ever thought about writing a book?'

'Christ, I wouldn't have a clue where to start. I know where I am with a script. Ninety minutes maximum.

You've usually got a tight budget, so that limits what you can do. And you have to keep to a certain amount of characters. Every time you put in a new character it costs money, so you have to make sure they are worth it.'

'I suppose I've never thought about it.'

'Whereas with a book – the world is your oyster. You can even go to the moon if you want and no one is going to shout at you.'

'I think my editor might shout if I put the moon in. I am very definitely not science fiction.' She took another sip of her drink. 'Well, I'm not anything at the moment, strictly speaking.'

He tutted. 'I think writer's block is an indulgence.'

Her eyes widened. 'Oh?'

'I mean, no other profession has it. You don't get dentists going *I simply can't pull this tooth.* Or a builder saying he can't lay a brick.'

Margot had to laugh. 'I suppose you're right.'

'I *am* right.' He was buttering a roll, and he pointed his knife at her. 'Just get on with it. There's no getting out of it, so you might as well.'

Margot felt peeved. She hadn't come here for a lecture. She'd come here for sympathy, or some sort of magical answer that she thought he might pull out of a hat. She hadn't expected to be spoken to like a schoolgirl dragging her feet over an English essay. She felt silly and foolish.

In her head, he had sympathised, and they had gone to the Beachcomber at the May Fair Hotel for consoling martinis and drowned their sorrows . . .

She felt a flutter of panic. She had somehow thought he might provide her with the answer. Telling her to get on with it was no use at all. She'd told herself that hundreds of times. She thought about the pile of envelopes Sally kept giving her and she felt sick. She still hadn't opened them. Well, she'd opened one and shoved it straight in the kitchen drawer. The rest she just piled up in her office.

The food came, but Margot barely touched her fish. There was a very nice bottle of white wine, so she drank two glasses very quickly to squash down her misgivings. She was just starting to relax, falling into that blurry comforting lunchtime drinking place, and to feel less intimidated. She put her elbow on the table and her head in her hand.

Terence leaned forward. Her heart pounded a little and she smiled up at him. It was a classic Margot move.

'Do you want a sweet?' he asked. 'Or coffee? Or brandy?'

'No. Thank you. I'm happy just to finish my wine.'

She picked up her glass, then frowned as Terence did a pen-signing signal to the waiter, asking for the bill.

'Do you have to go?'

'I'm afraid I do. I'm going to the theatre tonight, and I need to do some more work.'

Don't go, she wanted to plead. The script will wait.

'Oh.' She felt desperately disappointed. Just as she felt relaxed enough to start asking him more questions about himself . . . Oh dear – was he bored? He looked like the kind of man who had a low boredom threshold. Perhaps she should have been more forward? She had been un-usually reserved at lunch. She hadn't flirted or teased once.

She leaned forwards, her voice low. 'It's been a lovely lunch. We must do it again. I usually stay at Brown's. They have an excellent dining room.'

The waiter arrived with the bill, which he signed.

'So I believe,' he said, but he didn't indicate if he had

registered her meaning or wanted to take her up on her offer.

He stood up and held out his hand for her to shake. As if it had been a business meeting.

'Don't ever be afraid of your words,' he said. 'They are your gift to other people.'

And he left the table.

Margot stared after him. She felt dazed. No man had ever shut her out like that. Usually by now she would be getting improper suggestions, which she invariably turned down. She wasn't interested in anything more than a little light flirtation, which for her was an art form; almost a sport. She didn't know how *not* to flirt. But having met someone who seemed totally immune to her charms, she was intrigued. She felt a combination of indignation – *nobody* wasn't interested in Margot Willoughby.

'Everything all right, madam? Would you like some water?' The waiter was looking at her, concerned, and she realised she must look a little peculiar.

'I'm fine. Thank you.' She dismissed him and looked at her watch. It was only twenty past two. Their lunch had barely lasted an hour. She might as well go back to Paddington and get the train home. She didn't have the heart for shopping, and she definitely didn't want to pop in on Niggle or her editor, Fanny. They would only ask about the book.

The book that didn't even exist.

25

1967

After she had been at Hunter's Moon a month, Margot told Sally that she absolutely had to have the weekend off.

'But everyone still needs to eat!' protested Sally.

'But everyone needs a rest. Even you.'

'I think you should come with me and Phoebe to see The Lucky Charms,' said Alexander. 'I've managed to get them a slot at the Milk Bar in Soho. Every Saturday for the next two months. Tonight's the first one.'

'Can I come? Please?' demanded Annie. 'It will give me something to talk about at school.'

Margot, in a fit of parental responsibility, said Annie couldn't go unless Sally went.

'I don't trust you two.'

'Oh great. You don't trust your own children,' grumbled Phoebe.

'No. I don't,' said Margot. 'And I know Annie. She won't manage. She'll get there and she'll want to go home.'

'No, I won't.'

'Well, I'd love to go,' said Sally. 'And I don't mind looking after you. It'll probably be me who wants to go home.'

Phoebe looked at her. 'Do you want to choose something to wear?'

'Could I?'

'Of course!'

Sally went into the dining room and spent an hour trying on dresses and trouser suits and tunics and skirts all under Phoebe's critical eye. Phoebe wouldn't rest until Sally looked as if she had walked off the pages of a magazine. In the end, they settled on a burgundy paisley dress worn with a feather boa and a floppy felt hat.

'You look the bee's knees,' said Phoebe.

Her brothers wouldn't recognise her, thought Sally, gleeful. She'd always made an effort to look nice when she went out, but life with the Willoughbys was something else. Her boring old skirts and jumpers just wouldn't do.

'How much do I owe you?' she asked, but Phoebe waved her query away.

'If anyone asks, just tell them you've been dressed by Phoebe. I need to get my name out there. You can be my walking advert.'

Sally made a face. 'Really?'

She couldn't get to grips with this family. They were so kind and generous. Yet maddening.

They all set off for London in the Mini.

'Are we staying up in town?' asked Phoebe. 'It'll be too late to drive home.'

'We can say with D,' said Alexander. 'Her flatmates have all gone away for the weekend so there's plenty of room.'

'I thought you had broken up with her?'

'Yes. But you know. We're still friends.'

'Because she's got a big flat?'

'Because if I didn't stay with her she would go bananas.'

234

'You're using her, Beetle.'

'We've been friends since we were thirteen. I can't just banish her.'

'She won't get the message unless you cool it.'

'Well, where else are we going to stay? The four of us?'

'You're asking for trouble.' Phoebe sighed. 'She drives me mad.'

'Well, me too.'

'She goes into Biba every Saturday and buys up everything she can because her father gives her handfuls of money instead of love. And she looks awful in all of it.'

'Now that's not fair.'

'She hasn't got a clue about fashion.'

'That doesn't make her a bad person,' said Annie. 'I haven't got a clue either.' Annie was in jeans and a jumper, with no nod to fashion.

'Yes, but you don't swan around as if you're Jean Shrimpton when actually you look like the back of a bus.'

'Phoebe!' This was an insult too far for Alexander. 'You're just annoyed because you offered to make her an outfit for that wedding and she refused.'

'Yes. How rude. I could have made her look less like a galumphing heffalump, but that's fine. It's her prerogative.'

Phoebe looked out of the window, huffy. Annie giggled.

'I bet you can't wait to meet her, Sally.'

'D's all right. Her heart is in the right place,' said Alexander. 'But she does like to be the centre of attention and have things her way.'

'She's a spoilt cow,' said Phoebe.

'Phoebe! Enough.'

'Oh, so I'm not supposed to care if my brother's saddled with—'

'Enough!'

Sally couldn't help smiling. She loved their crazy arguing and the insults and the fact they all cared so very deeply for each other but pretended not to. She felt a bit sorry for the girl they were talking about. It made her remember the exchange in the café, the first day she had arrived. Hilly? Had that been the woman's name? It reminded her of Margot's warning, not to let Alexander break her heart. She had no intention of letting him do so. She very obviously wasn't his type. He went for sophisticated older women or rich girls. But she did love his company and was really pleased to have been asked to see the band. She had never seen a proper band, only awful amateur ones at the tennis club.

It was dark by the time they hit London, which was crammed with buses, taxis, scooters and cars, all hell bent on getting wherever they were going quicker than the next person. The pavements were crowded with people on a Saturday night out – going out for dinner or a drink or dancing or just soaking up the atmosphere. They passed Harrods, its windows all lit up.

'My clothes will be in there one day,' swore Phoebe.

They swooped around Hyde Park corner and up Piccadilly. Sally realised they weren't far from the Kitten Club, which was tucked away in a street off Park Lane, and she thought – how strange. It seems like a lifetime ago but it's only a month.

Piccadilly Circus was blazing with light, reigned over by a huge sign advertising Coca Cola.

Alexander drove three times around Eros, beeping his horn.

'Welcome to Swinging London, Sal!!'

Sally didn't think she had ever been happier as they zoomed up Regent Street.

'I hope those boys are ready. Last time I had to drag them out of a boozer on Carnaby Street.' He plunged off the main road and into the network of streets that was Soho, turning right left right left until he pulled up outside a murky looking nightclub with hundreds of posters stuck up on the walls outside.

'Here we are. The infamous Milk Bar. Because they serve anything but. Hold on to your hats, girls. And your knickers.' He jumped out of the car. There were already crowds of youngsters queueing up to get in, but Alexander barged his way to the front, gesturing to the girls to follow.

'Oi! Don't jump the queue,' said a feisty girl with a fetching beehive.

'We're management,' said Alexander, and the door was opened and they were ushered inside and plunged down into the basement.

It was the hottest, sweatiest, smokiest, noisiest place Sally had ever been. She loved it. There was loud music playing, and no one was standing still. They were either dancing or talking and laughing and everyone was drinking and smoking. She saw people looking them up and down as Alexander lead them over to a table – the girls to check out the competition and the boys to see what was on offer. Everyone looked so self-assured and up to the minute, but she felt confident in her outfit. Phoebe was clever. She knew exactly what suited.

Phoebe glided through the crowds like royalty. She was strikingly monochromatic, in a black tunic with black-and-white striped sleeves and white kinky boots, offset by her pale face and ridiculously long false eyelashes. Annie trailed behind her, clapping her hands over her ears. They arrived at a table at the back of the club where a very tall girl was drumming her nails on the table, looking annoyed.

'This is Diana,' said Alexander with a look that said *I know everything we said about her makes her sound awful but please be nice.*

Sally said hello. Diana looked her up and down and gave a tight smile. Phoebe was right. Diana might be dressed in the height of fashion, in a very short yellow dress with a chain around her waist, but she looked awkward. She was tall and loud and bossy, dictating where everyone should sit and what everyone should drink.

'Will you be all right?' asked Alexander. 'I need to go and see the lads in the dressing room. They're on in fifteen minutes.'

'Of course!'

Sally was entranced by the whole scene, and didn't feel intimidated in the least. After the sinister undertones of the Kitten Club, the Milk Bar seemed tame. Everyone was just out to have a good time.

'So you're the Willoughbys' housekeeper?' Diana was surveying her without a smile. She had awfully thin, over-arched eyebrows, which made her look supercilious.

'Yes. I've been with them about a month.'

Diana gave a sniff. 'None of our housekeepers ever looked like you.'

'Housekeepers don't all look the same, Diana,' said Phoebe. 'And Sally is a lifesaver. Hunter's Moon is transformed. Even Daddy's a bit in love with her.'

'Even?' Diana looked at Phoebe sharply.

'It's a turn of phrase,' sighed Phoebe.

Annie was making faces at Diana behind her back and Sally wanted to laugh, but she didn't want to goad the girl. She could see she was possessive and a bit drunk. She didn't want to cause any trouble.

When the Lucky Charms finally came on to much applause after a long wait, the excitement levels in the little club went through the roof. The band were dressed in matching buttoned up jackets and tight black trousers, and they rollicked their way through cover versions of the Kinks and the Rolling Stones. Alexander was grinning from ear to ear and pulled Sally on to the dance floor. She wasn't a bad dancer, but it didn't really matter anyway as the dance floor was so crowded there was little room to move.

'I'm trying to get them to write their own material,' he shouted over the music. 'That's where the big money will be, if they can write their own hits.'

'They're fabulous!'

'I could book them out every night for a year. But they won't make the big time unless they take the plunge. They won't listen to me, though.'

'Maybe they're quite happy? Less pressure?' Sally looked around the club. It must be great, making people smile and dance and have fun. She turned to find Diana looming over her.

'Bugger off, Mrs Danvers,' she said. 'It's my turn now.'

Sally melted away, but not before she'd seen the look of despair on Alexander's face as Diana threw her arms in the air and started to gyrate in front of him, totally oblivious to anyone around her.

It was after midnight before the band finally packed up and they left the Milk Bar. Outside, Soho was mysteriously quiet, like a party girl who has finally run out of steam. Sally shivered in the cold night air. It was freezing, coming out of the sweaty heat of the club.

'Pile in, everyone,' said Alexander. 'Quick, before D notices.'

It was too late. Diana came bursting out of the exit.

'Wait for me,' she said. 'You *are* coming back to mine?'

'No,' said Alexander. 'We have to get back home, I'm afraid.'

'Oh.' Diana's face fell. 'Well, can I come back with you?'

'I don't think that's a good idea.' Alexander braced himself.

Diana's face crumpled and for a second Sally felt sorry for her. It was quite humiliating, but she had set herself up for it.

'You bastard,' she hissed. 'You're just using me. You're just a sponger, Alexander Willoughby.'

'She's got a point,' murmured Phoebe. 'He does use people.'

'No, he doesn't,' said Annie, who was gripped by the drama. 'Some people *want* to be used. Diana definitely does.'

'Well, you'll have to give me a lift home. You *have* to. How else am I going to get back?'

Alexander sighed. 'OK.'

'I'll have to go in the front,' said Diana. 'I've got the longest legs.'

Phoebe, Annie and Sally squeezed into the back. Sally could see Annie poking the back of Diana's chair with her foot every now and again. She nudged her with her elbow to stop, but she could see why she was doing it and, as ever with Annie, she tried not to laugh.

The Mini raced back along Piccadilly, around Hyde Park Corner, down through Knightsbridge. Diana was pawing at Alexander, who was trying his best to be polite and not shrug her off, but in the end he couldn't stand it.

'D, I can't drive properly with you doing that.'

Diana folded her arms and tucked her chin into her neck, sulking. She knew her time was up.

The car headed out on to the Cromwell Road before veering right past the slumbering Natural History Museum. Sally recognised her surroundings, and her heart sank a little as they drove past the entrance to Russell Gardens. She imagined Barbara fast asleep, snoring away. Thank goodness she had got away.

Two minutes later they pulled up outside Diana's flat, which was on the ground floor of a gracious white Regency terrace with thick white pillars outside.

It must have been here that Alexander had been making his way from or to the night she found him in the gutter, Sally realised, but she didn't say anything. Instead, she looked at it in awe as Diana scrambled out of the front seat.

'Thanks for nothing,' she snarled at Alexander, slamming the door.

'She is so rude,' said Phoebe. 'Which just goes to show, money doesn't buy you manners.'

'It must be why Beetle won't ditch her, though,' added Annie. 'She reels him in with her money.'

Sally frowned, puzzled. Surely the Willoughbys had enough money of their own not to have their heads turned by someone else's? Although then she remembered the bills and the bank statements that kept arriving. Maybe there wasn't as much money as there seemed to be.

'I'm not interested in D's money,' protested Alexander. 'Anyway, she's as tight as a tick. She never pays for her own drinks. I do keep trying to get rid of her but she won't get the message. I don't know why I get involved with women. I really don't.'

'We're not all like that, I don't suppose,' ventured Sally.

Alexander started the car back up and spun the Mini round so it was facing the way they came.

'Yes, but the sensible ones are boring. Maybe there's a part of me that likes all the complications.'

'Well, that's your own fault, then,' said Phoebe.

'At least *Saturday Night Theatre*'s finished,' said Annie, waspish and owlish with tiredness. 'Can I get some sleep now?'

She fell asleep leaning against Sally's shoulder. As the Mini bowled home through the darkness, she felt her own eyes closing. And she thought – it's funny, I feel part of this family, even though I'm not.

When they got back home, the lights were still blazing and Dai and Margot were in the kitchen. The record player was on and there were several empty glasses on the table.

'Darlings! Let's have martinis,' said Margot.

'It's two o'clock in the morning.' Sally looked shocked.

'Who cares?' Margot unscrewed the lid of a bottle of Vermouth. 'Where's the gin? I wrote three chapters today and I'm celebrating.'

Sally saw that the chicken casserole she'd left Margot and Dai was untouched.

'You haven't eaten.'

'Oh shit,' said Margot. 'We forgot. Let's have it now. Come to think of it, I'm starving.'

So Sally heated up the casserole and served it out in bowls, and Margot sloshed gin and Vermouth into mismatched glasses.

'I don't think you should have one, Annie,' whispered Sally.

But Annie grabbed a glass anyway. 'It's part of my training plan,' she said.

Then Margot put 'Something Stupid' by Frank and Nancy Sinatra on the record player and handed Dai a wooden spoon to use as a microphone.

'Come on.'

And the two of them stood together by the Aga and sang along, slightly out of tune, but very charmingly, and pretending to gaze into each other's eyes, and suddenly Sally could see who Dai and Margot were and how much they loved each other really, even when she was being a bitch and he was being a grump.

Alexander had his hands over his ears. 'Make it stop,' he pleaded, but he was laughing.

It was noticeable, thought Sally, how the Willoughbys all came together when their parents were happy.

Later, as they went up the stairs to bed, Alexander grabbed Sally's hand.

'Come and talk to me,' he said. 'There's no way I'm going to sleep now. It's almost dawn. There's almost no point in going to bed.'

Sally wasn't sure what to do or say. Did he mean for her to go into his room? Yes, because that's where he was heading, looking over his shoulder to see if she was following.

26

1967

Sally sat gingerly on the end of his bed as Alexander stretched out on it and lit a cigarette. He threw her a pillow, and she tucked it behind her back and leaned against the wall. She liked his room. His bedcover was tartan, and the walls were dark red and covered in posters of bands and film stars. His curtains were wide open to the soft velvet night, the sky sprinkled with silver pinprick stars. They sat there in silence for a moment. It felt incredibly intimate. Sally felt as if they were alone in the world.

'I don't want you to get the wrong idea about me,' he said eventually. 'With girls, I mean. I seem to get myself into sticky situations but it's not as bad as it looks.'

'It's OK,' said Sally, wondering why he minded what she thought.

'That's it now,' he said. 'I'm going celibate. Till the end of the year. I can't take any more drama.'

Sally fiddled with her watch, winding it up, because she really didn't know what to say. This was all too awkward for words. She changed the subject quickly.

'Your parents seemed really happy tonight.'

'Oh, they're like Liz Taylor and Richard Burton. Either madly in love or at each other's throats. We're used to it.'

Sally went quiet. She thought about her own mum and

dad. Their marriage couldn't have been further from the Willoughbys'.

'My mum and dad weren't like yours at all. They never went to parties. Or even drank much. Maybe the odd sherry at Sunday lunch or Christmas.'

Her parents had worked hard to give Sally and her two brothers what they needed. They trusted each other and were kind. But something had come between them: something dark and dangerous. Something that had destroyed everything.

Perhaps it was because she was tired, perhaps it was the martini, but suddenly Sally felt overwhelmed by the memories. She sighed.

'I really miss my dad.'

Alexander stubbed out his cigarette and scooted down the bed to sit next to her. 'Of course you do. I'm sorry. I keep forgetting. It must be awful.'

'It's not just that. I miss my mum too and I need to go and see her.'

He took her hand in his fingers. 'I'll take you home to see your mum, if you like.'

'It's awful and I feel so guilty, but I can't face it.'

'Why not?'

'I can't face going back. And remembering.' She needed to tell him. She put a hand on her chest and took a deep breath. 'He didn't just die, my dad.'

'What do you mean?'

'He – he hanged himself.'

Alexander looked horrified. He ran a hand through his hair. 'Jesus. Why?'

Sally gave a despairing sigh. 'Money. Stupid bloody money. And none of us had any idea. We knew it was tough keeping the shop going, but he didn't tell anyone how close to the bone it was. Not my brothers. Or even Mum. He just sat there, worrying and worrying that it was all going to be taken away.'

'Poor bloke.'

'And he kept getting letters from the bank and he hid them all, because we found them after he died . . .' She stopped, took in a deep breath, and gulped. 'And one afternoon, Mum found him in the garage. He'd got a rope and tied it to the rafter . . .'

'Oh you poor baby.'

'I was at school when it happened. When I came home the ambulance was outside the front door. My mum was just standing there . . .'

She would never forget the terror she had felt: the combination of wild hope and utter despair as she ran to see what was happening, who it was. Even in her panic she didn't imagine something so devastating; so terrible. She had thought appendicitis or a broken arm. She would never forget the look on her mother's face as their eyes met. Standing on the pavement with her flowery pinny on, her socks pulled halfway up her legs and her slippers on, her preferred uniform when cooking tea.

Alexander was staring at her.

'You're so brave.'

'Not really.'

'Yes, you are. After everything you've been through, you come here and make our lives . . . a million times better.'

'You've made my life better too. All of you. I love it here.'

'Well, we all love you, Sally Huxtable.' He crooked his arm round her neck and gave her a playful hug.

She laughed. 'Just think, if I hadn't found you in the gutter, I'd still be in that awful flat.'

'Instead you're in a mad house. Lucky you.' Alexander jumped up. 'I'll put some music on. That'll cheer you up.'

'Won't you wake everyone?'

'I play records all night. No one can hear. What's your favourite band?'

'I don't know.'

'You must have a favourite band.'

'I haven't.' She tried to think. 'OK then. The Monkees.'

'I think you need educating.' He took a record out of its sleeve and put it on his turntable. 'Have you heard of David Bowie?'

'No.'

'He's going to be the next big thing, I can tell you. I got an early copy.'

They listened to a ridiculous song called The Laughing Gnome, which made them laugh as they played it over and over and over again and sang along, and Sally forgot her sadness.

'That's what music's for,' said Alexander. 'No one can live without music.'

Sally woke a couple of hours later, freezing cold. Alexander was curled up on the bed next to her where he had fallen asleep too. The turntable was still going round and round. She slipped off the bed, tugged the eiderdown and tucked it over him so he wouldn't get cold, and ran up to her own bedroom, hoping that none of the other Willoughbys would spot her leaving and get the wrong idea.

She got to her room unnoticed and slid under the

covers, shivering. Away from the distraction of Alexander she lay there, unable to sleep, going over that awful time, wondering if anyone could have done anything any differently.

Looking back, her dad hadn't been right for a while. Her mum had had her fears, but she'd kept them quiet. She'd put on a brave face for all of them, but she'd known about his dark moments, his never-ending worry about the shop. And, in hindsight, Sally could remember him withdrawing, his face haunted by what she now knew was a pernicious anxiety that pulled him down to somewhere he couldn't climb out of. And there were the rages – never directed at his wife or his children, but uncontrollable outbursts. A hole kicked in the kitchen door, a teapot hurled across the room. It had all got too much for him, the doctor said – but what? That was what no one could understand. He had a good business, a lovely wife, loving children, a nice house.

For twelve months afterwards, they all pulled together, Beverley and the boys and Sally. They didn't speak much about what had happened. Beverley worked her fingers to the bone managing it all. Running the shop and the house and keeping the boys in order. And Sally took her mum to visit her dad's grave every Sunday, even though Sally herself was furious with her dad for leaving her mum in the lurch like that. What kind of a husband did that, even if things were looking bleak?

Her mum couldn't ever sleep. She even got up for a cigarette in the middle of the night, She never got over finding her husband. It haunted her day and night. If only she'd gone to look for him earlier, she used to say. She'd had a feeling . . .

Sally had remained as stoic as she could throughout it all, and was as much help as she could be, taking over her mother's role when her mother didn't feel up to it. She had a naturally caring nature, and she worried about her brothers, and she was supremely capable, more than able to juggle schoolwork and housework. She took it on the chin when her exam results were not as good as expected, although after all that had happened no one expected brilliance. She ploughed on with her trademark optimism and cheerfulness, determined to make it all right.

She could have coped with the loss of her father. But there was worse to come. Their mother had never told them the extent of the debts their father had run up: the debts she was still struggling to pay off, the debts that had been responsible for his breakdown. She had remained tight-lipped, never complaining, never letting on. Eight months after their father died, the truth was finally uncovered. She'd taken out a massive mortgage on the house to cover their debt. And now the bank wanted it back.

It was losing the house that finally broke Sally's heart. She'd been able to hold it together while those familiar four walls were around them. Watching their things being taken out of their solid, comfortable red-brick home with its stained glass fanlight, and the cherry red front door being closed with an ominous finality, left her with a sense of desolation she almost couldn't bear. Her bedroom with the pink roses on the wall. The living room with the big fireplace, and the bay window where the Christmas tree used to go. The kitchen, which always smelled of something delicious, the kettle always on. It had been a house of constant noise and endless food, only really quiet from midnight, when their mother turned the last light out, to four in the morning, when the two boys got up to sort out the day's deliveries.

The Huxtables were homeless. There was no choice but to move in over the butcher's shop in the high street, which they rented – as long as they paid the rent, no one could take that away. The first floor had been used for storage: icy cold, no heating or water or electricity. And there were two attic rooms. They would manage. They all pulled together and fixed the place up. The toilet was outside – there was nothing much they could do about that - but they managed to get carpets and curtains and furniture upstairs and to make it into a makeshift home.

Sally looked at it and knew she couldn't live there. The boys were under enough pressure. She didn't want them to have to worry about her. Anyway, there was no room for her. There was one room for her mum, and one for Ray and Colin, until the time one of them got married and moved out.

She decided to go to London and make her fortune. She felt guilty leaving her mother, but she had the boys. She didn't need Sally so much.

Ray and Colin drove her to the station.

'Any trouble, Sal, just let us know. We'll come and sort it out.'

They would. She knew that. Her brothers had got her back. It was a good feeling, but not good enough for her to stay in Knapford, wrapping up slices of streaky bacon. London had called to her. She knew what would happen if she didn't go away. Not escape: that wasn't the right word; it was too dramatic. But she wanted more from life. She wanted to find out who and what she was.

And she was so glad she'd done it. Here, at Hunter's Moon, she was learning so much. About clothes and music and books and about how other people lived. Maybe Alexander was right. Maybe she was brave after all.

27

On Monday afternoon, Leo knew with a heavy heart that he had to go back to London. There were meetings he couldn't miss. He stood on the doorstep, looking out at the fields, a lively breeze skittering round him as if to jolly him along. He breathed in the air, filled with the scent of blossom and the possibility of a spring shower.

'Now I know,' he told his mum and dad as he said goodbye, 'I can make more time. And you must tell me if you need anything. I can be here in just over an hour.'

'We're going to keep life as normal as we can for as long as we can,' Sally told him.

'I know. But . . . you know where I am.'

'We're going to go up to Scotland and tell Jess next weekend.'

'Will you be all right? It's a long drive.'

'We'll break it up. Stop on the way. And we'll stay a few days.'

'If you want me to drive, I can take some time off.' He was going to have to learn to trust his team more and delegate. They were keen and bright and ready for the responsibility, he thought. He had chosen well.

'That's very kind,' said Alexander, grateful that he had such a thoughtful son. 'But we'll be fine.' He was dreading it. He hated the burden of having to tell people. The responsibility that what he was going to say was going to shatter their world. Not that he had an over-inflated opinion of himself, but no matter how you dressed it up, people were going to be devastated.

'Anything you want, you know that,' said Leo, before he got in the car. 'I'll come down and mow the lawns. Cut the hedges. Anything.'

'Come down for the sealed bids,' said Sally. 'We should decide together, as a family, who gets Hunter's Moon.'

The three of them stood in silence for a moment as they contemplated the finality of these words.

Then Leo got in his car, shut the door and drove off down the drive. He looked back in the rear-view mirror and saw his parents standing on the doorstep, holding hands. He wiped away the tears that sprang into his eyes and turned up the stereo very loud.

He had a couple of things he wanted to do before he made his way home.

He drove into Peasebrook and found a parking space on the high street. He remembered thinking how deathly dull the town was when he was a teenager and even in his twenties. There'd been nothing to divert him. Now, however, there was something wherever he looked. Peasebrook had got quite a name for itself as a gastro-destination – blackboards everywhere proclaimed 'artisan' or 'organic' or 'locally sourced'. Lots of people were moving here out of London because of the train service, and there were a substantial number of weekenders. Sleepy little Peasebrook was hip and happening in a countrified and whole-some way.

It could have been made for him, thought Leo with a wry grin, as he passed a bakery, the windows filled with loaves of sourdough and friands and tartiflettes. Maybe you always fell out of love with your home town and fell back in again when you realised its true worth?

Or needed it?

He slipped into a shop that was one of his favourite places in the world. The Peasebrook Cheesemonger had been going as long as he could remember, though he had only really taken any notice of it in the past ten years, since food had become his living; his life. He was always in charge of coming here and getting the supplies for Hunter's Moon at Christmas. Leo had done the shop's website for them a few years ago, and even though he'd been properly paid he was always loaded up with free cheese whenever he visited. Not that free cheese was his motive for coming in.

He breathed in the sharp, sweet, milky air as he walked in. Cheery-faced Jem was behind the counter, which was crammed with wheels of cheese in every shade from chalky white to a rich deep golden orange. Leo and Jem could talk for hours, and Jem always had something new for him to try.

'Hey, buddy.'

They high-fived each other over the counter, then chatted as Leo gave his order: a slice of Vignotte, a chunk of Berkswell and a wedge of sharp, ageing Cheddar.

'So what's new?'

'Just down for the weekend.' Leo didn't give anything away. News of Hunter's Moon's sale obviously hadn't reached Jem. 'What's going down in Cheese World?'

'I'm taking over from my old man soon. He's finally

retiring.' Jem gave a triumphant double thumbs-up.

'Cool. Well, if I can help . . .'

'You definitely can,' said Jem. 'I've got big plans.'

'Great. Let me help you make them bigger.'

'It's world domination, mate. Nothing else will do. Hey – you'll have to come and have dinner at my girlfriend's place. She's got a pop-up restaurant just round the corner.'

'A Deux? I've heard good things.'

'You'll be lucky if you can get in, but I can probably swing it for you.' Jem grinned proudly.

Leo took his selection of cheeses, all wrapped up and put in a brown paper bag with string handles.

'Awesome. I can't stop now as I'm on my way home, but let's catch up soon.'

'Here. One for the road.'

Jem ferreted in his refrigerator and handed him a small wooden box.

'It's an amazing goat's cheese from a local dairy. Tell me what you think.'

'Cheese from an amazing goat?' Leo grinned.

'Damn right.'

Who needed Borough Market? He was right on the ground here. He lifted the box in appreciation. 'Cheers.'

He left the shop. He felt good about the exchange. He loved the idea of Jem taking over from his dad and taking the shop to the next level. He started thinking about how he could help him with his marketing strategy. Peasebrook Cheese wouldn't have a big marketing budget but it was the sort of project Leo could get passionate about. Local, family business. He thought: maybe what's happened to Dad will mean a change of direction for me? Maybe it's time to come home?

Then he remembered – there wasn't going to be a home much longer.

Cathy tinged the bell that was hanging up on the wall of the office. They rang it every time they sold a house. Belinda heard it and came out of her office with a smile.

'The High House,' said Cathy triumphantly. 'Asking price. They want to exchange as soon as possible so their children can start at Peasebrook Primary in the summer term and get settled in.'

'Maybe we should have asked for more,' said Belinda.

'Nope,' said Cathy. 'You've got the price bang on and you know it.'

'You're right,' said Belinda. Being greedy could backfire.

'You know what this means,' said Cathy. 'Your Forever House fund has reached its target. We can start looking for a house for you.'

Cathy had been longing for this moment for years. She was as obsessed with finding Belinda a house as she was with finding her a man.

'You can start looking,' conceded Belinda, laughing. 'But I've got strict criteria.'

'I know,' said Cathy. 'Built before 1860, with parking, a small garden, a pantry, an airing cupboard . . . No flying freeholds or covenants.'

'What's the betting I end up in a modern penthouse?'

'I'm going to make you an appointment with the mortgage advisor.' Cathy opened up her web browser. 'You need to be good to go when you find the right one.'

'It's not going to happen overnight. It's got to be perfect.'

'Yes. So when you find it, you need to pounce.'

Belinda smiled. She knew Cathy was right. But she was a little bit scared. Now the time had come, she wasn't sure she was ready for the next step. Her own house: it was such a big commitment, a change of lifestyle. She would have to step out of her comfort zone. For heaven's sake, she told herself, what's the worst that can happen?

She looked out of the window. There was an enormous bouquet of wild roses tangled up with twigs and greenery walking up towards their office from the high street.

'Good grief,' she said. 'It's like that scene out of Macbeth.'

It was Leo behind the foliage, and he was definitely heading to the office.

'There you are. Proof that the law of attraction exists,' breathed Cathy. 'You have been doing it, like I told you?'

'Of course I haven't,' said Belinda, who had no truck with anything airy-fairy.

A sudden thought occurred to her – what if he'd persuaded his parents to take Hunter's Moon off the market and he was coming to break the news to her? All that hard work, for nothing.

Leo opened the door of the office and approached her with a wry smile, holding out the flowers.

'These are for you, to say thank you for being so fantastic over the weekend.'

'Goodness – there was absolutely no need.' But Belinda held out her arms for them nevertheless, breathing in their scent.

'I'm heading back up to London this afternoon, but I just wanted to say how much we appreciate your help. And I want to say sorry again for bursting in and causing a scene.'

'I think you were quite calm, all things considered,' said Belinda. 'How are your parents?'

A shadow flickered over Leo's face.

'Oh, I don't know. I hate leaving them. They've got to go and tell my sister. And I think the stress of selling the house is a strain. Not knowing how much they'll get.'

'Listen, I'm going to get them the very best price I can. Don't you worry.'

'I know. Thanks.' He looked resigned. 'I feel as if I've aged ten years over the weekend.'

'I'm sure . . .'

'Sorry. You don't want to hear all this—'

'It's fine. I'm happy to listen. It's hard for you, not having anyone to share it all with.'

She could see Cathy behind Leo, doing thumbs up signs, and nodding her head as if to say 'Go on'. She looked at her watch. It was nearly time to close. Cathy would shut up shop for her. She could ask him for a drink. They could go and have a glass of wine at the Peasebrook Arms before he headed back, chat things over. She could hear Bruce in her head, egging her on: 'Girl power, baby'.

'Listen, I'm finished for the day. Do you want to—'

She was about to suggest a drink when his phone rang. He looked apologetic. 'Sorry, I really need to get this.'

'No problem.'

His face lit up as he spoke to whoever was on the other end. 'I'm so glad you called me back. Can I drop in on my way home? I really need to see you . . . Yes. Put something nice in the fridge. I'll bring cheese . . . Fantastic. It will be about six. Lots of love.'

He stuffed his phone back in his pocket. 'Sorry. I

needed to catch her. She's very hard to pin down. You know what these career women are like.'

Belinda put her hands up with a wry smile as if to say 'guilty'.

'And I need to go. Listen, I'm sure I'll see you again in the next few weeks.'

'Sure. The deadline for the sealed bid is the Friday after next.'

'I'll be down for that, definitely. Crunch time, eh?'

'Yes.'

'Bye, then.'

'Bye. And thank you for the flowers . . .'

The door shut behind him. Belinda watched him head back down the road. She felt a little stab of disappointment. She was an idiot. Of course he was absolutely bound to have a glossy, leggy girlfriend called India or Tabitha who would curl herself around him tonight and give him comfort.

Cathy opened her mouth.

'Don't say anything,' said Belinda. 'He's got a girlfriend.'

Yet as she ploughed through the rest of the names on her list, she kept imagining Leo's future children sliding down the bannisters and tearing around on the lawn at Hunter's Moon, and it almost moved her to tears. She told herself to get a grip. It was lucky she wasn't a surgeon. If she got this involved with a house sale, what would she be like if it really was a matter of life and death?

Finding a parking space in Chiswick was always a game. Leo ended up about a quarter of a mile from where he was heading. His heart lifted slightly as he approached the house. He was happy to see the lights were on, so she was already home. He thought he might feel better once he'd told her. He'd had to hold everything in over the weekend. It had been exhausting. He'd got to the point where he didn't know what to think or feel, but he needed someone who understood him. Who he was close to. She was the one person in the world who always made him feel better when he had a problem. She always knew what to say, what to do. She was his rock, if he was honest. He didn't know what he would do without her.

He knocked on the door. He could hear her footsteps. Hear her sliding back the bolt.

And then he saw her face. Her dear face, which lit up in delight when she saw him. Her hair was all over the place, as it always was, one of her many pairs of glasses on top of her head. She was holding a glass of wine in one hand. He knew there'd be no supper on the go yet, but that was why he'd bought the cheese.

'Darling. It's so lovely to see you. Come in.'

'Oh Annie.' He put his arms around his aunt. 'Oh Annie – I don't know what to do.'

28

1967

As the cool of early spring edged into May and the sun became a more frequent visitor, Sally settled into life at Hunter's Moon. Although it was hard work and, sometimes, quite mundane, she found it surprisingly enjoyable running a big house. Having an unlimited budget made it easier, so if she wanted to order beef fillet or a new set of table linen, she could. And living with the Willoughbys was never dull. She loved getting involved in whatever Phoebe was creating, and was always a willing model. Alexander was embroiled in hawking her clothes around London and setting up summer bookings for the Lucky Charms, who seemed to be on the up. Annie was revising hard for her GCEs and would ask Sally to test her in the kitchen.

'Absolutely no one else is doing any revision at all. They say the exams are ages off. They all just loll around the common room smoking and listening to records. They take the mickey out of me.'

'Well, they're very silly,' said Sally. How could anyone be horrible to Annie? She was a darling.

'I'm dreading the sixth form.' Annie looked glum.

Sally was concerned, but there was no point in discussing it with anyone. Margot was on a roll with her book,

262

and seemed to be taking it very seriously, locking herself away in the coach house for hours on end. And Dai was a non-starter, out of touch with the real world and people's needs.

Dai always seemed to be at a loose end. He didn't say much. He just loomed in a gloomy way. He didn't seem to bother about shaving. Or possibly, Sally suspected, even washing. She wondered if he was depressed. She'd seen it in her father – the glum silences; the withdrawing; the apathy. Of course her dad had been under pressure. Dai didn't have any pressure at all, which was why it was a bit of a mystery that he seemed so down. He and Margot were very scratchy with each other. And if there was too much wine at dinner, things escalated quite rapidly. When he drank, Dai became more and more Welsh and more and more obnoxious, goading his wife.

'How's the poor man's Barbara Cartland, then?'

'At least I write,' she shot back. 'The poor man's Dylan Thomas isn't exactly prolific.'

Sally knew Dai had started it but she could see that Margot's words stung him and this was the root of his problem. She called upon her mother's boy-rearing tactics: fresh air and being given something to do about which they had no choice.

She tackled him one morning after breakfast.

'It's crazy,' she said. 'Me spending all this money on groceries when there's a beautiful garden out there. I wondered if you'd help me bring it back into action? It would be so lovely to have our own fresh vegetables.'

She gave him her most winning Sally smile. She knew perfectly well that it worked on men. It had always worked on her father and brothers. Dai sipped his tea then put his cup down.

'Come on, then,' he said. 'Show me what you want.'

They went out into the grounds and walked down to the walled garden, which was tucked away just below the coach house. It was a tangle of weeds and crumbling soft red bricks, dilapidated cold frames and a greenhouse full of broken glass.

'Bloody hell,' said Dai. 'It hasn't been touched for years. We had a gardener at one point but he had light fingers, not green ones.'

'It would be hard work to get it back to how it was, but it must have provided the house with all its produce once. Wouldn't it be lovely, to have our own fruit and vegetables? Nothing tastes better than a potato fresh from the ground.'

'I wouldn't know where to start.'

'Well, you'll need some tools. A hoe, a rake, a spade . . .' Sally was improvising madly. Her knowledge of gardening was sparse. 'Will you do it? It might be a bit late to start for some things, but we can try.'

Dai looked around the wildness, his hands in his pockets.

'I don't see why not.'

She went to the ironmonger's in Peasebrook and bought him everything he could possibly need – trowels and dibbers and gardening twine and a shiny wheelbarrow. She started saving all the vegetable peelings from the kitchen for a compost heap.

To her delight, Dai seemed to respond to her challenge. It was an enormous project and the work was quite back-breaking at times. He pulled out all the old vegetation and dug out the beds; repaired all the crumbling brick-work and replaced all the glass in the cold frames and the greenhouse.

They spent hours in the kitchen drinking tea and poring over seed catalogues, deciding which variety of green bean or tomato to try.

Margot was rather disparaging.

'We can find a gardener if you want,' she said. 'I never imagined I'd end up married to Percy Thrower.'

Dai looked at her. 'But I'm enjoying it.'

'Wait till you taste our first potatoes,' said Sally.

'*Our?*' said Margot, with a little more edge to her voice than was necessary.

For some reason, the garden captured Annie's imagination too. Sally was pleased. She was still worried about how unhappy Annie said she was at school, and how much she fretted about her exams.

Annie and Dai spent hours together, digging and planting. It seemed to give both of them a rhythm and a purpose to their life. It was the first place Annie ran to when she came home at weekends, to see what seedlings had sprouted while she had been away. Sally was relieved.

Sometimes it wasn't about revelry and partying and dressing up. Sometimes it was about the simple things.

One Sunday, Alexander took her up to Knapford to see her mum and brothers.

She cried when she saw them, of course. But she was happy to see her mum had a bit more life to her. She had lost the awful dark rings under her eyes, and she wasn't smoking so much. Time. There was a lot to be said for it. It had been over two years now and the shop was doing well. They'd made a lot of changes and got a lot of new customers. Ray had been out hustling for business and he was good at it.

And it turned out that there had been an insurance policy they didn't know her father had taken out. There had been some doubt over whether it would be paid out, but somehow the doctor had been involved and had managed to get a verdict of accidental death rather than suicide.

'It's not a fortune,' her mum told her. 'But it's keeping the wolf from the door.'

There was a ceremonial rib of beef for lunch, and Alexander joined them, even though Sally said he didn't have to; that he could come back later and get her. But he seemed happy to get his feet under her mum's table and share a beer with Colin and Ray.

'I didn't know anyone could make better roast potatoes than Sally,' he exclaimed as he scraped his plate clean.

Beverley glowed. Sally hid a smile. He knew how to charm her mother all right.

And her brothers seemed to like him, which was good. Ray and Colin could take scunners quite easily, and Sally was worried they would think he was a posh git, but they chatted away with him about football (she suspected Alexander was pretending to know more than he did).

After lunch she and her mum walked round to the churchyard to put a bunch of flowers on her dad's grave.

'Bloody silly sod,' said her mother, which was an improvement. The last time Sally had gone with her, her mother hadn't been able to speak for weeping.

'Poor old dad.'

There was a pause. 'I've been to the cinema with Artie from the King's Head,' said her mum.

Sally was astonished. This was the last thing she had expected. Beverley looked at her, unsure of her reaction.

'Mum, that's wonderful.' She nodded. 'Honestly. You deserve to have some fun.'

'He's an ugly bugger but he's very kind.'

Sally laughed. 'Looks mean nothing. Kindness is much more important.'

'I like *your* young man.' Her mum gave her a meaningful smile. 'He's *very* handsome.'

'He's not my young man, Mum,' Sally said. 'I just work for him.'

'Mmmm,' said her mother. 'We'll see.'

'See what?'

'We'll see. That's all.'

As they drove home, Sally felt her heart lighten. She was always so worried, that the shop would have to close, or that her mum would have a breakdown, and she'd felt so guilty about running away. But now she didn't have to.

'Thank you for taking me,' she said to Alexander as they drove back up the drive.

He stopped the car and looked at her. His gaze was intense, and she felt a bit nonplussed.

'I'd do anything for you, Sally. You know that. Anything.'

She thought he must feel sorry for her, after meeting her mum and seeing their predicament for himself.

'Mum's got a boyfriend,' she grinned. 'Who'd have thought it?'

Towards the end of May there was a heatwave and the swimming pool came into its own. The four of them spent hours on sunloungers, reading and listening to music and drinking home-made lemonade that Sally had made but Alexander insisted on lacing with vodka.

'You'll drown,' chided Sally, and ended up watering down the vodka without Alexander knowing. She really was too sensible, she thought.

'We need to start thinking about Mum's birthday,' said Phoebe. 'It's next month.'

'We always have a party,' Alexander told Sally.

'Another one?' They never seemed to need any excuse for carousing.

'This is a proper one. With invitations. And dressing up. It goes on all night.'

'Of course,' said Sally. The Willoughbys couldn't seem to discern between day and night. She sometimes found it exhausting.

'Books,' said Annie, who was re-reading Jane Eyre for the nth time for her English Lit exam. 'We should have books as the theme this year. I can't believe we've never done that before.'

'Last year was the Wild West,' said Phoebe. 'But too many people came on horses. It got a bit out of hand.'

'Books are pretty safe,' said Annie. 'Aren't they?'

'Books is brilliant,' said Phoebe. 'I'll do some invitations.'

'Won't it cost a lot?' asked Sally, worrying about the bills.

'Of course,' said Phoebe. 'But that doesn't matter.'

Sally thought it probably did, but she couldn't say anything. Discussing money really wasn't her place.

They heard shrieks coming from the garden. They looked up to see Margot racing down to the pool, waving her arms and yelling excitedly. She stood on the edge of the pool, facing outwards.

'I've finished it. I've bloody finished it!' she announced to them as they stared at her from behind their sunglasses.

Then she held out her arms and fell into the pool with a shriek.

Alexander, Phoebe and Annie jumped off their loungers and threw themselves into the pool after her.

Sally laughed as she watched them all leap around, splashing each other and duck diving.

She wondered what sort of a mother it was best to be? A crazy, beautiful career woman like Margot, or like her mum, solid and unchanging, always in the kitchen with a pinny on?

Maybe it was possible to be a bit of both?

29

1967

A fortnight after she had finished her book, Margot went up to town to have a meeting with Niggle. He'd asked to see her and she felt excited. The book she had delivered was the last one in her contract so they would no doubt be discussing the future, the way forward for Margot Willoughby. There would be a lovely lunch and champagne, of that she had no doubt. With the advent of such gorgeous weather, the hard work done (she intended to give herself the summer off and start work on the next book in September) and the prospect of a new book deal, she felt in a better mood than she had done for weeks.

She'd even been into the bank to allay the bank manager's fears with a clear conscience. He'd been frosty at first, but she had talked him round, and they were firm friends again by the time she'd left, and she'd promised his wife a signed copy of her new book. She felt much happier now she'd bought herself a bit of time. All those horrid letters that had been piling up could be forgotten about. They'd given her a burning feeling in her stomach every time she looked at them.

She was surprised to be shown into Niggle's office and asked to sit down. Usually they would walk out together and go to the latest restaurant for buzz and gossip. Margot was dressed in a lilac shift dress with a matching coat in anticipation of admiring glances.

Niggle looked at her over his glasses.

'I'm afraid Fanny isn't happy with *The Silver Brooch*.'

'What?' Margot frowned. 'Why on earth not?'

'For lots of reasons. Mainly because she thinks it's stale. Lacklustre.'

'Well, I can do another draft. Put in some sparkle.' Margot smiled at him brightly.

Niggle steepled his fingers. He looked grave. Niggle never looked grave.

'It's not just a question of sparkle. It's more than that. The plot's flimsy. There are no surprises. It's predictable. I'm sorry, Margot. There's not much point in me being euphemistic here, or trying to pretend it's salvageable.'

'Salvageable?' She felt her chest go tight with panic.

'It's for the bin, I'm afraid.'

'You don't mean it!'

'It's not a decision Fanny has made lightly. It's not in her interests for the book to go in the bin, because it means she will have a big gap in her Christmas publishing schedule. But there's no point in trying to breathe new life into it. It's a dead duck.'

Margot looked around his office as she tried to take in what he was saying. On the wall were framed copies of her book covers. Mingled in with other authors, yes, but there were more of hers than anyone's.

She was the jewel in Niggle's crown. A big, fat, sparkling diamond.

Her mind was racing. If the manuscript wasn't accepted she wouldn't get her delivery money. And if they didn't

publish it she wouldn't get her publication payment . . .
How much had the advance been? How much would she
have to pay back if the book was refused because it was
not up to standard? Well, she couldn't, and that was that.
Oh God, this wasn't happening. Nothing like this had
ever happened before. She was the golden goose. She was
Fanny's pet. What the hell were they going to live on if
she didn't get paid?

She'd already pinched some money out of Annie's post
office savings account to pay Sally, who needed cash. She
was intending to pay it back, of course.

She tried to smile.

'I think Fanny's being a bit doom and gloom. I've noticed she's been a bit hard on people lately. Get her to read
it again. I could send her some ideas to titivate it.'

'Margot.' Niggle looked at her and shook his head.

She could barely ask the question.

'Will I have to give the advance back?'

'Not yet. Not if you can deliver something . . . publishable. As soon as possible.'

'Publishable?' Margot was indignant. How dare they
question her? She had made thousands and thousands of
readers happy with her books.

She had to get out. She would get hysterical if she
didn't get out of this office. She picked up her bag,
stuffed her arms into the sleeves of her coat, pulled on her
gloves . . .

'Margot . . .'

The tears were coming. Tears of absolute rage and fury
at the injustice.

'I'm sorry. I have to go.'

She stumbled towards the door.

'Margot – come and see me when you've thought things through so we can decide what to do.'

She pulled on the door handle. She couldn't reply to him. She was too, too angry.

She ran through the streets. The implications of the revelation were too ghastly to contemplate. She thought of all the bills piling up. How had she cavalierly anticipated the arrival of her next payment wiping out all the debt? This was terrible. How many bills were there? And the bank? The house? What would happen? She couldn't think about it. She stopped at a phone box. Terence would calm her. He would have some sage advice. She had got into the habit of phoning him, on the pretext of talking about work. He always sounded pleased to hear from her but would only indulge her for a few minutes before calling off.

'Can you come and have a drink?' she blurted out as Terence answered the phone. 'I need you.'

His voice sounded amused. 'Well, that's quite a declaration.'

'It's not funny.'

'What's happened?'

She knew if she told him, he might dish out a few bon mots and tell her to get on with it. He was such a stoic. It was part of the attraction. He found her so . . . easy to resist. She was determined to work on him until he crumbled.

'Come to the Beachcomber. At the May Fair Hotel. I'll tell you there.'

'Margot. I'm working.'

'I don't care,' she said. 'This is a crisis.'

'I can't.' He would not be moved. 'Come to my house tomorrow morning. I'm taking you out for the day. Wear something warm. The forecast is terrible. And sensible shoes.'

Sensible shoes? She didn't have any sensible shoes. She heard him hang up. She threw the receiver back into the cradle and put her head in her arms, swallowed up with fury and despair.

She arrived at his house in Bloomsbury at nine thirty the next day. The weather had indeed turned. The glorious sunshine had been replaced by a gloomy sky that suited her mood. She had followed his instructions to the best of her sartorial ability: jeans and her lowest heels and a mac, because it looked as if it might rain any moment, and a headscarf and sunglasses. All eventualities covered.

He came out of his house with a picnic basket and led her to his Triumph Herald. She got in without question. She found it quietly thrilling, the way he took charge without saying much. It was such a relief for someone else to be driving things for once.

He was infuriatingly blasé about her bombshell when she told him about her meeting with Niggle.

'It's a blip. You've done it before so you can do it again. Your ability to write doesn't just disappear. I'm afraid it's just a question of knuckling down.'

'You don't understand!'

'Of course I bloody do.' He scowled. 'Stop whining and get on with it.'

'You're a bully.'

'You wanted my advice, didn't you? You know I wasn't going to stroke your arm and say *there, there*. Or tell you they were wrong and that your book is a work of genius. I'm a realist. A pragmatist. Don't come to me for platitudes.'

Margot looked at him. How had she ever thought he would be the person to turn to? He was giving her no comfort at all.

'Where are we going?'

'Wait and see.' He stared at the road ahead, not giving her an inch. It was too late to ask him to turn back. He would be even more cross. Margot huddled herself into her mac and leaned her head back. She would go to sleep. She was exhausted by it all, and talking to him was just making it worse.

She woke some time later and opened her eyes. They were parked up in front of a wide beach, covered in shingle. He led her to a ramshackle hut, the last in a row. He opened it with a key kept hidden under a large grey stone. Inside there was just enough room for a small table and a chair.

'This is my hideaway,' he told her. 'This is where I come when I need to clear my head. No distractions. No one to disturb me. Just me and my typewriter.'

Margot looked around. It wasn't the prettiest of beaches. The shingle was grey and cold to the touch. The sea and the sky matched it. Birds soared overhead, crying piteously.

'Where exactly are we?'

'Greystone Beach. On the Sussex coast.'

She looked out across the water and shivered. 'Very aptly named.'

What was he doing, dragging her here? She wanted to be with him in the Beachcomber, drinking cocktails. This was awful. Margot knew she was supposed to be charmed, but she wasn't.

They sat on a rug in front of the hut. Terence had made egg sandwiches and buttered some fruit cake. The salty breeze whipped around them as they ate.

'It's never warm here, even in the height of summer. But there's something bracing about it. Something that clears the mind and helps you focus. So if you want to lock yourself away here for a while, you can. Spend a couple of weeks away from your family and just get it done. Any time. The key's under the stone.'

She knew he was trying to help but she felt ungrateful. 'I'm never going to write another word again.'

Terence looked at her. 'Do you know what, Margot? Sometimes I think you just need to grow up. Or you might be in danger of losing everything.'

She dug her fingers into the stones. They were icy cold. 'There's something else,' she said.

'Let me guess,' he replied. 'You want to borrow some money?'

30

The deadline for sealed bids for Hunter's Moon was midday on Friday, two weeks after the open house.

Belinda was going to take all the bids over to Hunter's Moon to discuss the contenders with Sally and Alexander. Sealed bids were a balancing act. The best offer wasn't necessarily the highest. Besides, a sealed bid wasn't legally binding, so the buyer could still pull out at any point before contracts were exchanged, if something wasn't to their liking or if their circumstances changed.

She desperately hoped that whoever got Hunter's Moon both deserved and appreciated it. Time and again she had to remind herself not to get emotionally involved, but sometimes a house got under your skin and there was nothing you could do about it.

Three offers came in during the week, all for the asking price or over, and all in a strong position. Then two more were delivered first thing on Friday morning. Five decent offers was a solid result, and she felt pleased.

She was hugely relieved there was nothing from Natasha and Charlie. She had steeled herself to look at their registration document and do a thorough background check. There was no evidence of Charlie's name anywhere: it would obviously be bankrolled by Natasha's father. All right for some, thought Belinda. But then again, Natasha had ended up in rehab, so maybe having a rich daddy wasn't such a good thing.

She took a photocopy of all the offers and put them in the file she was taking to Hunter's Moon. Then she compiled a spreadsheet, outlining the amounts offered and all the other relevant details, so everyone could consider the bids at a glance. She tried to personalise each offer as much as she could in case the Willoughbys wanted to visualise who was to have their home: *couple with one child moving from London, three generation family from Birmingham.*

'Can you write to everyone who's made an offer and thank them?' she asked Cathy. 'Tell them we'll be in touch early next week when a decision has been made. Ask them please not to call us in the meantime. Send the letters out first class this afternoon. We don't want them pestering us all weekend.'

'Who do you think will get it?' asked Cathy.

'Probably the Shepherd's Bush lawyers.'

'Oh yes. The little boy was sweet.'

'Yes, and I got the impression they wanted more kids. Anyway, we'll have it wrapped up by the end of the week.'

'Do you think that's all the offers?'

Belinda shrugged. 'I don't know. I expect most people would want to get their bid in before now. It takes a bit of nerve to go right up to the wire.'

It was quarter past eleven. The hands of the clock swept nearer and nearer to midday. Belinda picked up her car keys.

'Just call me if any more offers come in,' she said. 'But I doubt they will.'

*

She headed out to Hunter's Moon with a heavy heart. All she could think of to lift her spirits was that The High House looked set to complete in six weeks. She'd been to view several houses already, but nothing was quite right. She was prepared to be patient. She had waited so long for this day, and worked so hard, nothing but the perfect house would do.

Hunter's Moon was looking more beautiful than ever when she arrived. Bright green buds and blossom abounded. Teddy nosed at her ankles anxiously as she got out of the car, as if to say 'There's something going on'.

As well as Sally, Alexander and Leo, Belinda was surprised to find two more members of the Willoughby family in the drawing room. Alexander introduced them.

'These are my sisters. Phoebe. And Annie.'

'Commonly known as The Afterthought.' Annie held out her hand. She was plain but smiley, in a grey jumper and trousers and flat boots, her hair scraped back in a ponytail and a pair of glasses perched on her head.

Phoebe was a total contrast: tall and slender with a chic short grey crop, a crisp white shirt under a mohair sweater and black palazzo pants. Her make-up was striking: heavily made-up eyes and dark red lipstick. She must be in her seventies, thought Belinda, but she looked as if she'd stepped out of the pages of a magazine.

'We've got the whole family embroiled, I'm afraid,' said Sally, who had brought in coffee and a plate of raspberry muffins.

'Of course,' said Annie. 'Leo was right. This is exactly what families are for.'

Belinda caught Alexander's eye. He gave a little shrug as if to say *what can you do*, but he was smiling.

'Just ignore us,' said Annie. 'We haven't come to tell Beetle and Sally what to do. Just give them our support.'

'I'm sure you'll throw the odd opinion in,' said Alexander. 'You'll find it impossible not to.'

'It's good to have everyone's input, surely?' said Annie. 'We all love the house. We care what happens.'

'Not as much as we care about Beetle and Sally, though,' said Phoebe. 'Let's not forget that.'

'Can you imagine,' said Leo sotto voce to Belinda, 'what it was like for poor Dad growing up here with those two?'

But he was smiling, and Belinda smiled back and said, 'I expect it was pretty wonderful.'

She cleared her throat. She looked at the clock on the mantelpiece. It was five to twelve. She hadn't heard anything from Cathy.

'We might as well start going through all the offers,' she said to everyone, and handed around photocopies of her spreadsheet. 'They're all pretty solid and all pretty much bang on the money. It's a question of time frame and personal choice, I suppose. If you want to narrow it down and make a shortlist, then meet the potential buyers, that's always an option—'

Her words were drowned out by the roar of a motorbike. She stopped and looked up, alert.

Everyone gravitated towards the window. There was an enormous Harley-Davidson Electra Glide pulling up outside the door.

'Bloody hell,' said Leo in admiration.

They all watched as a leather-clad courier made his way to the door. He was holding a large envelope.

'I'll go,' said Sally, and left the room.

Belinda's heart was thumping. She had thought she was out of the water, but she feared not.

Sally came back in with a thick cream envelope with a crest emblazoned in the top right hand corner.

'It's addressed for your attention, Belinda.'

Belinda felt as if she was being served with a writ as she took it.

She opened it, but she knew without looking this was the offer she had been dreading. The first page was a formal offer way beyond what anyone else had bid. It blew everyone else out of the water.

Attached to that was solicitor's details and evidence of cash in the bank from a Coutts account. The headed paper was from the company Belinda had already checked up on at Companies House during her initial research. Natasha's father.

It was a very businesslike offer of the kind estate agents could only dream of – no caveats or conditions or potential pitfalls, the contract to be exchanged at the Willoughbys' convenience.

Accompanying the official paperwork was a handwritten letter in pale blue ink. Belinda smoothed it out and began to read it aloud.

Dear Mr and Mrs Willoughby

Two years ago I was on the verge of totally destroying myself with drugs and alcohol. I was lucky enough to meet a wonderful man, and together we healed each other, through the power of mindfulness. From that day on I determined to help other people who had lost their way in life by opening a retreat.

I began my search for somewhere to fulfil my dream, and as soon as I saw Hunter's Moon I knew it was the one. Its quiet *calm and its beautiful setting would be the perfect environment for my clients' journeys back to a place of safety.*

I would pour my love into the house. The love that I can see it has been given over the years. I want to keep its beautiful aura so my guests can feel at home while they are on the bravest and most difficult quest they will ever make. I will use the walled garden to nourish them while they are there. They will breathe in the scent from the flowers you have planted. I will honour your memory every day during our rituals.

Hunter's Moon will be safe in my hands and in my heart.

Natasha

Belinda felt sick as she put the letter down.

This was the moment when she could reveal what she knew about Charlie and tell them all what he had done. Yet she also knew that what had happened between her and Charlie wasn't relevant. The difference between this offer and the next one down could make a real difference to the Willoughbys' lifestyle. She couldn't sabotage that just because of what had happened in her private life. It wasn't professional.

'Well, that's that, then,' said Alexander, shrugging. 'You can't argue with an offer like that.'

Belinda desperately hoped that someone would come up with an objection. Perhaps the Willoughbys would want Hunter's Moon to remain a family home? That was quite common with vendors.

'It does seem a waste,' said Annie. 'For the poor house to be teetotal. I mean, Hunter's Moon is all about drinking – Pimm's on the lawn and mulled wine in front of the fire and champagne in the bath.'

Phoebe made a face. 'Instead it's going to be all chanting and sun salutations and downward facing dog.'

'Truthfully,' said Alexander, 'I don't care what happens to it. If it's not ours then it's not ours. We just have to move on.'

'We'll always have the memories,' said Sally.

Belinda couldn't think of anything to say. The offer spoke for itself.

'Let me leave the offers with you. It's only fair you have a chance to sleep on it. I don't want to put you under any pressure.'

'Which would you go for?' Leo was pressing her for her opinion. 'I mean, there really is only one, isn't there? Can you see any snags? Any reason why not?'

This was the moment for her to voice her fears. To hint that perhaps the team behind the offer were not as solid as the paperwork might indicate. But that was only her experience, her opinion. It had no reflection on what was there in front of them in black and white.

'It's always a gamble,' she said finally. 'Things can always fall through right up to the moment of exchange.'

Sally chided her son. 'Leo, don't put Belinda under pressure.' She smiled at Belinda. 'We'll have a family chat and make our final decision then call you tomorrow.'

'Take as much time as you like. Whoever wants to buy it will wait a few days, I'm sure. I can tell everyone their offers are still under consideration.'

Belinda said her goodbyes to the family then Leo walked her out to her car.

'Thank you. I know your advice and guidance has made this easier for Mum and Dad. They feel very safe in your hands.'

'Thank *you*. I'm just sorry they're having to sell in the first place.'

She opened her car door. The two of them looked at each other. This was her chance to say something.

'There is one thing. I'm in a bit of a quandary,' she said.

'Go on.'

'That last offer? The girl who's buying it is engaged to my ex-husband.'

'Your ex-husband?'

He looked shocked, and Belinda felt as if he was looking at her with new eyes.

'It was a long time ago and it was only a short marriage. One of those youthful mistakes.'

'I've been lucky enough not to make one of those.' He smiled, and she thought he was trying not to judge.

'The thing is, I know he's bankrupt. His wine shop went bust just before we got divorced. Part of me feels I should tell your parents. Give them full disclosure. But the offer isn't actually from him. It's from Natasha and her father. So I don't want to put them off when it's such a lot of money.'

Leo frowned. 'Do you think the offer's sound?'

'As solid as it can be. He's got the funds. There's no mortgage to negotiate. I just feel guilty not giving them the heads up. But at the same time I don't want to put them off.'

'Don't say anything.' Leo was decisive. 'That's a lot of money. They're going to need it.' He put a reassuring hand on her shoulder. 'My decision. So no need to feel guilty.'

'Thank you. That's eased my conscience a bit.'

*

Leo looked down at his shoes and traced the gravel with his toe, his hands in his pockets.

'When it's all signed and sealed, maybe I could take you for a drink?'

'Oh.' She felt relieved that her failed marriage hadn't put him off.

'Or dinner. There's a little pop-up in Peasebrook I keep hearing great things about.'

'A Deux? Yes, it's supposed to be wonderful. I've never been.'

'Well, I think that would be the most perfect thank you.'

Belinda wasn't sure what to think. Did he really just want to say thank you or was this a date? She remembered the woman he was on his way to see the last time she'd seen him.

Maybe she should play it cool? She tried not to smile, because she could hear Bruce's voice in her head: 'Babe, he would not be asking you out if he didn't want to spend time with you. Trust me. No man saddles himself with a bird he doesn't fancy for an evening out.' And Cathy. 'It's the law of attraction, Belinda. The Universe has given him to you.'

Yet despite their voices trying to convince her, she didn't want to set herself up for a fall.

'Let's get the deal done first,' she said crisply. She slid into the driver's seat and put the keys in the ignition. 'I'll be in touch.'

She shut her door, started the engine and drove away.

As she made her way down the drive, she sorted through her thoughts. Her heart was still pounding from the un-expected thrill of Leo's invitation. Yet underlying that was a feeling of nausea and a bitter taste in her mouth.

Bloody Charlie Fox. As wily as his name, and who always landed with his bum in the honey. She could already imagine him parading the terrace, looking out over the rolling hills and smiling. Bastard, she thought as she pulled out of the drive and accelerated down the lane. Bastard bastard bastard.

His aunts descended on Leo as soon as he went back into the drawing room.

'Darling – she's a sweetheart. How about it?' Phoebe's eyes were sparkling with the intrigue.

'She's a smart cookie, too,' added Annie. 'And very pretty but she doesn't know it, which is always devastatingly attractive.'

'For heaven's sake, you two! When will you ever stop?'

Leo was used to his aunts' matchmaking; their eternal frustration at the fact he hadn't settled down.

'Maybe something good will come out of this bloody nightmare,' said Annie. 'Beetle, darling, should we have a farewell party?'

Leo looked at his dad. He looked tired and drawn. The emotion of the afternoon must have got to him, and his aunts were always exhausting even if they meant very, very well.

'I don't think so,' said Alexander. 'I think that would be an actual living hell. Even more than this already is.'

For once, Annie knew when to keep quiet.

31

1967

Phoebe had designed the most beautiful invitations to Margot's birthday party, in the shape of a book, in navy blue and silver and decorated with the moon and stars. There were over a hundred of them. Sally couldn't imagine knowing that many people.

'We ask everyone,' said Annie. 'Even the postman.'

'Parties are what we Willoughbys do best,' Phoebe added.

'I've never had one,' Sally admitted. 'Well, not unless you count a children's party, with pin the tail on the donkey and pass the parcel.'

'Watch and learn,' said Phoebe.

And so Sally watched in utter amazement as the Willoughbys galvanised themselves into the organisation. They all had a role and they all knew what to do.

'You'll be in charge of cooking,' said Alexander. 'We never do food, usually, so that'll make a change. I'm in charge of music. Phoebe does the decorating. Annie sorts out the practical stuff. Parking and so on. It's actually really easy. All you need is good weather, lots of booze and loads of guests.'

Yet again, they made it all seem so simple.

Margot just sat back and watched them get on with it, which was what she always did. Since her trip to the seaside with Terence, she'd been in a permanent state of semi-hysteria. She'd been to the doctor to get some tablets, some for daytime and some for night, so during the day her anxieties were kept at bay, and at night she could sleep. But she was mixing them with more drink than was probably sensible. Anything to blot out the horrible truth, that her words had dried up, that she was haemorrhaging money, and that Terence thought she was a fool. But she'd sent him a party invitation. He had come to her rescue, after all. His loan had bought her some time.

'I'm only lending it to you,' he'd said. 'Because I know you will come through in the end.'

That should have given her confidence, but of course it hadn't.

If she were sensible, she would cancel the party. It was going to cost a fortune. It always did. But if she did that, she would have to admit the truth to everyone. She hadn't told anyone else. Not even Dai. Especially not Dai.

What kind of marriage was that? she thought. When you couldn't share a catastrophe with your husband? He was obsessed with gardening. He scurried about in the most awful clothes and was always covered in mud. What bloody use was that?

There was another reason she hadn't told him; because deep down she was afraid he might be pleased she had failed. Pleased she could no longer queen it over him. The ultimate in Schadenfreude.

God, these pills were making her paranoid. She thought they were supposed to make her feel better. She tried to focus on the party. Phoebe had found a black silk 1920s dress in a shop on the King's Road and Margot had nabbed it.

'I'm going as Daisy Buchanan,' said Margot. 'Dai – you can be Jay Gatsby.'

'I'm not bloody dressing up as him,' he grumbled. 'I couldn't be less like Jay Gatsby.'

Margot eyed him critically.

'True,' she said. 'You can always go as Mr McGregor.'

Dai didn't rise to the bait.

Phoebe decided that the rest of them would go as characters from Alice in Wonderland.

'Sally, you will be a perfect Alice, with your hair. Alexander can be the Mad Hatter. I'll be the Red Queen. And Annie – you can be the White Rabbit.'

'I wanted to be the Lady of Shallot,' objected Annie. 'I was going to float in the swimming pool. Or Ophelia.'

That should be me, thought Margot. Perhaps that could be her swan song. A public suicide bid at her own party. She'd be doing them all a favour.

The party was to be on midsummer's day, starting at six in the evening and carrying on all night. The Lucky Charms were going to play and the fountain was to be filled with ice buckets full of champagne. Sally spent days roasting hams and sides of beef which she would lay out with bread and baked potatoes and salad. She had been to enough dos at the tennis club to know that stodge was essential if utter drunken carnage was to be avoided.

Everyone had very sweetly insisted she should ask her family to the party. Try as she might, she couldn't imagine Beverley and Ray and Colin dressed up and mingling on the lawn. But it would be unkind of her not to invite them. It's not as if she was ashamed of them.

'Thank you very much for asking,' her mother said when she telephoned. 'But Saturdays I go the cinema with Artie. And Ray and Colin play footie on a Sunday morning. I don't think they'll want to miss it.'

Sally felt a little relieved, and promised to go up and see them again soon.

There were other things giving her a sense of unease. Tensions were high between Margot and Dai. Margot seemed to resent the time he spent in the garden. And Sally suspected that Margot was getting to the post before she was, because there were never any bills amongst the letters any more. Not that it was any of her business, but she had been told at more than one shop that she couldn't have anything else on account until it had been settled. Margot kept promising and then forgetting.

The sense of excitement grew until the day dawned. Everyone the Willoughbys knew had been invited. Margot's publishing friends. Hers and Dai's friends from the old days. People who'd been to or who were still at Larkford. Most of Peasebrook, including the regulars at the White Horse. It was a funny mixture, which shouldn't work but somehow did, riff-raff mixing with the literary elite, all helped along by the alcohol.

By seven o'clock the lawns were crowded with colourful characters. There was Miss Havisham and the Artful Dodger; Hobbits and Gandalfs; King Arthur and a gaggle of Bennet sisters, and Sherlock Holmes. One woman had come as Sylvia Plath with a cardboard gas oven around her head, which Margot found witty if a trifle distasteful. One couple had come as Eeyore the donkey, in a pantomime costume, and they walked sombrely around the party with the head down, making people laugh.

Dai had slung a couple of dead pheasants around his neck.

'Mellors, I suppose?' said Margot, not very impressed with his efforts.

'He's more of a man than Gatsby ever was,' said Dai. He was very pleased with himself.

All Margot cared about was whether Terence was going to come. He was the only person on the planet who seemed to care about her. He understood her, even if he was tough on her. He'd phoned her several times to see if she was all right. He'd listened to her possible ideas for a new book, and encouraged her. Every time she came off the phone to him she felt galvanised, but then when she went to the typewriter, the enthusiasm had gone.

She needed him in her life. To keep her on track and guide her and nurture her.

She knew she was being ridiculous, but she told herself there was nothing wrong with daydreaming. It got her through her waking hours, which seemed endless. It was an antidote to the cocktail of panic, fear, dread and denial that churned up her stomach. The pills helped, but not as much as her fantasy.

Sally was laying out bowls of trifle she'd made for pudding, although she was pretty sure no one would bother to eat it, when a woman dressed as Scarlett O'Hara sidled up to her.

'It's Sally, isn't it?'

Sally peered at her, puzzled. The woman laughed and she finally recognised her. It was Hilly, the woman from the café she'd met on her first day.

'Hello,' she said. She was surprised to see her here after what Alexander had told her.

'You're hanging in there rather well. Three months? That must be a record.'

The Willoughbys had often talked about how hard they found it to keep staff. Sally laughed.

'Yes. I don't quite know how I've managed it.'

Hilly moved in closer. Sally could see she was rather drunk, but so was everyone, so it was hardly shocking.

'I managed six but of course it was a secret, so we hardly saw each other at all, really. My husband would have blown his head off.'

'Oh!' Sally realised she meant something else entirely. 'But I'm not—'

'He broke my heart, you know.' Hilly's brown eyes filled with tears. 'Like a lot of beautiful people, Alexander can be very cruel without realising.'

'He's always been very kind to me,' said Sally, stout in her defence.

'Oh, I know. He's absolutely charming. But he has a lot of his mother in him.'

Sally stared after her as she walked off in her green velvet ruffles.

She must be jealous.

Only there was nothing to be jealous of.

When Margot saw Terence, she thought she was going to faint. He was in a white tie and tails, his hair swept back, a coupe of champagne in his hand. How had he known to come as Jay Gatsby? She was certain she hadn't told him who she was going as. There was something serendipitous about it that thrilled her, and in that moment she realised her feelings for him were even more potent that she'd realised.

She walked over to him, smiling.

'How long have you been here? You should have come to find me. Are you being looked after?'

'We are,' he said, and he turned to hold his hand out to a figure who was approaching with two bowls of strawberries and cream.

It was another Daisy Buchanan. A slight figure in a silver dress and a sequined cap, her mouth a dark red bow. She looked enchanting. She made Margot feel bovine. And old. Terribly old. The girl couldn't be more than twenty-five or twenty-six.

'Ohhh,' she said as she approached Margot. 'I couldn't believe it when Terence said you were a friend of his. I am such a fan of your work. I used to read your books on the bus every day on the way into work. They are heaven! And thank you so much for inviting us to the party. It's wonderful.'

Margot's eyes were like chips of ice.

'This is my wife, Celia,' said Terence.

'How funny,' said Celia, 'that we're both Daisy Buchanan. What are the chances of that?'

Sally quickly forgot about her exchange with Hilly. She was having far too much fun. The Willoughbys paraded her proudly like a mascot and she was introduced to everyone. The sparkling wine cup she and Alexander had concocted and put into huge silver punch bowls made her feel slightly lightheaded but took away any shyness. She danced to the Lucky Charms, and never found herself short of partners.

There was only one moment that marred the evening, and that was when she slipped upstairs to use the bathroom and check on her make-up. She bumped into Dai coming out of his bedroom. He looked very drunk, and seemed in a dark mood, but when he saw her, his face lit up.

'Sally-Alice,' he slurred. 'Sally in Wonderland. You're an angel. You know that, don't you?'

He put his arms around her and went to kiss her. It was a gesture of fondness, she thought, even though he was a bit uncoordinated, so she gave him a kiss back on the cheek and laughed. The scent from the pheasants, strong and gamey, rose up and made her nauseous, so she pushed him away. The gesture seemed to alert him to his behaviour. He put his hands up.

'Sorry. I didn't mean . . . Sorry . . .'

She didn't know what to say. Dai looked mortified. It was a bit embarrassing. She was a bit tipsy herself. It would all be forgotten tomorrow, she decided. She'd forget it, anyway. There was no point in making a fuss.

Then she looked towards the stairs and saw Margot at the top, her hand on the bannister. She gave Sally such a knowing glance, as if to say she knew exactly what she was up to. Sally thought if she said anything it would only make things worse, so she turned and walked away towards the bathroom. She had done nothing wrong.

Margot cornered Terence by the swimming pool. No one had braved the water yet but if previous years were anything to go by, it would eventually be heaving. She had seen Celia on the dance floor, so she took her chance.

'You didn't tell me you were married.'

'I didn't know you didn't know.'

'She's young enough to be your daughter.'

He shook his head. 'I'm younger than I look and Celia's older than she looks. There's only seven years between us. That hardly makes me Humbert Humbert.'

'Sorry. I just . . .'

She realised she was about to cry. She'd had too many glasses of champagne. Every day she wanted to cry. The pills stopped her wanting to. But the drink brought back the desire. She shouldn't mix them.

'I think I'm in love with you,' she said, and Terence laughed.

She slapped him very hard, just once, around the face.

'What was that for?' He looked shocked.

'For not telling me.'

'What difference would it have made? You're married. We're both spoken for.'

'You made a fool of me.'

'Margot, I think you're making a perfectly good job of making a fool of yourself.'

'You've been phoning me. Why would you phone me if you weren't interested?'

He looked exasperated.

'If you must know, Niggle asked me to make sure you were all right. He's very worried about you.'

Margot stared at him in disbelief.

'I honestly thought you cared.'

'Margot, of course I care. We all do.'

She turned and walked away. She couldn't take one more moment of humiliation.

*

Half an hour later, Sally was looking for Annie. She hadn't seen her for ages. Most of the guests were hardened drinkers but she thought Annie probably hadn't had as much practice as everyone else, despite her training plan. She'd seen her drink at least three glasses of the wine cup, and it was lethal.

'Have you seen Annie?' she asked Margot. 'She's had quite a lot to drink. I'm worried she might be sick.'

'Oh for Christ's sake,' snapped Margot. 'Can't you drop the Girl Guide act for just one evening? It doesn't fool me.'

Sally decided to square up to her.

'There wasn't anything going on between me and Dai, if that's what you're worried about,' she told her. 'Honestly. He was just being friendly.'

Margot looked at her. Her eyes were glazed, almost blank. 'What a lovely view of the world you have,' she said dreamily. 'I'd give anything to swap places with you, darling Sally.'

She blew her a kiss and wandered off. She had taken off her shoes and was walking rather unsteadily.

Sally felt uncomfortable. She couldn't tell if Margot was being sarcastic or not. A man in a white tie and tails came and spoke in her ear.

'I think she's had a bit too much to drink.'

'I think everyone has,' said Sally, knowing she sounded prim.

She carried on looking for Annie, pushing through the crowds of people. Everyone was looking hot and dishevelled. Quite a few people were off balance and being very loud. It suddenly felt a bit hostile, and she felt panicky.

'Has anyone seen the White Rabbit?' she went around

asking, and everyone laughed, thinking it was a literary reference and not a genuine question.

Alexander came and grabbed her hand.

'Quick. I need cover. Hilly's on the warpath. She's had way too much to drink and her husband's here.'

Sally hesitated. If her husband wasn't here, might he be interested?

'I think I'm the only person who hasn't danced with you yet tonight,' he said. 'You are the belle of the ball.'

'I don't think so,' laughed Sally, but he pulled her through the crowds of people to the dance floor that had been cleared in the courtyard – the band were playing in the garage with the doors open. They were on top form, covering everyone's current favourites – 'I'm a Believer' and 'A Whiter Shade of Pale' and 'The Beat Goes On'. Sally span and twirled, loving the freedom of forgetting about everything just for a moment.

Then as the band started to play 'White Rabbit' by Jefferson Airplane it reminded her of Annie.

'I think I should go and look for Annie. I haven't seen her for ages.'

Alexander looked at her. 'Stop worrying about everyone else, will you?' he said. 'Annie will be fine.'

Sally shook her head. 'I'm worried about her.'

Alexander sighed. 'Oh, Sally.' Her heart thumped at the way he said her name. He picked up her hand. 'Come with me.'

Alexander led her down the garden, down behind the hedge into the secret spot where they all got changed for swimming because no one could see you in there.

He turned her and looked into her eyes.

'You have made such a difference to this family,' he

told her. 'The way you look out for us all. It's amazing. Everyone's so much happier. We all love having you here so much.'

Sally bit her lip. 'I'm not sure your mother does. She never seems happy.'

'That's the point of Mum. She thrives on pretending to be unhappy. And I promise you, if she didn't like you, you wouldn't still be here.'

He took her hand so their fingers were interlinked, and she felt his thumb trace patterns on her palm. His touch was so delicate but it reached right inside her and turned her upside down.

'Phoebe and Annie adore you like a sister. Dad is a new man. And I . . .'

He pulled her in so their foreheads were almost touching.

His hair was tangled up in hers. She could barely breathe and her heart skittered.

'What?' she whispered.

'Shhh,' was all he said in reply.

She felt his mouth on hers. It was soft and sweet. He began to kiss her, tiny kisses that made her melt.

Then she froze. The memory of Hilly's warning was still fresh. *Alexander can be cruel.* And Margot's words, when she arrived. *Annie says he can break three hearts before breakfast.*

She didn't want to be one of those women, like Hilly or Diana. She wasn't going to ruin her new life by getting involved with him. He would break her heart and she would lose her job. She imagined going back to Knapford after a taste of this exciting new world she'd been shown.

She wasn't going to risk leaving Hunter's Moon for anything. Not even Alexander.

'No!' She pulled away from him. 'This is all wrong.'

He took her head in his hands and turned her to face him. His expression was beseeching; his eyes dark with sincerity. 'No it's not.' He was stroking her hair and she could feel each strand ripple over her scalp.

'Please,' she said, in the most no-nonsense tone she could muster. 'Stop it now, before it goes too far.'

He pulled her in tight. 'But I need to tell you something.'

She could feel his heart beating. It was in time with hers. So fast, she thought. Their hearts were beating so fast.

Suddenly, a scream pierced through the night air.

'It's Mum!' screamed Annie. 'Mum's fallen in the pool. I can't get her out.'

Sally had never seen a man move as fast as Dai. He ran down across the lawns, pushing people out of the way, and jumped into the pool. Margot was at the deep end, her body limp and lifeless. He grabbed her, pulled her head out of the water. He was tall enough to stand up, and he heaved her over his shoulder, wading through the water, then passing her over to the outstretched hands of people on the side.

They lifted her out and laid her out. Annie was standing over her, sobbing uncontrollably. Dai was struggling to climb out of the pool with his wet clothes.

A man in a white suit stepped forward, pushing everyone out of the way. He bent over Margot and began to press her chest, pushing at it firmly, then sealed his mouth over hers to breathe into her.

Sally put her hands to her head. How could this have happened? She remembered her words that day by the pool – 'you'll drown'. Had it been a portent?

Oh God. Time was passing so slowly. Everyone had fallen silent. There was no noise except the sound of Annie sobbing.

Then suddenly Margot spluttered and sat up. She looked around, bewildered.

'What happened?' she said. 'I just thought I'd go for a little swim.'

32

A week before the contracts were due to be exchanged on Hunter's Moon, Cathy ushered a woman into Belinda's office. She was in a white silk dress, her hair in a long plait over one shoulder.

Belinda stood up with a welcoming smile.

'It's Natasha, isn't it?'

Natasha edged into the room and sat down in the chair opposite Belinda. She looked at her, her eyes wide. She had an air of serenity about her, but also one of vulnerability.

'Congratulations on Hunter's Moon,' said Belinda. 'I'm sure what you're going to do with it will be amazing.'

'I need you to tell me what happened between you and Charlie,' said Natasha. 'I know something happened. I could see the tension between you at the open house. Your face when you saw him. You were so shocked. He refused to tell me what went on between you. But I think something happened and I need to know.'

She tightened her fists, leaning forwards, beseeching.

'I'm about to make the biggest commitment of my life,' she went on. 'This retreat is a dream come true for me. It's about everything I believe in. And if Charlie and I are going to make a success of it, I have to believe in *him*.'

'Of course.' Belinda was thinking fast.

'But I'm not sure I trust him. I know he's had problems. That's nothing to be ashamed of. I've had problems myself. That's how we met. But I can't put up with lies. I won't be lied to.' She sighed. 'He's been drinking again. We both know that's something that could happen to either of us. But he's lying about it. He forgets that I know all the tricks.' She managed a self-deprecating laugh.

Belinda nodded. 'I know only too well about the drinking.'

'Tell me what happened.'

'It was all a very long time ago . . .' Should she tell Natasha the truth? Was what happened between Charlie and her relevant? Should his past be held against him?

She looked down at her desk. It was ironic that she had the paperwork for The High House in front of her. The offer letters and the notifications for the solicitors: it was all going ahead. She looked at the picture of the house on the brochure, and remembered how much she had loved it. How much losing it had hurt. And that had been down to Charlie.

Belinda thought if it were her, she would want to know.

'I'm just going to give you the facts,' said Belinda. 'I'm not going to give you an opinion or tell you what to do.'

'That's all I want,' said Natasha.

She didn't exaggerate, or paint Charlie any blacker than he needed to be. She just outlined the chain of events as they had happened.

When she had almost finished decorating The High House, the carpets were laid on the first two floors, and three days later Belinda still found the smell of the rubber backing made her feel sick. A thought occurred to her. She stood in the hallway, looking at the black-and-white tiles, the cornicing she had picked out in white, the glittering glass lamp that shone its light over the Wedgwood-blue walls and thought 'We're going to be a family'.

'Charlie,' she called, holding on to the curl of newel post at the bottom of the stairs. And when he appeared from the kitchen, glass in hand, she told him her suspicions.

He stared at her in disbelief. For a moment, she thought his expression was one of horror. It was just a split second, before his face broke into a beaming smile.

'My cup of happiness is overflowing,' he told her.

Belinda couldn't believe how lucky she was. She had the perfect house, the perfect job, and she was going to have a baby. Sometimes she felt overwhelmed when she looked at what she had. For all her planning, she had never imagined everything would fall into place so quickly.

But for some reason, a few more weeks into her pregnancy, things began to go wrong. Rumours of a property crash meant that everyone was putting their house on the market but no one was buying. Richard Mortlake was putting the pressure on her and Giles to get some commissions in, but you couldn't force people to buy. They had barely sold anything over the past few weeks. She hadn't told them she was pregnant yet – she didn't want to jinx it until her twelve-week scan – but she could see Giles looking at her strangely. And she overheard him talking to his father.

'I think Puss has got a bun in the oven.'

'Bugger,' said Richard. 'I don't want to be forking out for maternity leave, only for her to push out another one in eighteen months. Bloody women.'

Her mouth dropped open and her cheeks flushed red.

She wanted to go storming in on them – sexist bastards – but she didn't trust herself not to cry, because she cried at the drop of a hat at the moment.

At least Charlie had more clients than he knew what to do with, judging by the amount of time he spent with them.

And the house was a joy. Everyone who saw what she had done was green with envy. She insisted that it was because the house was already perfect, it had just needed all the awful things that had been done to it undoing, but she had a flair for just the right colour paint, the right amount of lighting, the little touches that lifted it from pleasing to spectacular.

She was in the top bedroom, the one that was destined to be the nursery, testing out scraps of wallpaper against the light, when she felt the first pain. She thought it must just be a twinge – she'd read they were only to be expected, so she rubbed her tummy and shifted her position.

Ten minutes later, she felt as if a knitting needle had been driven into her. She called Charlie repeatedly on her phone, but it went straight to voicemail.

'Charlie? Charlie, it's me – can you come home?' That was all she could manage to say. There was sweat breaking out on her brow. She could hardly breathe with the pain. She edged her way down the stairs, clinging on to the bannister, then collapsed at the bottom. She just managed to dial the emergency services.

In the back of the ambulance, she screamed with the pain. A paramedic tried to calm her while he did her obs.

'What's happening?'

No one answered her. She could sense by the atmosphere

this was an emergency. She heard the sirens go on. Tears and sweat poured down her face.

Everything happened too fast but not fast enough. She was bundled out of the ambulance and put onto a trolley. There were faces above her as she was wheeled down endless corridors, the strip lights overhead glaring into her eyes. She could barely breath for the pain.

'We're taking you into theatre, love,' said someone in a green uniform.

'Charlie. Where's Charlie?'

'We've called him.' Two people above her exchanged glances. They had masks on.

'Where is he? I need him here.'

They pushed through a set of double doors. The lights were even brighter. Someone took her hand and patted the back of it. But it wasn't for reassurance. She felt something go in. Something sharp.

There was a new voice. A woman. Calm. Authoritative.

'Belinda? I'm the anaesthetist. I need to ask you a few questions. When did you last eat?'

'Anaesthetist?' She tried to sit up, in panic. A nurse pushed her gently back down. Everyone around her was working quickly, getting things ready. There were machines, numbers, noises. Pain. Oh God the pain.

'When did you last eat?'

'Where's Charlie? What's happening?'

'We're helping you, love, but you need to calm down.'

'My baby. Is it my baby? Is my baby coming?' It couldn't be coming. It wasn't ready yet.

'Shhh, love.'

'Sweetheart, can you count backwards from ten for me?'

'No. I need my husband. I need him here. You can't . . .'

She felt ice in her veins. She looked at a screen next to her. There were green lines. They wavered, then melted into one and went black.

When she woke, she saw the concerned and kindly face of a nurse hovering over her. She sat by her bed.

'Oh love, here you are. You've been very lucky.'

'What?' Belinda tried to sit up but she couldn't. She seemed to be connected to wires. 'Where's Charlie?'

The nurse pressed her lips together. 'We've tried to contact him. We've left messages.'

Belinda tried to take this new information in, but her head was swimming.

'So . . . the baby?'

'I'm sorry, love. But like I said, you were lucky. You had an ectopic pregnancy.'

'I don't understand . . .'

'The doctor will be here to explain now you're awake. Try and rest, love.'

Dark panic washed over her. How could something so terrible happen? How could Charlie not be here? The doctor came and his words washed over her . . . ectopic . . . emergency . . . general anaesthetic . . . Fallopian tube . . . The story he was telling her became meaningless, because she knew the only bit of it she needed to know.

She had lost her baby.

She'd drifted off, because sleep was better than being awake. She heard Charlie's voice calling her name. She opened her eyes and he was there, next to the bed. He looked shamefaced and shambolic.

'Didn't you get my message?'

He couldn't meet her eye.

'I was out of signal.'

'You're lying.'

'I thought you wanted more wallpaper paste or something . . .'

She turned away from him and closed her eyes.

'How was I supposed to know?'

'They phoned you from here. The nurse told me she'd spoken to you and you were too drunk to understand what she was saying.'

'It was a bad line. I was with clients. I'm sorry, Belinda.' He sat on the edge of the bed next to her and patted her awkwardly. 'Look at you. I told you to take it easy.'

No, you didn't, she thought.

'Still, as long as you're all right. No harm done, eh? You'll just have to slow down a bit.'

She stared at him. He didn't know. He'd blundered in still drunk – she could smell it on him – and he didn't have a clue. He looked down at her, his face red and sweaty.

'Charlie.'

'What?'

She could only whisper it. 'I've lost the baby.'

He gaped at her. She shut her eyes. Where once she would have longed for his arms around her, now she wanted him as far away from her as possible. There was no comfort he could give her. Nothing would fill the emptiness she felt. She felt as if she could fall into the hole left inside her where her baby had been. She wanted to follow him, or her, into oblivion.

*

She took a fortnight off work to recuperate. She felt washed out and weak. She drifted around the house, getting on her own nerves. She didn't feel like herself at all. She didn't know how to address what had happened. She told herself she had to come to terms with the loss of the baby, but it was overwhelming. She sat in the nursery-that-wasn't and endless tears seemed to leak from her eyes when she didn't even think she was crying.

She could get pregnant again, she had been told, but with the loss of one tube it might take time. And she wasn't to try straight away.

She didn't want to try. The very thought of Charlie touching her was repulsive. She was shocked at how their loss had highlighted Charlie's shortcomings. Every day he seemed to become more and more useless. How on earth she could have thought he was capable of anything more than pouring a glass of wine was beyond her.

One night he got stuck into a bottle of gin in the kitchen and got even drunker than usual.

'It's all my fault,' he told her. 'The baby. I was scared. I didn't know how to be a dad. I . . .' He looked at her, and she knew she didn't want to hear what he was going to say. 'I wished that you weren't pregnant. I kept thinking maybe it was a false pregnancy or something. I made you lose the baby. Because I didn't want it!'

She looked at him, snivelling in the kitchen, his eyes red, his hair a mess. He couldn't have been further away from the twinkling, charming man she had met less than two years ago.

'Charlie,' she said, 'I had an ectopic pregnancy. It was nothing to do with you or what you thought about it. You didn't "make" it happen. So don't try and steal my own bloody miscarriage from me. It is not all about you.'

She went upstairs and that night he didn't come up to bed. She had no idea where he slept and nor did she care.

She had only been back to work for a week when Richard Mortlake called her in to his office. She hadn't given any details about what had happened to her – just the euphemism 'women's problems' was enough to make them recoil and not ask any more questions. She thought perhaps he was going to quibble about the time she had taken off, but she had a doctor's note.

He wasn't quibbling. Instead, he told her she was being made redundant.

'It's this bloody property crash. I'm sorry. But we can't afford to keep you on. We've only had one sale in the past fortnight.'

It didn't occur to him that there might be a correlation between her absence and the lack of sales. She looked at his smug face as he delivered the news. The Mortlakes would be all right. He was keeping his useless oaf of a son on. Of course he was. Did he know how many times she had covered Giles's back? How much she had taught him? Didn't he know that without her Giles was a glorified office boy? He had no rapport with clients, or any feel for what a property might be worth unless it was bog standard.

She wasn't going to go without a fight.

'I suppose this is about you not wanting to pay for maternity leave.'

Richard paled. 'What?'

'I overheard your conversation,' she said. 'When Giles said he thought I'd got a bun in the oven?'

She smiled at him sweetly.

Richard looked horrified.

'You must have misheard,' he blustered.

'No, I didn't. And I did have a 'bun in the oven'. So I think you might find if I took this to a tribunal—'

'Oh God, don't do that.'

'Well, in that case, shall we discuss my pay off?'

Richard swallowed.

'I imagine you will be quite generous?'

'That's blackmail.'

'How is it blackmail?' Belinda stared him out.

'You're taking advantage of the situation.'

She shrugged. She knew she had the upper hand.

'It's up to you. I'm quite happy to sue you if I have to.'

When she saw the size of her redundancy cheque, she laughed for the first time in weeks.

She didn't tell Charlie about her redundancy. She wanted to bide her time while she thought about what to do. And she didn't want him to know about her pay-off. She knew if Charlie got wind of it, he'd rip through it in no time. He didn't notice she wasn't going to work.

They were both in the same house, but they might have been in different countries. They were prowling around, lying to each other, biding their time, until something happened. Something would, Belinda knew. They were going to lose everything. She could feel it in her bones. But she didn't have any fight. The loss of her baby had taken her spirit with it. She didn't care about anything any more.

*

She was right to trust her instincts. The wine shop went bust. Of course it did.

'It's not my fault,' said Charlie, and Belinda couldn't even be bothered to roll her eyes, because of course it wasn't. Nothing was ever his fault.

She felt defeated. Gradually, everything she had worked and fought for was being eradicated. The baby was gone, her marriage was going – and she knew the house was next. Without her salary or his contribution, they couldn't pay the mortgage. She was struggling to get work with another estate agent because they were all in the same boat with the property crash, finding it impossible to sell houses, so no one was taking on new staff.

She wanted to wipe the slate clean and start again. This was purgatory, both of them in the house they had once loved and now couldn't afford.

They were skirting round each other in the kitchen one night. She had made a half-hearted effort to cook a spaghetti bolognese, but as she twisted her fork into her pasta and looked across the table at him staring glumly down into his bowl, she realised she wouldn't care if she never saw him again.

'I want a divorce,' she told him.

He stared at her. 'We'll have to sell the house.'

She wanted to throw the Parmesan grater at him. 'Of course we'll have to sell the house, Charlie. We'll have to sell it anyway. Neither of us is bringing any money in. You haven't even noticed I haven't been to work for the past month. That's how interested you are in me.'

He chewed on a string of spaghetti as he considered her words. She could see the cogs whirring in his brain.

'I'm entitled to half. It was me who found this place. If it wasn't for me . . .'

Me me me me me.

She got up and walked out of the room. She couldn't trust herself. She had no respect left for Charlie. How could she not have noticed that everything was always about him?

When they sold the house she walked away with fifteen hundred pounds. That was all that was left, after all the money she had put in – the deposit and the stamp duty – never mind all the work she'd done and the materials and labour she had paid for, because prices had plummeted since they had bought it.

She felt sick when the solicitor phoned to tell her the final amount and transfer the money into her account. What a fool she had been. She was never, ever going to let anyone put her in that position again. She was never going to be answerable to anyone either. From now on, she was going to do everything for herself and no one else.

She still had her redundancy money, which she'd squirrelled away. When Charlie had queried if she had got any, she faced him head on.

'Don't you dare have the gall to even ask,' she said, keeping her voice level even though she wanted to scream. 'Don't you *dare*.'

She had plans for that money. She wasn't ready to put it into action yet, because Belinda was watching and waiting for the right time and the right place.

The day they handed over the key to the house, she thought her heart was going to break. Charlie had vanished. The wine shop was abandoned. He hadn't come home for a week. She walked through the empty house, saying goodbye to each room. She still felt pride at what she had accomplished.

As she locked the front door for the last time, she looked up at The High House. She felt a million times worse about the loss of her home than the breakdown of her marriage. She turned and walked back up towards the high street with her head held high. No one could take away her achievement. She still had her wits and her unfailing courage. There might be a property crash, but no way was it going to last forever. And when things picked up, she was going to be ready.

'I'm so sorry about your baby,' said Natasha. 'I'm so sorry.' She was in tears. 'Thank you for being honest with me. I really appreciate it.'

Belinda smiled at her. Throughout her tale, she'd managed to stay composed. It was almost as if it had all happened to someone else.

'What do you think you'll do?'

Natasha looked around the office.

'I want to achieve. I want to do something I'm proud of. Like you have.'

'Do you think you'll go ahead with the retreat?'

'I need to think it over.'

'Of course.'

'I don't know if I'm strong enough to do it on my own.'

Belinda looked at her. 'Of course you are,' she told her. 'Of *course* you are. You can do, and be, anything you want. Don't let him break you. He didn't break me.' She leaned forward, her eyes shining. 'I got the last laugh, you know.'

*

She'd found the phone number she wanted amongst the pile of paperwork Charlie had left behind.

'I'm interested in the lease on the Peasebrook Wine Company premises. I gather they've been vacated?'

'Yes,' said the landlord. 'I can't get in touch with the owner. Slippery bugger hasn't paid his rent for six months. It might take a while to sort things out . . .'

'I can wait,' said Belinda. 'It's perfect for what I want.'

She screwed the landlord down on the price of a ten-year lease, because she knew he'd have difficulty letting it to anyone else in the current climate. And three weeks later, she took immense pleasure in changing the sign from *The Peasebrook Wine Company* to *Belinda Baxter Estate Agents*.

Natasha stared at her in admiration. 'You are a legend. And do you know what? You're going to meet somebody else, somebody amazing,' she said. 'You're going to meet somebody amazing and it will all be all right. I can feel it here.'

She placed her hand on her heart. Belinda smiled.

'Well, you too,' she said.

Charlie would probably see what she'd done today as revenge. But it wasn't. It was about protecting Natasha from going through what she'd had to go through.

Belinda was very aware she might have jeopardised the sale of Hunter's Moon. She felt a little bit sick, but it was out of her hands. All house sales were precarious, she reminded herself. All house sales had the potential to fall through at any minute. But she felt guilty that she hadn't been more transparent from the outset and given the Willoughbys the heads-up on Charlie. She'd wanted them to have the money. It hadn't been for her own gain. And Leo had reassured her she'd done the right thing.

Bloody money. The root of all evil.

33

1967

After the party, midsummer slid quietly into late summer: a shimmering August that turned the lawns brown.

Margot drifted around the house and garden in a state of torpor. Sally found her behaviour troubling and unsettling. She was distracted, moody, aimless. But at least there were no dramas. She seemed to have learned her lesson, after the swimming pool incident.

Dai, conversely, seemed to have come right out of his shell. He had even entered some of his vegetables into the village fete, which seemed to drive Margot into an utter fury.

'Can't you do something useful?' she hissed. 'Best fucking onions?'

'*Onion skins very thin, Mild weather coming in,*' was all Dai could say in reply.

She stared at him. 'I don't know what's happened to you.'

'I don't know what's happened to *you*,' he replied, and stomped off to the greenhouse.

Sally just felt sad for them. She knew he loved Margot. She had seen his panic that night. And she thought Margot loved Dai too.

There was one evening of respite, when Annie got her exam results, and got top marks in every subject.

Sally cooked Annie's favourite supper – roast chicken and mashed potato and cauliflower cheese – and made her a cake with twelve candles on, one for each subject. Margot ended up sitting on Dai's knee, hanging on to his neck and gazing up at him.

'Aren't we clever?' she said. 'Isn't she clever? Our little Afterthought.'

Sally suspected her amiable mood was down to getting the combination of pills and alcohol she was taking exactly right for once.

'Do I get a reward?' asked Annie.

'Of course, darling,' said Margot. 'What about a lovely diamond? Buy your clever daughter a diamond.'

She prodded Dai, who frowned. Margot knew he didn't have the means to buy Annie a diamond.

'I don't want a diamond,' said Annie. 'I want to go to the grammar school. Not horrible Larkford.'

Margot sighed. 'Not that again.'

She changed the subject as quickly as she could. Sally saw Annie's face fall, and felt sorry for her. She'd been a little quiet lately, not her usual self. She just read and slept. Sally supposed it was what she needed, after all that revision. She'd worked jolly hard.

She was glad to have Phoebe to distract her. Phoebe had taken her under her wing. The two of them went up to London on Saturdays, trawling the boutiques and cafés of Chelsea and Kensington, looking at what the girl on the street was wearing. Although she just wore her ordinary clothes at Hunter's Moon, Sally had begun to enjoy getting dressed up in the height of fashion and being admired when they went out. The two of them looked good together – Sally blonde and Phoebe dark. Sometimes they went out to night clubs and danced all night long. Alexander could get them in anywhere they wanted to go.

Sally learnt a lot from observation. What people were really like: the kind who were just out to have fun and the kind who were destructive. There were drugs, sometimes, though she and Phoebe never got mixed up in that crowd. And sex. There was a lot of sex going on around them. She often found herself the centre of attention. She was constantly being asked out and flirted with. But something inside was holding her back from making any commitment. She danced, had the occasional kiss, but no one interested her.

Alexander quite often came with them, but he had kept his distance from Sally since the party. He was still lovely to her, but they were never alone together, and she suspected that was deliberate on his part. He'd just been swept up in the moment that evening. He was still funny and sweet and kind and attentive, but he treated her no differently than he did Phoebe. Almost like a big brother. If anything he was protective, just like Ray and Colin would be.

And he was very busy. She could see that. The catalogue they'd made, with Sally on the cover, had got Phoebe taken on by three boutiques in London, so she was flat out sewing and getting more designs made for the next season. And the Lucky Charms were on tour, so he had to go away quite a lot.

*

Margot knew she was being a monster. She hated herself. She had lost control of everything and she didn't know what to do.

Every morning, she woke and wished she hadn't. Her palms felt sweaty, her heart felt heavy and her head was pounding.

Today she could hear cheery whistling. She slid out of bed and crept over to the window, squinting as she opened the curtain and sunlight streamed in. She winced. Whenever she surveyed the garden, snippets of the party came back to her. Most of them she didn't want to replay in her mind. Especially her finale. Everybody seemed to make such a fuss.

She could see Dai in the garden, trundling his bloody wheelbarrow. It was him whistling. What did he have to be so bloody happy about? She watched as Sally came out of the house and bounced over to him. He disappeared off and reappeared with a trug full of vegetables. Sally looked as if he had given her the Crown jewels, and he beamed with pride. The exchange made Margot feel sick. Why? Was she jealous? And if so, what of?

She never made Dai smile like that. Not any more.

She crept back to bed, fishing about in the drawer of the bedside table for her happy tablets. Well, not her happy tablets. Her not-utterly-suicidal tablets. Maybe she'd take two. That would take the edge off.

Annie came creeping in. She had been like a little shadow around her since the party, anxious and concerned. She sat on the edge of Margot's bed.

'Mummy, do I have to go back to Larkford? Please can't I go to school in Oxford? I want to stay here and look after you and I won't be any trouble. I *hate* it there. I really do.'

Margot couldn't think. She couldn't face making any decisions. And if she was honest, she didn't want Annie trailing around after her. It wasn't that she didn't love her. She adored her. It was just that she reminded her of how awful she was. What a bloody useless mother she'd been.

'But you did so well in your exams.' She stroked Annie's cheek. 'Stick it out, my darling. Only two more years.'

So Annie went back to school in September.

It was a couple of weeks into the term when Sally realised one Saturday that Annie hadn't got up by lunchtime, so Sally went into her bedroom to see if she was OK.

Annie was lying on her back staring at the ceiling.

'I'm pregnant,' she told Sally.

Sally could not have been more shocked. 'How?'

'The usual way.'

'I know but . . . who? Where? When? Oh darling.'

She threw her arms around the girl. Little Annie. It didn't seem possible.

'It was the party. The summer party. I planned it. I was determined to go back to school without my virginity. It's quite easy to get someone to do it to you, you know.'

Her little face was pale and earnest.

'I just thought if I lost my virginity I might become like the other girls at school. That maybe that was the missing piece of me. That maybe sleeping with someone would turn me into a somebody.'

'But you *are* a somebody. You're a very special somebody.'

'I'm not like everyone else. I don't care about clothes and make-up and what to do with my hair. I don't care about boys. I just don't!'

'It's OK.' Sally tried to stroke her hair and reassure her.

'It was horrid. I don't see the point. Just a load of grunting and thrashing about and jabbing his stupid horrid *thing*!' She threw her arms out in despair. 'I mean, what is all the fuss about?'

'I think perhaps it's about finding the right person.'

Annie just shuddered, then lay back on her bed.

'What am I going to do?' Her voice was very small. *She* was very small.

'Sweetheart, you need to tell me who the father is.'

'Oh, just some boy at the party. I think he came with the band. I don't even know his name or where to find him.'

'Would Alexander know him?'

Annie sat up in alarm.

'If you tell Beetle, I will die. You mustn't tell him. You absolutely mustn't. Promise?'

Sally could tell by the tone in her voice that she meant it.

'I promise. I'll have a think about what to do. But I don't want you to be frightened. Whatever happens, I won't let anybody make you do anything you don't want to. Don't you want to tell your mum?'

'Absolutely the last person on the planet who should know about this is Mummy. Promise me you won't tell her. Swear?'

Why was she so afraid of her mother finding out? Sally thought Margot would take it in her stride. She wasn't some old-fashioned, judgemental harridan.

'The thing is, I don't want to get rid of it. I know I was a mistake. They call me The Afterthought, but really they should call me The Mistake.'

'Oh darling.' Sally wrapped her arms around the girl

and pulled her in tight. 'No one could think you were a mistake. No one.'

Annie went back to school on Sunday night and Sally promised her they would talk about it the next weekend and make a plan.

Several times she went to talk to Margot, even though it would be breaking Annie's confidentiality, but Margot was totally preoccupied and seemed to look straight through Sally whenever she spoke to her. She was far too embarrassed to talk to Dai about it. And she knew Alexander wouldn't be able to cope. He would want to know who it was, and would want to go after them and probably kill them, and that really would be shutting the barn door.

In the end, she swore Phoebe to secrecy, because she couldn't think of the right thing to do and two heads were better than one.

Phoebe clapped her hand over her mouth when she heard. 'Oh the poor darling!'

'You mustn't tell her I told you.'

'Of course not. Maybe we should go and talk to Doctor Ponder?' Phoebe grimaced. 'Though I can't imagine talking to him about something like that. Should we tell Mum?'

'I promised Annie we wouldn't.'

'Mum would know what to do, though. I know you think she's as mad as a snake, but she can be good in a crisis.' Phoebe bit her lip. 'Well, other people's. She's not very good at her own.'

Sally sighed. 'Let's talk to Annie at the weekend. I'll have to tell her I've told you.'

*

It was Friday morning when Sally answered the phone in the hall at Hunter's Moon. She heard pips, and then Annie sounding very small indeed.

'Sally? I don't feel very well. I wonder if you could come and get me a bit early. But don't say anything to anyone. Just say it's a tummy bug.'

She was as white as a sheet when Sally collected her, and barely spoke on the way home. As they turned into the drive, she spoke.

'We don't have to worry any more, by the way.'

Sally stopped the car and stared at her. 'What?'

'The one good thing about Larkford is people always know people.'

'What have you done? What people?'

Annie took in a sharp breath and held her tummy. Sally frowned. Annie was in pain. Not feeling sick because she was pregnant.

'Darling?'

'It's OK because I went to someone very, very posh in Harley Street. Not a knitting needle job. I took some money out of my Post Office savings.' She frowned. 'It's funny because someone had taken some money out of it. Fifty pounds! Who would have done that?'

She seemed far more concerned about the money than what had happened to her.

'Oh God . . .' Sally's voice was strangled and there were tears pouring down her cheeks. 'Oh you poor darling. Why didn't you say? I would have come with you.'

'You wouldn't. You'd have stopped me. I know you would because you're a good person. And I'm not. I'm an awful person.' Annie shut her eyes and leant her head back. 'I just want to go to sleep for a week.'

'Let's get you into your room. Everyone's out. Have you got everything you need? Do I need to go to the chemist?'

'I've got bags of STs. And some pills.'

Sally got her up the stairs as quickly as she could before anyone saw her. If anyone was going to find out about it, it would be when Annie was fit enough to deal with the aftermath.

Luckily she had made all the beds earlier in the week, so she got her into a clean nighty and tucked her into fresh sheets, then brought her up a hot water bottle to hold against her tummy. She thought it would probably soothe it. She felt furious for poor little Annie. She told Margot that it was a stomach bug she had picked up at school. Margot just wrinkled her nose and said she hoped *she* didn't get it.

Annie went back to school the following Monday, with strict instructions from Sally to phone if she felt unwell.

The atmosphere in the house felt dark as the evening drew nearer. Sally and Dai were sharing a pot of tea in the kitchen and making a list of seeds they wanted to buy for next year from the catalogue when Margot came in, querulous and spoiling for a fight.

Sally looked at Margot and remembered she'd taken a call from the bursar of Larkford that morning.

'The bursar phoned this morning. I think you've forgotten to pay the school fees.'

'How is that any of your business?' Margot banged her teacup down. 'How dare you discuss my private affairs with the bursar?'

'I was just passing the message on.'

'You were prying.'

'No, I wasn't.'

'Margot. Leave the girl alone.' Dai shot his wife a warning scowl.

'No. I won't. I've got a few things to say, as it happens.' Margot pointed a finger at Sally. 'You've wormed your way into this family, haven't you? What are you hoping? That I'll leave and you can step into my shoes?'

'How dare you?' Sally's voice was low and trembling. She stood up and faced Margot. She wasn't afraid of her. 'You will not judge me. You are a terrible wife and you're a terrible mother. There are things going on under your nose that you have no idea about because you're only interested in yourself!'

She stopped. She mustn't say any more. She mustn't betray Annie.

'Oh, I know what's going on all right.' Margot pointed at Dai. 'He's besotted with you. He can't take his eyes off you. And you keep pandering to him. Snuggled up in the potting shed.'

'What?' said Sally. 'We're discussing radishes!'

'I saw you both at the party. If I hadn't come up the stairs, I know what would have happened. You must think I'm stupid.'

'I think you're a lot of things. Not stupid. But selfish. And uncaring. And—' She stopped as a thought occurred to her. 'Did you take that money out of Annie's savings account?'

She couldn't believe she'd said it. But she'd had enough of Margot's accusations.

'How dare you?' Margot's face was rigid with fury, her eyes blazing.

'You did. Didn't you? Because who else would it be?'

Margot shut her eyes and took a deep breath in. She opened her eyes again, and they had gone from blazing to icy.

'It was to pay you. Actually. Which was my mistake. I think you'd better go.'

'Yes,' said Sally. 'I think I had.'

'I'll telephone a taxi.'

'Where will she go?' Dai looked bewildered, unsure how the argument had escalated at such a furious rate.

'I don't care. But at least I won't have to look at you looking at her like a lovesick teenage boy.'

Dai stood up, towering over his wife.

'If I was in love with her, it wouldn't be a surprise – because she's the only person who cares about anyone or anything in this family. She's the glue that's been holding us together, and if you can't see that then you *are* stupid.'

Sally stepped between them. She was quite calm.

'Dai. It's fine. Please may I use the telephone to call my brothers? They can come and collect me from Paddington. It will only take me half an hour to pack.'

She ran out of the kitchen and up the stairs to her room.

Margot looked unsure of herself all of a sudden. She realised she had gone too far. But she was out of her depth. She was too afraid to back down.

In her room, Sally gathered her things together as quickly as she could. She couldn't keep this family together any more. She didn't have the strength. Everything was unravelling. Phoebe was in London. Alexander wasn't here – he was up in Nottingham or Northampton or somewhere with the Lucky Charms. Maybe it was best if she slipped away while he was gone, to avoid any awkward goodbyes.

Don't cry, Sally, she told herself. Margot Willoughby is not worth your tears.

An hour later a taxi drove up the drive and Sally put her case in the boot, then went round to the passenger seat.

Dai watched from the front steps.

'Oh, Margot,' he said. 'What have you done? What have you done?'

34

The day before the contracts were due to be exchanged on Hunter's Moon, Belinda was scouring the local paper and the Internet for houses.

Everything was in place for the sale to go through. It hadn't fallen through as she'd feared and in her head she silently cheered Natasha on, delighted she'd found the strength to go it alone.

The High House had completed the day before, which meant the money had been released and her fund had reached its target. She had been to view several houses in Peasebrook but none of them was quite right. She had waited so long she was only going to accept perfection.

Cathy was frowning at her computer screen.

'What is it?' asked Belinda, on alert.

Cathy grimaced, pressed a button, then reached over for the paper on which the email she had been reading had been printed. She handed it to Belinda.

It was from Natasha's solicitor.

'We regret to inform you that our clients no longer wish to proceed with the purchase of Hunter's Moon.'

That was it. No further explanation. Belinda knew that she didn't need one. She knew perfectly well why it wasn't going through. Her heart sank. She'd let the Willoughbys down.

'I'm so sorry,' said Cathy. 'Do you want me to start phoning the other interested parties?'

Belinda nodded. 'Let's see if we can salvage it.' She grabbed the spreadsheet with all the other offers on it. 'People are going to drop their price if they know we're desperate, so don't make it sound as if we are.'

'Are you going to tell the Willoughbys?'

'Not yet.' Belinda knew this was why she was good at her job. This was when she earned her commission. She was a firefighter.

By eight o'clock that evening, she was starting to feel defeated. She'd phoned every single person who had come to the open house. Most of them were pursuing other properties. Two were going to get back to her, but she didn't hold out much hope.

There was a tiny little bit of her that was pleased that Hunter's Moon might have a stay of execution. That the Willoughbys might have one last summer there. This deal might have collapsed, but she would be able to re-market it and get a buyer without much trouble. Just not in time to save the purchase of the Digby Hall property.

An email pinged into her inbox. It was from Natasha.

Dear Belinda,

I'm so sorry to pull out of buying Hunter's Moon. I was so inspired by you, and I really thought I was going to realise my dream. But I thought carefully about it and I decided it was too soon for such a big commitment. I need to discover more about myself and who I am and what I could be. Hopefully one day someone as brave as you. I know you will find someone else to buy Hunter's Moon. It is a very special house.

    With much love

    Natasha

It was such a sweet and heartfelt email, and Belinda could see Natasha had made the right decision. She composed a short reply wishing her the best of luck.

Then she leafed through the Hunter's Moon file, looking at Bruce's photographs. The fountain, the walled garden, the swimming pool, the little coach house . . .

She stopped and looked more closely at the photograph. She drew out the floor plan and looked at the measurements. Then she looked at the ordnance survey map where the boundaries of Hunter's Moon were outlined, tracing her finger along the lane.

She remembered Sally showing her inside the dusty cottage where Margot had written all her books. In the brochure she had described it as 'brimming with potential for a home office, party barn or ancillary accommodation.' It was small, but with the adjoining garages added in there was quite a lot of floor space. What if . . .?

Her heart was thumping. She could feel the same tingle of excitement she had felt when she first saw The High House. The possibilities. The potential. Her imagination started to work. A large kitchen dining room in the garage with a mezzanine floor. Bi-fold doors leading out into the courtyard. It wouldn't be huge, but it would be the perfect size for a single career girl.

She gathered up the papers and left the office. She ran down to the high street, over the bridge and along to the old glove factory. She pressed Bruce's buzzer, praying he was in.

'Babe! Come on up.' He sounded pleased to hear from her.

She went up to his apartment. He opened the door. She walked inside and stopped short. On the sofa was a woman, very tanned, with long dark hair. She was elegant and stylish in a very laid-back, arty way.

'I'm so sorry. I didn't know you had company.'

'Don't worry,' grinned Bruce. 'You know me. The more the merrier.'

The woman rolled her eyes and stood up, holding out her hand with a smile. 'Hi. I'm Martine.'

Belinda took her hand and looked between the two of them, but she didn't need to ask much. They had a glow that was unmistakeable. Bruce deserved someone lovely, and Martine looked more than capable of handling his capricious ways.

'I won't keep you long,' she said, pleased for her friend. 'I just want to pick your brains. I want you to tell me if I'm going mad.'

Belinda wasn't used to London traffic or London parking, but somehow she managed to navigate her way to Borough Market the next morning and nab a parking space in an NCP. She'd turned her idea over and over in her mind on the way up the motorway. It wasn't a flawless plan, but it ticked so many boxes she had to run it past him.

She ran through the market. She didn't have time to stop and look at all the enticing stalls, but she could smell roasting coffee and baking bread and bubbling paella all mixed up into one enticing scent. She searched the café fronts until she found the one she wanted, ran towards the door and pushed it open.

There he was, sitting at a table. He had a cup of coffee in front of him and was scrolling through his phone. He looked up and saw her, and he smiled and stood up.

'Thank you for agreeing to meet me.' Belinda flopped into the chair opposite, breathless from running.

'It's no problem. Can I get you a drink?'

She shook her head. 'Listen to what I've got to say first. I need to talk to you before I talk to your parents.'

'What's happened?'

'I'm afraid the sale has fallen through. The buyers have pulled out.'

'Oh shit.'

'This is exactly what I was worried would happen when I spoke to you. I'm really sorry.'

'Listen – it wasn't your fault. It could just as easily have gone through. Selling houses is a precarious business. It's a shame, but it's not as if there aren't other people keen to buy.'

'I know. I just don't know if they can come through in time for your parents to get Digby Hall.'

Leo grinned ruefully. 'I don't know that's such a bad thing. My parents took me to see it. I just can't imagine them there. And maybe this will give us time as a family to work out the best plan.' He leant his head in one hand. 'They were so determined to do this on their own, I think they rushed into things.'

'I have got an idea.' Belinda pulled out the file and put it on the table. 'I wanted to run it past you first.'

She opened the file and pulled out the Hunter's Moon

brochure, leafing to the page that showed the plot and the boundaries on a large-scale map. She spread it on the table in front of him.

'We know the main reason your parents are selling is to release some capital. I don't get the feeling they want to leave Hunter's Moon at all. They did a very good job of trying to convince themselves the new place was what they wanted, but I don't think either of them were that keen.'

'No,' said Leo. 'It was very much a means to an end.'

'OK. Listen,' said Belinda. 'Yes, the differential in price between Hunter's Moon and the new place would have left your parents with quite a bit of money to play with. But bear in mind they would also have high annual maintenance fees at Digby Hall. All those facilities aren't thrown in for nothing. And a big whack of stamp duty.'

'I'm not sure where this is going?'

Belinda paused for a moment. This was going to be make or break. Leo would either think she was mad or a genius.

'Do you think they'd be interested in me buying the coach house off them?'

'What?'

'I'm looking to buy my own place. If I converted the coach house it would be perfect for me. It's just the right size. And it's quite separate from the house.' She drew a blue line on the plans. 'You could put in a drive around the back, coming off the lane a little further up. So it would be completely cut off and you wouldn't notice I was there . . .'

She trailed off. Leo was staring at her.

'Carry on.'

'Obviously you'd have to get an independent valuation and not take my word for it. But selling the coach house would release about the same amount of cash. They could stay at Hunter's Moon and have money for any help they need, or any alterations they want to make.'

Leo sipped his coffee, tracing his finger over the plans in front of them.

'Sorry,' said Belinda. 'I know this is a bit out of the blue. But I wanted to talk it over with you first.'

'I know Dad doesn't want to leave Hunter's Moon. And I know he feels guilty about making Mum leave. She pretends it's fine, but I know she's gutted.'

He picked up the pen Belinda had been using and fiddled with it.

'I've been trying to reorganise my business so I can come down every weekend. I can come down Friday to Monday. Take the pressure off Mum. Sort out stuff that needs doing in the garden.' He swallowed. 'Maybe even move down full-time when things . . .'

He stopped. He was a little choked up, and Belinda saw the glitter of a tear.

She reached out her hand across the table and touched his. She held it there for a moment while he composed himself. After a few moments he turned his hand over and took hers. He squeezed it, tightly. And he didn't let go.

'I think it's an amazing idea,' he said.

She gave a shaky laugh. 'You know us wily estate agents. Always coming up with a plan to save the deal.'

He was staring at her. She blushed and looked away, unsure of herself.

'Shall we go and ask your parents what they think?'

Leo nodded.

'Can I have a lift with you? I can get the train back tomorrow morning.' He was still holding her hand.

'Of course.'

She took her hand away, gathered up all the paperwork and put it back in her bag. 'Ready?'

They fell into step together as they left the café. And as they walked down the road towards the car park, it seemed the most natural thing in the world for Belinda to put her arm in his. It was unspoken, but something had passed between them in the coffee shop.

The question stuck in her throat, but she had to ask it.

'Can I ask you something?'

'Of course.'

'Are you seeing anyone at the moment?'

He looked puzzled. 'You mean like a psychiatrist?'

She couldn't help laughing. 'No. I mean like a girl. A woman.'

'No. Not for a while, to be honest.'

'Only when you were in my office, when you brought me the flowers, you were going to see someone that night.' She had to be careful with her tone. She didn't want to sound too needy or hectoring.

'Was I?' He screwed up his face, trying to remember. 'Annie. That was my aunt. I was going to see Annie.' He gave her a nudge with his elbow. 'Idiot.' He was laughing. 'Why do you ask?' His tone was teasing.

'No reason.' She put on an innocent face. She felt her heart skip a beat and remembered the fortune cookie.

A dark stranger is going to enter your life and bring you untold happiness . . .

*

Sally and Alexander were alarmed at first when Leo and Belinda turned up together. But it took less than half an hour to explain Belinda's idea.

'I know it's not ideal, breaking up the property like this. But it can be quite separate. It's not as if you'd have a shared drive. And you'll still have some of the garages for your own use.'

When they'd agreed that Leo would arrange for an independent valuation of the coach house, Leo and Sally went to the kitchen to fetch some wine to toast the new beginning.

Alexander was sitting in his chair by the fire. He smiled at Belinda.

'You know, you remind me so much of Sally,' said Alexander. 'She was the one who rescued Hunter's Moon all those years ago. We nearly lost it then. In the autumn of 1967.'

'Tell me,' said Belinda, fascinated. She longed to hear the history of the house – she could see from the photos that were dotted around that it was a house of many stories.

Alexander sighed. 'It was awful at the time. My mother had a nervous breakdown. None of us had any idea what to do. The only one of any of us who ever had any common sense was Sally . . .'

35

1967

Alexander raged when he came back the next day and found out what Margot had done. He was even more angry than Dai had been.

'What were you thinking? She's the only person with a brain in this house. The only person who ever has a clue about anything.'

Margot just sat at the table looking blank.

'Darling, housekeepers are two a penny—'

Alexander thumped the table. Margot jumped.

'She was more than a housekeeper! She was . . .'

He cast about for the words.

'She was an angel.'

Margot just laughed. 'Oh God, don't tell me you're besotted too?'

Alexander put his face right up close to his mother's.

'She's worth a million of you.'

'Oh, right, so what I do counts for nothing. I only keep the roof over your head. Pay for everything. Including your ministering angel . . .'

Alexander picked up the glass in front of Margot. He stopped himself just in time from throwing its contents over her. Instead, he sniffed it.

He set it back on the table.

And he turned and left the room.

Outside, Alexander jumped into the Mini. By some miracle there was half a tank of petrol.

He felt sick with fear. Sally couldn't have gone. What was his mother thinking? And his useless father, standing by and letting it happen.

He realised he had set off without a map, but he thought he could remember the way to Knapford. Please let her have gone home, he thought. Please don't let her have headed off into London, where he might never find her.

In the kitchen, Margot was raging at Dai.

'You have no *idea* of the pressure I've been under all these years. I don't just pull those books like magic out of a hat. It's hard work. It's *bloody* hard work. And all I get from any of you is sarcastic remarks about how useless I am. But you don't mind the lifestyle and the parties and the *house*.'

This last word was on the borderline of hysterical. She was pulling open a drawer, digging around to find what she was looking for, hidden amongst some old table mats. She threw a letter at him.

'Well, there. The house is being taken off us. There's no money left. I haven't been paying the mortgage. The bank want it back. So you are all right. I *am* useless.'

She stormed out of the room.

Dai picked up the letter. It was from the bank manager. He could only pick out a few key words, his hands were shaking so much, but they were enough to show Margot was speaking the truth.

The bank was taking Hunter's Moon off them.

*

Alexander found his way to Knapford. He screeched up the high street, searching for the front of Huxtable's, trying to remember exactly how far up it was. There – with its red-and-white striped awning. He abandoned the car and went running into the shop.

Colin and Ray were behind the counter in their white coats and hats. They looked up as Alexander came in.

'Sally.' He looked at them. 'Please tell me she's here.'

He could tell by the way the two of them looked at each other that she was.

'I need to see her.'

'Sorry, mate,' said Colin, who was holding a nasty looking cleaver.

Alexander knew he couldn't get past either of them to the door that led to the flat. They were big, strong blokes. He wouldn't have a hope.

'Please. There's been an awful mistake. My mother's not very well and she may have said something to upset Sally. But we need her.'

Ray shook his head. 'She's home now, mate. We need her too. She's staying here.'

'Can I at least talk to her?'

Colin pointed his thumb out of the door. 'Hop it.'

Alexander crossed his arms. 'I'm not going until I've seen her.'

The brothers looked at each other. Colin put down his knife carefully and Ray wiped his hands on his apron. They both came around to Alexander's side of the counter and stood one either side of him.

'We can do this the easy way or the hard way.'

They each put a hand on his elbows. He was going to

be pushed out of the door any minute. There was no point in even—

'Wait.'

The three of them turned to see Sally in the door of the flat.

'It's OK. I'll talk to him.'

She nodded her head towards the door. 'Come on,' she said to Alexander. Her arms were folded and she didn't have her usual sunny smile. She led him around to the alley that ran alongside the butcher's shop.

'I can't stay any longer,' she said. 'I can't cope with it. It's all too much.'

Alexander was aware of people watching him, but he didn't care. This was the most important speech of his life and he couldn't mess it up.

'Sally. We need you. You have to come back. I know Mum went a bit crazy but she didn't mean it. Not really. She needs help. She's gone off the rails. And I know we can't sort things out without you. We've always been a bit useless, all of us. But ever since you arrived, our lives have been so much better. You've made us better people. We all love you. I know we do. Even Mum, really. She just doesn't know how to show it. She's always been like that. We all love you and we all need you, Sally.'

He stopped for a moment to see her reaction. She chewed on her thumbnail.

'Sally?'

She nodded. Alexander leapt forward and hugged her.

'You won't regret it, Sal. I promise.'

Sally and Alexander got back to the house just as dusk was starting to fall.

'I'm sure Mum will apologise,' said Alexander. 'She's one of those people that forgets arguments in about five minutes, and she doesn't have a clue that what she's said might hurt someone.'

'She doesn't have to do that,' said Sally. 'That would be too embarrassing for words.'

But as they went into the kitchen, they could sense that something was terribly wrong. Dai was at the table, his head in his hands. He looked up.

'Your mother's gone,' he said. 'She says she's never coming back.'

36

1967

They waited all night at Hunter's Moon for Margot to come back, but there was no sign of her in the morning.

'It's not like her,' said Phoebe, who had turned up late in the evening. 'She usually calms down pretty quickly.'

She and Sally and Alexander were drinking tea in the kitchen. Dai came in, holding several bottles of pills.

'I found these hidden in the bedside cabinet,' he said. 'I knew she popped the odd pill to make her sleep, but this many?'

There were several different kinds, but no one knew quite what they were for.

'Well, at least if they were in the drawer, she can't take them,' said Alexander.

'It does explain a lot, though,' said Phoebe. 'She has been pretty unbalanced. If she's been mixing these up, and drinking.'

'It's the worry about the house,' said Dai. He looked distressed, and showed them the letter from the bank.

'There's lots of those,' said Sally. 'I kept telling her to open them.'

'Will we lose Hunter's Moon?' asked Phoebe.

'We need to find her,' said Dai. 'But where do we

start? She could be anywhere. Who knows how her mind works?'

'Let's go and have a look in her study,' said Sally to Alexander. 'We might find something in there.'

Sally and Alexander searched through the piles of letters on Margot's desk, and dug through the drawers. Dozens of bills and red letters spilled out. Alexander looked more and more worried as the full picture came to light.

'Look at this,' Sally held out a handwritten letter.

'*Following on from our meeting at the party,*' read Alexander. He frowned and scanned the rest of it. '*I would like to take you out for lunch* – who the hell's Terence Miller?'

'I don't know,' said Sally. 'But I think we should go and see him.'

'We can't tell dad. He'd be terribly upset.'

'Let's tell him we're going to see Niggle. Or her publisher.'

Alexander folded the letter up and put it in his pocket. 'Will you come with me? Phoebe and Dad can wait here in case she turns up.'

'Of course.'

'Thank God Mum took the Mini. We can take the Jag.'

Bloomsbury was quiet and dignified in the autumn sunshine as Alexander drove up and down, looking for a parking space.

'There's one,' said Sally. 'And there's number eleven.'

They parked and walked along to Terence Miller's house. They stood on the doorstep. Sally rang the bell, squeezing Alexander's arm for reassurance, and they waited, not sure what to expect.

A tall man in glasses answered.

'Mr Miller?' asked Sally.

'Yes.' He looked between the two of them, frowning.

'We're looking for Margot Willoughby.'

'My mother,' added Alexander. 'She's disappeared from home and we're very worried about her.'

His frown deepened. 'Well, she's not here . . .'

'We found this, in her study.' Alexander held out the letter. 'It's from you.'

Terence scanned the lines. 'Yes.'

Alexander was frowning. Who was this man and what did he mean to his mother?

'Were you having an affair?'

Terence raised his eyebrows.

'No. I've got a perfectly lovely wife who I feel no need to be unfaithful to.'

'I think Alexander's a bit upset.' Sally felt the need to apologise. 'We just hoped you might have some idea where she was?'

'I'm afraid not. The last time I saw her was at her party. We've spoken on the phone a few times. We talk about work. That really is all there is to it.' He paused. He was thinking. 'Although there is somewhere she might be. I offered her the use of my hut any time she wanted it. At Greystone Beach. You could try there.'

Sally and Alexander looked at each other. 'It's worth a try,' said Sally. 'Could you give us directions?'

Terence drew them a rough map with a pencil and paper. 'It will take you about two hours to get there.'

'Not the way I drive,' said Alexander, who intended to put his foot down all the way.

*

The shingles were like ice: a freezing cold that worked its way right into her bones, gnawing at them, but she was too tired to care. She wondered about the imprint she would leave if she got up – the smooth dips where her shoulders, her hips, her calves had sunk in, leaving a perfect cast in the grey pebbles.

She had no intention of getting up, though. Her head throbbed from the bottle of wine she had drunk. She had hoped it might stop her thinking. But on the contrary it had made her think more. It seemed it was as impossible to stop thinking as it was to stop breathing.

She lay as still as she could and imagined pulling the sea over her head, like a blanket, shutting her eyes and giving in to sleep – but it wouldn't be just sleep. It would be something darker and deeper. And it would be forever. What a delicious thought.

How easy would it be? Could she just breathe it in, that soft water that was whispering to her? Could she let it fill her lungs until she breathed no more? Or would it hurt? She didn't want it to hurt. The whole point was for the pain to stop. She couldn't understand why she couldn't make it go away. She couldn't even describe it, but it held her down, the pain, as if her pockets were full of the stones she lay on. She couldn't push it away, no matter what she tried.

Everything was in ruins. Her career. Her marriage. Her family. Even her house. Everything she had spent her life fighting for had fallen apart. She couldn't do it any longer. There were too many obstacles and not enough hope. It was a relief, to realise she could give up. Sweet relief. And no doubt everyone else would feel the same, once they found out. It was the right thing to do for everyone.

She felt the first waves at her feet, kissing her toes and then running away. The waves would return, braver and braver, inching up her body. Maybe she should get up, she thought, but she didn't have the will or the strength. She gave a half-smile. As endings went, it was suitably romantic, though if it were one of her books, a shadow would be cast over her any minute, and she would look up in to the smouldering dark eyes of a fisherman who would scoop her up in his arms and carry her off to his cottage where they would fall madly in love and live happily ever after . . .

Maybe her death would herald a rise in sales? Niggle would be happy. Dear old Niggle. He'd done his best but it wasn't enough, and most of it was nothing to do with him. Not his responsibility. There was only so much you could ask of one person, and she had asked more than she should of him over the years.

She mustn't think about people. Thinking about people would make this too hard. She must think about nothing. Because that was all she wanted. To think about nothing, feel nothing, be nothing . . .

The waves were lapping her ankles now. How long it would take she had no idea. Besides, she was falling asleep, what with the wine and the pills and the tiredness, the all-consuming tiredness.

With luck, it would all be over by dusk.

She could hear nothing but the pounding of the waves. But then there was another sound. Footsteps on shingle, crunching towards her. It must be her fantasy fisherman.

But then she heard a cry, and her mother's instinct kicked in. Who was it? Phoebe? Annie? Alexander? But there was nothing she could do. She couldn't sit up. She was so cold. She was so very cold.

She looked up. She could see faces looming over her. 'Beetle?'

She managed a smile. And then she closed her eyes.

37

1967

Margot could sense somebody in the room. She didn't want to wake up. She was so deliciously cosy and warm. She had never thought she would be warm again. Whoever it was, was sitting on the edge of her bed. She stirred and turned over. Then opened her eyes. The light was bright. It must be daytime. She had no idea of the time, or how long she had slept.

It was Sally. She was holding out a cup, smiling.

'Beef tea.'

'Oh,' said Margot. She didn't have the energy to sit up. 'Thank you.'

She reached out a hand and touched Sally's arm. 'Put it on the bedside table.'

'I'm not going until you drink it.'

She knew that tone of voice. It was the voice Sally used when she wasn't going to take no for an answer.

'Let me put some pillows behind you and you can sit up.'

How could she be so weak? It was such a struggle. But eventually she managed it, and when she'd had a few sips of the tea – it was delicious – she felt stronger. Her head was starting to clear.

She was surprised to find that she could think straight. Although she had lots of questions.

'Where is everyone?'

'They're all waiting to come and see you. When you're ready.'

'Oh, yes please.' She wanted to see them, all of them. 'Do I look a fright?'

'You look very pale. Do you want lipstick?'

'Oh, I don't know that it matters. Does it?'

'Not at all.'

'I feel as if I've been asleep for weeks.'

'Three days, off and on. You were very lucky not to get pneumonia. We had to take you straight to hospital.'

Sally looked out of the window. It was there, in the hospital corridor, while they were waiting for the doctor to see Margot, that Alexander had taken her in his arms, had told her—

'I can't remember anything,' Margot said.

'You don't need to at the moment. You just need to rest.'

Margot looked around the room. 'Where's Dai? I need Dai.'

Suddenly, she did. She needed his big, bear presence and his comforting arms.

'I'll send him in,' said Sally.

Margot couldn't believe that Dai wanted to see her. She had a dim memory of saying terrible things to him. But all he wanted to do was hold her.

'Don't ever run away again, you.' He held her tight and kissed her head. 'Why didn't you tell me, Margot? I know you think I'm useless but I could have helped.'

'It was all too awful. And it was all my fault.'

'No. It was everyone's. We weren't pulling together. We were all in our own worlds.'

'The house,' said Margot. Memories were coming back to her gradually. She sat up in panic. 'What about the house?'

'Hey. Calm down, cariad.' His voice was soothing. 'I've sorted it all. Niggle came down yesterday and we had a meeting with the bank.'

'You did that?'

'I can wheel and deal when I want to.' Dai grinned. 'The agency have given the bank some money, offset against your future earnings.'

'Oh.' Margot's face clouded. 'But I can't write. I can't write any more.'

'Of course you can,' said Dai. 'Niggle's going to come and talk to you about it, when you're better. But really, you just need structure and discipline and a routine and not to start guzzling wine at ridiculous hours.'

Margot looked at him, horrified. 'Are you going to be my jailer?'

'If you can't do it by yourself. Yes.'

Margot was quiet for a moment.

'I love you, you know,' she said. 'I'm not sure I've been a terribly good wife.'

'Margot,' he said. 'I love you because you're crazy and mad. I'd be bored witless if you were dutiful and docile.' He smiled proudly. 'I've gone and got myself a job.'

Margot couldn't have been more shocked. 'An actual job?'

'I'm helping out in the gardens up at Peasebrook

Manor. It's not a lot of money, of course. But I thought I should put something in the pot.' He wiggled his fingers at her. 'It turns out I've got quite green fingers.'

Margot wound her fingers through his.

'I know I'm much to blame for all of this,' said Dai gruffly. 'I've been a difficult sod. Too proud and too up my own arse.'

'Christ,' said Margot, 'I think I get the prize for difficult. If we're going to have a competition.' She squeezed his fingers. 'Where've you been sleeping?'

'In one of the spare rooms.'

'Come back, would you? I like feeling you next to me in bed. It makes me feel safe.'

Dai was too choked to say that yes, of course he would come back.

Little Annie was next. She held on to her mother and wouldn't let go.

'Beetle said you would have drowned,' she told her. 'He said the tide was coming in so fast, you wouldn't have had a hope.'

Margot's memory was hazy. She had a dim idea that Greystone Beach came into the picture, but that was about it. 'Let's not think about it. Tell me something nice.'

Annie thought about it. 'I don't suppose you're interested in parsnips, much?'

'If they are parsnips you've grown, darling, then yes, I am.'

'You can remember I'm doing A levels, can't you? English, French and History. We're doing *Jude the Obscure* and it's just so sad. I could come and read it to you if you like. Anyone who reads *Jude the Obscure* will always feel better about life. It will cheer you up no end, because you'll know how lucky you are.'

'That would be lovely.'

Annie looked at her mother. She stood up and went to the dressing table. She came back with a lipstick.

'You really had better put this on, Mummy, or you'll frighten everyone.'

Phoebe was fizzing and bubbling with excitement.

'They want to put some of my clothes in a fashion show. In Chelsea. It's in a month's time. Please say you'll be better for it.'

'If I have to be wheeled in, I'll be there.'

'I'm nervous, though, Mum. If I bring all the things I've made up here, will you tell me what you think? Tell me if you think my clothes are awful.'

'They won't be. We'll have a dry run. Here. A fashion show at Hunter's Moon.'

Alexander was last.

'My lovely boy.' Margot's eyes were fluttering with tiredness by now. Her lids felt as heavy as lead, but she wanted to hold his hand and listen to him.

'Mum. There's something I need to talk to you about. It's about Sally.'

'Mmmm.'

'Are you listening? Because we need her here, and there's one way I can think of to keep her.'

Margot nodded. Her eyes were shut.

'If it wasn't for Sally, you wouldn't be here. And she's organised everything. She got Niggle to come down and talk to dad. She sent them to the bank. And she's been to the grammar school in Oxford and got Annie a place. She's refused to go back to Larkford . . .'

Alexander could see that his words were falling on deaf ears. His mother was fast asleep. He smiled. He could wait to tell her his plan.

The last part of his plan. The first part wasn't so interesting, though he was rather proud of himself. He'd signed up to do a business course at night school in Oxford. He'd been bumbling around, trying to pull off all these deals, but, to be honest, he hadn't a clue what he was doing. He needed to understand how money worked. And be a bit more businesslike. Know about profit and loss and tax and interest rates.

The truth was everyone at Hunter's Moon needed shaking up a bit. And it was Sally who'd made them realise that if they didn't sharpen up they could lose everything. That you couldn't just ignore your responsibilities and please yourself and open another bottle when the going got tough.

It was all going to be all right, though. He pulled the covers up and tucked his mother in and kissed her on the forehead.

Sally came in later in the afternoon with a huge bunch of red roses.

Margot had slept for another two hours. She felt a little stronger. She sat up.

'Who on earth are those from?'

Sally handed her an envelope. Margot tore it open. She recognised the writing straight away.

To Margot, I shall expect you back behind that typewriter

as soon as possible. No time off for bad behaviour. With much love and best wishes from Terence

'Cheek!' she said.

'He's phoned every day,' said Sally. 'He wants to come and see you but I won't let him just yet.'

Margot sighed. 'I just don't know that I'll ever be able to write another word ever again.'

Sally sat down on the bed beside her. 'Yes, you will. Why don't you try something new?'

'What do you mean?'

'Something fresh. Modern. Something me and Phoebe would read.'

Margot nodded. 'Maybe.'

'Something fun and exciting. About girls living in London. About their jobs and their clothes and their parties and their boyfriends. It can still be romantic.'

Margot began to think about it. She *could* imagine it. Girls like Phoebe and Sally sauntering up the Kings Road, laughing, going to meet their friends. Their hopes and dreams. Their lovers . . .

'*The Chelsea Girls,*' she murmured.

'There you are,' said Sally, delighted. 'I can see it on the shelves already.'

That night, there was an enormous moon, like a giant pearl, glowing silvery-white in the sky, lighting up the valley.

'Come outside with me,' whispered Alexander to Sally, and he took her by the hand and they stood outside staring up.

'Is that it?' asked Sally. 'Is that the hunter's moon?'

'Yes,' said Alexander. 'And I want you to stay here

354

forever, and see every hunter's moon that rises.' He paused. 'With me.'

Sally turned to face him, laughing. 'You sound like one of your mother's books.'

Then she stopped laughing, because he was looking at her intently, with the most serious expression on his face.

'Do you understand what I'm saying, Sally? I'm asking you to marry me. Will you marry me?'

Her face was bright in the moonlight, her eyes sparkling. She reached up a hand to touch his face, brushed the lock of dark hair out of his eyes.

'Of course. Of course I will.'

And the moon shone down, wrapping them in its silver light, and the night breeze rustled around them, and an owl hooted far down in the valley, but they saw nor felt nor heard any of it . . .

38

'That's a beautiful story,' sighed Belinda to Alexander. 'Every time this house thinks it can escape the Willoughbys' clutches, someone comes along to its rescue.' He pointed to a book on the mantelpiece. 'It's there, Margot's biggest seller. She got up out of her sick bed and wrote the whole thing before Christmas.'

Belinda picked up the book. It was a first edition of *The Chelsea Girls*. On the cover were two girls, one blonde, one dark, walking up the Kings Road in miniskirts and kinky boots. She smiled. 'I remember reading this at school. We learned a lot from this.'

'It was ahead of its time. It's almost a classic now.'

'Well, I hope this will be the right plan. The great thing is, you won't have burnt any bridges.'

'It will be a pleasure to have you as a neighbour.'

Alexander looked up at her and thought to himself that maybe she would be something more. That really would be his perfect ending.

Later, Leo walked her out to her car.

'It's all falling into place. The more I think about it, I'm going to keep the office in London, and get another one in Peasebrook. It was time I expanded anyway, so

I'm going to look for more clients in this area. There's loads of food businesses opening up. There'll be plenty of opportunity.'

'If I can help you with premises, just let me know!'

'You don't miss a trick, do you?'

'Never.'

They were standing very close together. Dusk was starting to fall and the air cooled around them. The scent of blossom hung heavy and promising. Time seemed to trickle by very slowly. Belinda ran a hand through her hair and took in a deep breath. She was going to ask him. That's what Bruce would tell her to do. And Cathy. They'd be telling her to go for it. Make the first move.

'Are you—'

'Are you free for dinner?' asked Leo, and she jumped. He'd beaten her to it. She laughed. She put her hands on his shoulders, then moved toward him. She breathed in that warm, spicy cologne that tantalised her whenever she was close to him. She felt the warm of Leo's hands sliding underneath her jacket and touching her waist. She moved in further, pressing her mouth to his neck and realised how much she had been longing to feel his skin on her lips. She could feel a pulse, tripping faster than a butterfly wing. Was it inside her, or him? They were so close she couldn't tell. She pushed herself against him, feeling herself come alive again, after all the years of numbness, a delicious molten pool deep inside her.

'I'm not sure,' she breathed, 'that we should even bother with dinner.'

*

Sally smiled as she stood by the drawing room window, about to draw the long velvet curtains to keep out the night. She reflected that there was nothing more satisfying as a mother than to see your children settle with someone who felt right.

She remembered Margot telling her that. Margot, who had left Sally and Alexander Hunter's Moon in her will 'because if it belongs to anyone, it belongs to Sally. She saved Hunter's Moon.' And now Belinda had done the same, in a way.

She felt a hand on her shoulder. Alexander. She turned to find him behind her, smiling at what he could see playing out on the driveway.

'I think she will be a very good thing for Leo,' he said. She noticed the slight lurch in his voice. The slurry suggestion that he might be a little drunk, one of the disease's signature signs. Was it more marked than it had been a week ago? Was this how life was going to be: analysing every sound, every move he made for signs of deterioration? Fear squeezed at her.

Sally turned and slid her arms around her husband's waist.

'It's OK,' he whispered, kissing the top of her head lightly.

Her love for him was still as strong as it ever had been. Her heart felt crushed with the enormity of what lay ahead. Yet in some ways, they were lucky. They had their wonderful family, and together they would face the pain, and make the very most of the precious time that was left. Who knew how long that would be?

She felt as safe in Alexander's arms as she ever had done. There was no place she would rather be. She couldn't imagine a time when she couldn't slide into his embrace for comfort. She determined to make the most of every kiss, every touch, every word as long as she had him. Her handsome, strong, funny, kind Beetle.

39

Four years later

Annie, in a black polo-necked dress and her trusty flat boots, her hair scraped back into a velvet band, climbed up into the pulpit. She paused for a moment, looking out at the congregation, then took a deep breath.

'Alexander, or Beetle as we always called him when we were growing up, was the most wonderful brother a girl could hope for. He would tease you, as all brothers should, but you never minded really. You knew that if you phoned him in the middle of the night, he would come and get you, no questions asked. He would lend you his last fiver, no questions asked. And when it really mattered, he told he loved you. Maybe not in those exact words, but when you were feeling small or alone or afraid, he would say something that made you feel you mattered. And he was funny and smart and so, so, so terribly handsome. I used to say that he could break three hearts before breakfast time without even knowing he was doing it. He could have had any girl in the world, but lucky for us all he fell in love with our beautiful, kind Sally.'

She smiled down at Sally in the front pew, then took in a deep breath.

'This poem was our mother's favourite, and she always said it was where she got the idea for his name. The poem's about losing a beetle, and that's what we've done. The very best Beetle that ever there was.'

Her clear true voice wavered just at the end, but she cleared her throat and picked up the old red copy of *Now We Are Six* and began to read:

'I found a little beetle . . .'

And as Annie read on, Belinda reached beside her and took Leo's hand in hers, and he gripped it tightly, facing forwards and staring at his aunt and trying not to cry.

Everyone came back to Hunter's Moon for the funeral tea after the service. Sally had tried to insist on doing it all herself, but Leo persuaded her that there were times when things were best left to the professionals, and a funeral was one of them, and the catering company had laid everything out on the table in the dining room.

And because they all felt Alexander's spirit, it wasn't a sombre occasion, but a merry one, as the guests mingled and swapped memories and stories and proposed endless toasts. Teddy was rushing around, excited by all the visitors, licking up any falling crumbs. But he knew something was wrong. He knew someone was missing.

'That was a wonderful tribute,' said Leo to Annie.

'I'm going to miss my big brother,' she said, and she looked around the hall. 'Do you know, it feels like only yesterday he'd come down those stairs in his mohair suit with his car keys jangling, off on some jaunt. I can't believe I won't see him again.'

'I know,' said Leo, and sighed. He didn't much want to think about it. He put his arm around his aunt, and for a moment she rested her head on his shoulder as they both thought about the man who had meant so much to them.

Annie had taken Leo aside the afternoon before.

'I want to lend you some money,' she told him. 'So you and Belinda can buy out Sally. It's the right thing to do. We need to keep Hunter's Moon in the family. And I know you can't afford it at the moment. When Margot left Sally the house, she gave Phoebe and me the royalties from her backlist. I've done rather well with mine. I invested them wisely. And I can't think of any better way of spending that money than lending it to you, interest free. I've thought about it long and hard. I still earn good money and I don't need much and my house is bought and paid for. I would be leaving it to you anyway, as you're my godson, but you might as well have it now . . .'

Leo looked at her in astonishment. 'You don't have to do that.'

'There is a condition,' she grinned. 'That you keep my old room for me. I won't ever turn up unannounced—'

'You will be welcome any time. *Any* time,' said Leo.

Belinda had stopped off at Cathy's house on the way back from the funeral to pick up Clementine.

'She's been an absolute angel,' Cathy assured her, handing over the little girl.

Clementine was dressed in a grey corduroy pinafore dress with a red spotty blouse underneath, her shiny dark hair tied in tiny plaits. Everyone had agreed that a funeral service was no place for a little one, but that she would be a welcome distraction back at the house afterwards. She had brought her grandfather great joy in his last years, although she would probably never remember him.

And now Belinda took her daughter's hand and led her out of the house and down across the lawn. She felt an overwhelming sense of peace as she helped Clementine down the stone steps then lifted her on to the edge of the fountain to look at the fish. She and Leo and Sally had had a long talk the evening before, curled up on the sofas in front of the fire in the drawing room.

Annie's offer meant their dream could be realised much sooner than they thought. Together with the sale of Leo's flat and a mortgage raised on their joint salaries, they could now afford to buy Hunter's Moon from Sally, who would move into the coach house. She still couldn't believe it and yet, in some ways, it felt as if it was meant to be. There was lots of red tape to get through yet, and inheritance tax issues to sort out, but to all intents and purposes the house was theirs. And of course they would make it open to the whole family, as it always had been, for that was the point.

And although she wasn't a Willoughby by blood, Belinda still felt as if she belonged, just as much as Sally did.

She lifted Clementine down from the fountain then turned and looked back at Hunter's Moon. Its windows glowed bright in the evening sun as it began to set, and the house seemed to be speaking to her:

'Today may be sad, and sadness has its place in our hearts, but it must not live on. It must move aside for joy and happiness and new beginnings. But I will be here throughout both your sadness and your joy, my walls wrapped tightly around you. I will be your comfort and your place of safety. I will be here for you forever.

Your forever house.'

Take a sneak peek at Veronica Henry's
charming, cheeky story

A COUNTRY CHRISTMAS

The perfect book to curl up with . . .

Honeycote may appear to be the perfect English village,
but what scandals hide beneath the surface?

The Liddiards have a wonderful life at Honeycote
House: endless guests, parties and family fun. But
unbeknownst to his wife Lucy, Mickey Liddiard
has a few secrets.

He's going to make some changes, though. He owes
it to Lucy and the children, even if it will take more
than just willpower.

After all, it's impossible to keep secrets in a village as
small as Honeycote . . .

I

A single bell tolled out with authoritative finality. Eye-watering winter sunshine drenched the little churchyard at Honeycote, highlighting the dewy cobwebs that stretched from grave to grave. A mound of earth indicated the most recent, the latest in a line of Liddiards that stretched back hundreds of years.

He craned his neck to assess the turnout. They were all there. Patrick, seemingly unperturbed, the only betrayal of any emotion being the speed at which he smoked his cigarette before tossing the nub end into the freshly dug hole. Sophie and Georgina stood behind him, unnaturally pale in their black school coats, lending an air of Victorian melodrama to the tableau. He thought this was probably their first funeral, if you didn't count the elaborate arrangements they'd made for various guinea pigs and goldfish over the years. Kay was chic in rigidly tailored black, a huge hat and impossibly high heels – he knew she'd be wearing stockings. Lawrence was at her side, etiquette requiring them to be united. Even Cowley was there from the bank, in a shapeless suit, his Christmas Biro clipped into the top pocket, no doubt luxuriating in a morning away from his desk: this was about as much fun as Cowley ever had.

And Lucy. She'd rejected widow's weeds in favour of palest grey, her only concession to mourning a black velvet ribbon that held back her curls. She was wearing a pearl necklace he'd given her the Christmas before, an over-generous gesture he hadn't been able to afford. As ever.

As she arrived at the graveside to stand beside his brother,

James, there was just time for him to notice her slipping her hand into his before the vicar started intoning the familiar words.

As the first clod of earth began to hit the coffin, Mickey Liddiard summoned up every last drop of energy from his bones and pushed. But the lid of the coffin was stout, hewn from a mighty oak, and wouldn't give...

'Mickey! Mickey!'

Lucy anxiously shook her husband awake. She could feel his heart hammering as he thrashed beside her. He sat bolt upright, drenched in sweat, and looked at her in alarm.

'You've had one of your dreams again.'

Mickey slumped back on the pillows, relief that it was all over flooding through him. But Lucy could still sense anxiety.

'What on earth were you dreaming about? You were tossing and turning—'

'I don't know.' Mickey feigned puzzlement. He could remember only too well. 'You know what dreams are like. You wake up and they're gone.'

It was the third time this week he'd had the dream, or one like it. He'd wondered about having it analysed, but thought perhaps the meaning wasn't all that hidden and that quite simply he had a fear of dying and nobody giving a toss. He screwed up his eyes to look at the clock. 'What's the time?'

Lucy stretched out her arm and turned the miniature carriage clock to face her. 'Nearly six.' She frowned as Mickey threw back the blankets. 'You don't need to get up yet, surely?'

'I need a shower.'

She watched his shadowy outline pad across the room and pull back the heavy, interlined curtains, letting the very first fingers of early morning light in. She could see him clearly now. He was tall, broad-shouldered, and with still no sign of a middle-age spread despite having celebrated his forty-third birthday six months before. He had just enough gravitas in his features to stop him looking boyish, but he had a bloom of youth that he didn't deserve and that his contemporaries resented given his lifestyle – no thickening middle or thinning hair as yet, not even a sprinkling of grey in his thick brown hair.

He was definitely a handsome man in anyone's books, but as he gazed out of the window there was a frown marring his features that Lucy didn't like. She suddenly felt a need to reassure both him and herself. This wasn't the first time she'd woken him from a nightmare lately. She patted the empty space in the bed beside her.

'Come back to bed.'

Mickey shook his head. He was wide awake now, the adrenaline from the dream still pumping through his body, and his head was already whirling with the problems the day held in store for him. He reflected grimly that he had no respite these days, only a brief half-hour after the first few glasses of wine, in that mellow period between being relaxed and becoming totally plastered. Why could he never stop at that point? Why did he insist on getting completely shit-faced, so he became melancholy, his fears waxed rather than waned and his sleep was troubled?

He turned to look at his wife. She was wearing the necklace she'd had on in the dream, and didn't look a day older than the day he'd married her. But then why should she? She had nothing to worry about. She knew nothing of his problems, that was for sure.

**Escape to the country this Christmas
with Veronica Henry!**

About
VERONICA HENRY

Veronica Henry worked as a scriptwriter for *The Archers*, *Heartbeat* and *Holby City*, amongst many others, before turning to fiction. She won the 2014 RNA Novel of the Year award for *A Night on the Orient Express*. Veronica lives with her family in a village in north Devon.

Find out more at www.veronicahenry.co.uk

Sign up to her Facebook page
www.facebook.com/veronicahenryauthor

Or follow her on Twitter @veronica_henry
and Instagram @veronicahenryauthor

Discover Your Next Read from
VERONICA HENRY

Home isn't always where the heart is . . .

Jamie Wilding's return home is not quite going
to plan. A lot has changed in the picturesque
Shropshire village of Upper Faviell since she
left after the death of her mother. Her father
is broke and behaving like a teenager. Her best
friend's marriage is slowly falling apart. And the
man she lost her heart to years ago is trying to
buy her beloved family home.

As Jamie attempts to fix the mess, she is forced
to confront a long-standing family feud and the
truth about her father, before she can finally
listen to her own heart.

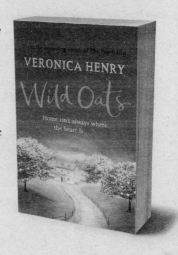

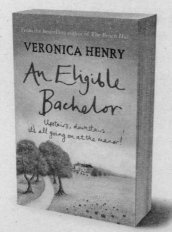

**Upstairs, downstairs . . . it's all going
on at the manor**

When Guy wakes up with a terrible hang-over
and a new fiancée, he tries not to panic. After
all, Richenda is beautiful, famous, successful . .
. what reason could he have for doubts?

As news of the engagement between the
heir of Eversleigh Manor and the darling of
prime-time television spreads through the
village, Guy wonders if he's made a rash
decision. Especially when he meets Honor, a
new employee of the Manor who has a habit
of getting under his skin. But Honor has her
own troubles – a son who's missing, and an
ex-boyfriend who has made an unexpected
reappearance . . .

It was the opportunity of a lifetime – a rundown hotel in Cornwall, just waiting to be brought back to life

When the rundown Rocks Hotel comes up for auction in Mariscombe, Lisa and her boyfriend George make a successful bid to escape and live the dream. But their dream quickly becomes a nightmare. Their arch-rival, Bruno Thorne, owner of Mariscombe Hotel, seems intent on sabotage.

Meanwhile, local chambermaid Molly is harbouring a secret that will blow the whole village apart. Then an unexpected visitor turns up on the doorstep. It seems everyone in Mariscombe is sailing a little too close to the rocks . . .

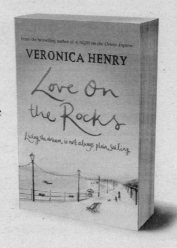

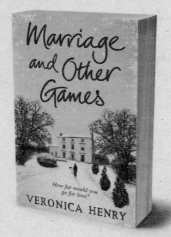

How far would you go for love: a white lie, a small deceit, full-scale fraud . . . ?

When Charlotte Briggs' husband Ed is sent down for fraud, she cannot find it in her heart to forgive him for what he has done. Ostracised from their social circle, she flees to the wilds of Exmoor to nurse her broken heart. But despite the slower pace of life, she soon finds that she is not the only person whose life is in turmoil.

On Everdene Sands, a row of beach huts holds the secrets of the families who own them

'FOR SALE: a rare opportunity to purchase a beach hut on the spectacular Everdene Sands. "The Shack" has been in the family for fifty years, and was the first to be built on this renowned stretch of golden sand.'

Jane Milton doesn't want to sell her beloved beach hut, which has been the heart of so many family holidays and holds so many happy memories. But when her husband dies, leaving her with an overwhelming string of debts, she has no choice but to sell.

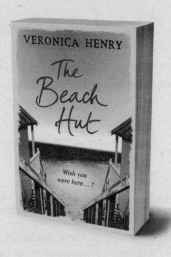

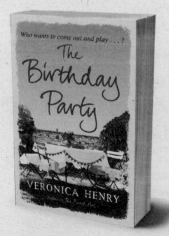

Secrets, rivalry, glamour – it's time for the party of the year . . .

Delilah has lived out her tempestuous marriage to hell-raiser Raf in the glare of the media spotlight. Now planning a milestone birthday, she has more on her mind than invitations.

Raf has been offered a part in a movie he can't refuse. But will he succumb to the temptations he's struggled to resist for the last ten years?

Delilah's three daughters are building careers of their own, only too aware that the press are waiting for them to slip up. For the Rafferty girls might look like angels, but they are only human.

It's the perfect recipe for a party like no other . . .

A short break can become the holiday of a lifetime

In a gorgeous quay-side hotel in Cornwall, the long weekend is just beginning . . .

Claire Marlowe owns 'The Townhouse by the Sea' with Luca, the hotel's charismatic chef. She ensures everything runs smoothly – until an unexpected arrival checks in and turns her whole world upside down.

And the rest of the guests arrive with their own baggage…

Here are affairs of the heart, secrets, lies and scandal– all wrapped up in one long, hot weekend.

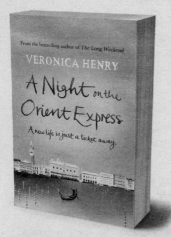

Get ready for the journey of a lifetime

The Orient Express. Luxury. Mystery. Romance.

For one group of passengers settling in to their seats and taking their first sips of champagne, the journey from London to Venice is more than the trip of a lifetime.

A mysterious errand; a promise made to a dying friend; an unexpected proposal; a secret reaching back a lifetime. As the train sweeps on, revelations, confessions and assignations unfold against the most romantic and infamous setting in the world.

Return to Everdene Sands, setting for the *The Beach Hut*, and discover secrets, love, tragedy and dreams. It's going to be a summer to remember . . .

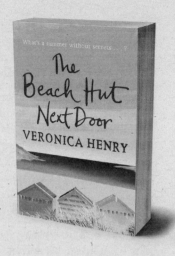

Summer appeared from nowhere that year in Everdene and for those lucky enough to own one of the beach huts, this was the summer of their dreams.

For Elodie, returning to Everdene means reawakening the memories of one summer fifty years ago. A summer when everything changed. But this summer is not all sunshine and surf — as secrets unfold, and some lives are changed for ever . . .

Pennfleet might be a small town, but there's never a dull moment in its narrow winding streets . . .

Kate has only planned a flying visit to clear out the family home after the death of her mother. When she finds an anonymous letter, she is drawn back into her own past.

Single dad Sam is juggling his deli and two lively teenagers, so romance is the last thing on his mind. Then Cupid fires an unexpected arrow — but what will his children think?

Nathan Fisher is happy with his lot, running picnic cruises up and down the river, but kissing the widow of the richest man in Pennfleet has disastrous consequences.

Vanessa knows what she has done is unseemly for a widow, but it's the most fun she's had for years. Must she always be on her best behaviour?

Everyone has a story . . . but will they get the happy ending they deserve?

Emilia has just returned to her idyllic Cotswold hometown to rescue the family business. Nightingale Books is a dream come true for book-lovers, but the best stories aren't just within the pages of the books she sells — Emilia's customers have their own tales to tell.

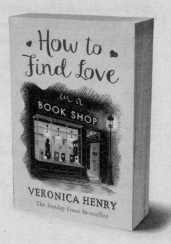

There's the lady of the manor who is hiding a secret close to her heart; the single dad looking for books to share with his son but who isn't quite what he seems; and the desperately shy chef trying to find the courage to talk to her crush . . .

And as for Emilia's story, can she keep the promise she made to her father and save Nightingale Books?